The Flag of Distress
A Story of the South Sea

by

Captain Mayne Reid

Double9
BOOKS

The Flag of Distress
A Story of the South Sea
by Captain Mayne Reid

ISBN: 978-93-61425-57-8

Published by

DOUBLE 9 BOOKS

2/13-B, Ansari Road
Daryaganj, New Delhi – 110002
info@double9books.com
www.double9books.com
Tel. 011-40042856

ABOUT THE AUTHOR

Thomas Mayne Reid, an Irish-American novelist, participated in the Mexican–American War. His numerous books on American life discuss colonial policy in the American colonies, the horrors of slave labor, and the lifestyles of American Indians. "Captain" Reid created adventure stories similar to those of Frederick Marryat and Robert Louis Stevenson. They were primarily situated in the American West, Mexico, South Africa, the Himalayas, and Jamaica. He admired Lord Byron. Dion Boucicault turned his anti-slavery novel Quadroon (1856) into a drama called The Octoroon (1859), which was staged in New York. Reid was born in Ballyroney, a hamlet near Katesbridge in County Down, Northern Ireland, as the son of Rev. Thomas Mayne Reid Sr., a senior clerk of the General Assembly of the Presbyterian Church in Ireland, and his wife. Reid's father intended him to become a Presbyterian pastor, so he enrolled at the Royal Belfast Academical Institution in September 1834. He stayed for four years, but lacked the ambition to finish his studies and graduate. He returned to Ballyroney to teach at a school.

CONTENTS

Chapter One
A Chase

In mid-ocean—the Pacific. Two ships within sight of one another, less than a league apart. Both sailing before the wind, running dead down it with full canvas spread—not side by side, but one in the wake of the other.

Is it a chase? To all appearance, yes; a probability strengthened by the relative size and character of the vessels. One is a barque, polacca-masted, her masts raking back with the acute shark's-fin set supposed to be characteristic of piratical craft. The other is a ship, square-rigged and full sized; a row of real, not painted, ports, with a gun grinning out of each, proclaiming her a man-of-war.

She is one—a frigate, as any seaman would say, after giving her a glance. And any landsman might name her nationality. The flag at her peak is one known all over the world: it is the ensign of England.

If it be a chase, she is the pursuer. Her colours might be accepted as surety of this, without regard to the relative position of the vessels; which show the frigate astern, the polacca leading.

The latter also carries a flag—of nationality not so easily determined. Still it is the ensign of a naval power, though one of little note. The five-pointed white star, solitary in a blue field, proclaims it the standard of Chili.

Why should an English frigate be chasing a Chilian barque? There is no war between Great Britain and this, the most prosperous of the South American republics; instead, peace-treaties, with relations of the most amicable kind. Were the polacca showing colours blood-red, or black, with death's-head and cross-bones, the chase would be intelligible. But the bit of bunting at her masthead has nothing on its field either of menace or defiance. On the contrary, it appeals to pity, and asks for aid; for it is an ensign reversed—in short, a *signal of distress*.

And yet the craft so signalling is on the scud before a stiff breeze, with all sail set, stays taut, not a rope out of place!

Strange this. So is it considered by every one aboard the man-of-war, from the captain commanding to the latest joined "lubber of a landsman"—a thought that has been in their minds ever since the chase commenced.

For it *is* a chase: that is, the frigate has sighted a sail, and stood towards it. This without changing course; as, when first espied, the stranger, like herself, was running before the wind. If slowly, the pursuer has, nevertheless, been gradually forging nearer the pursued; till at length the telescope tells the latter to be a barque—at the same time revealing her ensign reversed.

Nothing strange in this, of itself; unfortunately, a sight too common at sea. But that a vessel displaying signals of distress should be carrying all sail, and running away, or attempting to do so, from another making to relieve her—above all, from a ship bearing the British flag—this *is* strange. And just thus has the polacca been behaving—still is; sailing on down the wind, without slacking haulyards, or lessening her spread of canvas by a single inch!

Certainly the thing seems odd. More than that—mysterious.

To this conclusion have they come on board the warship. And, naturally enough; for there is that which has imbued their thoughts with a tinge of superstition.

In addition to what they see, they have something *heard*. Within the week they have spoken two vessels, both of which reported this same barque, or one answering her description: "*Polacca-masted, all sail set, ensign reversed.*"

A British brig, which the frigate's boat had boarded, said: That such a craft had run across her bows, so close they could have thrown a rope to her; that at first no one was observed on board; but on her being hailed, two men made appearance, both springing up to the main-shrouds; thence answering the hail in a language altogether unintelligible, and with hoarse croaking voices that resembled the barking of muzzled mastiffs!

It was late twilight, almost night, when this occurred; but the brig's people could make out the figures of the men, as these clung on to the ratlines. And what seemed as surprising as their odd speech was, that both appeared to be clothed in skin-dresses, covering their bodies from head to foot!

Seeing the signal of distress, the brig's commander would have sent a boat aboard; but the barque gave no chance for this—keeping on without slacking sail, or showing any other sign of a wish to communicate!

Standing by itself, the tale of the brig's crew might have been taken for a sailor's yarn; and as they admitted it to be "almost night," the obscurity would account for the skin-clothing. But coupled with the report of another vessel, which the frigate had afterwards spoken—a whaler—it seemed to receive full corroboration. The words sent through the whaler's trumpet were:—

"Barque sighted, latitude 10 degrees 22 minutes South, longitude 95 degrees West. Polacca-masted. All sail set. Ensign reversed. Chilian. Men seen on board covered with red hair, supposed skin-dresses. Tried to come up, but could not. Barque a fast sailer—went away down wind."

Already in receipt of such intelligence, it is no wonder that the frigate's crew feel something more than mere curiosity about a vessel corresponding to the one of which these queer accounts have been given. For they are now near enough the barque to see that she answers the description: "Polacca-masted—all sail set—ensign reversed—Chilian."

And her behaviour is as reported: sailing away from those who would respond to her appealing signal, to all appearance endeavouring to shun them!

Only now has the chase in reality commenced. Hitherto the frigate was but keeping her own course. But the signal of distress, just sighted through the telescope, has drawn her on; and with canvas crowded, she steers straight for the polacca.

The latter is unquestionably a fast sailer; but although too swift for the brig and whaler, she is no match for the man-of-war. Still she makes quick way, and the chase is likely to be a long one.

As it continues, and the distance does not appear very much, or very rapidly, diminishing, the frigate's people begin to doubt whether she will ever be overtaken. On the fore-deck the tars stand in groups, mingled with marines, their eyes bent upon the retreating craft, making their comments in muttered tones, many of the men with brows o'ercast. For a fancy has sprung up around the forecastle, that the chased barque is no barque at all, but a *phantom*! This is gradually growing into a belief; firmer as they draw nearer, and with naked eye note her correspondence with the reports of the spoken vessels.

They have not yet seen the skin-clad men—if men they be. More like, imagine some, they will prove *spectres*!

While on the quarterdeck there is no such superstitious thought, a feeling almost as intense agitates the minds of those there assembled. The captain, surrounded by his officers, stands glass in hand gazing at the sail ahead. The frigate, though a fine sailer, is not one of the very fastest, else she might long ago have lapped upon the polacca. Still has she been gradually gaining, and is now less than a league astern.

But the breeze has been also declining, which is against her; and for the last half-hour she has barely preserved her distance from the barque.

To compensate for this, she runs out studding-sails on all her yards, even to the royals; and again makes an effort to bring the chase to a termination. But again to suffer disappointment.

"To no purpose, now," says her commander, seeing his last sail set. Then adding, as he casts a glance at the sky, sternwards, "The wind's going down. In ten minutes more we'll be becalmed."

Those around need not be told this. The youngest reefer there, looking at sky and sea, can forecast a calm.

In five minutes after, the frigate's sails go flapping against the masts, and her flag hangs half-folded.

In five more, the canvas only shows motion by an occasional clout; while the bunting droops dead downward.

Within the ten, as her captain predicted, the huge warship lies motionless on the sea—its surface around her smooth as a swan-pond.

Chapter Two
A Call for Boarders

The frigate is becalmed—what of the barque? Has she been similarly stayed in her course?

The question is asked by all on board the warship, each seeking the answer for himself. For all are earnestly gazing at the strange vessel regardless of their own condition.

Forward, the superstitious thought has become intensified into something like fear. A calm coming on so suddenly, just when they had hopes of overhauling the chase! What could that mean? Old sailors shake their heads, refusing to make answer; while young ones, less cautious of speech, boldly pronounce the polacca to be a spectre!

The legends of the *Phantom Ship* and *Flying Dutchman* are in their thoughts, and on their lips, as they stand straining their eyes after the still receding vessel; for beyond doubt she is yet moving on with waves rippling around her!

"As I told ye, mates," remarks an old tar, "we'd never catch up with that craft—not if we stood after her till doomsday. And doomsday it might be for us, if we did."

"I hope she'll hold her course, and leave us a good spell behind," rejoins a second. "It was a foolish thing followin' her; for my part, I'll be glad if we never do catch up with her."

"You need have no fear about it," says the first speaker. "Just look! She's making way yet! I believe she can sail as well without a wind as with one."

Scarce are the words spoken, when, as if to contradict them, the sails of the chased vessel commence clouting against the masts; while her flag falls folded, and is no longer distinguishable either as signal of distress, or any other. The breeze that failed the frigate is also now dead around the barque, which, in like manner, has been caught in the calm.

"What do you make her out, Mr Black?" asks the frigate's captain of his first, as the two stand looking through their levelled glasses.

"Not anything, sir," replies the lieutenant; "except that she should be Chilian from her colours. I can't see a soul aboard of her. Ah, yonder! Something shows over the taffrail! Looks like a man's head! It's down again—ducked suddenly."

A short silence succeeds, the commanding officer, busied with his binocular, endeavouring to catch sight of the thing seen by his subordinate. It does not appear again.

"Odd!" says the captain, resuming speech; "a ship running up signals of distress, at the same time refusing to be relieved! Very odd, isn't it, gentlemen?" he asks, addressing himself to the group of officers now gathered around; who all signify assent to his interrogatory.

"There must be something amiss," he continues. "Can any of you think what it is?"

To this there is a negative response. They are as much puzzled as himself—mystified by the strange barque, and more by her strange behaviour.

There are two, however, who have thoughts different from the rest—the third lieutenant, and one of the midshipmen. Less thoughts than imaginings; and these so vague, that neither communicates them to the captain, nor to one another. And whatever their fancies, they do not appear pleasant ones; since on the faces of both is an expression of something like anxiety. Slight and little observable, it is not noticed by their comrades standing around. But it seems to deepen, while they continue to gaze at the becalmed barque, as though due to something there observed. Still they remain silent, keeping the dark thought, if such it be, to themselves.

"Well, gentlemen," says the commanding officer to his assembled subordinates, "I must say this *is* singular. In all my experience at sea, I don't remember anything like it. What trick the Chilian barque—if she be Chilian—is up to, I can't guess; not for the life of me. It cannot be a case of piracy. The craft has no guns; and if she had, she appears without men to handle them. It's a riddle all round; to get the reading of which, we'll have to send a boat to her."

"I don't think we'll get a very willing crew, sir," says the first lieutenant jestingly. "Forward, they're quite superstitious about the character of the stranger. Some of them fancy her the *Flying Dutchman*. When the boatswain pipes for boarders, they'll feel as if his whistle were a signal for them to walk the plank."

The remark causes the captain to smile, as also the other officers; though two of the latter abstain from such cheerful demonstration—the third lieutenant and midshipman, already mentioned, on both of whose brows the cloud still sits, seeming darker than ever.

"It's a very remarkable thing," observes the commander, musingly, "how that sort of feeling still affects the forecastle! For your genuine British tar, who'll board an enemy's ship, crawling across the muzzle of a shotted gun, and has no fear of death in human shape, will act like a scared child when it threatens him in the guise of his Satanic majesty! I have no doubt, as you say, Mr Black, that our lads forward are a bit shy about boarding yonder vessel. Let me show you how to send their shyness adrift. I'll do that with a single word!"

The captain steps forward, his subordinates following him. When within speaking distance of the fore-deck, he stops, and makes sign he has something to say. The tars are all attention.

"Men!" he exclaims, "you see that barque we've been chasing; and at her masthead a flag reversed—which you know to be a signal of distress? That is a call never to be disregarded by an English ship, much less an English man-of-war. Lieutenant! order a boat lowered, and the boatswain to pipe for boarders. Those of you who wish to go, muster on the main-deck."

A loud "hurrah!" responds to the appeal; and, while its echoes are still resounding through the ship, the whole crew comes crowding towards the main-deck. Scores of volunteers present themselves, enough to man every boat in the frigate.

"So, gentlemen!" says the captain, turning to his officers with a proud expression on his countenance, "there's the British sailor for you. I've said he fears not man. And, when humanity makes call, as you see, neither is he frightened at ghost or devil!"

A second cheer succeeds the speech, mingled with good-humoured remarks, though not much laughter. The sailors simply acknowledge the compliment their commanding officer has paid them, at the same time feeling that the moment is too solemn for merriment; for their instinct of humanity is yet under control of the weird feeling.

As the captain turns aft to the quarter, many of them fall away toward the fore-deck, till the group of volunteers becomes greatly diminished. Still there are enough to man the largest boat in the frigate, or fight any crew the chased craft may carry, though these should prove to be pirates of the most desperate kind.

Chapter Three
Forecastle Fears

"What boat is it to be, sir?"

This question is asked by the first lieutenant, who has followed the captain to the quarter.

"The cutter," replies his superior; "there seems no need, Mr Black, to send anything larger, at least till we get word of what's wanted. Possibly it's a case of sickness—scurvy or something. Though that would be odd too, seeing how the barque keeps her canvas spread. Very queer altogether!"

"Is the doctor to go?"

"He needn't, till we've heard what it is. He'd only have to come back for his drugs and instruments. You may instruct him to be getting them ready. Meanwhile, let the boat be off, and quick. When they bring back their report we'll see what's to be done. The cutter's crew will be quite sufficient. As to any hostility from those on board the stranger, that's absurd. We could blow her out of the water with a single broadside."

"Who's to command the boat, sir?"

The captain reflects, with a look cast inquiringly around. His eye falls upon the third lieutenant, who stands near, seemingly courting the glance.

It is short and decisive. The captain knows his third officer to be a thorough seaman; though young, capable of any duty, however delicate or dangerous. Without further hesitation he assigns him to the command of the cutter.

The young officer enters upon the service with alacrity—as if moved by something more than the mere obedience due to discipline. He hastens to the ship's side to superintend the lowering of the boat. Nor does he stand at rest, but is seen to help and hurry it, with a look of restless impatience in his eye, and the shadow still observable on his brow.

While thus occupied, he is accosted by another officer, one yet younger than himself—the midshipman already mentioned.

"Can I go with you?" the latter asks, as if addressing an equal.

"Certainly, my dear fellow," responds the lieutenant, in like familiar tone. "I shall be only too pleased to have you. But you must get the captain's consent."

The young reefer glides aft, sees the frigate's commander upon the quarterdeck, and saluting, says:

"Captain, may I go with the cutter?"

"Well, yes," responds the chief; "I have no objection." Then, after taking a survey of the youngster, he adds, "Why do you wish it?"

The youth blushes, without replying. There is a cast upon his countenance that strikes the questioner, somewhat puzzling him. But there is no time either for further inquiry or reflection. The cutter has been lowered, and rests upon the water. Her crew is crowding into her; and she will soon be moving off from the ship.

"You can go, lad," assents the captain. "Report yourself to the third lieutenant, and tell him I have given you leave. You're young, and, like all youngsters, ambitious of gaining glory. Well; in this affair you won't have much chance. I take it. It's simply boarding a ship in distress, where you're more likely to be a spectator to scenes of suffering. However, that will be a lesson for you; therefore you can go."

Thus authorised, the mid hurries away from the quarterdeck, drops down into the boat, and takes seat alongside the lieutenant, already there.

"Shove off!" commands the latter; and with a push of boat-hook, and plashing of oars, the cutter parts from the ship's side, cleaving the water like a knife.

The two vessels still lie becalmed, in the same relative position to one another, having changed from it scarce a cable's length. And stem to stern, just as the last breath of the breeze, blowing gently against their sails, forsook them.

On both, the canvas is still spread, though not bellied. It hangs limp and loose, giving an occasional flap, so feeble as to show that this proceeds not from any stir in the air, but the mere balancing motion of the vessels. For there is now not enough breeze blowing to flout the long feathers in the tail of the Tropic bird, seen soaring aloft.

Both are motionless; their forms reflected in the water, as if each had its counterpart underneath, keel to keel.

Between them, the sea is smooth as a mirror—that tranquil calm which has given to the Pacific its distinctive appellation. It is now only disturbed, where furrowed by the keel of the cutter, with her stroke of ten oars, five on each side. Parting from the frigate's beam, she is steering straight for the becalmed barque.

On board the man-of-war all stand watching her—their eyes at intervals directed towards the strange vessel. From the frigate's forward-deck, the men have an unobstructed view, especially those clustering around the head. Still there is nearly a league between, and with the naked eye this hinders minute observation. They can but see the white-spread sails, and the black hull underneath them. With a glass the flag, now fallen, is just distinguishable from the mast along which it clings closely. They can perceive that its colour is crimson above, with blue and white underneath—the reversed order of the Chilian ensign. Its single star is no longer visible, nor aught of that heraldry, which spoke so appealingly. But if what they see fails to furnish them with details, these are amply supplied by their excited imaginations. Some of them can make out men aboard the barque—scores, hundreds! After all, she may be a pirate, and the upside-down ensign a decoy. On a tack, she might be a swifter sailer than she has shown herself before wind; and, knowing this, has been but "playing possum" with the frigate. If so, God help the cutter's crew?

Besides these conjectures of the common kind, there are those on the frigate's fore-deck who, in very truth, fancy the polacca to be a spectre. As they continue gazing, now at the boat, now at the barque, they expect every moment to see the one sink beneath the sea; and the other sail off, or melt into invisible air! On the quarter, speculation is equally rife, though running in a different channel. There the captain still stands surrounded by his officers, each with glass to his eye, levelled upon the strange craft. But they can perceive nought to give them a clue to her character; only the loose flapping sails, and the furled flag of distress.

They continue gazing till the cutter is close to the barque's beam. For then do they observe any head above the bulwarks, or face peering through the shrouds!

The fancy of the forecastle seems to have crept aft among the officers. They, too, begin to feel something of superstitious fear—an awe of the uncanny!

Chapter Four
The Cutter's Crew

Manned by ten stout tars, and as many oars propelling her, the cutter continues her course with celerity. The lieutenant, seated in the stern-sheets, with the midshipman by his side, directs the movements of the boat; while the glances of both are kept constantly upon the barque. In their eyes is an earnest expression—quite different from that of ordinary interrogation.

The men may not observe it; if they do, it is without comprehension of its meaning. They can but think of it as resembling their own, and proceeding from a like cause. For although with backs turned towards the barque, they cast occasional glances over their shoulders, in which curiosity is less observable than apprehension.

Despite their natural courage, strengthened by the late appeal to their humanity, the awe is strong upon them. Insidiously returning as they took their seats in the boat, it increases as they draw farther from the frigate and nearer to the barque. Less than half-an-hour has elapsed, and they are now within a cable's length of the strange vessel.

"Hold!" commands the lieutenant.

The oar-stroke is instantly suspended, and the blades held aloft. The boat gradually loses way, and at length rests stationary on the tranquil water.

All eyes are bent upon the barque; glances go searchingly along her bulwarks, from poop to prow.

No preparations to receive them! No one appears on deck—not a head raised over the rail!

"Barque ahoy!" hails the lieutenant.

"Barque ahoy!" is heard in fainter tone; but not in answer. Only the echo of the officer's voice, coming back from the hollow timbers of the becalmed vessel! There is again silence, more profound then ever. For the sailors in the boat have ceased talking; their awe, now intense, holding them speechless and as if spellbound!

"Barque ahoy!" again shouted the lieutenant, louder than before, but with like result. As before, he is only answered by echo. There is either nobody on board, or no one who thinks it worth while to make rejoinder.

The first supposition seems absurd, looking at the sails; the second equally so, regarding the flag at the main-royal masthead, and taking into account its character.

A third hail from the officer, this time vociferated in loudest voice, with the interrogatory added:

"Any one aboard there?"

To the question no reply, any more than to the hail.

Silence continues—stillness profound, awe-inspiring. They in the boat begin to doubt the evidence of their senses. Is there a barque before their eyes? Or is it all an illusion? How can a vessel be under sail—full sail—without sailors? And if any, why do they not show at her side? Why have they not answered the hail thrice given; the last time loud enough to be heard within the depths of her hold? It should have awakened her crew, even though all were asleep in the forecastle!

"Give way again!" cries the lieutenant. "Bring up on the starboard side, coxswain! Under the forechains."

The oars are dipped, and the cutter moves on. But scarce is she in motion, when once more the officer commands "Hold!"

With his voice mingle others, coming from the barque. Her people seem at length to have become aroused from their sleep, or stupor. A noise is heard upon her deck, as of a scuffle, accompanied by cries of strange intonation.

Presently two heads, apparently human, show above the bulwarks; two faces flesh-coloured, and thinly covered with hair! Then two bodies appear, also human-like, save that they are hairy all over—the hair of a foxy red! They swarm up the shrouds; and clutching the ratlines shake them, with quick violent jerks; at the same time uttering what appears angry speech in an unknown tongue, and harsh voice, as if chiding off the intruders. They go but a short way up the shrouds, just as far as they could spring from the deck, and only stay there for an instant; then dropping down again, disappear as abruptly and unceremoniously as they had presented themselves!

The lieutenant's command to "Hold!" was a word thrown away. Without it the men would have discontinued their stroke. They have done so: and sit with bated breath, eyes strained, ears listening, and lips mute, as if all had been suddenly and simultaneously struck dumb. Silence throughout the boat—silence aboard the barque—silence everywhere: the only sound heard being the "drip-drop" of the water as it falls from the feathered oar-blades.

For a time the cutter's crew remains mute, not one essaying to speak a word. They are silent, less from surprise than sheer stark terror. Fear is depicted on their faces and observable in their attitudes, as no wonder it should. What they have just seen is sufficient to terrify the stoutest hearts—even those of tried tars, as all of them are. A ship manned by hairy men—a crew of veritable Orsons! Certainly enough to startle the most phlegmatic mariner, and make him tremble as he tugs at his oar. But they have ceased tugging at their oars, and hold them, blades suspended. Almost the same is their breath. One alone, at length, musters sufficient courage to mutter:

"Gracious goodness, shipmates! what can it all mean?"

He receives no answer, though his question brings the silence to an end. It is now further broken by the voice of the lieutenant, as also that of the midshipman. They do not speak simultaneously, but one after the other. The superstitious fear pervading the minds of the men does not extend to them. They too have their fears, but of a different kind, and from a different cause. As yet neither has communicated to the other what he himself has been thinking; the thoughts of both being hitherto vague, though every moment becoming more defined. And the appearance of the red men upon the ratlines—strange to the sailors—seems to have made things more intelligible to them. Judging by the expression upon their faces, they comprehend what is puzzling their companions. And with a sense of anxiety more than fear—more of doubt than dismay.

The lieutenant speaks first, shouting in command:

"Give way! Quick! Pull in! Head on for the forechains!"

He acts in an excited manner, appearing nervously impatient. And, as if mechanically, the midshipman repeats the order, imitating the mien of his superior. The men execute it, but slowly, and with seeming reluctance. They know their officers to be daring fellows, both. But now they deem them rash, even to recklessness. For they cannot comprehend the motives urging them to action. Still they obey; and the prow of the boat strikes the barque abeam.

"Grapple on!" commands the senior officer soon as touching.

A boat-hook takes grip in the chains; and the cutter, swinging round, lies at rest alongside.

The lieutenant has already risen to his feet, as also the mid. Ordering only the coxswain to follow, they spring to the chains, lay hold, and lift themselves aloft.

Obedient to orders, the men remain in the boat, still keeping seat on the thwarts, in wonder at the bold bearing of their officers—at the same time admiring it.

Chapter Five
A Feast Unfinished

Having gained the bulwarks, the two officers, balancing themselves on the rail, look down over the decks of the polacca. Their glances sweep these forward, aft, and amidships—ranging from stem to stern, and back again.

Nothing seen there to explain the strangeness of affairs; nothing heard. No sailor on the fore-deck, nor officer on the quarter! Only the two queer creatures that had shown themselves on the shrouds. These are still visible, one of them standing by the mainmast, the other crouching near the caboose. Both again give out their jabbering speech, accompanying it with gestures of menace.

Disregarding this, the lieutenant leaps down upon the deck, and makes towards them; the mid and coxswain keeping close after.

At their approach, the hirsute monsters retreat; not scared-like, but with a show of defiance, as if disposed to contest possession of the place. They give back, however, bit by bit, till at length, ceasing to dispute, they shuffle off over the quarter, and on to the poop.

Neither of the two officers pays any attention to their demonstrations; and the movement aft is not made for them. Both lieutenant and midshipman seem excited by other thoughts—some strong impulse urging them on. Alone is the coxswain mystified by the hairy men, and not a little alarmed; but, without speaking, he follows his superiors.

All continue on toward the quarterdeck, making for the cabin-door. Having boarded the barque by the forechains, they must pass the caboose going aft. Its sliding panel is open, and when opposite, the three come to a stand. They are brought to it by a faint cry, issuing out of the cook's quarters.

Looking in, they behold a spectacle sufficiently singular to detain them. It is more than singular—it is startling. On the bench, in front of the galley-fire—which shows as if long-extinguished—sits a man, bolt upright, his back against the bulkhead. Is it a man, or but the semblance of one? Certainly it is a human figure; or, speaking more precisely, a human skeleton with the skin still on; this black as the coal-cinders in the grate in front of it!

It is a man—a negro. And living; since at sight of them he betrays motion, and makes an attempt to speak.

Only the coxswain stays to listen, or hear what he has to say. The others hurry on aft, making direct for the cabin, which, being between decks, is approached by a stairway.

Reaching this, they rush down, and stand before the door, which they find shut. Only closed, not locked. It yields to the turning of the handle; and, opening, gives them admission.

They enter hastily, one after the other, without ceremony or announcement. Once inside, they as quickly come to a stop, both looking aghast. The spectacle in the caboose was nought to what is now before their eyes. That was but startling; this is appalling.

It is the main-cabin they have entered; not a large one, for the polacca has not been constructed to carry passengers. Still is it snug, and roomy enough for a table six feet by four. Such a one stands in the centre, its legs fixed in the floor, with four chairs around it, similarly stanchioned.

On the table there are decanters and dishes, alongside glasses and plates. It is a dessert service, and on the dishes are fruits, cakes, and sweetmeats, with fragments of the same on the plates. The decanters contain wines of different sorts; and there are indications of wine having been poured out into the glasses—some of them still containing it. There are four sets, corresponding to the four chairs; and, to all appearance, this number of guests have been seated at the table. But two of the chairs are empty, as if those who occupied them had retired to an inner state-room. It is the side-seats that are vacant, and a fan lying on one, with a scarf over the back of that opposite, proclaim their last occupants to have been ladies.

Two guests are still at the table; one at its head, the other at the foot, facing each other. And such guests! Both are men, though, unlike him in the caboose, they are white men. But, like him, they also appear in the extreme of emaciation: jaws with the skin drawn tightly over them, cheekbones prominent, chin protruding, eyes sunken in their sockets!

Not dead neither; for their eyes, glancing and glaring, still show life. But there is little other evidence of it. Sitting stiff in the chairs, rigidly erect, they made no attempt to stir, no motion of either body or limbs. It would seem as if from both all strength had departed, their famished figures showing them in the last stages of starvation. And this in front of a table furnished with choice wines, fruits, and other comestibles—in short, loaded with delicacies!

What can it mean?

Not this question, but a cry comes from the lips of the two officers, simultaneously from both, as they stand regarding the strange tableau. Only for an instant do they thus stand. Then the lieutenant, rushing up the stair, and on to the side, shouts out—

"Back to the ship, and bring the doctor! Row with all your might, men. Away!"

The boat's people, obedient, pull off with alacrity. They are but too glad to get away from the suspected spot. As they strain at their oars, with faces now turned towards the barque, and eyes wonderingly bent upon her, they see nought to give them a clue to the conduct of their officers, or in any way elucidate the series of mysteries, prolonged to a chain and still continuing. One imbued with a belief in the supernatural, shakes his head, saying—

"Shipmates! we may never see that lieutenant again; nor the young reefer, nor the old cox—never!"

Chapter Six
"A Phantom Ship—Sure!"

During all this while those on board the man-of-war have been regarding the barque—at the same time watching with interest every movement of the boat.

Only they who have glasses can see what is passing with any distinctness. For the day is not a bright one, a haze over the sea hindering observation. It has arisen since the fall of the wind, perhaps caused by the calm; and, though but a mere film, at such far distance interferes with the view through their telescopes. Those using them can just tell that the cutter has closed in upon the strange vessel, and is lying along under the foremast shrouds, while some of her crew appear to have swarmed up the chains. This cannot be told for certain. The haze around the barque is more dense than elsewhere, as if steam were passing off from her sides, and through it objects show confusedly.

While the frigate's people are straining their eyes to make out the movement of their boat, an officer, of sharper sight than the rest, cries out—

"See! the cutter coming back!"

All perceived this, and with some surprise. It is not ten minutes since the boat grappled on to the barque. Why returning from her so soon?

While they are conjecturing as to the cause, the same officer again observes something that has escaped the others. There are but *eight* oars, instead of ten—the regulation strength of the cutter—and ten men where before there were thirteen. Three of the boat's crew must have remained behind.

This causes neither alarm, nor uneasiness, to the frigate's officers. They take it that the three have gone aboard the barque, and for some reason, whatever it be, elected to stay there. They know the third lieutenant to be not only a brave man, but one of quick decision, and prompt also to act. He has boarded the distressed vessel, discovered the cause of distress, and sends the cutter back to bring whatever may be needed for her. Thus reasons the quarterdeck.

It is different on the fore, where apprehensions are rife about their missing shipmates—fears that some misfortune has befallen them. True, no shots have been heard nor flashes seen. Still they could have been killed without firearms. Savages might use other, and less noisy, weapons.

The tale of the skin-clad crew gives colour to this supposition. But then the "cutters" went armed—in addition to their cutlasses, being provided with pikes and boarding-pistols. Had they been attacked, they would not have retreated without discharging these last—less likely leaving three of their number behind. Besides no signs of strife or struggle have been observed upon the barque.

All the more mystery; and pondering upon it, the frigate's crew are strengthened in their superstitious faith. Meanwhile, the cutter is making way across the stretch of calm sea that separates the two ships, and although with reduced strength of rowers, cleaves the water quickly. The movements of the men indicate excitement. They pull as if rowing in a regatta! Soon they are near enough to be individually recognised, when it is seen that neither of the two officers is in the boat! Nor the coxswain—one of the oarsmen having taken his place at the tiller.

As the boat draws nearer, and the faces of the two men seated in the stern-sheets can be distinguished, there is observed upon them an expression which none can interpret. No one tries. All stand silently waiting till the cutter comes alongside, and sweeping past the bows, brings up on the frigate's starboard beam, under the main-chains.

The officers move forward along the gangway, and stand looking over the bulwarks; while the men come crowding aft, as far as permitted.

The curiosity of all receives a check—an abrupt disappointment. There is no news from the barque, save the meagre scrap contained in the lieutenant's order: "Back to the ship, and bring the doctor."

Beyond this the cutter's crew only knew that they have seen the hairy men. Seen and heard them, though without understanding a word of what these said. Two had sprung upon the shrouds, and shouted at the cutter's people, as if scolding them off!

The tale spreads through the frigate, fore and aft, quick as a train of powder ignited. It is everywhere talked of, and commented on. On the quarter, it is deemed strange enough; while forward, it further intensifies the belief in something supernatural.

The tars give credulous ear to one who cries out: "That's a phantom ship—sure!"

Their other comrade repeats what he said in the boat, and in the self-same words:

"Shipmates, we may never see that lieutenant again, nor the young reefer, nor the old cox—never!"

The boding speech appears like a prophecy, on the instant realised. Scarce has it passed the sailor's lips, when a cry rings through the frigate that startles all on board, thrilling them more intensely than ever.

While the men have been commenting upon the message brought back from the barque, and the officers are taking steps to hasten its execution—the doctor getting out his instruments, with such medicines as the occasion seems to call for—the strange vessel has been for a time unthought of.

The cry now raised recalls her, causing all to rush towards the frigate's side, and once more bend their eyes on the barque.

No, not *on* her; only in the direction where she was last seen. For, to their intense astonishment, *the polacca has disappeared!*

Chapter Seven
A Black Squall

The surprise caused by the disappearance of the strange vessel is but short-lived; explained by that very natural phenomenon—a fog. Not the haze already spoken of; but a dense bank of dark vapour that, drifting over the surface of the sea, has suddenly enveloped the barque within its floating folds.

It threatens to do the same with the frigate—as every sailor in her can perceive. But though their wondering is at an end, a sense of undefined fear still holds possession of them. Nor is this due to the fast approaching fog. That could not frighten men who have dared every danger of the deep, and oft groped their way through icy seas shrouded in darkness almost amorphous.

Their fears spring from the old fancy, that the other phenomena are not natural. The fog of itself may be; but what brings it on, just then, at a crisis, when they were speculating about the character of the chased vessel, some doubting her honesty, others sceptical of her reality, not a few boldly pronouncing her as a phantom? If an accident of nature, certainly a remarkable one.

The reader may smile at credulity of this kind; but not he who has mixed among the men of the forecastle, whatever the nationality of the ship, and whether merchantmen or man-of-war. Not all the training of naval schools, nor the boasted enlightenment of this our age, has fully eradicated from the mind of the canvas-clad mariner a belief in something more than he has seen, or can see—something *outside* nature. To suppose him emancipated from this would be to hold him of higher intelligence than his fellow-men, who stay ashore ploughing the soil, as he does the sea. To thousands of these he can point, saying: "Behold the believers in supernatural existences— in spirit-rappings—ay, in very ghosts; this not only in days gone by, but now—now more than ever within memory of man!" Then let not landsmen scoff at such fancies, not a whit more absurd than their own credence in spiritualism.

Aside from this sort of feeling in the warship, there is a real and far more serious cause for apprehension, in which all have a share—officers as men. A fog is before their eyes, apparently drifting towards them. It has curtained the other vessel, spreading over her like a pall, and will surely do the same with their own. They perceive, also, that it is not a fog of the ordinary kind, but one that portends storm, sudden and violent. For they are threatened by the *black squall* of the Pacific.

Enough in its name to cause uneasiness about the safety of their ship; though not of her are they thinking. She is a strong vessel, and can stand the sea's buffetings. Their anxiety is more for their shipmates, whose peril all comprehend. They know the danger of the two vessels getting separated in a fog. If they should, what will be the fate of those who have gone aboard the barque? The strange craft had been signalling distress. Is it scarcity of provisions, or want of water? In either case she will be worse off than ever. It cannot be shortness of hands to work her sails, with these all set! Sickness then? Some scourge afflicting her crew—cholera, or yellow fever? Something of the kind seems probable, by the lieutenant sending back for the doctor—and the doctor only.

Conjecturing ends, and suddenly. The time for action has arrived. The dark cloud comes driving on, and is soon around the ship, lapping her in its damp murky embrace. It clings to her bulwarks, pours over her canvas still spread, wetting it till big drops clout down upon the deck.

It is no longer a question of the surgeon starting forth on his errand of humanity, nor the cutter returning to the becalmed barque. There would be no more likelihood of discovering the latter, than of finding a needle in a stack of straw. In such a fog, the finest ship that ever sailed sea, with the smartest crew that ever vessel carried, would be helpless as a man groping his way in dungeon darkness.

There is no more thought of the barque, and not much about the absent officers. Out of sight, they are for a time almost out of mind. For on board the frigate every one has enough to do looking after himself and his duties. Almost on the instant of her sails being enveloped in vapour, they are struck by a strong wind, coming from a quarter directly opposite to that for which they have been hitherto set.

The voice of her commander, heard thundering through a trumpet, directs all canvas to be instantly taken in.

The order is executed with the promptness peculiar to a man-of-war; and soon after, the huge ship is tossing amid tempestuous waves, with only storm-sails set.

A ship under storm-canvas is a sight always melancholy to the mariner. It tells of a struggle with wind and wave, a serious conflict with the elements, which may well cause anxiety.

And such is the situation of the British frigate, soon as surrounded by the fog. The sea, lately tranquil, is now madly raging; the waves tempest-lashed, their crests like the manes of white horses going in headlong gallop. Amid them the huge war-vessel, but the moment before motionless—a leviathan, apparently the sea's lord—is now its slave, and soon may be its victim. Dancing like a cork, she is buffeted from billow to billow, or bounding into the trough between, as if cast there in scorn.

The frigate's crew is now fully occupied taking care of her, without time to think about any other vessel—even one flying a flag of distress. Ere long they may have to hoist the same signal themselves. But there are skilled seamen aboard, who well know what to do—who watch and ward every sea that comes sweeping along. Some of these tumble the big ship about, till the steersmen feel her going almost regardless of the rudder.

There are but two courses left for safety, and her captain weighs the choice between them. He must "lie to," and ride out the gale, or "scud" before it. To do the latter may take him away from the strange vessel—now no longer seen—and she may never be sighted by them again. Ten chances to one if she ever would; for *she* may not elect to run down the wind. Even if she did, there would be but slight hope of overhauling her—supposing the storm to continue for any considerable time. The probabilities are that she will lie to. As the naval lieutenant will no doubt have control, he would order her sails to be taken in. Surely he will not think of parting from that spot.

Thus reflecting, the frigate's captain determines upon "lying to," and keep as near the place as possible. Everything has been made snug, and the ship's head set close to wind.

Still, aboard of her, brave hearts are filled with fears and forebodings, not for themselves, but the safety of their shipmates on the barque. Both of the absent officers are favourites with their comrades of the quarter, as with the crew. So too the coxswain who accompanies them. What will be their fate?

All are thinking of it, though no one offers a surmise. No one can tell to what they have committed themselves. 'Tis only sure, that in the tempest now raging there must be danger to the stranger craft, without counting that signalised by the reversed ensign—without thought of the mystery already enwrapping her. The heart of every one on board the warship is beating with humanity, as pulsing with pent-up fear. And while the waves are pitching her almost on her beam-ends—while winds are rattling loud amidst her rigging—a yet louder sound mingles with their monotone. It is given out at regularly measured intervals: for it is the *minute-gun* which the frigate has commenced firing—not as a signal of distress, asking for assistance, but one of counsel and cheer, seeking to give it. Every sixty seconds, amidst the wild surging of waves, and the hoarse howling of winds, the louder boom of cannon breaks their harsh continuity.

The night comes down, adding to the darkness, though not much to the dilemma in which the frigate is placed. The fog and storm combined have already made her situation dangerous as might be; it could not well be worse.

Both continue throughout the night. And on through it all she keeps discharging her signal-guns, though no one thinks of listening for a response. In all probability there is no cannon aboard the barque—nothing that could give it.

Close upon the hour of morning, the storm begins to abate, and the clouds to dissipate. The fog seems to be lifting, or drifting off to some other part of the ocean.

And with hope again dawning comes the dawn of day. The frigate's people—every man of them, officers and tars—are upon deck. They stand along the ship's sides, ranged in rows by the bulwarks, looking out across the sea. There is no fog now—not the thinnest film. The sky is clear as crystal, and blue as a boat-race ribbon fresh unfolded; the sea the same, its big waves no longer showing sharp white crests, but rounded, and rolling lazily along. Over these the sailors look, scanning the surface. Their gaze is sent to every quarter—every point of the compass. The officers sweep the horizon with their glasses, ranging around the circle where the two blues meet. But neither naked eye nor telescope can discover aught there. Only sea and sky; an albatross with pinions of grand spread, or a tropic bird, its long tail-feathers trailing train-like behind it. No barque, polacca-rigged or otherwise—no ship of any kind—no sign of sail—no canvas except a full set of "courses" which the frigate herself has now set. She is alone upon the ocean—in the mighty Pacific—a mere speck upon its far-stretching illimitable expanse.

Every man upon the war-vessel is imbued with a strange sense of sadness. But all are silent—each inquiring of himself what has become of the barque, and what the fate of their shipmates.

One alone is heard speaking aloud, giving expression to a thought, seeming common to all. It is the sailor who twice uttered the prediction, which, for the third time, he repeats, now as the assertion of a certainty. To the group gathered around him he says:—

"Shipmates, we'll never see that lieutenant again, nor the young reefer, nor the old cox—never!"

Chapter Eight
A Fleet of many Flags

Scene, San Francisco, the capital of California. Time, the autumn of 1849; several weeks anterior to the chase recounted.

A singular city the San Francisco of 1849; very different from that it is to-day, and equally unlike what it was twelve months before the aforesaid date, when the obscure village of Yerba Buena yielded up its name, along with its site, entering on what may be termed a second genesis.

The little *pueblita*, port of the Mission Dolores, built of sun-dried bricks—its petty commerce in hides and tallow represented by two or three small craft annually arriving and departing—wakes up one morning to behold whole fleets of ships sailing in through the "Golden Gate," and dropping anchor in front of its shingly strand. They come from all parts of the Pacific, from all the other oceans, from the ends of the earth, carrying every kind of flag known to the nations. The whalesman, late harpooning "fish" in the Arctic ocean, with him who has been chasing "cachalot" in the Pacific or Indian; the merchantman standing towards Australia, China, or Japan the traders among the South Sea Islands; the coasters of Mexico, Chili, Peru; men-o'-war of every flag and fashion, frigates, corvettes, and double-deckers; even Chinese junks and Malayan prahus are seen setting into San Francisco Bay, and bringing to beside the wharfless beach of Yerba Buena.

What has caused this grand spreading of canvas, and commingling of queer craft? What is still causing it; for still they come! The answer lies in a little word of four letters; the same that from the beginning of man's activity on earth has moved him to many things—too oft to deeds of evil—*gold*. Some eighteen months before the Swiss emigrant Sutter, scouring out his mill-race on a tributary of the Sacramento River, observes shining particles among the mud. Taking them up, and holding them in the hollow of his hand, he feels that they are heavy, and sees them to be of golden sheen. And gold they prove, when submitted to the test of the alembic.

The son of Helvetia discovered the precious metal in grains, and nuggets, interspersed with the drift of a fluvial deposit. They were not the first found in California, but the first coming under the eyes of European settlers—men imbued with the energy to collect, and carry them to the far-off outside world.

Less than two years have elapsed since the digging of Sutter's mill-race. Meantime, the specks that scintillated in its ooze have been transported over the ocean, and exhibited in great cities—in the windows of brokers, and bullion merchants. The sight has proved sufficient to thickly people the banks of the Sacramento—hitherto sparsely settled—and cover San Francisco Bay with ships from every quarter of the globe.

Not only is the harbour of Yerba Buena crowded with strange craft, but its streets with queer characters—adventurers of every race and clime— among whom may be heard an exchange of tongues, the like never listened to since the abortive attempt at building the tower of Babel.

The Mexican mud-walled dwellings soon disappear—swallowed up and lost amidst the modern surrounding of canvas tents, and weather-board houses, that rise as by magic around them. A like change takes place in their occupancy. No longer the tranquil interiors—the *tertulia*, with guests sipping aniseed, curacoa, and Canario—munching sweet cakes and *confituras*. Instead, the houses inside now ring with boisterous revelry, with a perfume of mint and Monongahela; and although the guitar still tinkles, it is almost inaudible amid the louder strains of clarionet, fiddle, and French horn.

What a change in the traffic of the streets! No more silent, at certain hours deserted for the *siesta*, at others trodden by sandalled monks and shovel-hatted priests—both bold of gaze, when passing the dark-eyed damsels in high shell-combs and black silk mantillas; bolder still, saluting the brown-skinned daughters of the aboriginal wrapped in their blue-grey *rebozos*. No more trodden by garrison soldiers in uniforms of French cut and colour; by officers glittering in gold lace; by townsmen in cloaks of broadcloth; by country gentlemen (haciendados) on horseback; and herdsmen, or small farmers (rancheros) in their splendid Californian costume.

True, some of these are still seen, but not as of yore, swaggering and conspicuous. Amid the concourse of new-comers they move timidly, jostled by rough men in red flannel shirts, buckskin and blanket coats, with pistols in their belts, and knives hanging handy along their hips. By others equally formidable, in Guernsey frocks, or wearing the dreadnought jacket of the sailor; not a few scarce clothed at all, shrouding their nakedness in such rags as remain after a long journey overland, or a longer voyage by sea.

In all probability, since its beginning, the world never witnessed so motley an assemblage of men, tramping through the streets of a seaport town, as those seen in Yerba Buena, rebaptised San Francisco, in the year of our Lord 1849.

And perhaps never a more varied display of bunting in one bay. In all certainty, harbour never held so large a fleet of ships with so few men to man them. At least one-half are crewless, and a goodly portion of the remainder almost so. Many have but their captains and mates, with, it may be, the carpenter and cook. The forecastle fellows are ashore, and but few of them intend returning aboard. They are either gone off to the gold-diggings, or are going. There has been a general *debandade* among the Jack-tars—leaving many a merry deck in forlorn and silent solitude.

In this respect there is a striking contrast between the streets of the town and the ships lying before it. In the former, an eager throng, pushing, jostling, surging noisily along, with all the impatience of men half-mad; in the latter, tranquillity, inaction, the torpor of lazy life, as if the vessels—many of them splendid craft—were laid up for good, and never again going to sea. And many never did—their hulks to this day, like the skeletons of stranded whales, are seen lying along that beach which was once Yerba Buena!

Chapter Nine
A Brace of British Officers

Notwithstanding the abnormal condition of naval affairs above described, and the difficulties to be dealt with, not all the vessels in San Francisco Bay are crewless. A few still retain their full complement of hands—these being mostly men-of-war, whose strict discipline prevents desertion, though it needs strategy to assist. They ride at anchor far out, beyond swimming distance from the beach, and will not allow shore-boats to approach them. The tar who attempts to take French leave will have a severe swim for it; perchance get a shot sent after, that may send him to the bottom of the sea. With this menace constantly before their minds, even California's gold does not tempt many to run the dangerous gauntlet.

Among the craft keeping up this iron discipline is one that bears the British flag—a man-of-war, conspicuous by her handsome hull and clean tapering spars. Her sails are stowed snug, lashed neatly along the yards; in her rigging not a rope out of place. Down upon her decks, white as holystone can make them, the same regularity is observable; every rope coiled, every brace trimly turned upon its belaying-pin. It could not be otherwise with the frigate *Crusader*, commanded by Captain Bracebridge—a sailor of the old school, who takes a pride in his ship. He has managed to retain his crew—every man-Jack of them. There is not a name on the frigate's books but has its representative in a live sailor, who can either be seen upon her decks, or at any moment summoned thither by the whistle of the boatswain. Even if left to themselves, but few of the "crusaders" would care to desert. Gold itself cannot lure them to leave a ship where things are so agreeable; for Captain Bracebridge does all in his power to make matters pleasant, for men as well as officers. He takes care that the former get good grub, and plenty of it—including full rations of grog. He permits them to have amusements among themselves; while the officers treat them to *tableaux-vivants*, charades, and private theatricals. To crown all, a grand ball has been given aboard the ship, in anticipation of her departure from the port— an event near at hand—at which more than one of her officers have made acquaintances they would wish to meet again—two of them desiring this with longings of a special kind. These last have fallen in love with a brace of shore damsels, with whom they had danced, and done a little flirting at the ball.

It is the third day after, and these love-struck gentlemen are standing upon the poop-deck, conversing about it. They are apart from their comrades—purposely, since their speech is confidential. Both are young men; the elder, by name Crozier, being a year or two over twenty; while the younger, Will Cadwallader, is almost as much under it. Crozier has passed his term of probationary service, and is now "mate;" while the other is still but a "midshipmite." And a type of this last, just as Marryat would have made him; bright face, light-coloured hair, curling over cheeks ruddy as the bloom upon a Ribston pippin. For he is Welsh, with eyes of that turquoise blue often observed in the descendants of the Cymri, and hair of aureous hue.

Quite different is Edward Crozier, who hails from an ancestral hall in the East Riding of York. His hair, also curling, is dark brown; his complexion in correspondence. Moustaches already well grown. An acquiline nose and broad jaw-blades denote resolution—a character borne out by the glance of an eye that shows no quailing. He is of medium size, with a figure denoting strength, and capable of great endurance—in short, carrying out any resolve his mind may make. In point of personal appearance he is the superior; though both are handsome fellows, each in his own style.

And as the styles are different, so are their dispositions—these rather contrasting. Crozier is of a serious, sedate turn and, though anything but morose, rarely given to mirth; while, from the countenance of Cadwallader the laugh is scarce ever absent, and the dimple on his cheek—to employ a printer's phrase—appears stereotyped. With the young Welshman a joke might be carried to extremes, and he would only seek his *revanche* by a lark of like kind. But with him of Yorkshire, practical jesting would be dangerous.

Notwithstanding this difference of disposition, the two officers are fast friends; a fact perhaps due to the dissimilitude of their natures. When not separated by their respective duties, they keep habitually together on board the ship, and together go ashore. And now, for the first time in the lives of both, they have commenced making love together. Fortune has favoured them in this, that they are not in love with the same lady. Still further, that their sweethearts do not dwell apart, but live under the same roof, and belong to one family. They are not sisters, for all that; nor yet cousins, though standing in a certain relationship. One is the aunt of the other.

Such kinship might argue inequality of age. There is none, however, or only a very little: scarce so much as between the young officers themselves. The aunt is but a year or so the senior of her niece. And as Fate has willed, the lots of the lovers have been cast to correspond in proper symmetry and proportion. Crozier is in love with the former—Cadwallader with the latter.

Their sweethearts are both Spanish, of the purest blood, the boasted *sangre azul*. They are, respectively, daughter and grand-daughter of Don Gregorio Montijo, whose house can be seen from the ship: a mansion of imposing appearance, in the Mexican *hacienda* style, set upon the summit of a hill, at some distance inshore, and southward from the town.

While conversing, the young officers have their eyes upon it—one of the two assisting his vision with a telescope. It is Cadwallader who uses the instrument.

Holding it to his eye, he says:

"I think I can see them, Ned. At all events, there are two heads on the house-top, just showing over the parapet. I'll take odds it's them, the dear girls. I wonder if they see us."

"I should say, not likely; unless, as yourself, they're provided with a telescope."

"By Jove! I believe they've got one. I see something glance. My Iñez has it to her eye, I'll warrant."

"More likely it's my Carmen. Give me that glass. For all those blue eyes you're so proud of, I can sight a sail farther than you."

"A sail, yes; but not a pretty face, Ned. No, no; you're blind to beauty; else you'd never have taken on to the old aunt, leaving the niece to me. Ha, ha, ha!"

"Old, indeed! She's as young as yours, if not younger. One tress of her bright amber hair is worth a whole head of your sweetheart's black tangle. Look at that!"

He draws out such a tress, and unfolding, shakes it tauntingly before the other's eyes. In the sun it gleams golden, with a radiance of red; for it is amber colour, as he has styled it.

"Look at this!" cries Cadwallader, also exhibiting a lock of hair. "You thought nobody but yourself could show love-locks. This to yours, is as costly silk alongside cheap cotton."

For an instant each stands caressing his particular favours; then both burst into laughter, as they return them to their places of deposit.

Crozier, in turn taking the telescope, directs it on the house of Don Gregorio; after a time saying:

"About one thing you're right, Will: those heads are the same from which we've had our tresses. Ay, and they're looking this way, through glasses; perhaps, expecting us soon. Well; we'll be with them, please God, before many hours; or it may be minutes. Then, you'll see how much superior bright amber is to dull black—anywhere in the world, but especially in the light of a Californian sun."

"Nowhere, under either sun or moon. Give me the girl with the crow-black hair!"

"For me, her whose locks are red gold!"

"Well; *cada uno a su gusto*, as my sweetheart has taught me to say in her soft Andalusian. But now, Ned, talking seriously, do you think the governor will give us leave to go ashore?"

"He must; I know he will."

"How do you know it?"

"Bah! *ma bohil*; as our Irish second would say. You're the son of a poor Welsh squire—good blood, I admit. But I chance to be heir to twice ten thousand a year, with an uncle in the Admiralty. I have asked leave for both of us. So, don't be uneasy about our getting it. Captain Bracebridge is no snob; but he knows his own interests, and won't refuse such fair request. See! There he is—coming this way. Now for his answer—affirmative, you may rely upon it."

"Gentlemen," says the captain, approaching, "you have my permission to go ashore for the day. The gig will take you, landing wherever you wish. You are to send the boat back, and give the coxswain orders where, and when, he's to await you on return to the ship. Take my advice, and abstain from drink—which might get you into difficulties. As you know, just now San Francisco is full of all sorts of queer characters—a very Pandemonium of a place. For the sake of the service, and the honour of the uniform you wear, steer clear of scrapes—and above all, give a wide berth to *women*."

After thus delivering himself, the captain turns on his heel, and retires—leaving mate and midshipman to their meditations.

They do not meditate long; the desired leave has been granted, and the order issued for the gig to be got ready. The boat is in the water, her crew swarming over the side, and seating themselves upon the thwarts.

The young officers only stay to give a finishing touch to their toilet, preparatory to appearing before eyes whose critical glances both more fear than they would the fire of a ship's broadside.

Everything arranged, they drop down the man-ropes and seat themselves in the stern-sheets; Crozier commanding the men to shove off.

Soon the little gig is gliding over the tranquil waters of San Francisco Bay; not in the direction of the landing-wharf, but for a projecting point on the shore, to the south of, and some distance outside, the suburbs of the town. For, the beacon towards which they steer is the house of Don Gregorio Montijo.

Chapter Ten
A Pair of Spanish Señoritas

Don Gregorio Montijo is a Spaniard, who, some ten years previous to the time of which we write, found his way into the Republic of Mexico, afterwards moving on to "Alta California." Settling by San Francisco Bay, he became a *ganadero*, or stock-farmer—the industry in those days chiefly followed by Californians.

His grazing estate gives proof that he has prospered. Its territory extends several miles along the water, and several leagues backward; its boundary in that direction being the shore of the South Sea itself; while a thousand head of horses, and ten times the number of horned cattle, roam over its rich pastures.

His house stands upon the summit of a hill that rises above the bay—a sort of spur projected from higher ground behind, and trending at right angles to the beach, where it declines into a low-lying sand-spit. Across this runs the shore-road, southward from the city to San José, cutting the ridge midway between the walls of the house and the water's edge, at some three hundred yards distance from each.

The dwelling, a massive quadrangular structure—in that Span-Moriscan style of architecture imported into New Spain by the *Conquistadores*—is but a single storey in height, having a flat, terraced roof, and inner court: this last approached through a grand gate entrance, centrally set in the front façade, with a double-winged door wide enough to admit the coach of Sir Charles Grandison.

Around a Californian country-house there's rarely much in the way of ornamental grounds—even though it be a *hacienda* of the first-class. And when the headquarters of a grazing estate, still less; its inclosures consisting chiefly of "corrals" for the penning and branding of cattle, these usually erected in the rear of the dwelling. To this almost universal nakedness the grounds of Don Gregorio offer some exception. He has added a stone fence, which, separating them from the high road, is penetrated by a portalled entrance, with an avenue that leads straight up to the house. This, strewn with snow-white sea-shells, is flanked on each side by a row of *manzanita* bushes—a beautiful indigenous evergreen. Here and there a clump of California bays, and some scattered peach-trees, betray an attempt, however slight, at landscape gardening.

Taking into account the grandeur of his house, and the broad acres attached to it, one may safely say, that in the New World Don Gregorio has done well. And, in truth, so has he—thriven to fulness. But he came not empty from the Old, having brought with him sufficient cash to purchase a large tract of land, as also sufficient of horses and horned cattle to stock it. No needy adventurer he, but a gentleman by birth; one of Biscay's bluest blood—hidalgos since the days of the Cid.

In addition to his ready-money, he also brought with him a wife—Biscayan as himself—and a daughter, at the time turned eight years old. His wife has been long ago buried; a tombstone in the cemetery of the old Dolores Mission commemorating her many virtues. Since, he has had an accession to his contracted family circle; the added member being a grand-daughter, only a year younger than his daughter, but equally well grown—both having reached the ripest age of girlhood. It is scarce necessary to add, that the young ladies, thus standing in the relationship of aunt and niece, are the two with whom Edward Crozier and Willie Cadwallader have respectively fallen in love.

And while mate and midshipman are on the way to pay them a promised visit—for such it is—a word may be said about their personal appearance. Though so closely allied, and nearly of an age, in other respects the two differ so widely, that one unacquainted with the fact would not suspect the slightest kinship between them.

The aunt, Doña Carmen, is of pure Biscayan blood, both by her father's and mother's side. From this she derives her blonde complexion, with that colour of hair so admired by Mr Crozier; with the blue-grey eyes, known as "Irish"—the Basques and Celts being a kindred race. Her Biscayan origin has endowed her with a fine figure of full development, withal in perfect feminine proportions; while her mother has transmitted to her what, in an eminent degree, she herself possessed—beauty of face and nobleness of feature.

In the daughter neither has deteriorated, but perhaps improved. For the benignant clime of California has such effect; the soft breezes of the South Sea fanning as fair cheeks as were ever kissed by Tuscan, or Levantine wind.

A chapter might be devoted to the charms of Doña Carmen Montijo, and still not do them justice. Enough to say, that they are beyond cavil. There are men in San Francisco who would dare death for her sake, if sure of her smile to speak approval of the deed; ay, one who would for as much do murder!

And in that same city is a man who would do the same for Iñez Alvarez—though she has neither blonde complexion, nor blue eyes. Instead she is a *morena*, or brunette, with eyes and hair of the darkest. But she is also a beauty, of the type immortalised by many bards—Byron among the number, when he wrote his rhapsody on the "Girl of Cadiz."

Iñez is herself a girl of Cadiz, of which city her father was a native. The Conde Alvarez, an officer in the Spanish army, serving with his regiment in Biscay, there saw a face that charmed him. It belonged to the daughter of Don Gregorio Montijo—his eldest and first-born, some eighteen years older than Carmen. The Andalusian count wooed the Biscayan lady, won, and bore her away to his home. Both have gone to their long home, leaving their only child inheritress of a handsome estate. From her father, in whose veins ran Moorish blood, Iñez inherits jet-black eyes, with lashes nearly half-an-inch in length, and above them brows shaped like the moon in the middle of her first quarter. Though in figure more slender than her aunt, she is quite Carmen's equal in height, and in this may some day excel; since she has not yet attained her full stature.

Such are the two damsels, who have danced with the young British officers, and made sweet havoc in their hearts. Have the hearts of the *señoritas* received similar hurt in return? By listening to their conversation we shall learn.

Chapter Eleven
Mutual Admissions

The dwelling of Don Gregorio Montijo, as already stated, is terrace-topped, that style of roof in Spanish countries termed *azotea*. This, surrounded by a parapet breast-high—beset with plants and flowering shrubs in boxes and pots, thus forming a sort of aerial garden—is reached by a stone stair, the *escalera*, which leads up out of the inner court, called *patio*. During certain hours of the day, the azotea is a favourite resort, being a pleasant place of dalliance, as also the finest for observation—commanding, as in this case it does, a view of the country at back, and the broad bay in front. To look upon this last have the two "señoritas," on the same morning, ascended—soon after breakfast, which in all parts of Spanish America is eaten at the somewhat late hour of 11 a.m.

That they do not intend staying here long, is evident from the character of their dresses. Both are costumed and equipped for the saddle; having hats of vicuña wool on their heads, riding-whips in their hands, and spurs on their heels; while in the courtyard below stand four horses, saddled and bridled, champing their bits, and impatiently pawing the flagged pavement.

Since all the saddles are such as are usually ridden by men, it may be supposed only men are to be mounted, and that the ladies' horses have not yet been brought out of the stable. This would naturally be the conjecture of a stranger to Spanish California. But one *an fait* to its fashions would draw deductions differently. Looking at the spurred heels upon the house-top, and the saddled horses below, he would conclude that two of the steeds were intended to be ridden by the ladies; in that style of equitation with which the famed Duchesse de Berri was accustomed to astonish the Parisians.

The other two horses, having larger and somewhat coarser saddles, are evidently designed for gentlemen; so that the cavalcade will be symmetrically composed—two and two of each sex.

The gentlemen have not yet put in an appearance; but who they are may be learnt from the dialogue passing between the two ladies. From their elevated, position they can see the rapidly growing city of San Francisco, and the shipping in its harbour—north-east, and a little to their left. But there are several vessels riding at anchor out in front of them; one a warship, towards which the eyes of both keep continuously turning, as though they expected a boat soon to put off from her side.

As yet none such has been seen; and, withdrawing her gaze from the warship, Iñez opens the conversation by a question—

"Is it really true that we're going back to Spain?"

She has been in California only a short time, since the death of her father and mother, which placed her under the guardianship of Don Gregorio. But though here, lovers have been all the while sighing around her, she longs to return to her dear Andalusia. Therefore has she asked the question with more than a common interest.

"Quite true;" says Carmen, giving the answer, "and I'm sorry it is so."

"Why should you be sorry?"

"There are many reasons."

"Give one."

"I could give twenty."

"One will be sufficient—if good."

"They're all good."

"Let me hear them, then."

"First of all, I like California—I love it. Its fine climate, and bright blue sides."

"Not a bit brighter, or bluer, than those of Spain."

"Ten times brighter, and ten times bluer. The skies of the Old-World are to those of the New as lead to *lapis lazuli*. In that respect, neither Spain nor Italy can compare with California. Its seas, too, are superior. Even the boasted Bay of Naples would be but a poor pond alongside that noble sheet of water, far-stretching before our eyes. Look at it!"

"Looking at it through *your* eyes, I might think so; not through mine. For my part, I see nothing in it to be so much admired."

"But something *on* it; for instance, that grand ship out yonder. Come, now; confess the truth! Isn't that something to admire?"

"But she don't belong to your bay," replies the Andalusian.

"No matter. There is on it now, and in it—the ship I mean—somebody who, if I mistake not, has very much interested somebody else—a certain Andalusian lady, by name Iñez Alvarez."

"Your words will answer as well for a Biscayan lady—by name Carmen Montijo."

"Suppose I admit it, and say yes? Well; I will. There *is* one in yonder ship who has very much interested me. Nay, more; I admire—ay, love him! You see I'm not ashamed to confess what the world affects to consider a weakness. We of the Celtic race don't keep secrets as you of the further South; half Moors, as you are. For all, *sobrina*, you haven't kept yours; though you tried heard enough. I saw from the first you were smitten with that young English officer, who has hair the exact colour of a carrot!"

"It isn't anything of the kind. His hair is of a much more becoming hue than that of the other English officer, who's taken your fancy, *tia*."

"Nothing to compare with it. Look at this. There's a curl; one of the handsomest that ever grew on the head of man! Dark and glossy, as the coat of the fur-seal. Beautiful! I could kiss it over, and over again!"

While speaking, she does so.

"And look at this!" cries the other, also drawing forth a lock of hair, and displaying it in the sunlight, "See how it shines—like tissue of gold! Far prettier than that you've got, and better worth kissing."

Saying which she imitates the example set her, by raising the tress to her lips, and repeatedly kissing it.

"So, so, my innocent!" exclaims Carmen, "you've been stealing too?"

"As yourself!"

"And, I suppose, you've given him a love-lock in exchange?"

"Have you?"

"I have. To you, Iñez, I make no secret of it. Come, now! Be equally candid with me. Have you done so?"

"I've done the same as yourself."

"And has your heart gone with the gift? Tell the truth, *sobrina*."

"Ask your own, *tia*; and take its answer for mine."

"Enough, then; we understand each other, and shall keep the secret to ourselves. Now let's talk of other things; go back to what we began with—about leaving California. You're glad we're going?"

"Indeed, yes. And I wonder you're not the same. Dear old Spain, the finest country on earth! And Cadiz the finest city."

"Ah! about that we two differ. Give me California for a country, and San Francisco for a home; though it's not much of a city yet. It will, ere long;

and I should like to stay in it. But that's not to be, and there's an end of the matter. Father has determined on leaving. Indeed, he has already sold out; so that this house and the lands around it are no longer ours. As the lawyers have the deed of transfer, and the purchase money has been paid, we're only here on sufferance, and must soon yield possession. Then, we're to take ship for Panama, go across the Isthmus and over the Atlantic Ocean; once more to renew the Old-world life, with all its stupid ceremonies. How I shall miss the free wild ways of California—its rural sports—with their quaint originality and picturesqueness! I'm sure I shall die of *ennui*, soon after reaching Spain. Your Cadiz will kill me."

"But, Carmen; surely you can't be happy here—now that everything is so changed? Why, we can scarce walk out in safety, or take a promenade through the streets of the town, crowded with those rude fellows in red-shirts, who've come to dig for gold—Anglo-Saxons, as they call themselves."

"What! You speaking against Anglo-Saxons! And with that tress treasured in your bosom—so close to your heart!"

"Oh! *he* is different. He's not Saxon, but Welsh—and that's Celtic, the same as you Biscayans. Besides, he isn't to be ranked with that rabble, even though he were of the same race. The Señor Cadwallader is a born hidalgo."

"Admitting him to be, I think you do wrong to these red-shirted gentry, in calling them a rabble. Rough as they may appear, they have gentle hearts under their coarse homespun coats. Many of them are true bred-and-born gentlemen; and, what's better, behave as such. I've never received insult from them—not even disrespect—though I've been among them scores of times. Father wrongs them too: for it is partly their presence here that's causing him to quit California—as also many others of our old families. Still, as we reside in the country, at a safe distance from town, we might enjoy immunity from meeting *los barbaros*, as our people are pleased contemptuously to style them. For my part, I love dear old California, and will greatly regret leaving it. Only to think; I shall never more behold the gallant *vaquero*, mounted on his magnificent steed, careering across the plain, and launching his lazo over the horns of a fierce wild bull, ready to gore him if he but miss his aim. Ah! it's one of the finest sights in the world—so exciting in this dull prosaic age. It recalls the heroic days and deeds of the Great Conde, the Campeador, and Cid. Yes, Iñez; only in this modern transatlantic land—out here, on the shores of the South Sea—do there still exist customs and manners to remind one of the old knight-errantry and times of the troubadours."

"What an enthusiast you are! But apropos of your knights-errant, yonder are two of them, if I mistake not, making this way. Now, fancy yourself on the donjon of an ancient Moorish castle, salute, and receive them accordingly. Ha, ha, ha!"

The clear ringing laugh of the Andalusian is not echoed by the Biscayan. Instead, a shadow falls over her face, as her eyes become fixed upon two mounted figures just distinguishable in the distance.

"True types of your Californian *chivalry!*" adds Iñez ironically.

"True types of Californian *villainy!*" rejoins Carmen, in serious earnest.

Chapter Twelve
A Couple of Californian "Caballeros"

The horsemen, so oddly commented upon, have just emerged from the suburbs of San Francisco, taking the road which leads southward along shore.

Both are garbed in grand style, in the national costume of that country, which, in point of picturesqueness is not exceeded by any other in the world.

They wear the wide trousers (*calzoneras*), along the outer seams lashed with gold lace, and beset with filigree buttons; the snow-white drawers (*calzoncillas*) here and there puffing out; below, *botas* and spurs—the last with rowels several inches in diameter, that glitter like great stars behind their heels. They have tight-fitting jackets of velveteen, closed in front, and over the bosom elaborately embroidered; scarfs of China crape round their waists, the ends dangling adown the left hip, terminating in a fringe of gold cord; on their heads *sombreros* with broad brim, and band of bullion— the *toquilla*. In addition, each has over his shoulders a *manga*—the most magnificent of outside garments, with a drape graceful as a Roman *toga*. That of one is scarlet-coloured, the other sky-blue. Nor are their horses less grandly bedecked. Saddles of stamped leather, scintillating with silver studs—their cloths elaborately embroidered; bridles of plaited horse-hair, jointed with tags and tassels; bits of the Mamaluke pattern, with check-pieces and curbs powerful enough to break the jaw at a jerk.

The steeds thus splendidly caparisoned are worthy of it. Though small, they are of perfect shape—pure blood of Arabian sires, transmitted through dams of Andalusia. They are descended from the stock transported to the New World by the *Conquistadores*; and the progenitor of one or other may have carried Alvarado or Sandoval—perhaps Cortez himself.

The riders are both men of swarthy complexion, with traits that tell of the Latinic race. Their features are Spanish; in one a little more pronounced than the other. He who wears the sky-coloured cloak has all the appearance of being Mexican born. The blood in his veins giving the brown tinge to his skin, is not Moorish, but more likely from the aborigines of California. For all this, he is not a true *mestizo*; only one among whose remote ancestry an

Indian woman may have been numbered; since the family-tree of many a proud Californian has sprung from such root. He is of medium size, with figure squat and somewhat square, and sits his horse as though he were part of the animal. If seen afoot his legs would appear bowed, almost bandied, showing that he has spent the greater part of his life in the saddle. His face is flat, its outline rounded, the nose compressed, nostrils agape, and lips thick enough to suggest the idea of an African origin. But his hair contradicts this—being straight as needles, and black as the skin of a Colobus monkey. More like he has it from the Malays, through the Californian Indian—some tribes of which are undoubtedly of Malayan descent.

Whatever the mixture in his blood, the man is himself a native Californian, born by the shores of San Francisco Bay, on a *ganaderia*, or grazing estate. He is some twenty-six or seven years of age, his name Faustino Calderon— "Don" by ancestral right, and ownership of the aforesaid *ganaderia*.

He in the scarlet *manga*, though but a few years older, is altogether different in appearance, as otherwise; personally handsomer, and intellectually superior. His features better formed, are more purely Spanish; their outline oval and regular the jaws broad and balanced; the chin prominent; the nose high, without being hooked or beaked; the brow classically cut, and surmounted by a thick shock of hair, coal-black in colour, and waved rather than curling. Heavy moustaches on the upper lip, with an imperial on the under one—the last extending below the point of the chin—all the rest of his face, throat, and cheeks, clean shaven. Such are the facial characteristics of Don Francisco de Lara, who is a much larger, and to all appearance stronger, man than his travelling companion.

Calderon, as said, is a gentleman by birth, and a *ganadero*, or stock-farmer, by occupation. He inherits a considerable tract of pasture-land, left him by his father—some time deceased—along with the horses and horned cattle that browse upon it. An only son, he is now owner of all. But his ownership is not likely to continue. He is fast relinquishing it, by the pursuit of evil courses—among them three of a special kind: wine, women, and play—which promise to make him bankrupt in purse, as they already have in character. For around San Francisco, as in it, he is known as *roué* and reveller, a debauchee in every speciality of debauch, and a silly fellow to boot. Naturally of weak intellect, and dissipation has made it weaker.

Of as much moral darkness, though different in kind, is the character of Don Francisco de Lara—"Frank Lara," as he is familiarly known in the streets and saloons. Though Spanish in features, and speaking the language, he can also talk English with perfect fluency—French too, when called upon, with a little Portuguese and Italian. For, in truth, he is not a Spaniard, but only so by descent, being a Creole of New Orleans—that cosmopolitan city *par excellence*—hence his philological acquirements.

Frank Lara is one of those children of chance, wanderers who come into the world nobody knows how, when, or whence; only, that they are in it; and while there, performing a part in accordance with their mysterious origin—living in luxury, and finding the means for it, by ways that baffle conjecture.

He is full thirty years of age; the last ten of which he has spent on the shores of San Francisco Bay. Landing there from an American whaling-vessel, and in sailor costume, he cast off his tarry "togs," and took to land-life in California. Its easy idleness, as its lawlessness, exactly suited his natural inclinations.

Similar inclinings and pursuits, at an early period brought him and Calderon in contact; and certain relations have been established between them; in other words, they have become united in a business partnership—a *bank*; of that species known as *"monté"* bank.

Since the discovery of the gold *placers*, the streets of San Francisco have been crowded with men mad after the precious metal; among them some who do not desire to undergo the toil of sifting it out of sand, or washing it from river-mud. They prefer the easier, and cleaner, method of gathering it across the green baize of a gambling table.

To accommodate such gentry, Francisco de Lara has established a *monté* bank, Faustino Calderon being his backer. But though the latter is the moneyed man, and has supplied most of the cash to start with, he does not show in the transaction. He is only as the sleeping partner; De Lara, with less reputation at stake, being the active and ostensible one.

As yet Faustino Calderon has not come within the category of the professional gamester, and respectability does not repel him. His dissipated habits are far from exceptional, and his father's good name still continues to throw its *aegis* over him. Under it he is eligible to Californian society of the most select kind, and has the *entrée* of its best circles.

And so also Don Francisco de Lara—in a different way. Wealth has secured him this; for although anything but rich, he has the repute of being so, and bears evidence of it about him. He is always stylishly and fashionably attired; his shirt of the finest linen, with diamond studs sparkling in its front. Free in dispensing gratuities, he gives to the poor and the priests—finding this last kind of largess a good speculation. For, in California, as in other Catholic countries, the dispenser of "Peter's Pence" is sure of being held in high estimation. Frank Lara so dispenses with a liberal hand; and is therefore styled "Don" Francisco—saluted as such by the sandalled monks and shovel-hatted priests who come in contact with him.

In addition to all, he is good-looking and of graceful deportment, without being at all a dandy. On the contrary he carries himself with earnest air, calm and cool, while in his eyes may be read the expression—*noli me tangere*. A native of New Orleans, where duels occur almost daily, he is up in the *art d'escrime*; and since his arrival in California has twice called out his man—on the second occasion killing him.

Escroc as the French might call him; "blackleg" in the English vocabulary; "sport" in American phrase, Frank Lara is a man with whom no one who knows him likes to take liberties.

Such are the two men whom Iñez Alvarez has facetiously styled types of Californian "chivalry," while Carmen Montijo has more correctly described them as typical of its "villainy." And yet to make call on this very Iñez, and this same Carmen, the gentlemen so differently designated are now on their way!

Chapter Thirteen
Confession of Fear

After having delivered their speeches, so nearly alike in sound, yet so opposed in sense, the two girls stand for a short time silent, their faces turned toward the approaching horsemen. These are still more than a mile off, and to the ordinary eye only distinguishable as mounted men wearing cloaks—one of scarlet colour, the other sky-blue. But despite the distance, the others easily identify them, simultaneously, and in tone contemptuous, pronouncing their names.

"Yes," says Carmen, now speaking in full assurance, with a lorgnette raised to her eyes—hitherto bent upon the British warship, "in all California there are no truer types of what I've called them. Do you think they're coming on to the house, Iñez?"

"'Tis very likely; I should say, almost certain."

"What can be bringing them?" mechanically queries Carmen, with an air of increased vexation.

"Their horses, aunt," rejoins the niece, jestingly.

"Don't jest, *niña*! It's too serious."

"What's too serious?"

"Why, these fellows coming hither. I wonder what they can be wanting?"

"You needn't wonder at that," says Iñez, still speaking jocularly. "I can tell you what one of them wants, that one Don Francisco de Lara. He is desirous to have a look at the mistress of this mansion."

"And Don Faustino Calderon is no doubt equally desirous to look at her niece," retorts the other in like bantering tone.

"He's quite welcome. He may look till he strains his ugly eyes out. It won't make any impression on me."

"I'm sorry I can't say the same for Don Francisco. On me, his looks *do* make impression—far from pleasant."

"It wasn't always so, *tia*?"

"No, I admit. I only wish it had been."

"But why?"

"Because, now I shouldn't need to be afraid of him."

"Afraid of him! Surely you are not that?"

"Well, no—not exactly afraid—still—"

She speaks hesitatingly, and in disjointed phrases, her head drooping down. Then a quick change comes over her countenance, and, bending closer to the other, she asks, "Can I trust you with a confidence, Iñez?"

"Why need you ask that? You've already trusted me with one—in telling me you love Don Eduardo."

"Now I give you another—by telling you I once loved Don Francisco."

"Indeed!"

"No, no!" rejoins Carmen quickly, and as half-repenting the avowal. "Not *loved* him—that's not true, I only *came near it.*"

"And now?"

"I hate him!"

"Why, may I ask? What has changed you?"

"That's easily answered. When I first met him I was younger than now; a mere girl, full of girlish fancies—romantic, as called. I thought him handsome; and in a sense so he is. In person, you'll admit, he's all man may, or need, be—a sort of Apollo, or Hyperion. But in mind—ah, Iñez, that man is a very Satyr—in heart and soul a Mephistopheles."

"But why should you be afraid of him?"

Carmen does not reply promptly. Clearly, she has not yet bestowed the whole of her confidence. There is something withheld.

Iñez, whose sympathies are now enlisted, presses for *the* explanation.

"Carmen—dear Carmen! tell me what it is. Have you ever given Don Francisco a claim to call you his *novia?*"

"Never! Neither that, nor anything of the kind. He has no claim, and I no compromise. The only thing I've reason to regret is, having listened to his flattering speeches without resenting them."

"Pst! What does that signify? Why, Don Faustino has made flattering speeches to me—scores of them—called me all sorts of endearing names—does so whenever we two are together alone. I only laugh at him."

"Ah! Faustino Calderon is not Francisco de Lara. They are men of very different dispositions. In the behaviour of your admirer there's only a little of the ludicrous; in that of mine, there may be a great deal of danger. But let us cease discussing them. There's no time for that now. The question is, are they coming to call on us?"

"I think there can be no question about it. Very likely they've heard that we're soon going away, and are about to honour us with a farewell visit."

"Supposing they should stay till our English friends arrive!"

"Let them—who cares? I don't."

"But I do. If papa were at home, I mightn't so much mind it. But, just now, I've no desire to see Señor De Lara alone—still less while being visited by Eduardo. They're both *demonios*, though in a different way."

"Look yonder!" exclaims Iñez, pointing towards the British frigate, where a boat is in the water under her beam. The sun, reflected from dripping oar-blades, tells them to be in motion.

While the girls continue gazing, the boat is seen to separate from the ship's side, and put shoreward, straight towards the sand-pit which projects in front of Don Gregorio's dwelling. The rowers are all dressed alike, the measured stroke of their oars betokening that the boat belongs to the man-o'-war. But the young ladies do not conjecture about this; nor have they any doubt as to the identity of two of the figures seated in the stern-sheets. Those uniforms of dark blue, with the gold buttons, and yellow cap-bands, are so well known as to be recognisable at any distance to which love's glances could possibly penetrate. They are the guests expected, for whom the spare horses stand saddled in the *patio*. For Don Gregorio, by no means displeased with certain delicate attentions which the young British officers have been paying to the female members of his family, has invited them to visit him—ride out along with the ladies, and, on return, stay to dinner. He knows that a treat of this kind will be pleasing to those he has asked; and, before leaving home, had given orders for the steeds to be saddled.

It is not the first time Crozier and Cadwallader have been to the Spaniard's house, nor the first to stretch their limbs under his dining-table, nor the first for them to have held pleasant converse with the *señoritas*, and strolled along solitary paths, opportune for the exchange of those love-locks. But it may be the last—at least during their sojourn in California. For in truth is it to be a farewell visit.

But with this understanding, another has been entered into. The acquaintance commenced in California is to be renewed at Cadiz, when the *Crusader* goes thither, which she is ere long expected to do. But for such anticipation Carmen Montijo and Iñez Alvarez would not be so high-hearted at the prospect of a leave-taking so near. Less painful on this account, it might have been even pleasant, but for what they see on the opposite side — the horsemen approaching from the town. An encounter between the two pairs gives promise to mar the happy intercourse of the hour.

"They'll meet—they must!" says Carmen, apprehensively.

"Let them!" rejoins Iñez, in a tone of nonchalance. "What if they do?"

"What! They may quarrel. I'm almost sure they will."

"No fear for that; and, if they should, where's the danger? You, such a believer in the romantic—stickler for old knight-errantry—instead of regretting it, should be glad! Look there! Lovers coming from all sides — suitors by land and suitors by sea! Knights terrestrial, knights aquatic. No lady of the troubadour times ever had the like; none ever honoured by such a rivalry! Come, Carmen, be proud! Stand firm on your castle-keep! Show yourself worthy to receive this double adoration!"

"Iñez, you don't know the danger."

"There is none. If they should come into collision, and have a fight, let them. I've no fear for mine. If Willie Cadwallader isn't a match for Faustino Calderon, then he's not match, or mate, for me—never shall be."

"*Sobrina*! you shock me. I had no idea you were such a *demonia*. The Moorish blood, I suppose. Your words make me almost as wicked as yourself. It isn't for that I'm afraid. I've as much confidence in my lover as you in yours. No fear that Señor Crozier will cower before Francisco de Lara. If he do, I shall take back my heart a second time, and carry it unscathed to Cadiz!"

Chapter Fourteen
A Sweet Pair of Suitors

While the young ladies upon the house-top are discussing the characters of De Lara and Calderon, these worthies, in return, are conversing of them, and in a strain which bodes little good to Iñez, with much evil to Carmen. That the visit designed for them is of no ordinary nature, but for an all important purpose, can be gleaned from the speech passing between the two horsemen as they ride along the road.

De Lara commences it by remarking:—

"Well, friend Faustino, from something you said before setting out, I take it you're going to Don Gregorio's on an errand very similar to my own? Come, *camarado!* declare it!"

"Declare yours!"

"Certainly. I shall make no secret of it to you; nor need I. Why should there be any between us? We've now known one another long enough, and intimately enough, to exchange confidences of the closest kind. To-day mine is—that I mean proposing to Don Gregorio's daughter—offering her my hand in marriage."

"And I," returns Calderon, "intend doing the same to his grand-daughter."

"In that case, we're both in the same boat; and, as there's no rivalry between us, we can pull pleasantly together. I've no objection to being your uncle; even admitting you to a share in the old Spaniard's property—proportioned to your claims of kinship."

"I don't want a dollar of the Don's money; only his grand-daughter. I'm deeply in love with her."

"And I," continues De Lara, "am just as deeply in love with his daughter—it may be deeper."

"You couldn't. I'm half-mad about Iñez Alvarez. I could kill her—if she refuse me."

"I *shall* kill Carmen Montijo—if she refuse *me.*" The two men are talking seriously, or seem so. Their voices, the tone, the flashing of their eyes, the expression upon their faces, with their excited gesticulation—all show them to be in earnest.

At the last outburst of passionate speech they turn in their saddles, and look each other in the face. De Lara continues the dialogue:

"Now, tell me, Faustino; what hope have you of success?"

"For that, fair enough. You remember the last *fandango* held at Don Gregorio's—on the day of the cattle-branding!"

"Certainly I do. I've good reason to remember it. But go on."

"Well, that night," proceeds Calderon, "I danced twice with Iñez, and made many sweet speeches to her. Once I went farther, and squeezed her pretty little hand. She wasn't angry, or at all events didn't say or show it. Surely, after such encouragement, I may ask that hand in marriage—with fair presumption of not being refused. What's your opinion?"

"Your chances seem good. But what about himself. He'll have something to say in the matter."

"Too much, I fear; and that's just what I do fear. So long as his bit of grazing-land was worth only some thirty thousand dollars, he was amiable enough. Now that by this gold discovery it's got to be good value for eight or ten times the amount, he's become a different man, and in all likelihood will go dead against me."

"Like enough; it's the way of the world. And therefore, on that account, you needn't have a special spite against the Señor Montijo. You're sure no one else stands between you and your sweetheart? Or is there something in the shape of a rival?"

"Of course there is—a score of them, as you ought to know; same as with yourself, De Lara. Suitors have been coming and going with both, I suppose, ever since either was old enough to receive them. The last I've heard of paying attentions to Iñez is a young naval officer—a midshipman on board a British man-of-war now lying in the harbour. Indeed there are two of them spoken of; one said to be *your* rival, as the other is mine. Shall I tell you what's been for some time the talk of the town? You may as well know it, if you don't already."

"What?" asks the Creole, excitedly.

"Why, that the one represented as your competitor has cut out all Carmen's other admirers—yourself among the rest."

Bitter words to the ear of Francisco de Lara, bringing the red colour to his cheeks, as if they had been smitten by a switch. With eyes flashing, and full of jealous fire, he exclaims:

"If that be so, I'll do as I've said — "

"Do what?"

"*Kill Carmen Montijo!* I swear it. I'm in earnest, Calderon, and mean it. If it be as you've heard, I'll surely kill her. I've the right to her life — by her giving me the right to her love."

"But did she do that? Has she ever confessed to loving you?"

"Not in words, I admit. But there are other signs of assent strong as speech, or the hand-squeezings you speak of. Carmen Montijo may be cunning. Some call her a coquette. All I know is, that she has led me to believe she loved me; and if she's been playing a false game, she shall rue it, one way or the other. This day I'm determined to ascertain the truth, by offering her my hand, as I've said, and asking hers. If she refuse it, then I'll know how things stand, and take steps for squaring accounts between us. She shall find that Frank Lara is not the sort of man to let one of womankind either laugh at, or play tricks with him."

"I admire your spirit, *amigo*. I catch courage from it, and will imitate your action. If it turn out that Iñez has been trifling with me, I'll — well, we must first find what answer there is for us; which we shall, I suppose, soon after ascending yonder hill. One of us may be accepted, the other rejected. In that case, one will be happy, the other wretched. Or both may be accepted, and then we'll both be blessed. Taking things at their worst, and that we both get refused — what then? Despair, and a speedy end, I suppose?"

"The last, if you like, but not the first. When despair comes to Frank Lara, death will come along with it, of soon after. But we waste time talking; let us forward and learn our fate!"

With stroke of spur, urging their horses into a gallop, the two hasten on; in the countenances of both a cast showing them half-hopeful, half-doubting — such as may be seen when men are about to make some desperate attempt, with uncertainty as to the result. On Calderon's, notwithstanding his assumed levity, the expression is almost despairing; on that of De Lara it is more defiant and demon-like.

Chapter Fifteen
A Rude Rencontre

Having steeled themselves to the reception of their rival suitors, with brave words one supporting the other, the two girls remain upon the *azotea*. Meanwhile, the man-o'-war's boat has been drawing in towards the beach, heading for a little embayment, formed by the shore-line and the sand-bar already spoken of.

The horsemen advancing from the town-side do not see it; nor can the crew of the boat perceive them. The land-ridge is between the two parties, its crest concealing them from one another.

They are approaching it at a like rate of speed; for although the horses appear to be in a gallop, it is only a fancy gait fashionable among Spanish-Americans, its purpose to exhibit equestrian skill. For the two horsemen looking up the hill, have seen heads on the house-top, and know that ladies' eyes are upon them.

Surreptitiously goaded by the spur, their steeds plunge and curvet, apparently progressing at a rapid pace, but in reality gaining little ground.

After a time both parties disappear from the eyes of those on the *azotea*. They have gone under the brow of the hill, which, overhanging for a short distance, shuts out a view of the road, as also the sea-shore, along the sand-spit.

Unseen from above, the man-o'-war's boat beaches, and the two officers spring out upon the strand. One of them turning, says something to the coxswain, who has remained in the stern-sheets, with the tiller-ropes in hand. It is an order, with instructions about where and when he is to wait for them on return to the ship.

"At the new wharf in the harbour," Crozier is heard to say; for it is he who commands.

His order given, the boat shoves off, and is rowed back towards the ship; while the officers commence climbing the slope, to get upon the shore-road.

At the same time the horsemen are ascending from the opposite side.

Soon both parties are again within view of those on the house-top; though neither as yet sees the other, or has any suspicion of such mutual proximity. The crest of the ridge is still between, but in a few seconds more they will sight one another.

The men afoot are advancing at about the same rate of speed as those on horseback. The latter have ceased showing off, as if satisfied with the impression they must have made, and are now approaching in tranquil gait, but with an air of subdued triumph—the mock modesty of the *matador*, who, with blood-stained sword, bends meekly before the box where beauty sits smiling approbation.

The two pedestrians climb the hill less ceremoniously. Glad to stretch their limbs upon land—"shake the knots out of their knees," as Cadwallader gleefully remarks—they eagerly scale the steep. Not silent either, but laughing and shouting like a couple of schoolboys abroad for an afternoon's holiday.

Suddenly coming within view of the house, they bring their boisterous humour under restraint at sight of two heads above the parapet. For they know to whom these belong, and note that the faces are turned towards them.

At the same instant the horsemen also see the heads, and observe that the faces are *not* turned towards *them*. On the contrary, *from* them, the ladies looking in another direction.

Some chagrin in this. After all their grand caracolling, and feats of equitation, which must have been witnessed by the fair spectators.

At what are these now gazing? Is it a ship sailing up the bay, or something else on the water? No matter what, and whether on land, or water; enough for the conceited fellows to think they are being slightingly received.

Disconcerted, they seek an explanation, mutually questioning one another. But before either can make answer in speech, they have it under their eyes—in the shape of a brace of British naval officers.

Like themselves, the latter have just reached the summit of the ridge, and are moving on towards Don Gregorio's gate. It is midway between; and keeping on at the same rate of speed, the two pairs will meet directly in front of it.

Before that moment, neither has ever set eyes on the other. Notwithstanding, there is an expression on the faces of all four, which tells of mutual recognition, and of no friendly nature.

Calderon whispers to De Lara:

"The English officers!"

Cadwallader says, *sotto-voce* to Crozier:

"The fellows we've heard about—our rivals, Ned, like ourselves, I suppose, going to visit the girls."

De Lara makes no response to Calderon. Neither does Crozier to Cadwallader. There is not time. They are now close up to the gate, and there is only its breadth between them.

They have arrived there at the same instant of time, and simultaneously make stop. Face to face, silence on both sides, neither word nor salute offered in exchange. But looks are quite as expressive—glances that speak the language of jealous rivalry—of rage with difficulty suppressed.

It is a question of precedence, as to who shall first pass into the entrance. Their hesitation was not from any courtesy, but the reverse. The men on horseback look down on those afoot contemptuously, scornfully. Threateningly, too; as though they had thoughts of riding over, and trampling them under the hoofs of their horses. No doubt they would like to do it, and might make trial, were the young officers unarmed. But they are not. Crozier carries a pistol—Cadwallader his midshipman's dirk, both weapons conspicuous outside their uniforms.

For a period of several seconds' duration, the rivals stand *vis-à-vis*, neither venturing to advance. Around them is a nimbus of angry electricity, that needs but a spark to kindle it into furious flame. A single word will do it. This word spoken, and two of the four may never enter Don Gregorio's gate—at least not alive.

It is not spoken. The only thing said is by Crozier to Cadwallader—not in a whisper, but aloud, and without regard to what effect it may have on the enemy.

"Come along, Will! We've something better to do than stand shilly-shallying here. Heave after me, shipmate!"

Crozier's speech cut the Gordian knot; and the officers, gliding through the gateway, advance along the avenue.

With faces now turned towards the house, they see the ladies still upon the *azotea*.

Soon as near enough for Carmen to observe it, Crozier draws out the treasured tress, and fastens it in his cap, behind the gold band. It falls over his shoulder like a cataract of liquid amber.

Cadwallader does likewise; and from his cap also streams a tress, black as the plumes of a raven.

The two upon the house-top appear pleased by this display. They show their approval by imitating it. Each raises hand to her riding-hat; and when these are withdrawn, a curl of hair is seen set behind their *toquillas*—one chestnut-brown, the other of yellowish hue.

Scarce is this love-telegraphy exchanged, when the two Californians come riding up the avenue, at full speed. Though lingering at the gate, and still far-off, De Lara had observed the affair of the tresses, clearly comprehending the symbolism of the act. Exasperated beyond bounds, he can no longer control himself, and cares not what may come.

At his instigation, Calderon spurs on by his side, the two tearing furiously along. Their purpose is evident: to force the pedestrians from the path, and so humble them in the eyes of their sweethearts.

On his side, Crozier remains cool, admonishing Cadwallader to do the same. They feel the power of possession: assured by those smiles, that the citadel is theirs. It is for the outsiders to make the assault.

"Give a clear gangway, Will!" counsels Crozier; "and let them pass. We can talk to the gentlemen afterwards."

Both step back among the *manzanita* bushes, and the *ginetes* go galloping past; De Lara on Crozier's side scowling down, as if he would annihilate the English officer with a look. The scowl is returned with interest, the officer still reserves speech.

On the other edge of the avenue the action is a little different. The midshipman, full of youthful freak, determines on having his "lark." He sees the chance, and cannot restrain himself. As Calderon sweeps past, he draws his dirk, and pricks the Californian's horse in the hip. The animal, maddened by the pain, springs upward, and then shoots off at increased speed, still further heightened by the fierce exclamations of his rider, and the mocking laughter of the mid.

Under the walls the two horsemen come to a halt, neither having made much by their bit of rude bravadoism. And they know they will have a reckoning to settle for it—at least De Lara does. For on the brow of Crozier, coming up, he can read a determination to call him to account. He is not flurried about this. On the contrary, he has courted it, knowing himself a skilled swordsman, and dead shot. Remembering that he has already killed his man, he can await with equanimity the challenge he has provoked. It is not fear has brought the pallor to his cheeks, and set the dark seal upon his brow. Both spring from a different passion: observable in his eyes as he turns them towards the house-top. For the ladies are still there, looking down.

Saluting, he says:

"Dona Carmen, can I have the honour of an interview?"

She thus interrogated does not make immediate answer. Spectator of all that has passed, she observes the hostile attitude between the two sets of visitors. To receive both at the same time will be more than embarrassing. With their angry passions roused to such a pitch, it must end in a personal encounter.

Her duty is clear. She is mistress of the house, representing her father, who is absent. The English officers are there by invitation. At thought of this she no longer hesitates.

"Not now, Don Francisco de Lara," she says, replying to his question; "not to-day. I must beg of you to excuse me."

"Indeed!" rejoins he sneeringly. "Will it be deemed discourteous in me to ask why I am denied?"

It is discourteous; and so Doña Carmen deems it. Though she does not tell him as much in words, he can take it from her rejoinder.

"You are quite welcome to know the reason. We have an engagement!"

"Oh! an engagement!"

"Yes, sir, an engagement," she repeats, in a tone telling of irritation. "Those gentlemen you see are our guests. My father has invited them to spend the day with us."

"Ah! your father has invited them! How very good of Don Gregorio Montijo, extending his hospitality to *gringos*! And Doña Carmen has added her kind compliments with earnest entreaties for them to come, no doubt?"

"Sir!" says Carmen, no longer able to conceal her indignation, "your speech is impertinent—insulting. I shall listen to it no longer."

Saying which, she steps back, disappearing behind the parapet—where Iñez has already concealed herself, at the close of a similar short, but stormy, dialogue with Calderon.

De Lara, a lurid look in his eyes, sits in his saddle as if in a stupor. He is roused from it by a voice, Crozier's, saying:

"You appear anxious to make apology to the lady? You can make it to *me*."

"*Caraji!*" exclaims the gambler, starting, and glaring angrily at the speaker. "Who are you?"

"One who demands an apology for your very indecorous behaviour."

"You'll not get it."

"Satisfaction, then."

"That to your heart's content."

"I shall have it so. Your card, sir?"

"There; take it. Yours?"

The bits of cardboard are exchanged; after which De Lara, casting another glance up to the *azotea*—where he sees nothing but blank wall—turns his horse's head; then spitefully plying the spur, gallops back down the avenue—his comrade close following.

Calderon has not deemed it incumbent upon him to demand a card from Cadwallader. Nor has the latter thought it necessary to take one from him; the mid is quite contented with that playful prod with his dirk.

The young officers enter the house, in cheerful confidence. They have lost nothing by the encounter, and those inside will still smilingly receive them—as indeed they do.

Chapter Sixteen
A Ship without Sailors

Among the vessels lying in the harbour of San Francisco is one athwart whose stern is lettered the name *El Condor*.

She is a ship of small dimensions—some five or six hundred tons—devoted to peaceful commerce, as can be told by certain peculiarities of rig and structure, understood by the initiated in nautical affairs.

The name will suggest a South American nationality—Ecuadorian, Peruvian, Bolivian, or Chilian—since the bird after which she has been baptised is found in all these States. Columbia and the Argentine Confederation can also claim it.

But there is no need to guess at the particular country to which the craft in question belongs. The flag suspended over her taffrail declares it, by a symbolism quite intelligible to those who take an interest in national insignia.

It is a tricolour—the orthodox red, white, and blue—not, as with the French, disposed vertically, but in two horizontal bands; the lower one crimson red, the upper half-white, half-blue—the last contiguous to the staff, with a single five-pointed star set centrally in its field. This disposition of colours proclaims the ship that carries them to be Chilian.

She is not the only Chilian craft in the harbour of San Francisco. Several others are there showing the same colours; brigs, barques, schooners, and ships. For the spirited little South American Republic is as prosperous as enterprising, and its flag waves far and wide over the Pacific. With its population of skilled miners, it had been among the first of foreign states in sending a large representative force to "cradle" the gold *placers* of California, and not only are its ships lying in the bay, but its *guasos* and *gambusinos* in goodly number tread the streets of the town; while many of the dark-eyed damsels, who from piazzas and balconies salute the passer-by with seductive smiles, are those charming little Chileñas that make havoc with the heart of almost every Jack-tar who visits Valparaiso.

On the ship *El Condor* we meet not much that can be strictly called Chilian; little besides the vessel herself and the captain commanding her. Not commanding her sailors: since there are none upon her hailing from Chili or elsewhere. Those who brought the *Condor* into San Francisco Bay have abandoned her—gone off to the gold-diggings! Arriving in the heat of the *placer-fever*, they preferred seeking fortune with pick, shovel, and pan, to handling tarry ropes at ten dollars a month. Almost on the instant of the ship's dropping anchor they deserted to a man, leaving her skipper to himself, or with only his cook for a companion.

Neither is the latter Chilian, but African—a native of Zanzibar. No more the two great monkeys, observed gambolling about the deck; for the climate of Chili, lying outside the equatorial belt, is too cold for indigenous *quadrumana*.

Not much appearing upon the *Condor* would proclaim her a South American ship; and nothing in her cargo, for a cargo she carries. She has just arrived from a trading voyage to the South Sea Isles, extending to the Indian Archipelago, whence her lading—a varied assortment, consisting of tortoise-shell, spices, mother-of-pearl, Manilla cigars, and such other commodities as may be collected among the Oriental islands. Hence also the *myas* monkeys—better known as orang-outangs—seen playing about her deck. These she has brought from Borneo.

Only a small portion of her freight had been consigned to San Francisco; this long ago landed. The rest remains in her hold for further transport to Valparaiso.

How soon she may arrive there, or take departure from her present anchorage, is a question that even her skipper cannot answer. If asked, he would most probably reply, "*Quien sabe?*" and, further pressed, might point to her deserted decks, offering that as an explanation of his inability to satisfy the inquirer.

Her captain—Antonio Lantanas by name—is a sailor of the Spanish-American type; and being this, he takes crosses and disappointments coolly. Even the desertion of his crew seems scarcely to have ruffled him; he bears it with a patient resignation, that would be quite incomprehensible to either English or Yankee skipper. With a broad-brimmed *jipi-japa* hat shading his swarth features from the sun, he lounges all day long upon the quarterdeck, his elbows usually rested upon the capstan-head; his sole occupation rolling and smoking paper cigarritos, one of which is usually either in his fingers, or between his lips. If he at any time varies this, it is to eat his meals, or to take a turn at play with his pet monkeys.

These creatures are male and female, both full of fun in their uncouth fashion; and Captain Lantanas takes it out of them by occasionally touching their snouts with the lit end of his cigarette, laughing to see them scamper off, scared at the (to them) singular, and somewhat painful, effect of fire.

His meals are served regularly three times a day, and his cook—the aforesaid negro, black as the tar upon the rattlin ropes—after having served them, returns to an idleness equalling his own. He too, has his diversion with the orangs, approaching much nearer to them in physical appearance, and for this reason, perhaps, a more congenial playmate.

Once a day the skipper steps into his gig, and rows himself ashore. But not to search for sailors. He knows that would be an idle errand. True, there are plenty of them in San Francisco; scores parading its streets, and other scores seated, or standing, within its taverns and restaurants. But they are all on the spree—all rollicking, and if not rich, hoping soon to be. Not a man of them could be coaxed to take service on board an outbound ship for wages less than would make the voyage little profitable to her owner.

As the Chilian skipper is not only master, but proprietor of his own craft, he has no intention to stir under the circumstances; but is contented to wait till times change, and tars become inclined again to go to sea. When this may be, and the *Condor* shall spread her canvas wings for a further flight to Valparaiso, he has not the remotest idea. When he enters the town, it is to meet other skippers with ships crewless as his own, and exchange condolences on their common destitution.

On a certain day—that on which we are introduced to him—he has not sculled himself ashore, but abides upon his vessel, awaiting the arrival of one who has sent a message forewarning him of an intended visit.

Although San Francisco is fast becoming transformed into an American city, and already has its half-dozen newspapers, there is among these a small sheet printed in Spanish, by name *El Diario*. In it Captain Lantanas has advertised his vessel, for freight or passage, bound for Valparaiso, and to call at intermediate ports—Panama among the number. The advertisement directs reference to be made to a shipping-agent, by name Don Tomas Silvestre.

In answer to it, the Chilian has received a letter from a gentleman who had already communicated with the agent, and who has promised to present himself on board the *Condor* by 12 mid-day of this same day.

Although a stranger to the port of San Francisco, Captain Lantanas has some knowledge of his correspondent; for Don Tomas has the day before informed him that a gentleman from whom he may expect to hear—the same whose name is signed to the letter—is a man of immense wealth; a landed proprietor, whose acres lie contiguous to the rising city of San Francisco, and for this reason enormously increased in value by the influx of gold-seeking immigrants. What this important personage may want with him, Lantanas cannot tell; for Silvestre himself has not been made aware of it—the gentleman declining to state his business to any other than the captain of the ship.

On the morning of the appointed day, leaning as usual against his capstan, and puffing his paper cigar, the Chilian skipper is not in a mood for playing with his monkey pets. His mind is given to a more serious matter, his whole thoughts absorbed in conjecturing for what purpose his unknown correspondent may be seeking the interview.

He is not without surmises, in which he is assisted by something he has heard while mixing in Spanish circles ashore—this, that the landowner in question has lately sold his land, realising a very large sum—half a million dollars being the amount stated. Furthermore, that being a Peninsular Spaniard, and neither Mexican nor Californian, he is about to return to Spain, taking with him his household gods—Lares, Penates, and all.

These could not be stowed in a single state-room, but would require a whole ship, or a goodly portion of one. The *Condor* has still plenty of room to spare. Her hold is not half full; and her cabin has accommodation for one or two passengers. May it be on this business his correspondent is coming aboard.

So Captain Lantanas interrogates himself, while standing upon his quarterdeck, and with the glowing coal of his cigarrito sending off his hairy familiars, who, in their play, at times intrude upon him.

It pleases him to think he may have surmised correctly; and, while still indulging in conjectures, he sees that which puts an end to them—a shore-boat, with a single pair of rowers, and a gentleman—evidently a landsman—seated in the stern-sheets, to all appearance coming on for the *Condor*.

Captain Lantanas steps to the side of his ship; and, standing in her waist, awaits the arrival of his visitor.

As the boat draws near he makes out a man, dressed in semi-Californian costume, such as is worn by the higher class of *haciendados*. The skipper can have no doubts about who it is. If he has, they are soon set at rest; for the boat touching the ship's side is instantly made fast; the *haciendado* mounts the man-ropes; and, stepping down upon the deck, hands Captain Lantanas his card.

He who has thus presented himself is a man in years well up to sixty, and somewhat above medium height. Taller than he appears, through a slight stoop in the shoulders. His step, though not tottering, shows vigour impaired; and upon his countenance are the traces of recent illness, with strength not yet restored. His complexion is clear, rather rubicund, and in health might be more so; while his hair, both on head and chin—the latter furnished with a long flowing beard—is snow-white. It could never have been very dark, but more likely of the colour called sandy. This, with greyish-blue eyes, and features showing some points of Celtic conformation, would argue him either no Spaniard, or if so, one belonging to the province of Biscay.

This last he is; for the correspondent of Captain Lantanas is Don Gregorio Montijo.

Chapter Seventeen
A Charter-Party

Soon, as assured—by a glance at the card given him—that his visitor is the gentleman who has written to appoint an interview, Captain Lantanas politely salutes; and *jipi-japa* in hand, stands waiting to hear what the *haciendado* may have to say.

The latter, panting after the effort made in ascending the man-ropes, takes a moment's time to recover breath. Then, returning the skipper's bow, he says, interrogatively:—

"Captain Lantanas, I presume?"

"Si, señor," responds the master of the *Condor*, with a bow of becoming humility to one reputed so rich. Then adding: "*A dispocion de V.*"

"Well, captain," rejoins Don Gregorio, "I shall take it for granted that you know who I am. Don Tomas Silvestre has informed you, has he not?"

"He has, señor."

"And you received my letter?"

"Si, señor."

"That's all right, then. And now to proceed to the business that has brought me aboard your ship. Having seen your advertisement in the *Diario*, I communicated with Don Tomas; but only so far as to get your correct address, with some trifling particulars. For the rest, I've thought it best to deal directly with yourself; as the matter I have in hand is too important to be entrusted to an agent. In short, it requires confidence, if not secrecy, and from what I've heard of you, Señor Lantanas, I feel sure I can confide in you."

"You compliment me, Señor Montijo."

"No, no; nothing of the kind. I but speak from the account Silvestre has given me of your character. But now to business. Your ship is advertised for freight, or passage?"

"Either, or both."

"Bound for Valparaiso and intermediate ports?"

"Anywhere down the coast."

"Have you passengers already engaged?"

"Not any as yet."

"How many can you take?"

"Well, señor, to speak truth, my craft is not intended to carry passengers. She's a trading-vessel, as you see. But if you'll step down to the cabin, you can judge for yourself. There's a saloon—not very large, it is true—and sleeping accommodation for six—two snug staterooms that will serve, if need be, for ladies."

"That'll do. Now about the freight. Don Tomas tells me you have some cargo aboard."

"A portion of my ship is already occupied."

"That won't signify to me. I suppose there's enough room left for something that weighs less than a ton, and isn't of any great bulk. Say it will take a score or two of cubic feet. You can find stowage for that?"

"Oh, yes, that and much more."

"So far good. And you can accommodate three passengers: a gentleman and two ladies? In short, myself and the female members of my family—my daughter and grand-daughter?"

"Will the Señor Montijo step into the *Condor's* cabin, and see for himself?"

"By all means."

Captain Lantanas leads down the stairway, his visitor following.

The saloon is inspected; after it the sleeping-rooms, right and left.

"Just the thing," says Don Gregorio, speaking as in soliloquy, and evidently satisfied. "It will do admirably," he adds, addressing himself to the skipper. "And now about terms. What are they to be?"

"That, señor, will depend on what is wanted. To what port do you wish me to take you?"

"Panama. 'Tis one of the ports mentioned in your advertisement?"

"It is, señor."

"Well, for this freight—as I've told you, about a ton, with some trifling household effects—and the three passengers, how much?"

"The terms of freight, as you may be aware, are usually rated according to the class of goods. Is it gold, señor? From your description. I suppose it is."

The skipper has guessed aright. It is gold, nearly a ton of it, accruing to Don Gregorio from the sale of his land, for which he has been paid in dust and nuggets, at that time the only coin in California—indeed, the only circulating medium, since notes were not to be had.

"Suppose it to be gold," he answers guardedly, "how much then?"

The *ex-ganadero* is by no means a niggardly man; still, he would like to have his treasure transported at a rate not exorbitant. And yet he is anxious about its safety; and for this reason has resolved to ship it with secrecy in a private trading-vessel, instead of by one of the regular liners, that have already commenced plying between San Francisco and Panama. He has heard that these are crowded with miners returning home; rough fellows, many of them queer characters—some little better than bandits. He dislikes the idea of trusting his gold among them, and equally his girls, since no other ladies are likely to be going that way. He has full faith in the integrity of Captain Lantanas; knows the Chilian to be a man of gentle heart—in fact, a gentleman. Don Tomas has told him all this.

Under the circumstances, and with such a man, it will not do to drive too hard a bargain; and Don Gregorio, thus reflecting, at length confesses his freight to be gold bullion, and asks the skipper to name his terms.

Lantanas, after a moment spent in mental calculation, says:

"One thousand dollars for the freight, and a hundred each for the three passages. Will that satisfy you, señor?"

"It seems a large sum," rejoins Don Gregorio. "But I am aware prices are high just now; so I agree to it. When will you be ready to sail?"

"I am ready now, señor—that is, if—"

"If what?"

Lantanas, remembering his crewless ship, does not make immediate answer.

"If," says the Spaniard, noticing his hesitation, and mistaking the reason—"if you're calculating on any delay from me, you needn't. I can have everything on board in three or four days—a week at the utmost."

The skipper is still silent, thinking of excuses. He dislikes losing the chance of such a profitable cargo, and yet knows he cannot name any certain time of sailing, for the want of hands to work his vessel.

There seems no help for it but to confess his shortcomings. Perhaps Don Gregorio will wait till the *Condor* can get a crew. The more likely, since every other vessel in port is in a similar predicament.

"Señor," he says at length, "my ship is at your service; and I should be pleased and proud to have you and your ladies as my passengers. But there's a little difficulty to be got over before I can weigh anchor."

"Clearance duties—port dues to be paid. You want the passage-money advanced, I presume? Well, I shall not object to prepaying it in part. How much will you require?"

"*Mil gracias*, Señor Montijo. It's not anything of the kind. Although far from rich, thank Heaven, neither I nor my craft is under embargo. I could sail out of San Francisco in half-an-hour, but for the want of—"

"Want of what?" asks Don Gregorio in some surprise.

"Well, señor—sailors."

"What! Have you no sailors?"

"I am sorry to say, not one."

"Well, Captain Lantanas, I thought it strange observing nobody aboard your ship—except that black fellow. But I supposed your sailors had gone ashore."

"So have they, señor; and intend staying there. Alas! that's the trouble. They've gone off to the gold-diggings—every one of them, except my negro cook. Likely enough, I should have lost him too, but he knows that California is now part of the United States, and fears that some speculating Yankee might make a slave of him, or that perchance he might meet his old master: for he has had one."

"How vexatious all this!" says Don Gregorio. "I suppose I shall have to look out for another ship."

"I fear you'll not find one much better provided than mine—as regards sailors. In that respect, to use a professional phrase, we're all in the same boat."

"You assure me of that!"

"I do, señor."

"I can trust you, Captain Lantanas. As I have told you, I'm not here without knowing something of yourself. You have a friend in Don Tomas Silvestre?"

"I believe I have the honour of Don Tomas's friendship."

"Well, he has recommended you in such terms that I can thoroughly rely upon you. For that reason, I shall now make more fully known to you why I wish to travel by your ship."

The Chilian skipper bows thanks for the compliment, and silently awaits the proffered confidence.

"I've just sold my property here, receiving for it three hundred thousand dollars in gold-dust—the same I intended for your freight. It is now lying at my house, some three miles from town. As you must be aware, captain, this place is at present the rendezvous of scoundrels collected from every country on the face of the habitable globe, but chiefly from the United States and Australia. They live, and act, almost without regard to law; such judges as they have being almost as great criminals as those brought before them. I feel impatient to get away from the place; which under the circumstances, you won't wonder at. And I am naturally anxious about my gold. At any hour a band of these lawless ruffians may take it into their heads to strip me of it—or, at all events, attempt to do so. Therefore, I wish to get it on board a ship—one where it will be safe, and in whose captain I can thoroughly confide. Now, you understand me?"

"I do," is the simple response of the Chilian. He is about to add that Don Gregorio's property, as his secret, will be safe enough, so far as he can protect it, when the latter interrupts him by continuing:

"I may add that it is my intention to return to Spain, of which I am a native—to Cadiz, where I have a house. That I intended doing anyhow. But now, I want to take departure at once. As a Spaniard, señor, I needn't point out to you, who are of the same race, that the society of California cannot be congenial—now that the rowdies of the United States have become its rulers. I am most anxious to get away from the place, and soon as possible. It is exceedingly awkward your not having a crew. Can't something be done to procure one?"

"The only thing is to offer extra pay. There are plenty of sailors in San Francisco; for they've not all gone to gather gold. Some are engaged in scattering it. Unfortunately, most are worthless, drunken fellows. Still it is possible that a few good men might be found, were the wages made sufficiently tempting. No doubt, an advertisement in the *Diario*, offering double pay, might attract as many as would be needed for working my ship."

"How much would it all amount to?"

"Possibly an extra thousand dollars."

"Suppose I pay that, will you engage the whole ship to me? That is, take no other passengers, or wait for any more freight, but sail at once—soon as you've secured a crew? Do you agree to these terms?"

"Si, señor; they are perfectly satisfactory."

"I'll be answerable for the extra wages. Anything to get away from this Pandemonium of a place."

"In that case, señor, I think we'll have no great difficulty in procuring hands. You authorise me to advertise for them?"

"I do," answers Don Gregorio.

"Enough!" rejoins the skipper. "And now, Señor Montijo, you may make your preparations for embarking."

"I've not many to make; nearly all has been done already. It's only to get our personal baggage aboard, with the freight safely stowed. By the way," adds the Biscayan, speaking *sotto-voce*, "I wish to ship the gold as soon as possible, and without attracting attention to it. You understand me, captain?"

"I do."

"I shall have it brought aboard at night, in a boat which belongs to Silvestre. It will be safer in your cabin than anywhere else—since no one need be the wiser about the place of deposit."

"No one shall, through me."

"That I feel certain of, Señor Lantanas. Don Tomas is your endorser; and would be willing to be your bondsman, were it needed—which it is not."

Again the *Condor's* captain bows in acknowledgment of the confidence reposed in him; and after some further exchange of speech, respecting the shipment of the treasure, and the writing out an advertisement, which Don Gregorio is to *get* inserted in the *Diario*, the latter returns to his boat, and is rowed back to the shore; while the Chilian lights a fresh cigarette, and with elbows rested on the capstan-head, resumes his customary attitude of *insouciance*, from which he had been temporarily roused.

Chapter Eighteen
In Search of a Second

Just about the time Don Gregorio is taking leave of Captain Lantanas, the two unwelcome, as unreceived, visitors are turning their backs upon his house.

De Lara feels his discomfiture the keenest. His heart is harrowed with mingled emotions—passions of varied complexion, all evil. His lips are livid with rage, his brow black with chagrin, while his eyes fairly scintillate with unsatisfied vengeance.

While returning along the avenue he neither looks back, nor up. Not a syllable escapes him; with glance upon the ground, he rides in sullen silence.

After clearing the entrance-gate, and again upon the outside road, he turns face toward the dwelling whose hospitality has been so insultingly denied him. He sees nought there to soothe, but something which still further afflicts him. Four horses are filing out through the front gate, conducted by grooms. They are saddled, bridled, ready for being mounted. To his practised eye, their caparison tells that they are intended only for a short excursion, not a journey. And though their saddles are in shape nearly alike, he knows that two of them are to be mounted by men, the other two to carry ladies.

"The señoritas are going out for a ride—a *paseo de campo*—accompanied by their English guests," observes Calderon.

Simultaneously, as instinctively, de Lara arrives at this conclusion. Both now know why they were not received; a knowledge which, instead of tranquillising their chafed spirits, but maddens them the more. The thought of their sweethearts being escorted by these detested rivals, riding along wild unfrequented paths, through trees overshadowing, away from the presence of spying domestics, or the interference of protecting relatives, beyond the eyes and ears of every one—the thought that Carmen Montijo and Iñez Alvarez are setting out on an excursion of this kind, is to Francisco de Lara and Faustino Calderon bitter as deadliest poison.

And reflection embitters it the more. The excursionists will have every opportunity of wandering at will. They will become separated; and there can be no doubt as to how the partition will be made; the older of the two officers will pair off with Doña Carmen, the younger with Doña Iñez. Thus, they will ride unmolested, unobserved; converse without fear of being overheard; clasp hands without danger of being seen—perhaps exchange kisses! Oh, the dire, desperate jealousy! Even the dull brain and cold heart of Calderon are fired by these reflections. They sting him to the quick. But not as De Lara; for not as De Lara does he love.

After gazing for a while at the house—at the horses and grooms—at the preparations that are being made for mounting—noting their magnificent style—with a last glance such as Satan gave when expelled from Paradise, the Creole drives the spur deep into his horse's ribs, and dashes off down the hill the Californian after.

At its bottom they again come to a halt, being now out of sight of the house. Facing toward his companion, De Lara says:

"We're in for a fight, Faustino; both of us."

"Not both. I don't think I'm called upon to challenge that youngster. He's but a boy."

"He's been man enough to insult you; and, if I mistake not, you'll find him man enough to meet you."

"I don't see that he *did* insult me."

"Indeed; you don't? Sticking your horse, as if it were a pig, and sending him off in a stampede that well nigh dismounted you; all before the face of your lady-love—right under her eyes! You don't deem that an insult, eh?"

"But you must remember I gave him provocation. At your bidding, I all but rode over him. Looking at it in that light, he's in a sense excusable for what he did. Besides, he only meant it as a joke. Didn't you see, when it was all over, how he laughed at it?"

"Not at *it*, but at *you*. So did your sweetheart, *amigo*. As we reined up under the walls, I could see her long lashes drooping down, the eyes looking disdain at you, with her pretty lips pouting in very scorn. You're evidently out of her good graces, and you'll have to do something ere you can reinstate yourself."

"Do you really think so?"

"I am sure of it. Never surer of anything in my life."

"But what would you have me to do?"

The Flag of Distress | 81

"You ought to know without asking me. Call out the cub, and *kill* him—if you can. What I design doing with my gentleman."

"Ah! you're a dead shot; and that makes all the difference. These Anglo-Saxons always use pistols; and if I challenge him, he'll have the choice of weapons."

"Quite true. With me it will be different. I took care to *give* the affront, and you should have done the same. Seeing you got the worst of it, you ought to have followed up your first dash at him by something besides—a slap across the cheek, or a cut with your whip."

"I'm sorry now I didn't give him one or the other."

"Well, you may find an opportunity yet. For my quarrel, I don't care a toss whether it be settled with swords or pistols. We Creoles of Louisiana are accustomed to the use of either weapon. Thanks to old Gardalet of the Rue Royale, I've got the trick of both; and am equally ready to send a half-ounce of lead, or twelve inches of steel, through the body of this Britisher. By the way, what's his name?"

The speaker pulls out the card given him by the English officer, and glancing at it, answers his own question: "Edward Crozier, H.M.S. *Crusader*."

"Ha! Mr Ned Crozier!" he exclaims, speaking in plain English, the sight of the card seemingly giving a fresh fillip to his spleen; "you've had your triumph to-day. 'Twill be mine to-morrow. And, if my fortune don't fail me, there'll be an empty seat at the mess-table of the ship *Crusader*."

"You really intend fighting him?"

"Now, Don Faustino Calderon, why do you ask that question?"

"Because I think all might be arranged without—"

"Without what? Speak out, man!"

"Why, without any spilling of blood."

"You may arrange it that way, if you like. Your quarrel is a distinct one, and I've nothing to do with it—having my own hands full. Indeed, if they were empty, I'm not so sure I should be your second—talking as you do. However, that's not the purpose now. In answer to your first question, I can only say what I've said before. I not only intend fighting this Crozier, but *killing* him. True, I may fail in my intention; if so, there's an end of it, and of *me*. For, once on the ground, I don't leave it a living man, if he do. One or both of us shall stay there, till we're carried off—feet-foremost."

"*Carramba!* your talk gives one the trembles. It's not pleasant to think of such things, let alone doing them."

"Think your own way, and welcome. To me it would be less pleasant to leave them undone; less now, than ever in my life. After what I've gone through, I don't care much for character—in truth, not a straw. That's all stuff and pretension. Money makes the man, and without it he's nothing; though he were a saint. Respectability—bah! I don't value it a *claco*. But there's a reputation of another kind I *do* value, and intend to preserve. Because in my world it counts for something—has counted already."

"What is that?"

"Courage. Losing it, I should lose everything. And in this very city of San Francisco, I'd be only a hound where I'm now a hunter; barked at by every cur, and kicked by every coward who choose to pick a quarrel with me."

"There's no danger of that, Don Francisco. All who have had dealings with you know better. There's little fear of any one putting a slight upon *you*."

"There would be, if I refused to fight this fellow. Then you'd see the difference. Why, Faustino Calderon. I couldn't sit at our monté table, and keep the red-shirts from robbing us, if they didn't know 'twould be a dangerous game to play. However, it isn't *their* respect I value now, but that of one very different."

"Of whom?"

"Again you ask an idle question; so idle, that I don't believe you care a straw for Iñez Alvarez—or know what love is."

"What has she to do with it?"

"She—nothing. That's true enough. I don't care aught for her, or what she might think of me. But I do care for Carmen Montijo; above all things I value her good opinion. At least, so far, that she sha'n't think me either a fool or a coward. She may be fancying me the first; but if so, she'll find herself mistaken. At all events, she'll get convinced I'm not the last. And if it be as rumour reports, and as you say you've heard, that she's given her heart to this *gringo*, I'll take care she don't bestow her *hand* upon him—not while I live. When I'm dead, she can do as she likes."

"But after what's passed, will you ever speak to her again?"

"Ay, that will I—in a way that'll make her listen to me."

"But, surely, you don't still intend proposing to her?"

"Perhaps. Though not till I've finished this affair with the fellow who interrupted me. Yes; I'll give her every chance to save herself. She shall say yea, or nay, in straight speech, and in so many words. After that, I'll understand how to act. But come! we're wasting time. A duel's a thing won't do to dally over. Do you intend to meet your man, or not?"

"I'd rather not," replies the poltroon, hesitatingly; "that is, if the thing can be arranged. Do you think it can, De Lara?"

"Of course, it can; your *thing*, as you call it; though not without disgrace to you. You should fight him, Faustino."

"Well; if you say I should, why, I suppose I must. I never fired a pistol in my life, and am only second-rate with the sword. I can handle a *macheté*, or a *cuchilla*, when occasion calls for it; but these weapons won't be admitted in a duel between gentlemen. I suppose the sailor fellow claims to be one?"

"Undoubtedly he does, and with good reason. An officer belonging to a British man-of-war would call you out for questioning his claim to the epithet. But I think you underrate your skill with the small-sword. I've seen you doing very well with that weapon—at Roberto's fencing-school."

"Yes; I took lessons there. But fencing is very different from fighting."

"Never mind. When you get on the duelling-ground, fancy yourself within the walls of Roberto's shooting-gallery, and that you are about to take a fresh lesson in the *art d'escrime*. About all, choose the sword for your weapon."

"How can I, if I am to be the challenger?"

"You needn't be. There's a way to get over that. The English officers are not going straight back to their ship; not likely before a late hour of the night. After returning from their ride, I take it they'll stay to dinner at Don Gregorio's; and with wine to give them a start, they'll be pretty sure to have a cruise, as they call it, through the town. There, you may meet your man; and can insult him, by giving him a cuff, spitting in his face—anything to put the onus of challenging upon him."

"*Por Dios!* I'll do as you say."

"That's right. Now let us think of what's before us. As we are both to be principals, we can't stand seconds to one another. I know who'll act for me. Have you got a friend you can call upon?"

"Don Manuel Diaz. He's the only one I can think of."

"Don Manuel will do. He's a cool hand, and knows all the regulations of the *duello*. But he's not at home to-day. As I chance to know, he's gone to a *funcion de gallos* at Punta Pedro; and by this time should be in the cock-pit."

"Why can't we go there? Or had we better send?"

"Better send, I think. Time's precious—at least mine is. As you know, I must be at the monté table soon as the lamps are lit. If I'm not, the bank will go begging, and we may lose our customers. Besides, there's my own second to look up, which must be done this day before I lay a hand upon the cards. What hour is it? I've not brought my timepiece with me."

"Twelve o'clock, and a quarter past," answers Calderon, after consulting his watch.

"Only that! Then we'll have plenty of time to get to Punta Pedro, and witness a main. Don Manuel has a big bet on his *pardo*. I'd like myself to stake a doubloon or two on that bird. Yes, on reflection, we'd better go to the *pelea de gallos*. That will be the surest way to secure the services of Diaz. *Vamonos!*"

At this the two intending duellists again set their steeds in motion; and, riding for a short distance along the shore-road, turn into another, which will take them to Punta Pedro.

With jealous anger still unappeased, they urge their horses into a gallop, riding as if for life, on an errand whose upshot may be death—to one or both of them.

Chapter Nineteen
A "Paseo de Caballo"

The promontory called Punta Pedro is not in San Francisco Bay, but on the outside coast of the Pacific. To reach it from the former, it is necessary to traverse the dividing ridge between the two waters—this a spur of the "Coast Range," which, running higher as it trends southward, is known to Spanish Californians as the San Bruno Mountains.

Punta Pedro abuts from their base into the ocean; the coast in this quarter being bold and picturesque, but almost uninhabited. Here and there only the solitary hut of a seal-hunter, or fisherman, with a small collection of the same near the point itself, bearing its name, and a somewhat indifferent reputation. The Anglo-Saxon gold-seekers do not go there; it is only frequented by the natives.

From San Francisco to Punta Pedro the road runs past Dolores—an ancient mission of the Franciscan monks, whose port was, as already stated, Yerba Buena, previous to becoming re-christened San Francisco.

This route De Lara and Calderon have taken, getting into it by a cross-cut; and along it they continue to ride, still at a gallop, with faces set for Dolores.

They are not the only equestrians moving along that road. The dust kicked up by their horses hoofs has just settled down when a second party appears, going in the same direction, though at a gentler gait; for it is a cavalcade composed partly of ladies.

It is a quartette, two of each sex; and as the horses are the same already seen standing saddled in the courtyard of Don Gregorio's house, it is not necessary to give the names of the riders. These can be guessed.

Doña Carmen is carrying out the instructions left by her father, who, Californian fashion, supposed he could give his sailor-guests no greater treat than a *paseo de caballo*, including an excursion to the old Dolores Mission, without a visit to which no exploration of the country around San Francisco can be considered complete. It is not the least of California's "lions."

Like most Spanish-American ladies, Don Gregorio's daughter takes delight in the saddle, and spends some part of each day in it. An accomplished *equestrienne*, she could take a five-barred gate, or a bullfinch, with any of the hunting Dianas of England; and, if she has not ridden to hounds, she has chased wild horses, mounted on one but little less wild. That on which she now sits seems but half-tamed. Fresh from the stable, he rears and pitches, at times standing erect on his hind legs. For all, his rider has no fear of being unhorsed. She only smiles, pricks him with the spur, and regardlessly cuts him with her *cuarto*.

Much after the same fashion acts Iñez, for she, too, has learned the Californian style of equitation.

The two present a picture that, to the eye unaccustomed to Mexican habits, might seem somewhat *bizarre*. Their mode of mount—as already said, *à la Duchesse de Berri*—their half-male attire, hats of vicuña wool, *calzoncillas* lace-fringed over their feet, buff boots, and large rowelled spurs—all these give them an air of *bizarrerie*, at the same time a pleasing picturesqueness; and, if appearing bold, still beautiful, as the South Sea wind flouts back the limp brims of their sombreros, and tosses their hair into dishevelment, while the excitement of the ride brings the colour to their cheeks—with flashes, as of fire, from their eyes.

The young English officers regard them with glances of ardent admiration. If they have been but smitten before, they are getting fast fixed now; and both will soon be seriously in love. The *paseo de caballo* promises to terminate in a proposal for a longer journey in companionship—through life, in pairs.

They are thus grouped: Crozier alongside Carmen—Cadwallader with Iñez. The officers are in their uniforms—a costume for equestrian exercise not quite shipshape as they would phrase it. On horseback in a naval uniform! It would not do riding thus on an English road; there the veriest country lout would criticise it. But different in California, where all ride, gentle or simple, in dresses of every conceivable cut and fashion, with no fear of being ridiculed therefor. None need attach to the dress worn by Edward Crozier. His rank has furnished him with a frock-coat, which, well-fitting, gives a handsome contour to his person. Besides, he is a splendid horseman—has followed hounds before he ever set foot aboard a ship. Carmen Montijo perceives this; can tell it with half a glance; and it pleases her to reflect that her escorting cavalier is equal to the occasion. She believes him equal to anything.

With the other pair the circumstances are slightly different. Will Cadwallader is no horseman, having had but scant practice—a fact patent to all—Iñez as the others. Besides, the mid is dressed in a pea-jacket; which, although becoming enough aboard ship, looks a little *outré* in the saddle, especially upon a prancing Californian steed. Does it make the young Welshman feel ashamed of himself? Not a bit. He is not the stuff to be humiliated on the score of an inappropriate costume. Nor yet by his inferiority in horsemanship, of which he is himself well aware. He but laughs as his steed prances about—the louder when it comes near pitching him.

How does he appear in the eyes of Iñez Alvarez? Does she think him ridiculous? No. On the contrary, she seems charmed, and laughs along with him—delighted by his *naïveté*, and the courage he displays in not caring for consequences. She knows he is out of his own element—the sea. She believes that on it he would be brave, heroic; among ropes the most skilled of reefers; and if he cannot gracefully sit a home, he could ride big billows, breasting them like an albatross.

Thus mutually taking each other's measure, the four equestrians canter on, and soon arrive at the mission.

But they do not design to stay there. The ride has *been* too short, the sweet moments have flown quickly; and the summit of a high hill, seen far beyond, induces them to continue the excursion.

They only stop to give a glance at the old monastery, where Spanish monks once lorded it over their copper-skinned neophytes; at the church, where erst ascended incense, and prayers were pattered in the ears of the aborigines—by them ill understood.

A moment spent in the cemetery, where Carmen points out the tomb enclosing the remains of her mother, dropping a tear upon it—perhaps forced from her by the reflection that soon she will be far from that sacred spot—it may be, never to revisit it!

Away from it now; and on to that hill from which they can descry the Pacific!

In another hour they have reined up on its summit, and behold the great South Sea, stretching to far horizon's verge, to the limit of their vision. Before them all is bright and beautiful. Only some specks in the dim distance—the lone isles of the Farrallones. More northerly, and nearer, the "Seal" rocks and that called *Campana*—from its arcade hollowed out by the wash of waves, giving it a resemblance to the belfry of a church. Nearer still, below a belt of pebbly beach, a long line of breakers, foam-crested, and backed by a broad reach of sand-dunes—there termed *medanos*.

Seated in the saddle, the excursionists contemplate this superb panorama. The four are now together, but soon again separate into pairs, as they have been riding along the road. Somehow or other, their horses have thus disposed themselves: that ridden by Crozier having drawn off with the one carrying Carmen; while the steed so ill-managed by Cadwallader has elected to range itself alongside that of Iñez.

Perhaps the pairing has not been altogether accidental. Whether or no, it is done; and the conversation, hitherto general, is reduced to the simplicity of dialogue.

To report it correctly, it is necessary to take the pairs apart, giving priority to those who by their years have the right to it.

Crozier, looking abroad over the ocean, says—

"I shall ere long be upon it." He accompanies the speech with a sigh.

"And I, too," rejoins Carmen, in a tone, and with accompaniment, singularly similar.

"How soon do you think of leaving California?" queries the young officer.

"Oh, very soon! My father is already making arrangements, and hopes being able to set sail in a week, if not less. Indeed, he has this day been to see about taking passages to Panama. That's why he was not at home to receive you; leaving me to do the honours of the house, and apologise for his seeming rudeness."

For that not much apology was needed, thinks Crozier, who is for a time silent, not knowing what next to say. Love, reputed eloquent, is oft the reverse; and though opening the lips of a landsman, will shut those of men who follow the sea. There is a remarkable modesty about the latter more than the former—in the presence of women. Why, I cannot tell; only knowing that as a rule it is so; and certainly in the case of Edward Crozier.

In time he gets over his embarrassment, so far as to venture upon an interrogatory, not very pertinent—

"I suppose, Doña Carmen, you are very happy at the prospect of returning to Spain?"

"No, indeed," answers Don Gregorio's daughter. "On the contrary, it makes me rather melancholy. I love dear California, and could live in it all my life. Couldn't you?"

"Under certain circumstances, I could."

"But you like the country, don't you?"

"I do, now. In ten days from this time, I shall no longer care for it—not three straws."

"Why do you say that, Don Eduardo? There's an enigma in your words. Please explain them?"

While asking the question, her grey-blue eyes gaze into his, with an expression of searching eagerness—almost anxiety.

"Shall I tell you why, señorita!"

"I have asked you, señor."

"Well, then, I like California now, because it contains the fairest object on earth—to me the dearest—the woman I love. In ten days or less, by her own showing, she will be away from it; why should I care for it then? Now, Doña Carmen, I've given you the key to what you've called an enigma."

"Not quite. Perhaps you will pardon a woman's curiosity, if I ask the name of the lady who thus controls your likes and dislikes."

Crozier hesitates, a red spot flushing out upon his cheek. He is about to pronounce a name—perhaps make a speech, the most important he has ever made in his life—because laden with his life's happiness, or leading to the reverse. What if it should be coldly received?

But no; he cannot be mistaken. Her question, so quaintly, yet so impressively put—surely courts the answer he intends giving? And he gives it without further reflection—her own name, not an added word.

"Carmen Montijo."

"Eduardo," she asks, after a pause, dropping the Don, "are you in earnest? Can I take this as true? Do not deceive me—in honour do not! To you—and I truly tell you—I have surrendered all my heart. Say that I have yours!"

"I have said it, Carmen," he too adopting the familiar language of love. "Have I not?"

"Sincerely?"

"Look in my eyes for the answer."

She obeys; and drawing closer, tiny gaze into one another's eyes; the flashes from the blue crossing and commingling with those from the brown. Neither could mistake the meaning of the glance, for it is the true light of love, pure as passionate.

Not another word passes between them. The confession, with its dreaded crisis, is passed; and, with hearts quivering in sweet content, they turn their thoughts to the future, full of pleasant promise.

Near by are two other hearts, quite as happy as theirs; though after a scene less sentimental, and a dialogue that, to a stranger overhearing it, might appear to be in jest. For all, in real earnest, and so ending—as may be inferred from the young Welshman's final speech, with the reply of his Andalusian sweetheart:

"Iñez, you're the dearest girl I've met in all my cruisings. Now, don't let us beat about any longer, but take in sail, and bring the ship to an anchor. Will you be mine, and marry me?"

"I will."

No need to stay longer there—no object in continuing to gaze over the ocean.

The horses seem instinctively to understand this; and, turning together, set their heads for home.

Chapter Twenty
Pot Valiant

The bright Californian sun is declining towards the crest of the Coast Range, when two horsemen, coming from the Pacific side, commence ascending the ridge.

As the sultry hours have passed, and a chill breeze blows from the outside ocean, they have thrust their heads through the central slits of their cloaks—these being *mangas*—leaving the circular skirts to droop down below their knees—while draping back, cavalry fashion, over the hips of their horses. The colours of these garments—one scarlet, the other sky-blue—enable us to identify the wearers as Don Francisco de Lara and Don Faustino Calderon; for in truth it is they, returning from the *pelea de gallos* at Punta Pedro.

They have seen Diaz, and arranged everything about the duel. Faustino has finally determined upon fight. Instigated by his more courageous confederate, and with further pressing on the part of Diaz—a sort of Californian bravo—his courage has been at length screwed up to the necessary pitch; and kept there by the potent spirit of Catalonian brandy, found freely circulating around the cock-pit.

A flask of the *Catalan* he has brought away with him, and at intervals takes a pull from it, as he rides along the road. Under its influence he becomes pot valiant; and swears, if he can but again set eyes upon the English *guardia-marina*, he will affront him in such fashion as to leave him no loophole of escape from being the challenger. *Carrai!* he will do as De Lara has recommended: cuff the young officer, kick him, spit in his face, anything to provoke the *gringo* to a fight—that yellow-haired cub without *bigots* or beard. And if the cur won't fight, then he shall apologise—get down upon his knees, acknowledge him, Faustino Calderon, the better man, and for ever after surrender all claim to the smiles, as to the hand, of Iñez Alvarez!

With such swaggering talk he entertains his companion, as the two are returning to town.

De Lara, less noisy, is nevertheless also excited. The fiery alcohol has affected him too. Not to strengthen his courage; for of this he has already enough; but to remove the weight from off his soul, which, after the scene at Don Gregorio's, had been pressing heavily upon it. Six hours have since elapsed, and for the first three he had been brooding over his humiliation, his spirit prostrate in the dust. But the *Catalan* has again raised it to a pitch of exultation; especially when he reflects upon the prospect of the sure and speedy vengeance he is determined to take.

It does not occur to him to doubt of success. With thorough reliance on his skill as a swordsman, he feels sure of it. Though also a good shot, he prefers the steel for his weapon; like most men of the southern Latinic race, who believe Northerners to be very bunglers at sword-play, though admitting their superiority in the handling of the pistol. As things stand, unlike his comrade Calderon, he will have the choice of weapons. His intended antagonist was the first to demand the card, and must needs be challenger.

As the two ride on, they talk alternately, both giving vent to their spleen—the man of courage, as the coward. If not so loud, or boastingly, as his companion, De Lara expresses himself with a more spiteful and earnest determination; repeating much of what he has already said at an earlier hour, but with added emphasis. Once he sees the English officer at his rapier's point, he will show him no mercy, but run him through, without the slightest compunction. In vain may his adversary cry "Quarter." There can be none conceded, after what has that day passed between them.

"*Maldita*! it shall be a duel to the death!" he exclaims, after having given way to a series of threats, the words pronounced with an *empressement* that tells him to be truly, terribly in earnest.

They have been carrying on this excited dialogue, as their horses climbed the slope from the Pacific side, its steepness hindering them from going at their usual gait—a gallop. On rising the ridge's crest, and catching sight of San Francisco, with its newly painted white walls, and shining tin roofs, reflected red in the rays of the setting sun, De Lara, suddenly remembering the pressure upon him as to time, strikes the spur sharp against his horse's ribs, and puts the animal to speed. The other imitating his example, they dash on towards Dolores.

They have no intention to make stop at the mission; but, on reaching it, they draw up; obedient to the hail of a man seen standing in the door of a little tavern, or *tinacal*, frequented by the lower class of native Californians.

A rough, swarthy-skinned fellow, in a garb that proclaims his calling to have connection with the sea, though not that of a sailor. He may be a shore-boatman—perhaps a *piscador*—though, judging by his general appearance, and the uncanny cast of his countenance, he might well pass for a pirate.

Stepping a few paces out from the *tinacal*, he salutes the two horsemen, who have halted in the middle of the road to await his approach. Despite his coarse, brutal aspect, and common habiliments, he is evidently on terms of familiarity with both—the style of his salutation showing it. It is with De Lara, however, his business lies, as signified by his saying:

"I want a word with you, Don Francisco."

"What is it, Rocas?" asks the Creole. "Anything about *seal-skins?*" laying a significant emphasis on the last word.

"*Carramba!* No. Something of more importance than that."

"Money, then?"

"Money."

"Do you wish our speech to be private?"

"Just now, yes. Perhaps, in time, Don Faustino—"

"Oh!" interrupts the *ganadero*, "don't let me stand in the way. I'll ride slowly on; you can overtake me, Don Francisco."

"Do," says De Lara, at the same time stooping down in his saddle, and continuing the conversation with Rocas, in tone so low as to prevent their speech being overheard by other queer-looking customers who have just stepped out of the *tinacal*, and stand loitering at its door.

Whatever Rocas may have said, it appears to make a vivid impression on the gambler. His eyes kindle up with a strange light, in which surprise is succeeded by an expression of cupidity; while his manner proclaims that the revelation made to him is not only important, as he has been forewarned, but also pleasing.

Their muttered dialogue is of brief duration; ending with a remark which shows it to be only preliminary to a further and more prolonged conference.

"I shall be with you to-morrow, by mid-day." It is De Lara who has said this; after which adding: "*Adios, Don Rafael! Hasta mañana!*" he gives his horse the spur, and gallops to overtake his travelling companion; Rocas sauntering back towards the *tinacal*.

Chapter Twenty One
A "Golpe de Caballo"

On coming up with the *ganadero*, De Lara rides on silently by his side, without exhibiting any desire to satisfy the other's curiosity. He but piques it by saying, that Rocas has a made communication of an intensely interesting kind; which he will impart to him, Faustino, in due time; but now there are other matters of more importance to be attended to. The fighting is before them; and that cannot be set aside.

Calderon wishes it could: for the flask has been for a time forgotten, and the spirit has been getting cold within him.

"Take another pull!" counsels his companion; "you may need it. We'll soon be in the town, and, perhaps, the first man we meet there will be your yellow-haired rival."

Scarcely have the words passed De Lara's lips when something in front fixes his attention, as also that of his companion. At some distance along the road a cloud of dust is ascending; in its midst a darker nucleus, distinguishable as the forms of horses with riders on their backs. There appear to be four of them, filed two and two.

Plying their spurs, and galloping closer, the gamblers perceive that this equestrian party is proceeding in the same direction as themselves—towards the town.

But they are soon near enough to know that such is not their destination. For, despite the enshrouding dust, they have no difficulty in identifying the individuals before them. The horses are the same seen that morning, saddled and bridled, in front of Don Gregorio's house. Two of the riders are Carmen Montijo and Iñez Alvarez; the other two—

At this point conjecture terminates. De Lara, certain, and no longer able to control himself, cries out:

"*Carajo!* it's they returning from their excursion—paired off, as I supposed they would be! So, Calderon, you have your chance sooner than you expected. And without seeking it—a lucky omen! There's your rival, riding by the side of your sweetheart, and pouring soft speech into her ear! Now's your time to set things straight—insult him to your heart's content. I feel like giving a fresh affront to mine."

He draws rein, bringing his horse to a halt. The *ganadero* does the same. Scanning the equestrians ahead, they see them two and two, each pair some ten or twelve paces apart from the other. Crozier and Carmen are in the advance, Cadwallader and Iñez behind.

De Lara looks not at the latter couple; his eyes are all upon the former, staring with fixed intensity, full of jealous fire, in a glare such as only a tiger might give, on seeing Carmen Montijo turn towards her escorting cavalier, and bend over—he to her—till their heads are close together, and their lips seemingly in contact!

"*Carrai!* they're kissing!" he exclaims, in a tone of bitter exasperation.

He can bear it no longer. With a shout, half angry, half anguished, he digs the spur deep, and dashes forward.

The clattering of hoofs behind first warns Cadwallader, who is nearest to the noise. For, up to this time, the lovers, absorbed in sweet converse, dreamed not of danger.

The young Welshman, glancing back, sees what it is, at the same time hears De Lara's wild cry. Intuitively he understands that some outrage is intended—a repetition of the morning's work, with doubtless something more.

Quickly he draws his dirk: not now to be used in sport, for the mere pricking of a horse, but in serious earnest, to be buried in the body of a man—if need be. This resolve can be read in his attitude, in his eyes, in his features. These no longer bent in the laugh of a reckless boy, but the rigid, resolute determination of a man. Badly as he sits his horse, it will not do now to dash against him. The collision may cost life—in all likelihood, that of the aggressor.

De Lara sweeps past the midshipman without saying a word; without even taking notice of him. His affair is with one further on.

But now Calderon is coming up, clearly with the intent to assault, as shown in his eyes.

Suddenly, however, their expression changes at sight of the bared blade. Again that diabolical dirk! Despite a pull he has just taken from the flask, his courage fails him; and crestfallen, as a knight compelled to lower his plume, he too passes Cadwallader, without a word—riding on after De Lara.

He overtakes the latter in time to be spectator of a scene; in its commencement somewhat similar to that enacted by himself, but with a very different termination.

Crozier, whose ear has also caught the sounds from behind, draws bridle, and looks back. He sees De Lara making towards him; and, at a glance, divines the intent. It is a *golpe de caballo*, or collision of horses—a common mode of assault among Spanish Californians.

Instead of turning aside to avoid it, he of Shropshire determines on a different course. He knows he is upon a strong horse, and feels confident he can stay there.

With this confidence he faces towards the advancing enemy, and after taking true bearing, spurs straight at him.

Breast to breast the horses meet, shoulder to shoulder the men. Not a word between these themselves, both too maddened to speak. Only a cry from Carmen Montijo, a shriek from Iñez Alvarez, heard simultaneously with the shock.

When it is over, Don Francisco de Lara is seen rolling upon the road— his horse kicking and sprawling in the dust beside him.

Regaining his feet, the gambler rushes to get hold of a pistol, whose butt protrudes from his saddle-holster.

He is too late: Cadwallader has come up; and, dropping down out of his saddle, as if from a ship's shrouds, makes himself master of the weapon.

Disarmed, his glittering attire dust-bedaubed, De Lara stands in the middle of the road, irresolute, discomfited, conquered. He can do nothing now, save storm and threaten—interlarding his threats with curses— "*Carajos!*" spitefully pronounced.

The ladies, at Crozier's request, have ridden on ahead, so that their ears are not offended.

After listening to the ebullition of his impotent spleen—Cadwallader all the while loudly laughing—Crozier, in serious tone, says:

"Don Francisco De Lara—for your card tells me that is your name— take a sailor's advice: go quietly to your quarters; stow yourself out of sight;

and stay there till your temper cools down. We don't want you to walk. You shall have your horse, though not your shooting-iron. That I shall take care of myself, and may return it to you when next we meet. The same advice to you, sir," he adds, addressing Calderon, who stands near equally cowed and crestfallen.

After dictating these humiliating conditions—which, *nolens volens*, the defeated bravos are obliged to accept—the young officers leap back into their saddles, and trot off to rejoin the ladies.

Having overtaken these, they continue their homeward ride, with no fear of its being again interrupted by a "*golpe de caballo.*"

Chapter Twenty Two
"Hasta Cadiz!"

On leaving Captain Lantanas, the *ex-ganadero* returns to his house—though not direct. He has business to transact in the town, which stays him. He has to see Don Tomas Silvestre, the shipping-agent, and give directions about inserting the advertisement for sailors. That is an affair that will occupy only a few minutes. But he has another with the agent of a more important kind. He is personally acquainted with Silvestre, who is, like himself, a Peninsular Spaniard and Biscayan. Don Gregorio knows he can trust him, and does—telling him all he has told Lantanas, making further known the arrangement he has entered into for passages to Panama, and instructing him to assist the Chilian skipper in procuring a crew.

The more confidential matter relates to the shipment of his gold-dust. He trembles to think of the risk he runs of losing it. San Francisco is filled with queer characters—men who would stick at nothing.

Don Tomas knows this without being told. And the thought haunts the Biscayan like a spectre, that he will have his treasure taken from him by theft, burglary, or bold open robbery.

He has good reason for so apprehending. Among the latest accessions to the population of San Francisco all three classes of criminals are represented, and in no stinted numbers. There are ticket-of-leave men from Australia, jail-birds from the penitentiaries of the States, 'scape-the-gallows customers from every quarter of the globe; to say nothing of the native bandits, of which California has its share. If known to these that yellow metal, to the value of three hundred thousand dollars, was lying unguarded in the house of Don Gregorio Montijo, it would not be there many days or nights. Its owner has done what he could to keep this a secret; but the sale and transfer of his land have leaked out, as also the handsome price obtained, and paid over to him; hence a natural inference that the cash must be deposited somewhere.

And everyone well knows it will be in gold-dust; since banks have not yet been established, and there are not obtainable notes enough in San Francisco to cover a tenth part of the amount. He had tried to convert it thus—as more convenient for carriage and safety—but failed.

In fine, after confiding his fears to Silvestre, and taking counsel from him, he decides upon the plan, already in part communicated to Captain Lantanas—of having the endangered gold-dust secretly conveyed to the *Condor* that very night. Don Tomas will provide the boat, with a trusty sailor-servant he has attached to his establishment, to assist in the removal and rowing. They can take it aboard without passing through the town, or at all touching at the port. The boat can be brought to the beach below Don Gregorio's house, and the gold quietly carried down to it. Thence they can transport it direct to the ship. Once there, Lantanas will know how to dispose of it; and surely it will be safe in his custody—at all events, safer there than anywhere else in San Francisco. So thinks Don Gregorio, the ship-agent agreeing with him.

Soon everything is settled; for they spend not many minutes in discussing the matter. The *ex-ganadero* knows that by this time his house will be empty, excepting the servants: for the ride on which his girls have gone was arranged by himself, to gratify his expected visitors. He thinks apprehensively of the unprotected treasure, and longs to be beside it. So, remounting the stout cob that brought him to town, he rides hastily home.

On arrival there, he retires to his sleeping apartment; where he spends the remainder of the day, having given strict orders not to be called, till the party of equestrians comes back.

But although confining himself to the chamber, he does not go to bed, nor otherwise take repose. On the contrary, he is busy throughout the whole afternoon, getting ready his treasure for surreptitious transport, for it is there in the room—has been ever since it came into his possession. Almost fearing to trust it out of his sight, he sleeps beside it.

Some of it is in bags, some in boxes; and he now rearranges it in the most convenient form for carriage to the Chilian ship, and safe stowage in her cabin-lockers.

He has not yet completed his task, when he hears the trampling of hoofs on the gravelled sweep outside. The riding-party has returned.

The *saguan* bell rings; the heavy door grates back on its hinges; and, soon after, the horses, with the riders still on their backs, stand panting in the *patio*.

The master of the house sallies forth to receive his guests. He sees them hastening to assist the ladies in dismounting. But before either cavalier can come near them, both leap lightly out of their saddles; then, gliding into the corridor, fling their arms around Don Gregorio's neck—daughter and grand-daughter alike calling him "papa."

They are effusively affectionate—more than usually so—for this night both have a favour to ask of him. And he knows, or can guess, what it is. He has not been blind to what has been passing between them, and the young English officers. He suspects that vows have been exchanged—a double proposal made—and anticipates a demand upon himself to sanction it.

In both cases he is prepared to do this. For he is not unacquainted with either the character, or social standing, of those seeking an alliance with him. He has been aboard the British frigate, and from Captain Bracebridge obtained information on these points. Satisfactory in every sense. Both the young officers bear an excellent reputation. Though differing in other respects, they are alike skilled in their profession—each "every inch a seaman," as their commander worded it. Besides, both are of good family— Cadwallader moderately rich—Crozier in prospect of being immensely so—either of them fit mate for the proudest señora in Spain. Don Gregorio's reason for supposing that on this day engagements have been entered into, is, that the young officers are about to take departure from the port. The *Crusader* is under Admiralty orders to sail for the Sandwich Islands, soon as a corvette coming thence reaches San Francisco. Captain Bracebridge has been commissioned by the British Government to transact some diplomatic business with King Kamehameha. That done, he is to look in at the ports of Panama and Callao; then home—afterwards to join the Mediterranean squadron. As the *Crusader*, on her way to the Mediterranean, will surely call at Cadiz, the vows this day exchanged on the shore of the Pacific, can be thus conveniently renewed on the other side of the Atlantic.

At dinner—which is served soon after and in sumptuous style—Don Gregorio makes his guests aware of the fact, that he has secured passages for Panama, and may leave San Francisco soon as they. He confides to them the secret of his having chartered the Chilian ship—in short, telling them all he has told her captain—echoing the lament made by the latter about his difficulty in obtaining a crew.

"Perhaps," rejoins Crozier, after hearing this, "I can help your skipper to at least one good sailor. Do you think, Will," he continues, addressing himself to the young Welshman, "that Harry Blew is still in San Francisco, or has he gone off to the diggings?"

"I fancy he's still here," responds Cadwallader. "He was aboard the frigate only the day before yesterday—having a shake hands with his old comrades of the forecastle."

"Who is the Señor Bloo?" inquires their host.

"A true British tar—if you know what that means, Don Gregorio— lately belonging to our ship, and one of the best sailors on our books. He's off them now, as his time was out; and like many another, though not better man, has made up his mind to go gold-seeking on the Sacramento. Still, if he be not gone, I think we might persuade him to take a trip on the craft you speak of. It was once Harry's sinister luck to slip overboard in the harbour of Guaymas—dropping almost into the jaws of a *tintorero* shark—and my good fortune to be able to rescue him out of his perilous plight. He is not the man to be ungrateful; and, if still in San Francisco, I think you may count upon him for taking service on board this Chilian vessel. True, he's only one, but worth two—ay, ten. He not only knows how to work a ship's sails, but on a pinch could take a lunar, and make good any port in the Pacific."

"A most valuable man!" exclaims Don Gregorio; "would be worth his weight in gold to Captain Lantanas. I'm sure the Chilian skipper would at once make him his mate. Do you suppose you can find him?"

"If in San Francisco, yes. We shall search for him this very night; and, if found, send him either to the Chilian skipper or to the shipping-agent you've spoken of—Silvestre. By the way, what's his address?"

"Here," answers Don Gregorio, drawing forth a card, and handing it across the table to Crozier. "That's the place where Don Tomas transacts business. It's but a poor little shed down by the beach, near the new pier, lately constructed. Indeed, I believe he sleeps there—house-rent in San Francisco being at present something fabulous."

"This will do," says Crozier, putting the card into his pocket. "If Henry Blew can be found, he won't be far from Silvestre's office—if not this night, by early daybreak to-morrow morning."

It is not the custom of either Spaniards, or Spanish-Americans, to tarry long over the dinner-table. The cloth once removed, and the ladies gone, a glass or two of Port, Xeres, or Pedro Ximenes, and the gentlemen also retire; not for business, but recreation out of doors, so pleasant in southern climes.

Dona Carmen and her niece have ascended to the *azotea*, to enjoy the sweet twilight of a Californian summer; whither they are soon followed by Crozier and Cadwallader.

The master of the house has for a time parted with them—under the excuse of having affairs to attend to. It is to complete the packing of his gold-dust. But before leaving the *sala de comer*, and while emptying their last glass together, he has been approached by his sailor-guests on that subject uppermost in their thoughts, and dearest to their hearts. Asked if he be agreeable to become the father-in-law of one, and the—Cadwallader had difficulty in finding a word for it—*grandfather-in-law* of the other, to both interrogatories he has given the same answer—"Yes."

No wonder that, with bright faces and bounding step, the young officers rush out, and up to the *azotea*, there to rejoin the señoritas.

Their tale told to the latter—who have been awaiting them in anxious expectation—will save both a world of confusion and blushes. No need now for *them* to talk to "papa." His consent has been obtained—they are aware he will keep his word.

Again the four, now formally betrothed, separate into twos, taking opposite sides of the aerial garden.

They converse about the far future—that awaiting them at Cadiz. But the ladies cannot overlook, or forget, some perils more proximate. The retrospect of the day throws a shadow over the morrow. That encounter with De Lara and Calderon cannot end without further action. Not likely; and both aunt and niece recall it, questioning their now affianced lovers—adjuring them to refrain from fighting.

These reply, making light of the matter, declaring confidence in their own strength and skill, whatever be the upshot—at length, so assuring their sweethearts, that both believe them invincible, invulnerable. What woman who does not believe the same of him who holds her heart?

Time passes; the last moments speed silently, sweetly, in the old, old ecstasy of all-absorbing, time-killing love.

Then the inevitable *"Adios!"* though sounding less harshly by favour of the appended phrase—*"Hasta Cadiz!"*

Chapter Twenty Three
On Pleasure Bent

The clocks of San Francisco are striking the hour of ten. The moon has risen over Monte Diablo, and sends her soft mellow beams across the waters of the bay, imparting to their placid surface a sheen as of silver. The forms of the ships at anchor are reflected as from a mirror; their hulls, with every spar, stay, and brace, even to the most delicate rope of their rigging, having a duplicated representative in the fictitious counterfeit beneath. On none is there any canvas spread; and the unfurled flags do not display their fields, but hang motionless along masts, or droop dead down over taffrails.

Stillness, almost complete, reigns throughout; scarce a sound proceeding either from the ships inshore, or those out in the offing; not even the rattle of a chain dropping or weighing anchor, the chant of a night-watch at the windlass, or the song of jovial tar entertaining his messmates as they sit squatted around the forecastle stair.

Unusual this silence at such an early hour, though easily accounted for. That there are so few noises from the ships in San Francisco Bay, is explained by the fact of their being but few men to make them—in many cases not a single soul aboard. All have deserted; either for good, and are gone to the "diggings," or only for the night, to take part in the pleasures and dissipations of the town. Now and then a boat may be seen, putting off from, or returning to, the side of some vessel better manned—by its laborious movement, and the unmeasured stroke of oars, telling that even it lacks a full complement of crew.

Inside the town, everything is different. There, noises enough, with plenty of people; crowded streets, flashing lights, and a Babel-like confusion of voices. It is now the hour when iniquity has commenced its nightly career, or, rather, reached its full flush; since in San Francisco certain kinds of it are carried on throughout all hours of the day. Business houses are closed; but these are in small proportion to the places of pleasure, which keep their doors and windows wide open, and where dissipation reigns paramount, as permanent. Into the gambling-saloons go men laden with gold-dust, often coming out with their wallets lighter than when they went in, but their hearts a deal heavier. After toiling for months up to their middle, in the chill waters of streams that course down from the eternal snows of the Sierra Nevada, working, washing—while so occupied, half-starving—they return to San Francisco to scatter in a single night—oft in one hour—the hoarded gatherings of a half-year!

Into this pleasure-seeking city are about to enter two personages of very different appearance from those usually seen loitering in its saloons or hastening through its streets; for they are young officers belonging to a British frigate—Edward Crozier and William Cadwallader. They are returning to their ship; not directly, as they were rowed ashore, but through the town; Crozier having ordered the boat to be brought to one of the rough wooden wharfs recently erected.

They are advancing along the shore-road, afoot; having declined their host's offer of horses—both saying they would prefer to walk; Cadwallader adding, in his favourite sailor phrase, that he wished to "kick the knots out of his legs"—a remark but obscurely comprehensible to Don Gregorio.

For some time after leaving the Spaniard's house, not a word passes between them. Each is occupied with his own thoughts, the sacredness of which keeps him silent; absorbed in reflections, about that tender, but painful parting, speculating on what may be before them in the far uncertain future.

For a time, nought intrudes upon their reverie, to disturb its natural course. The sough of the tidal surf breaking upon the beach, the occasional cry of a soaring sea-bird, or the more continuous and melancholy note of the chuck-will's-widow, do not attract their attention. They are sounds in consonance with their thoughts, still a little sad.

As they draw nearer to the city, see its flashing lights, and hear its hum of voices, other and less doleful ideas come uppermost, leading to conversation. Crozier commences it:

"Well, Will, old fellow, we've made a day of it!"

"That we have—a rousing, jolly day. I don't think I ever enjoyed one more in my life."

"Only for its drawbacks."

"You mean our affair with those fellows? Why, that was the best part of it—so far as fun. To see the one in the sky-blue wrap, after I'd dirked his horse, go off like a ship in a gale, with nobody at the helm! By Jove! it was equal to old Billy Button in the circus. And then the other, you bundled over in the road, as he got up looking like a dog just out of a dust-bin! Oh!

'twas delicious! The best shore adventure I've had since leaving home—something to talk about when we get aboard the ship."

"Ay, and something to do besides talking. We've got a little writing to do; at least I have—a bit of a letter to this swaggerer, Mr Francisco de Lara."

"But, surely, you don't intend challenging him—after what's happened?"

"Surely I do. Though, to say the truth, I've no great stomach for it, seeing the sort he is. It's *infra dig* having to fight one's inferior, though it be with sword or pistol. It feels like getting into a row with roughs in some slum of a seaport."

"You're right there; and as to calling the fellow out, I'd do nothing of the kind, Ned. He's a bad lot; so is the other. Blackguards both, as their behaviour has shown them. They don't deserve to be treated as gentlemen."

"But we're in California, Will; where the code of the duello takes in such as they. Here even thieves and cut-throats talk about protecting their honour, as they term it; ay, and often act up to their talk. I've been told of a duel that took place not long since between two professional gamblers, in which one of them was shot dead in his tracks. And only the other day a judge was called out by a man he had tried, and convicted, of some misdemeanour! Well, the judge not only went, but actually killed the cad who'd stood before him as a criminal! All that seems very absurd, but so it is. And if this scarlet-cloaked cavalier don't show the white-feather, and back out, I'll either have to kill, or cripple him; though like as not he may do one or the other for me."

"But don't you think, Ned, you've had enough out of him?"

"In what way?"

"Why, in the way of *revanche*. For my part, I should decidedly say you had by far the best of it. After your first encounter in the morning, I thought differently; and would have so counselled you. Then the insult offered you remained unpunished. The other has put a different face on the affair; and now that he's got more than he gave, I think you should rest satisfied, and let things stand as they are—if he do. Certainly, after that knock and tumble, it's his place to sing out."

"There's something in what you say, Will. And now, on reflection, I'm not so sure that I'll take further trouble about the fellow, unless he insist on it; which he may not, seeing he's unquestionably base coin—as you say, a blackguard. He appears a sort of Californian bravo; and if we hadn't secured his pistol, I suppose he'd have done some shooting with it. Well, we'll see whether he comes to reclaim it. If he don't, I shall have to send it to him. Otherwise, he may have us up before one of these duelling justices on a charge of robbing him!"

"Ha, ha, ha! That would be a rare joke; an appropriate ending to our day's fun."

"Quite the contrary. It might be serious, if it should reach the ears of Bracebridge. The old disciplinarian would never believe but that we'd been in the wrong—taken the fellow's pistol from him for a lark, or something of that sort. True, we could have the thing explained, both to the San Francisco magistrate, and the frigate's captain; but not without an exposure of names and circumstances. That, though it might be proper enough, would be anything but a pleasant finale to our day's fun, as you call it."

"Well, I know what will," rejoins Cadwallader, after listening patiently to his comrade's explanatory speech, "and that's a glass of something good to drink. Those sweet Spanish wines of Don Gregorio have made me thirsty as a fish. Besides, parting with dear Iñez has got my heart down, and I need something to stir it up again."

"All right, my hearty!" exclaims Crozier; for the jest's sake, talking sailor-slang—"I'm with you in that way. For this day at least we've had enough of war, and, shall I say, women?"

"No—no!" protests Cadwallader; "that would be an ungallant speech, after what's passed. We could never have enough of them—at least, not I."

"Why, Will, we've grown wonderfully sentimental, and in such a short time! Well, let's drop the subject of woman, and end our day with the third of three w's—wine."

"Agreed!" responds the young Welshman. "But, for my part, I'd prefer ending it with a different tipple, which has also a w for its initial letter—that's whisky. If we could only get a glass of good Scotch or Irish malt in this mushroom city, it would make a new man of me—which just now I need making. As I tell you, Ned, my heart's down—dead down to the heels of my boots. I can't say why, but there it is; and there I suppose, it'll stay, unless Dutch courage come to the rescue."

"Well, you'll soon have an opportunity of getting that. As you see, we are in the suburbs of this grand city, partly constructed of canvas; where, though food may be scarce, and raiment scanty, there's liquor in abundance. In the *Parker House*, which is, I believe, its best hotel, we'll be sure of finding almost every beverage brewed upon the earth—among them your favourite whisky, and mine—'Bass's Bitter.'"

"Again the Spanish saw, '*Cada uno a su gusto*,' as just now my sweetheart said, after I had kissed the dear girl six times in succession. But let us step out."

"Don't be in such hot haste. You forget we've something to do; which must be done first—before everything else."

"What?"

"Look up Harry Blew; find him, if we can; and coax him to take service in this Chilian ship."

"He won't require much coaxing, once you say the word. The old salt is anything but ungrateful. Indeed, his regard for you, ever since you saved him from that shark, is more like real gratitude than anything I ever saw. He fairly worships you, Ned. He told me the day before he left the *Crusader*, that parting with you was the only thing which greatly grieved him. I saw the tears trickling down his cheeks, as you shook hands with him over the rail. Even then, if you'd said stay, I believe he'd have turned back into his old berth."

"I didn't, because I wished him to do better. You know he'd have a splendid chance here in California—to get rich by gold-digging, which no doubt he might, like a great many other humble sailors as himself. But now, this other chance has turned up in his favour, which I should say is surer. Don Gregorio has told us he can get from the Chilian captain almost any pay he may please to ask; besides, a fair likelihood of being made his first mate. That would suit Harry to a hair; in my opinion, answering his purpose far better than any gold-washing speculation. Though a man of first rating aboard ship, he's a mere child when ashore; and would be no more able to protect himself against the land-sharks of San Francisco, than he was to get out of the way of that sea-skimmer at Guaymas. Even if he should succeed in growing rich up the Sacramento River, I'd lay large odds, he'd be back here in port, and poor as ever, within a week. We must save him from that if we can. His natural element is the ocean. He has spent the greater part of his life on it, and here's a fine opportunity for him to return to, and stay upon it. That for life, if he likes, with better prospects than he could ever have had on board a man-o'-war. The question is, how we shall be able to find him in this rookery of a place. Did he say anything, when you saw him, about where he was sojourning!"

"By Jove! he just did. Now, I recall our conversation, I remember him telling me that he was staying at a sort of a boarding-house, or restaurant, called the 'Sailor's Home,' though he made no mention of the street. But, if I mistake not, I know the place, and can steer pretty straight for it."

"Straight or crooked, let's set head for it at once. We've plenty of time, if that were all. I told the coxswain not to come for us till well after eleven. I want to see something of this queer Californian life, of which I haven't had much experience yet."

"The same with myself."

"Well, we may never again get such a chance. Indeed, it's not likely we'll be allowed another night ashore, before the *Crusader* sails. Therefore, let us make hay while the sun shines, or, to speak less figuratively, a little merriment by the light of the moon. We've been either savage, or sentimental, all the day, and need changing our tune."

"You're right about that; but the music is not likely to be made by moonlight—not much of it. See those great clouds rolling up yonder! They'll be all over the sky in ten minutes' time, making it black as a pot of pitch."

"No matter; for what we want, gas-light will serve as well; and there's plenty of that in San Francisco. Now for Harry Blew. After him, whisky punches at the *Parker*."

"And after that?"

"A *Hell*, if you feel that way inclined."

"Surely, Ned, you don't want to go gambling!"

"I want to see life in San Francisco, as I've said; and, as you know, gambling's an important part of it. Yes; I wish to inspect the elephant, and I don't mind making an attempt to draw the teeth of the tiger. *Allons!* or, as I should say, in the softer language of Andalusia, *Nos vamos!*"

Thus jocosely terminating the conversation, the young officers continue on at increased speed, and are soon threading the streets of San Francisco in search of the "Sailor's Home."

Chapter Twenty Four
A Tar of the Olden Type

Harry Blew is a tar of the true man-o'-war type; this of the time when sailors were sailors, and ships were oak, not iron. Such ships are scarce now; but scarcer still the skilled men who handled their ropes, and kept everything taut and trim—in short, the true tars.

Than Harry, a finer specimen of the foremast-man never reefed topsail, or took his glass of grog according to allowance. Of dark complexion naturally, exposure to sun, sea, and storm has deepened it, till his cheeks and throat are almost copper-coloured; somewhat lighter in tint upon Sundays, after they have had their hebdomadal shave. His face is round, with features fairly regular, and of cheerful cast, their cheerfulness heightened by the sparkle of keen grey eyes, and two rows of sound white teeth, frequently, if not continuously shown in smile. A thick shock of curling brown hair, with a well-greased ringlet drooping down over each eyebrow, supports a round-rimmed, blue-ribboned hat, well aback on his head. His shaven chin is pointed and prominent, with a dimple below the lip; while the beardless jaws curve smoothly down to a well-shaped neck, symmetrically set upon broad shoulders, that give token of strength almost herculean. Notwithstanding an amplitude of shirt-collar, which falls back full seven inches, touching the shoulder-tips, the throat and a portion of the expansive chest are habitually exposed to view; while on the sun-browned skin of the latter may be seen a tattooed anchor. By its side, but not so openly exhibited, is the figure of a damsel done in dark blue—no doubt a souvenir, if not the exact similitude, of a sweetheart—some Poll of past time, or perhaps far-off port.

But there is a doubt whether Harry's heart has been true to her. Indeed, a suspicion of its having been false cannot fail to strike any one seeing him with his shirt-sleeves rolled up, since upon the flat of his right fore-arm is the image of another damsel, done more recently, in lighter blue, while on the left is a Cupid holding an unbent bow, and hovering above a pair of hearts, which his arrow has just pierced, impaling them through and through!

All those amorous emblems would seem to argue our true tar inconstant as the wind, with which he has so oft to contend. But no, nothing of the kind. Those well acquainted with him and his history can vouch for it, that he has never had a sweetheart save one—she represented in that limning of light blue; and to her he has been true as steel, up to the hour of her death, which occurred just as she was about to become Mrs Blew.

And that sad event has kept him a bachelor up to the present hour of his life. For the girl on his breast in dark blue is a merely mythical personage, though indelibly stained into his skin by a needle's point and a pinch of gunpowder—done by one of his man-o'-war shipmates while he was still only a sailor-lad.

He is now forty years of age, nearly thirty of which he has passed upon the sea, being off it only in short spells while his ship lay in port. And he has seen service on several vessels—corvettes, frigates, double and treble deckers—all men-of-war, in which he has thrice circumnavigated the globe.

For all, he is yet hale, hearty, and in the perfect plenitude of his strength; only with a slight stoop in the shoulders, as if caught from continually swarming up shrouds, or leaning over the yard while stowing sails. This gives him the appearance of being shorter than he really is: for when straightened up, with back well braced, he stands six feet in his stockings. And his limbs show symmetrical proportion. His duck trousers, fitting tightly over the hips, display a pair of limbs supple and muscular, with thighs that seem all sinew from skin to bone.

In spite of his sterling qualities as a seaman, and noble character as a man, Harry has never risen to any rank in the service. With him has it been literally true, "Once a sailor, still a sailor;" and though long ago rated an A.B. of the first order, above this he has not ascended a single step. Were he to complain, which he rarely ever does, he would in all probability say, that his non-promotion has been due to independence of spirit, or, shaping it in his own phraseology, owing to his not having "bootlicked the swabs above him." And there is some truth in this, though another reason might be assigned by those disposed to speak slightingly of him; this, that although liking salt water, he has a decided antipathy to that which is fresh, unless when taken with an admixture of rum. Then he is too fond of it. But it is his only fault, barring which, a better man than Harry Blew—and, when sober, a steadier—never trod the deck of ship.

As already said, he has trod many, the latest being that of the *Crusader*, in which vessel he has spent five years of his life. His engagement terminating almost on the very day she dropt anchor before San Francisco, he has been set free, either to stay in the ship, by entering his name upon her books for a fresh period of service, or step out of her, and go cruising on his own account, whithersoever he may wish.

Taking into consideration the state of things in San Francisco just at this time, it is not strange his having elected to leave the ship. It would be stranger if he had even hesitated about it, though this he had indeed done, for some days lingering with mind only half made up. But the golden lure proved at length too temptingly attractive, and, yielding to it, he took a last leave of his old shipmates, was rowed ashore, and has since been sojourning at the "Sailor's Home"—for he is still there, as Cadwallader rightly surmised—there in a very miserable state of mind, not knowing how his wretchedness will be relieved.

Chapter Twenty Five
The Sailor's Home

There is a "Sailor's Home," or "Snug Harbour" tavern in every seaport town, often anything but home, or harbour, in a pleasant sense. This of San Francisco, 1849, is a hostelry, half eating-house, half drinking-saloon, of somewhat unpretentious appearance—being a rough, weather-boarded building, without planing, or paint, and only two storeys in height. But if low in stature, it is high enough in its charges, as Harry Blew has learnt long since; these being out of all proportion to the outside appearance of the place, or its interior accommodation; though quite in keeping with the prices of other like houses of entertainment in the Pacific seaport.

Harry's original intention was to make only a short stay at the "Sailor's Home"—just long enough to put him through a bit of a spree; for which twelve months' pay, received from the frigate's purser at parting, had amply provided him. Then he would start off for the Feather River, or some other tributary stream of the Sacramento, where gold was being gathered, or dug for.

The first part of this programme he has already carried out, with something besides; that something being the complete expenditure of all his pay—every shilling he received from the ship, and in an incredibly short space of time. He had been scarcely six days ashore when he discovers his cash exchequer quite cleared out. As for credit, there is no such thing in San Francisco. A shop parcel sent home always comes conspicuously marked C.O.D.—"Cash on Delivery."

Since landing, he has not very carefully kept his dead-reckoning, and is at first somewhat surprised to find himself so far out in it. He has plunged his hands into his pockets without encountering coin. He searches in his sea-chest and every other receptacle where he has been accustomed to carry, with similar disappointing result. What can have become of his twelve months' wage, drawn on the day he left the *Crusader*? It has all disappeared!

No wonder he is unable to account for its disappearance; for ever since that day he has been anything but himself—in short, has given way to dissipation of longer continuance than ever before in his life. It has lasted six days, with most part of six nights, at the end of which time he has only pulled up for want of the wherewith to continue it—credit being denied him at the very counter over which he has passed all his pay.

Impecuniosity is an unpleasant predicament in any country, and at all times; but in the San Francisco of 1849 it was a positive danger—where six dollars were demanded, and obtained, for the most meagre of meals; the same for sleeping on a blanketless bed, in a chilly night, within a rough weather-boarded room, or under the yet thinner shelter of a canvas tent. It was a boon to be allowed to lie on the lee-side of a wooden-walled stable; but cost money for the privilege of sleeping in a stall, with straw litter for couch, and the radiating heat from the horses in lieu of coverlet.

In the necessity of seeking some such indifferent accommodation, Harry Blew finds himself, on the seventh night after having received his discharge from the *Crusader*. And as he has now got somewhat sobered, with brain clear enough to think, it occurs to him that the time is come for carrying out the second part of his programme—that is, going on to the gold-diggings.

But how to get off, and get there? These are separate questions, to neither of which can he give a satisfactory answer. Passage to Sacramento, by steamer, costs over a hundred dollars, and still more by stage-coach. He has not a shilling—not a red cent; and his sea-kit sold would not realise a sum sufficient to pay his fare, even if it (the kit) were free. But it is not. On the contrary, embargoed, "quodded," by the keeper of the "Sailor's Home," against a couple of days' unpaid board and lodging—with sundry imbibings across the counter, scored on the slate.

The discharged man-o'-war's man sees himself in a nasty dilemma— all the more from its having a double horn. He can neither go to the gold-diggings, nor stay in the "Sailor's Home." Comparatively cheap as may be this humble hostelry, it is yet dear enough to demand ten dollars a day for indifferent bed and board. Both have been thought bad enough by Harry Blew, even though only a foremast-man. But he is threatened with a still worse condition of things. Inappropriate the title bestowed on his house, for the owner of the "Home" has not the slightest hospitality in his heart. He has discovered that his English guest is "dead broke," drawing his deductions from the two days' board, and as many nights' bed, remaining unpaid.

There is a notice conspicuously posted above the bar that "scores must be settled daily." And Harry having disregarded this, has received private, but positive, notice of another kind; to the effect that he is forthwith to discontinue taking a seat at the *table-d'hôte*, as also to surrender up his share of the bed he has been occupying, for he has not had a complete couch to himself. At this the discharged man-o'-war's man has shown no anger, nor does he feel in any way affronted. He has that correct sense common to sailors, with most others trained by travel in strange lands, and knows that when cash is not forthcoming, credit cannot be expected. In California, as elsewhere, such is the universal and rigorous custom, to which man must resign himself. The English sailor is only a bit sorry to think he has expended his cash so freely; a little repentant at having done it so foolishly; and, on the whole, a good deal downhearted.

But there is a silver lining to the cloud. The *Crusader* is still in port, and not expected to sail for some days. He may once more place his name upon the frigate's books, and rejoin her. He knows he will not only be received back by her commander, but welcomed by all his old officers and shipmates. A word spoken to the first boat coming ashore, and all will be well. Shall he speak such word? That has become the question. For in this, as every other step in life, there is a *pro* and *contra*. Humiliating the thought of going back to service on the ship, after taking leave of everybody aboard; returning to a dingy forecastle hard, and the handling of tarry ropes, after the bright dreams he had been indulging in; to forego the gathering of gold-dust, and the exchanging it for doubloons or dollars; in short, turning his back upon fortune—the prospect of a life competence, perhaps plenitude of wealth, with its resulting ease and idleness—and once more facing stormy seas, with only hard knocks and laborious work in store for him the remainder of his life!

While the sovereigns were still clinking in his pockets, this was the dark side of the picture—towards Sacramento, the bright one. Now that the pockets are empty, everything seems changed, and the golden sheen lies on the side of the ship.

Still the sailor hesitates how to decide. Despite the pressure upon him, he ponders and reflects; as he does so, plunging his hands into his pockets, apparently searching for coin. It is merely mechanical, for he knows he has not a shilling.

While thus occupied, he is seated in the little sanded bar-room of the "Home" alone with the bar-keeper; the latter eyeing him with anything but a sympathetic air. For the book is before him, showing that indebtedness for bed and board—to say nothing of the unsettled bar-score—and the record makes a bar-sinister between them. Another drink could not be added now, even though but a bottle of ginger-beer. The door of credit is closed, and only cash could procure an extension of that hospitality hitherto scant enough.

The sailor thinks. Must he surrender? Give up his dreams of fingering yellow gold, and return to clutching black shrouds? A glance at the grim, unrelaxed, and unrelenting visage of the bar-keeper decides him.

His decision is expressed in characteristic speech, not addressed to the drink-dispenser, nor aloud, but in low, sad soliloquy:

"Wi' me, I see, the old sayin's to stan' good—'Once a sailor, still a sailor.' Harry Blew, there be no help for't, ye maun steer back for the *Crusader!*"

Chapter Twenty Six
Opportune Visitors

Having resolved upon returning to his ship—and that very night, if he can but get a boat—Harry Blew is about to sally forth into the street, when his egress is unexpectedly prevented. Not by the landlord of the "Sailor's Home," nor his representative behind the bar. These would only be too glad to get rid of a guest with two days' reckoning in arrear. For they have surreptitiously inspected his sea-chest, and found it to contain a full suit of "Sunday go-ashores," with other effects, which they deemed sufficient collateral security for the debt. And as it has been already hypothecated for this, both Boniface and bar-keeper would rather rejoice to see their sailor-guest clear out of the "Home" for good, leaving the chest behind him. On this condition they would be willing to wipe out the debt, both boarding and bar-score. Harry has no thought of thus parting with his kit. Now that he has made up his mind to return to the *Crusader*, a better prospect is opened up to him. He has hopes that on his making appearance aboard, and again entering his name on the frigate's books, the purser will advance him a sum sufficient to release his retained chattels. Or, he can in all likelihood collect the money among his old messmates. Not for this reason is he so anxious to reach the ship that night, but because he has no other chance of having any place to sleep in—save the street. The tavern-keeper has notified him, in plain terms, that he must peremptorily leave; and he is about to act upon the notification, and take departure, when prevented, as already said.

What now hinders him from going out of the "Home" is a man coming into it; or rather two—since two shadows have suddenly darkened the door, and are projected across the sanded floor of the bar-room. Not like shadows in the eyes of Harry Blew, but streaks of brightest sunlight! For in the individuals entering he recognises two of his officers; one of them his best friend, who saved his life. Crozier and Cadwallader have discovered him.

At sight of them the discharged sailor salutes promptly, and with as much respect as if all were on the quarterdeck of the *Crusader*. But with much more demonstration; for their well-timed appearance draws from him an exclamation of joy. Jerking off his straw hat, and giving a twitch to one of his brow-locks, he bobs his head several times in succession, with a simultaneous back-scrape of his foot upon the floor.

His obeisance ended, he stands silently awaiting whatever communication the young officers have to make. He is already aware that their business is with himself: for the bar-room is but dimly lit, and Crozier, while crossing its threshold, not at once recognising him, had called out:

"Is there a sailor staying here, by name Harry Blew!"

"Ay, ay, sir!" was the prompt response, the sailor himself giving it, along with the salutation described.

During the short interval of silence that succeeds, Harry's heart can be distinctly heard beating. Lately depressed—"Down in the dumps," as he himself would word it—it is now up in his throat. The sight of his patron, the saver of his life, is like having it saved a second time. Perhaps they have come to ask him to rejoin the ship? If so, 'tis the very thing he was thinking of. He will not anticipate, but waits for them to declare their errand.

"Well, Harry, old boy," says Crozier, after warmly shaking the sailor's hand, "I'm right glad to find you here. I was afraid you'd gone off to the diggings."

"True, Master Ed'ard; I did intend standin' on that tack, but ha'n't been able to get under way, for want o' a wind."

"Want of a wind? I don't quite understand you."

"Why, you see, sir, I've been a little bit spreeish since comin' ashore, and my locker's got low—more'n that, it's total cleared out. Though I suppose there be plenty of gold in them diggin's, it takes gold to get there; and as I ha'n't any, I'm laid up here like an old hulk foul o' a mud bank. That's just how it be, gen'lemen."

"In which case, perhaps you mightn't feel indisposed to go to sea again?"

"Just the thing I war thinkin' o', Master Ed'ard. I'd a'most made up my mind to it, sir, an' war 'bout startin' to try get aboard the old *Crusader*, and askin' your honour to ha' my name entered on her books again. I'm willin' to join for a fresh tarm, if they'll take me."

"They'd take, and be glad to get you, Harry; you may be sure of that. Such a skilled sailor need never be without a ship, where there's a British man-of-war within hailing distance. But we don't want you to join the *Crusader*."

"How is that, sir?"

"Because we can help you to something a little better. At least, it will be more to your advantage in a pecuniary sense. You wouldn't mind shipping in a merchant-vessel, with wages three or four times as much as you can get in a man-of-war? How would you like that, Harry?"

"I'd like it amazin'ly, sir. And for the matter o' being a merchanter, that's neither here nor there, so long's *you* recommend it. I'll go as cook, if you tell me to."

"No, no, Harry, not that," laughingly replies the young officer. "That would never do. I should pity those who had to eat the dishes you'd dress for them. Besides, I should be sorry to see you stewing your strength away in front of a galley-fire. You must do better than that; and it chances I'm authorised to offer you something better. It's a berth on board a trading-ship, and one with some special advantages. She's a Chilian vessel, and her captain is, I believe, either Chilian or Spanish. That won't make any difference to you?"

"Not a doit, sir. I don't care what the ship's colours be, nor what country her skipper, so long's he allows good wages an' plenty o' grub."

"And plenty of grog too, Harry?"

"Ay, ay, sir. I confess to a weakness for that—leastways the reg'lar three times a day."

"No doubt you'll get it, as often as you've a mind. But, Harry, I have a word to say about that. Besides my interest in your own welfare, I've another and more selfish one in this Chilian ship. So has Mr Cadwallader. We both want you to be on your best behaviour during the trip you're to take in her. On board will be two lady passengers, as far as Panama; for the ship is bound thither, and for ports beyond—I believe as far as Valparaiso. But the ladies are to land at Panama; and, so long as they're with you, you must do everything in your power to make things agreeable for them. If they should ever be in any danger—from storm, shipwreck, or otherwise—you'll stand by them?"

"Yes, Harry," adds Cadwallader, "you'll do that, won't you?"

"Lor', your honours!" exclaims the sailor, showing surprise. "Sure ye needn't put sich a questin to me—a British man-o'-war's man? I'd do that much, anyhow, out o' sheer starn sense o' duty. But when it comes to takin' care o' two ladies—to say nothin' about theer bein' so young, and so beautiful—"

"Avast, Harry! How do you know they are either one or the other?" asks Crozier, surprised; Cadwallader repeating the question.

"Lor' love ye, masters! Do ye think a common sailor han't got eyes in his head, for anythin' but ropes an' tar? You forget I war o' the boat's crew as rowed two sweet creeturs on board the *Crusader*, the night o' the grand dancin'; and arterward took the same ashore, along wi' two young gen'lemen, as went to see 'em home. Sure, sirs, actin' cox on that occasion, I couldn't help hearin' some o' the speeches as passed in the starn-sheets— tho' they wur spoken in the ears of the señoritas, soft as the breeze that fanned their fair cheeks, an' brought the colour out on 'em red as Ribston pippins."

"Avast again, you rascal! So you've been eavesdropping, have you? I quite forgot you understood Spanish."

"Only a trifle, Master Ed'ard."

"Too much for that occasion."

"Ah! well, your honour, it may stand me in good stead now—aboard the ship you speak o'."

"Well, Harry, I'm not going to scold you, seeing that you couldn't help hearing what you did. And now, I may as well tell you that the young ladies you saw that night in the boat *are* the same who are to be the passengers in the Chilian ship. You'll take good care of them, I know."

"That you may depend on, sir. Any one as touches hair o' their heads, to do 'em an injury, 'll have to tear the whole o' his off the head o' Harry Blew. I'll see 'em safe to Panama, or never show myself there. I promise that; an' I think both your honours 'll take the word of a British man-o'-war's man."

"That's enough—perfectly satisfactory! Now to give you the necessary directions about joining this ship. She's lying at anchor somewhere about in the bay. I didn't think of getting her name, but you'll find her easily enough. An' you needn't go in search of her till you've seen the gentleman whose name is upon this card. You see: 'Don Tomas Silvestre,' a ship-agent. His office is down in one of the streets by the strand. Report yourself to him first thing in the morning. In all likelihood he'll engage you on sight, make out your papers, and give you full directions for getting aboard the ship. It appears she's short of hands; indeed, even without a single sailor. *And,* by the way, Harry, if you apply soon enough, it's good as certain you'll be made mate—first at that; all the more from your being able to speak Spanish. It's too late for you to do anything about it to-night; but don't oversleep yourself. Be at the ship-agent's to-morrow betimes."

"Ye can trust me for that, sir. I'll show my figurehead there first thing in the mornin'. No fears o' any one getting theer afore me, if they've not gone a'ready."

"I think no one will be before you—I hope not. Send us word how you have succeeded, as the *Crusader* will likely be in port long enough for us to hear from you. Still, as she may sail on short notice, we may not see you again. Remember, then, what we've said about the señoritas. We shall rely upon your fidelity."

"An' well may ye, masters. You can both trust your lives to Harry Blew, an' those of them as is dear to you."

"All right, old boy!" exclaims Crozier, satisfied. "We must now part; but let's hope we'll meet again. When you get back to England you know where to find me. So, good-bye! Give us a grip of your honest fist, and God bless you!"

Saying this, he grasps the horny hand of the sailor, and warmly presses it. The pressure is returned by a squeeze that gives assurance of more than ordinary friendship. It is the grip of true gratitude; and the look which accompanies it tells of a devoted friendship, bordering on adoration.

Cadwallader also exchanges a like parting salutation; after which, the young officers start off, to continue their cruise through the streets of "Frisko."

Chapter Twenty Seven
An Inhospitable Hostelry

Harry Blew stands in the doorway of the "Sailor's Home," watching the two gentlemen as they walk away, his eyes glowing with gratitude and sparkling with joy. And no wonder, considering the change in his situation brought about by their influence. Ten minutes before, his spirits were at the lowest and darkest. But the prospect of treble, or quadruple pay on board a snug ship, though it be a trading-vessel, with the additional chance of being mate instead of foremast-man, has given him a fillip, not only restoring them to their ordinary condition of cheeriness, but raising them to the highest exaltation.

The only damper is regret at parting with the fine young fellow who has done so much for him. But he has passed through that already, when separating from his ship, and can now better bear it under the reflection that, though apart from his patron, he will have an opportunity of doing something to show his gratitude. He knows how much Crozier is interested in the wellbeing of Carmen Montijo—for Harry has been made acquainted with her name, as also that of Iñez Alvarez—and to be entrusted with a sort of guardianship over these young ladies is a proud thought to the ex-man-o'-war's man—a fine feather in his cap.

To carry out the confidence thus reposed in him will be a labour of love; and he vows in his heart it shall be done, if need be, at the risk of life.

Indeed, the interview just ended has made a new man of him in more senses than one; for upon the spot he registers a mental resolve to give up dram-drinking for ever, or at all events till he has seen his charge—the two Spanish señoritas—safe landed at Panama, and the Chilian ship snug in the harbour of Valparaiso. After that, he is less sure that he may not again go upon a spree, and possibly a big one.

Heaving a sigh as the English officers pass out of sight, he turns back into the bar-room. It is no longer a question of his going aboard the *Crusader*.

He must remain ashore, to be up betimes in the morning, so that he may be early at the office of the ship-agent.

And now, again, a shadow, though only a slight one, comes over his countenance. He has still before him the undetermined question, where he is to sleep. Notwithstanding his fine prospects for the future, the present is still unchanged, and yet unprovided for.

Unfortunately, he did not think of this while the officers were with him, else a word would have made all well. Either of them, he doubted not, would have relieved his necessities had they been but told of them. Too late now; they are gone out of sight, out of hail, and whether he cannot tell or guess; and to attempt searching for them in such crowded streets would be only a waste of time.

While thus ruefully reflecting, he is confronted by the bar-keeper, whose usually grave countenance is now beset with smiles. The fellow has got it into his head that his sailor-guest is no longer impecunious. The navy gentlemen just gone have no doubt been to engage him for their ship, and perhaps made him an advance of wages.

"Well, my salt," says he, in a tone of jocular familiarity, "I guess you've got the shiners now, an' kin settle up your score?"

"No, indeed, sir," answers Harry, more than ever taken aback; "I'm sorry to say I ha'n't."

"You hain't! Then what hev them gold-buttoned fellers been palaverin' ye about?"

"Not about money, master. Them's two o' the officers belongin' to my old ship—the British frigate *Crusader*. An' fine young fellows they be too."

"Much good their finikin fineness seems to hev done you! So they hain't gin you nuthin' better than their talk, hev they? Nuthin' besides?"

"Nothing besides," rejoins Blew, restraining his temper, a little touched by the bar-keeper's inquisitiveness, as also his impertinent manner.

"Nuthin' but fine words, eh? Well, thar's plenty o' them 'bout hyar, but they won't butter no parsnips; and let me tell you, my sailor-man, they won't pay your board bill."

"I know that," returns the other, still keeping his temper. "But I hope to have money soon."

"Oh! that's been your story for the last two days; but it won't bamboozle me any longer. You get no more credit here."

"Can't I have supper, and bed for another night?"

"No; that you can't—not so much as a shake-down."

"I'll pay for them first thing in the mornin'."

"You'll pay for 'em this night—now, if you calc'late to get 'em. An' if you've no cash, tain't any use talkin'. What d'ye think we keep a tavern for? 'Twould soon be to let—bar, beds, and all—if we'd only such customers as you. So, the sooner you slope, the better the landlord 'll like it. He's jest gin me orders to tell ye to clar out."

"It's gallows hard, master," says Harry, heaving a sigh; "the more so, as I've got the promise o' a good berth 'board a ship that's down in the harbour. The gentlemen you seed have just been to tell me about it."

"Then why didn't they give you the money to clar your kit?"

"They'd have done that—no doubt of it—if I'd only thought o' askin' them. I forgot all about it."

"Ah, that's all very fine—a likely tale; but I don't believe a word of it. If they cared to have you in their ship, they'd have given you the wherewithal to git there. But, come! it's no use shilly-shallyin' any longer. The landlord won't like it. He's gin his orders sharp: Pay or go."

"Well, I suppose I must go."

"You must; an', as I have already said, the sooner you're off the better."

After delivering this stern ultimatum, the bar-keeper jauntily returns behind his bar, to look more blandly on two guests who have presented themselves at it, called for "brandy smashes," and tossed down a couple of dollars to pay for them.

Harry Blew turns towards the door; and, without saying another word, steps out of the room.

Once on the street, he does not stop or stand hesitating. The hospitality of the so-called "home" has proved a sorry sham; and, indignant at the shabby treatment received, he is but too glad to get away from the place. All his life used to snug quarters in a fine ship's forecastle, with everything found for him, he has never before experienced the pang of having no place to lay his head. He not only feels it now, in all its unpleasantness, but fancies the passers-by can tell all about the humiliating position he is placed in.

Haunted by this fancy—urged on by it—he quickens his steps; nor stays them till out of sight of the "Sailor's Home," out of the street in which the detestable tavern stands. He even dislikes the idea of having to go back for his chest; which, however, he must some time do.

Meanwhile what is to become of him for the remainder of that night? Where is he to obtain supper, and a bed? About the latter he cares the least; and having had no dinner and but a spare breakfast he is hungry—half-famished—and could eat a pound or two of the saltest and toughest junk ever drawn out of a ship's cask.

In this unhappy frame of body as of mind he strays on along the street. There is no lack of food before his eyes, almost within reach of his hand; but only to tantalise, and still further whet the edge of his appetite. Eating-houses are open all around him; and under their blazing gas-jets he can see steaming dishes, and savoury joints, in the act of being set upon tables surrounded by guests seeming hungry as himself, but otherwise better off. He, too, might enter there without fear of being challenged as an intruder; for among the men inside are many in coarse garb, some of them not so respectably apparelled as himself. But what would be the use of his going into a restaurant without even a penny in his pockets? He could only gaze at dishes he may not eat, and dare not call for. He remembers his late discomfiture too keenly to risk having it repeated.

Thus reflecting, he turns his back upon the tables so temptingly spread, and keeps on along the street.

Again the double question recurs: Where is he to get supper, and where sleep?

And again he regrets not having given his confidence to the young gentlemen, and told them of the "fix" he was in. Either would have relieved him on the instant, without a word. But it is too late now to think of it, or hope seeing them in the streets. By this time, in all likelihood, they have started back to their ship.

How he wishes himself aboard the *Crusader*! How happy he would feel in her forecastle, among his old shipmates! It cannot be; and therefore it is idle to ponder upon it.

What on earth is he to do?

A thought strikes him.

It is of the ship-agent whose card Crozier left with him, and which he has thrust into his coat-pocket. He draws the bit of pasteboard out, and holds it up to a street-lamp, to make himself acquainted with the ship-agent's address. The name he remembers, and needs not that.

Though but a common sailor, Harry is not altogether illiterate. The seaport town where he first saw the light had a public school for the poorer people, in which he was taught to read and write. By the former of these elementary branches—supplemented by a smattering of Spanish, picked up in South American ports—he is enabled to decipher the writing upon the card—for it is in writing—and so gets the correct address, both the street and number.

Having returned it to his pocket, he buttons up his dreadnought; and, taking a fresh hitch at his duck trousers, starts off again—this time with fixed intent: to find Don Tomas Silvestre.

Chapter Twenty Eight
The "Hell" El Dorado

A Monté Bank in the city of San Francisco, in the establishment y-cleped "El Dorado" — partly drinking-house, for the rest devoted to gambling on the grandest scale. The two are carried on simultaneously, and in a large oblong saloon. The portion of it devoted to Bacchus is at the end farthest from the entrance-door; where the shrine of the jolly god is represented by a liquor-bar extending from side to side, and backed by an array of shining bottles, glittering glasses, and sparkling decanters; his "worship" administered by half-a-dozen "bartenders," resplendent in white shirts with wrist ruffles, and big diamond breast-pins — real, not paste!

The altar of Fortuna is altogether of a different shape and pattern, occupying more space. It is not compact, but extended over the floor, in the form of five tables, large as if for billiards; though not one of them is of this kind. Billiards would be too slow a game for the frequenters of "El Dorado." These could not patiently wait for the scoring of fifty points, even though the stake were a thousand dollars. "No, no! *Monté* for me!" would be the word of every one of them; or a few might say "*Faro*." And of the five tables in the saloon, four are for the former game, the fifth furnished for the latter; though there is but little apparent difference in the furniture of the two; both having a simple cover of green baize, or broadcloth, with certain crossing lines traced upon it, that of the Faro table having the full suite of thirteen cards arranged in two rows, face upwards and fixed; while on the Monté tables but two cards appear thus — the Queen and Knave; or, as designated in the game — purely Spanish and Spanish-American — "Caballo" and "Sota." They are essentially card games, and altogether of chance, just as is the casting of dice.

Other gambling contrivances have place in the "El Dorado;" for it is a "hell" of the most complete kind; but these are of slight importance compared with the great games, Monté and Faro — the real *pièces de résistance* — while the others are only side-dishes, indulged in by such saunterers about the saloon as do not contemplate serious play. Of all, Monté is the main attraction, its convenient simplicity — for it is simple as "heads or tails" — making it possible for the veriest greenhorn to take part in it, with as much likelihood of winning as the oldest *habitus* of the hell. Originally Mexican, in many of the western states it has become Americanised.

Of the visible insignia of the game, and in addition to the two cards with their faces turned up, there is a complete pack, with several stacks of circular-shaped and variously coloured pieces of ivory—the "cheques" or counters of the game. These rest upon the table to the right or left of the dealer—usually the "banker" himself—in charge of his "croupier," who pays them out, or draws them in, as the bank loses or wins, along with such coin as may have been staked upon the *albur*.

Around the table's edge, and in front of each player, is his own private pile, usually a mixture of doubloons, dollars, and ivory cheques, with bags or packets of gold-dust and nuggets. Of bank-notes there are few, or none—the currency of California being through the medium of metal; at this date, 1849, most of it unminted, and in its crude state, as it came out of the mine, or the river's mud. By the croupier's hand is a pair of scales with weights appertaining; their purpose being to ascertain the value of such little gold packages as are "punted" upon the cards—this only needed to be known when the bank is loser. Otherwise, they are ruthlessly raked in alongside the other deposits, without any note made of the amount.

The dealer sits centrally at the side of the table, in a grand chair, cards in hand. After shuffling, he turns their faces up, one by one, and with measured slowness. He interrupts himself at intervals as the face of a card is exposed, making a point for or against him in the game. Calling this out in calm voice and long-drawn monotone, he waits for the croupier to square accounts; which the latter does by drawing in, or pushing out, the coins and cheques, with the nimbleness of a presti-digitateur. Old bets are rearranged, new ones made, and the dealing proceeds.

Around the tables sit, or stand, the players, exhibiting a variety of facial types, and national costumes. For there you may see not only human specimens of every known nationality, but of every rank in the social scale, with the callings and professions that appertain to it; an assemblage such as is rarely, if ever, observed elsewhere: gentlemen who may have won university honours; officers wearing gold straps on their shoulders, or bands of lace around the rims of their caps; native Californians, resplendent in slashed and buttoned velveteens; States' lawyers, and doctors, in sober black; even judges, who that same morning were seated upon the bench—may be all observed at the Monté table, mingling with men in red flannel shirts, blanket coats, and trousers tucked into the tops of mud-bedaubed boots; with sailors in pea-jackets of coarse pilot, or Guernsey smocks, unwashed, unkempt, unshorn; not only mingling with, but jostled by them—rudely, if occasion call.

All are on an equality here; no class distinction in the saloon "El Dorado;" for all are on the same errand—to get rich by gambling. The gold gleaming over the table is reflected in their faces. Not in smiles, or cheerfully; but by an expression of hungry cupidity—fixed, as if stamped into their features. No sign of hilarity, or joyfulness; not a word of badinage passing about, or between; scarce a syllable spoken, save the call-words of the dealer, or an occasional remark by the croupier, explanatory of some disputed point about the placing, or payment, of stakes.

And if there be little light humour, neither is there much of ill-manners. Strangely assorted as is the motley crowd—in part composed of the roughest specimens of humanity—noisy speech is exceptional, and rude or boisterous behaviour rare. Either shown would be resented, and soon silenced; though, perhaps, not till after some noises of still louder nature—the excited, angry clamour of a quarrel, succeeded by the cracking of pistols; then a man borne off wounded, in all likelihood to die, or already dead, and stretched along the sanded floor, to be taken unconcernedly up, and carried feet-foremost out of the room.

And yet, in an instant, it will all be over. The gamesters, temporarily attracted from the tables, will return to them; the dealing of the cards will be resumed; and, amidst the chinking of coin, and the rattling of cheques, the sanguinary drama will not only cease to be talked about, but thought of. Bowie-knives and pistols are the police that preserve order in the gambling-saloons of San Francisco.

Although the "El Dorado" is owned by a single individual, this is only as regards the house itself, with the drinking-bar and its appurtenances. The gaming-tables are under separate and distinct proprietorship; each belonging to a "banker," who supplies the cash capital, and other necessaries for the game—in short, "runs" the table, to use a Californian phrase. As a general rule, the owner of a table is himself the dealer, and usually, indeed almost universally, a distinguished "sportsman"—this being the appellation of the Western States' professional gambler, occasionally abbreviated to "sport." He is a man of peculiar characteristics, though not confined to California. His "species" may be met with all over the United States, but more frequently in those of the south and south-west; the Mississippi valley being his congenial coursing-ground, and its two great metropolitan cities, New Orleans and Saint Louis, his chief centres of operation. Natchez, Memphis, Vicksburg, Louisville, and Cincinnati permanently have him; but places more provincial, he only honours with an occasional visit. He is encountered aboard all the big steamboats—those called "crack," and carrying the wealthier class of passengers; while the others he leaves to the more timid and less noted practitioners of his calling.

Wherever seen, the "sport" is resplendent in shirt-front, glittering studs, with a grand cluster of diamonds on his finger sparkling like star, or stalactite, as he deals out the cards. He is, in truth, an *elegant* of the first water, apparelled and perfumed as a D'Orsay, or Beau Brummell; and, although ranking socially lower than these, with a sense of honour quite as high, perhaps higher than had either.

Chapter Twenty Nine
A Monté Bank in Full Blast

In the hell "El Dorado," as already said, there are five gambling tables, side by side, but with wide spaces between for the players. Presiding over the one which stands central is a man of about thirty years of age, of good figure, and well-formed features—the latter denoting Spanish descent—his cheeks clean shaven, the upper lip moustached, the under having a pointed imperial or "goatee," which extends below the extremity of his chin. He has his hat on—so has everybody in the room—a white beaver, set upon a thick shock of black wavy hair, its brim shadowing a face that would be eminently handsome, but for the eyes, these showing sullen, if not sinister. Like his hair, they are coal-black, though he rarely raises their lids, his gaze being habitually fixed on the cards in his hands. Only once has he looked up and around, on hearing a name pronounced bearing an odd resemblance to that of the game he is engaged in, though merely a coincidence. It is "Montijo." Two native Californians standing close behind him are engaged in a dialogue, in which they incidentally speak of Don Gregorio. It is a matter of no moment—only a slight allusion—and, as their conversation is almost instantly over, the Monté dealer again drops his long dark lashes, and goes on with the game, his features resuming their wonted impassibility.

Though to all appearance immobile as those of the Sphinx, one watching him closely could see that there is something in his mind besides Monté. For although the play is running high, and large bets are being laid, he seems regardless about the result of the game—for this night only, since it has never been so before. His air is at times abstracted—more than ever after hearing that name—while he deals out the cards carelessly, once or twice making mistakes. But as these have been trifling, and readily rectified, the players around the table have taken no particular notice of them, nor yet of his abstraction. It is not sufficiently manifest to attract attention; and with the wonderful command he has over himself, none of them suspect that he is at that moment a prey to reflections of the strongest and bitterest kind.

There is one, however, who is aware of it, knowing the cause; this, a man seated on the players' side of the table, and directly opposite the dealer. He is a personage of somewhat squat frame, a little below medium height, of swarth complexion, and straight black hair; to all appearance a *native* Californian, though not wearing the national costume, but simply a suit of dark broadcloth. He lays his bet, staking large sums, apparently indifferent as to the result; while at the same time eyeing the deposits of the other players with eager, nervous anxiety, as though their losses and gains concerned him more than his own—the former, to all appearance, gladdening, the the latter making him sad!

His behaviour might be deemed strange, and doubtless would, were there any one to observe it. But there is not; each player is absorbed in his own play, and the calculation of chances.

In addition to watching his fellow-gamesters around the table, the seemingly eccentric individual ever and anon turns his eye upon the dealer—its expression at such times being that of intense earnestness, with something that resembles reproof—as if he were annoyed by the latter handling his cards so carelessly, and would sharply rebuke him, could he get the opportunity without being observed. The secret of the whole matter being, that he is a sleeping partner in the Monté bank—the moneyed one too; most of its capital having been supplied by him. Hence his indifference to the fate of his own stakes—for winning or losing is all the same to him—and his anxiety about those of the general circle of players.

His partnership is not suspected; or, if so, only by the initiated. Although sitting face to face with the dealer, no sign of recognition passes between them, nor is any speech exchanged. They seem to have no acquaintance with one another, beyond that begot out of the game.

And so the play proceeds, amidst the clinking of coin, and clattering of ivory pieces, these monotonous sounds diversified by the calls "Sota" this, and "Caballo" that, with now and then a "Carajo!" or it may be "Just my luck!" from the lips of some mortified loser. But, beyond such slight ebullition, ill-temper does not show itself, or, at all events, does not lead to any altercation with the dealer. That would be dangerous, as all are aware. On the table, close to his right elbow, rests a double-barrelled pistol, both barrels of which are loaded. And though no one takes particular notice of it, any more than it were a pair of snuffers on their tray, or one of the ordinary implements of the game, most know well enough that he who keeps this standing symbol of menace before their eyes is prepared to use it on slight provocation.

It is ten o'clock, and the bank is in full blast. Up to this hour the players in one thin row around the tables were staking only a few dollars at a time—

as skirmishers in advance of the main army, firing stray shots from pieces of light calibre. Now the heavy artillery has come up, the ranks are filled, and the files become doubled around the different tables—two circles of players, in places three, engaging in the game. And instead of silver dollars, gold eagles and doubloons—the last being the great guns—are flung down upon the green baize, with a rattle continuous as the firing of musketry. The battle of the night has begun.

But Monté and Faro are not the only attractions of the "El Dorado." The shrine of Bacchus—its drinking-bar—has its worshippers as well; a score of them standing in front of it, with others constantly coming and going.

Among the latest arrivals are two young men in the attire of navy officers. At a distance it is not easy to distinguish the naval uniforms of nations—almost universally dark blue, with gold bands and buttons. More especially is it difficult when these are of the two cognate branches of the great Anglo-Saxon race—English and American. While still upon the street, the officers in question might have been taken for either; but once within the saloon, and under the light of its numerous lamps, the special insignia on their caps proclaim them as belonging to a British man-of-war. And so do they—since they are Edward Crozier and Willie Cadwallader.

They have entered without any definite design, further than, as Crozier said, to "have a shy at the tiger." Besides, as they have been told, a night in San Francisco would not be complete without a look in upon "El Dorado."

Soon as inside the saloon, they step towards its drinking-bar, Crozier saying—

"Come, Cad! let's do some sparkling."

"All right," responds the descendant of the Cymri, his face already a little flushed with what they have had at the *Parker*.

"Pint bottle of champagne!" calls Crozier.

"We've no pints here," saucily responds the bar-tender—a gentleman in shirt-sleeves, with gold buckles on his embroidered braces—too grand to append the courtesy of "sir."

"Nothing less than quarts," he deigns to add.

"A quart bottle, then!" cries Crozier, tossing down a doubloon to pay for it. "A gallon, if you'll only have the goodness to give it us."

The sight of the gold coin, with a closer inspection of his customers, and perhaps some dread of a second sharp rejoinder, secures the attention of the dignified Californian Ganymede, who, re-using his hauteur, condescends to serve them.

While drinking the champagne, the young officers direct their eyes towards that part of the saloon occupied by the gamesters; where they see several clusters of men collected around distinct tables, some sitting, others standing. They know what it means, and that there is Monté in their midst.

Though Cadwallader has often heard of the game, he has never played it, or been a spectator to its play. Crozier, who has both seen and played it, promises to initiate him.

Tossing off their glasses, and receiving the change—not much out of a doubloon—they approach one of the Monté tables—that in the centre of the saloon, around which there are players, standing and sitting three deep.

It is some time before they can squeeze through the two outside concentric rings, and get within betting distance of the table. Those already around it are not men to be pushed rudely apart, or make way for a couple of youngsters, however imposing their appearance, or impatient their manner. A mere officer's uniform is not much there, no matter the nationality. Besides, in the circle are officers of far higher rank than they, though belonging to a different service: naval captains and commanders, and of army men, majors, colonels—even generals. What care these for a pair of boisterous subalterns? Or what reck the rough gold-diggers, and stalwart trappers, seen around the table, for any or all of them? It is a chain, however ill-assorted in its links, not to be severed *sans cérémonie*; and the young English officers must bide their time. A little patience, and their turn will come too.

Practising this, they wait for it with the best grace they can. And not very long. One after another the more unfortunate of the gamesters get played out; each, as he sees his last dollar swept away from him by the ruthless rake of the croupier, heaving a sigh, and retiring from the table; most of them with seeming reluctance, and looking back, as a stripped traveller at the footpad who has turned his pockets inside out.

Soon the outer ring is broken, leaving spaces between, into one of which slips Crozier, Cadwallader pressing in along side of him.

Gradually they squeeze nearer and nearer, till they are close to the table's edge.

Having, at length, obtained a position, where they can conveniently place bets, they are about plunging their hands into their pockets for the necessary stakes, when all at once the act is interrupted. The two turn towards one another with eyes, attitude, everything expressing not only surprise, but stark, speech-depriving astonishment.

For on the opposite side of the table, seated in a grand chair, presiding over the game, and dealing out the cards, Crozier sees the man who has been making love to Carmen Montijo—his rival of the morning—while, at the same instant. Cadwallader has caught sight of *his* rival—the suitor of Iñez Alvarez!

Chapter Thirty
Fighting the Tiger

At sight of De Lara and Calderon, the English officers stand speechless, as if suddenly struck dumb; for a pang has shot through their hearts, bitter as poison itself.

Crozier feels it keenest, since it is an affair which most concerns him. The suitor of Carmen Montijo a "sport" —a common gambler!

Cadwallader is less affected, though he too is annoyed. For although Calderon is in the circle of outside players—apparently a simple *punter*, like the rest—the companionship of the morning, with the relations existing between the two men, tell of their being socially the same. He already knows his rival to be a blackguard; in all likelihood he is also a blackleg.

Quick as thought itself, these reflections pass through the minds of the young Englishmen; though for some time neither says a word—their looks alone communicating to each other what both bitterly feel.

Fortunately, their surprise is not noted by the players around the table. Each is engrossed in his own play, and gives but a glance at the new-comers, whose naval uniforms are not the only ones there.

But there are two who take note of them in a more particular manner: these, Faustino Calderon and Francisco de Lara. Calderon, looking along the table—for he is on that same side—regards them with glances furtive almost timid. Very different is the manner of De Lara. At sight of Crozier he suspends the deal, his face suddenly turning pale, while a spark of angry light flashes forth from his eyes. The passionate display is to all appearance unobserved; or, if so, attributed to some trifling cause, as annoyance at the game going against him. It is almost instantly over; and the disturbed features of the Monté dealer resume their habitual expression of stern placidity.

The English officers having recovered from their first shock of astonishment, also find restored to them the faculty of speech; and now exchange thoughts, though not about that which so disturbs them. By a sort of tacit understanding it is left to another time, Crozier only saying—

"We'll talk of it when we get aboard ship. That's the place for sailors to take counsel together, with a clear head, such as we will want. At this precious minute, I feel like a fish out of water."

"By Jove! so do I."

"The thing we're both thinking of has raised the devil in me. But let us not bother about it now. I've got something else in my mind. I'm half-mad, and intend *fighting the tiger*."

"Fighting the tiger! What do you mean by that, Ned? I don't quite comprehend."

"You soon will. If you wish it, I'll give you a little preliminary explanation."

"Yes, do. Perhaps I can assist you."

"No, you can't. There's only one who can."

"Who is he?"

"It is not a he, but a she: the Goddess of Fortune. I intend soliciting her favours; if she but grant them, I'll smash Mr De Lara's Monté bank."

"Impossible! There's no probability of your being able to do that."

"Not much probability, I admit. Still there's a possibility. I've seen such a thing done before now. Bold play and big luck combined will do it. I'm in for the first; whether I have the last, remains to be seen. In any case, I'll either break the bank, or lose all I've got on me — which by chance is a pretty big stake to begin with. So here goes!"

Up to this time their conversation has been carried on in a low tone; no one hearing or caring to listen to it — all being too much absorbed in their own calculations to take heed of the bets or combinations of others. If any one gives a glance at them, and sees them engaged in their *sotto-voce* dialogue, it is but to suppose they are discussing which card they had best bet upon — whether the *Sota* or *Caballo*; and whether it would be prudent to risk a whole dollar, or limit their lay to the more modest sum of fifty cents.

They who may have been thus conjecturing, with everybody else, are taken by surprise, in fact, somewhat startled, when the older of the two officers, bending across the table, tosses a hundred pound Bank of England note upon the baize, with as much nonchalance as if it were but a five-dollar bill!

"Shall I give you cheques for it?" asks the croupier, after examining the crisp note — current over all the earth — and knowing it good as gold.

"No," answers Crozier; "not yet. You can give that after the bet's decided—if I win it. If not, you can take the note. I place it on the Queen, against the Knave."

The croupier, simply nodding assent, places the note as directed.

During the interregnum in which this little episode occurs, the English officers, hitherto scarce noticed, are broadly stared at, and closely scrutinised—Crozier becoming the cynosure of every eye. He stands it with a placid tranquillity, which shows him as careless about what they may think him, as he is of his cash.

Meanwhile, the cards have had a fresh shuffle, and the deal begins anew; all eyes again turning upon the game. In earnest expectancy; those who, like Crozier, have placed upon the Queen, wishing her to show her face first. And she does.

"*Caballo en la puerta mozo!*" (The Queen in the door wins) cries the dealer, the words drawled out with evident reluctance, while a flash of fierce anger is seen scintillating in his eyes.

"Will you take it in cheques?" asks the croupier addressing himself to Crozier, after settling the smaller bets. "Or shall I pay you in specie?"

"You needn't pay yet. Let the note lie. Only cover it with a like amount. I go it double, and again upon the Queen."

Stakes are re-laid—some changed—others left standing or doubled, as Crozier's, which is now a bet for two hundred pounds.

On goes the game, the piece of smooth pasteboard slipping silently from the jewelled fingers of the dealer, whose eye is bent upon the cards, as if he saw through them—or would, if he could. But whatever his wish, he has no power to change the chances. If he have any professional tricks, there is no opportunity for him to practise them. There are too many eyes looking on; too many pistols and bowie-knives about; too many men ready to stop any attempt at cheating, and punish it, if attempted.

Again he is compelled to call out:

"*Caballo en la puerta mozo!*"

"Now, sir," says the croupier to Crozier, after settling other scores, "you want your money, I suppose?"

"Not yet. I'm not pressed, and can afford to wait. I again go double, and am still contented with my Queen."

The dealing proceeds; with four hundred pounds lying on the *Caballo* to Crozier's account—and ten times as much belonging to other bettors. For now that the luck seems to be running with the Englishman, most lay their stakes beside his.

Once again: "*Caballo en la puerta mozo!*"

And again Crozier declines to take up his bet.

He has now eight hundred pounds sterling upon the card—sixteen hundred on the turn of the game—while the others, thoroughly assured that his luck is on the run, double theirs, till the bets against the bank post up to as many thousands.

De Lara begins to look anxious, and not a little downhearted. Still more anxious, and lower in heart, appears him seated on the opposite side—Calderon; for it is his money that is moving away. He is visibly excited. On the contrary, Crozier is as cool as ever, his features set in a rigid determination to do what he promised—break the bank, or lose all he has got about him. The last, not likely yet, for soon again comes the cry:

"*The Queen winner!*"

There is a pause longer than usual, for the settling of such a large score; and after it an interval of inaction. The dealer seems inclined to discontinue; for still lying upon the Queen is Crozier's stake, once more doubled, and now counting three thousand two hundred pounds!

Asked if he intends to let it remain, he replies sneeringly:

"Of course I do; I insist upon it. And once more I go for the Queen. Let those who like the Knave better, back him!"

"Go on! Go on!" is the cry around the table, from many voices speaking in tone of demand.

De Lara glances at Calderon furtively, but, to those observing it, with a look of interrogation. Whatever the sign, or answer, it decides him to go on dealing.

The bets are again made; to his dismay, almost everybody laying upon the Queen, and, as before, increasing their stakes. And in like proportion is heightened the interest in the game. It is too intense for any display of noisy excitement now. And there is less throughout the saloon; for many from the other tables, as all the saunterers, have collected round, and standing several deep, gaze over one another's shoulders, with as much eager earnestness as if a man were expiring in their midst.

The ominous call at length comes—not in clear voice, or tone exultant, but feeble, and as if rung reluctantly from the lips of the Monté dealer. For it is again a verdict adverse to the bank:

"*Caballo en la puerta mozo!*"

As De Lara utters the words, he dashes the cards down, scattering them all over the table. Then rising excitedly from his chair, adds in faltering tone:

"Gentlemen, I'm sorry to tell you the bank's broke!"

Chapter Thirty One
A Plucky "Sport"

"The bank's broke!"

Three words, that, despite their bad grammar, have oft—too oft—startled the ear, and made woe in many a heart.

At hearing them, the gamesters of the "El Dorado" seated around Frank Lara's Monté table spring to their feet, as if their chairs had suddenly become converted into iron at white heat. They rise simultaneously, as though all were united in a chain, elbow and elbow together.

But while thus gesturing alike, very different is the expression upon their faces. Some simply show surprise; others look incredulous; while not a few give evidence of anger.

For an instant there is silence—the surprise, the incredulity, the anger having suspended speech. This throughout the saloon; for all, bar-drinkers as well as gamesters, have caught the ominous words, and thoroughly understand their import. No longer resounds the chink of ivory cheques, or the metallic ring of doubloons and dollars. No longer the thudding down of decanters, nor the jingle of glasses. Instead, a stillness so profound that one entering at this moment might fancy it a Quakers' meeting, but for the symbols seen around—these, anything but Quakerish. Easier to imagine it a grand gambling-hell, where dealers, croupiers, players, and spectators have all been suddenly turned to stone, or have become figures in wax-work.

The silence is of the shortest—as also the immobility of the men composing the different groups—only for a half-score seconds. Then there is noise enough, with plenty of gesticulation. A roar arises that fills the room; while men rush about wildly, madly, as if in the courtyard of a lunatic asylum. Some show anger—those who are losers by the breaking of the bank. Many have won large bets, their stakes still lying on the table, which they know will not be paid. The croupier has told them so, confessing his cash-box cleared out at the last settlement; even this having been effected with the now protested ivory cheques.

Some gather up their gold or silver, and stow it in safety, growling, but satisfied that things are no worse. Others are not so lenient. They do not believe there is a good cause for the suspension, and insist on being paid in full. They rail at the proprietor of the bank, adding menace. De Lara is the man thus marked. They see him before them, grandly dressed, glittering with diamonds. They talk of stripping him of his *bijouterie*.

"No, gentlemen!" he exclaims, with a sardonic sneer. "Not that, if you please—not yet. First hear me, and then it will be time for you to strike."

"What have you to say?" demands one, with his fists full of ivory counters, unredeemed.

"Only that I'm not the *owner* of this bank, and never have been."

"Who is, then?" ask several at the same time.

"Well; that I can't tell you just now; and, what's more, I *won't*. No, that I won't."

The gambler says this with emphasis, and an air of sullen determination, that has its effect upon his questioners—even the most importunate. For a time it stays their talk, as well as action.

Seeing this, he follows it up with further speech, somewhat mere conciliatory.

"As I've said, gentlemen, I'm not the owner of this concern—only the dealer of the cards. You ask, who's proprietor of the smashed table. It's natural enough you should want to know. But it's just as natural that it ain't my business to tell you. If I did, it would be a shabby trick; and, I take it, you're all men enough to see it in that light. If there's any who isn't, he can have my card, and call upon me at his convenience. My name's Francisco de Lara—or Frank Lara, for short. I can be found here, or anywhere else in San Francisco, at such time as may suit anxious inquirers. And if any wants me now, and can't wait, I'm good this minute for pistols across that bit of board we've just been seated at. Yes, gentlemen! Any of you who'd relish a little amusement of that kind, let him come on! It'll be a change from the Monté. For my part, I'm tired of shuffling cards, and would like to rest my fingers on a trigger. Which of you feels disposed to give me the chance? Don't all speak at once!"

No one feels disposed, and no one speaks; at least in hostile tone, or to take up the challenge. Instead, half a score surround the "sport," and not only express their admiration of his pluck, but challenge him to an encounter of drinks, not pistols.

Turning towards the bar, they vociferate "Champagne."

Contented with the turn things have taken, and proud at the volley of invitations, De Lara accepts; and soon the vintage of France is seen effervescing from a dozen tall glasses, and the Monté dealer stands drinking in the midst of his admirers.

Other groups draw up to the bar-counter, while twos and solitary tipplers fill the spaces between.

The temple of Fortuna is for a time deserted, her worshippers transferring their devotion to the shrine of Bacchus. The losers drink to drown disappointment, while the winners quaff cups in the exhilaration of success.

If a bad night for the bank, it is a good one for the bar. Decanters are speedily emptied, and bottles of many kinds go "down among the dead men."

The excitement in the "El Dorado" is soon over. Occurrences of like kind, but often of more tragical termination, are too common in California to cause any long-sustained interest. Within the hour will arise some new event, equally stirring, leaving the old to live only in the recollection of those who have been active participants in it.

So with the breaking of Frank Lara's bank. A stranger, entering the saloon an hour after, from what he there sees, could not tell, neither would he suspect that an incident of so serious nature had occurred. For in less than this time the same Monté table is again surrounded by gamesters, as if its play had never been suspended. The only difference observable is that quite another individual presides over it, dealing out the cards, while a new croupier has replaced him whose cash receipts so suddenly ran short of his required disbursements.

The explanation is simply that there has been a change of owners, another celebrated "sport" taking up the abandoned bank and opening it anew. With a few exceptions the customers are the same, their number not sensibly diminished. Most of the old players have returned to it, while the places of those who have defected, and gone off to other gambling resorts, are filled by fresh arrivals.

A small party of gentlemen, who think they have had play enough for that night, have left the "El Dorado" for good. Among these are the English officers, whose visit proved so prejudicial to the interests of the place.

De Lara, too, and Calderon, with other confederates, have forsaken the saloon. But whither gone no one knows, or seems to care; for the fortunes of fallen men soon cease to interest those who are themselves madly struggling to mount up.

Chapter Thirty Two
A Supper Carte-Blanche

On parting from the "El Dorado," Crozier and Cadwallader do not go directly aboard the *Crusader*. They know that their boat will be awaiting them at the place appointed. But the appointment is for a later hour; and as the breaking of the Monté bank, with the incidents attendant, occupied but a short while, there will be time for them to see a little more of San Francisco life. They have fallen in with several other young officers, naval like themselves, though not of their own ship, nor yet their own navy, or nation, but belonging to one cognate and kindred—Americans. Through the freemasonry of their common profession, with these they have fraternised, and it is agreed they shall all sup together. Crozier has invited the Americans to a repast the most *recherché*, as the costliest, that can be obtained at the grandest hotel in San Francisco, the *Parker House*. He adds humorously, that he is able to stand the treat. And well he may; since, besides the English money with which he entered the "El Dorado," he has brought thousands of dollars out of it, and would have brought more had all the ivory cheques been honoured. As it is, his pockets are filled with notes and gold; as also those of Cadwallader, who helps him to carry the shining stuff. Part of the heavy metal he has been able to change into the more portable form of bank-notes. Yet the two are still heavily weighted—"laden like hucksters' donkeys!" jokingly remarks Cadwallader, as they proceed towards the *Parker*.

At the hotel a private room is engaged; and, according to promise, Crozier bespeaks a repast of the most sumptuous kind, with *carte-blanche* for the best wines—champagne at three guineas a bottle, hock the same, and South-side Madeira still more. What difference to him?

The supper ordered in the double-quick soon makes its appearance. Sooner in San Francisco than in any other city in the world; in better style, too, and better worth the money; for the Golden City excels in the science of gastronomy. Even then, amidst her canvas sheds, and weather-boarded houses, could be obtained dishes of every kind known to Christendom, or Pagandom: the *cuisine* of France, Spain, and Italy; the roast beef of Old England, as the pork and beans of the New; the *gumbo* of Guinea, and *sauerkraut* of Germany, side by side with the swallow's-nest soup and sea-slugs of China. Had Lucullus but lived in these days, he would have forsaken the banks of the Tiber, and made California his home.

The repast furnished by the *Parker House*, however splendid, has to be speedily despatched; for unfortunately time forbids the leisurely enjoyment of the viands, to a certain extent marring the pleasure of the occasion. All the officers, American as English, have to be on their respective ships at the stroke of twelve.

Reluctantly breaking up their hilarious company, they prepare to depart.

They have forsaken the supper-room, and passed on to the outer saloon of the hotel; like all such, furnished with a drinking-bar.

Before separating, and while buttoning up against the chill night-air, Crozier calls out:

"Come, gentlemen; one more glass! The stirrup-cup!"

In San Francisco this is always the wind up to a night of revelry. No matter how much wine has been quaffed, the carousal is not deemed complete without a last "valedictory" drink taken standing at the bar.

Giving way to the Californian custom, the officers range themselves along the marble slab; bending over which, the polite bar-keeper asks:

"What is it to be, gentlemen?"

There is a moment of hesitation, the gentlemen—already well wined—scarce knowing what to call for. Crozier cuts the Gordian knot by proposing:

"A round of punches *à la Romaine!*"

Universal assent to this delectable drink; as all know just the thing for a night-cap.

Soon the cooling beverage, compounded with snow from the Sierra Nevada, appears upon the counter, in huge glasses, piled high with the sparkling crystals; a spoon surmounting each—for punch *à la Romaine* is not to be drunk, but eaten.

Shovelling it down in haste, adieus are exchanged, with a hearty shake of hands. Then the American officers go off, leaving Crozier and Cadwallader in the saloon; these only staying to settle the account.

While standing by the bar, waiting for it to be brought, they cast a glance around the room. At first careless, it soon becomes concentrated on a group seen at some distance off, near one of the doors leading out, of which there are several. There are also several other groups; for the saloon is of large dimensions, besides being the most popular place of resort in San Francisco. And for San Francisco the hour is not yet late. Along the line of the drinking-bar, and over the white-sanded floor, are some scores of people of all qualities and kinds, in almost every variety of costume; though they who compose the party that has attracted the attention of the English officers show nothing particular—that is, to the eye of one unacquainted with them. There are four of them, two wearing broadcloth cloaks, the other two having their shoulders shrouded under *serapes*. Nothing in all that. The night is cold, indeed wet, and they are close to the door, to all appearance intending soon to step out. They have only paused to exchange a parting word, as if they designed to separate before issuing into the street.

Though the spot where they stand is in shadow—a folding screen separating it from the rest of the saloon—and it is not easy to get sight of their faces—the difficulty increased by broad-brimmed hats set slouchingly on their heads, with their cloaks and serapes drawn up around their throats—Crozier and Cadwallader have not only seen, but recognised them. A glance at their countenances, caught before the muffling was made, enabled the young officers to identify three of them as De Lara, Calderon, and the *ci-devant* croupier of the Monté bank. The fourth, whose face they have also seen, is a personage not known to them; but, judging by his features, a suitable associate for the other three.

Soon as catching sight of them, which he is the first to do, Crozier whispers to his companion:

"See, Will! Look yonder! Our friends from the 'El Dorado!'"

"By Jove! them, sure enough. Do you think they've been following us?"

"I shouldn't wonder. I was only surprised they didn't do something, when they had us in their gambling den. After the heavy draw I made on Mr Lara's bank, I expected no less than that he'd try to renew his acquaintance with me; all the more from his having been so free of it in the morning. Instead, he and his friend seemed to studiously avoid coming near us—not even casting a look in our direction. That rather puzzled me."

"It needn't. After what you gave him, I should think he'll feel shy of another encounter."

"No; that's not it. Blackleg though the fellow be, he's got game in him. He gave proof of it in the 'El Dorado,' defying, and backing everybody out. It was an exhibition of real courage, Will; and, to tell the truth, I couldn't help admiring it—can't now. When I saw him presiding over the gambling table, and dealing out the cards, I at once made up my mind that it would never do to meet him—even if he challenged me. Now, I've decided differently;

and if he call me out, I'll give him a chance to recover a little of his lost reputation. I will, upon my honour."

"But why should you? A 'sport,' a professional gambler! The thing would be simply ridiculous."

"Nothing of the kind—not here in California. On the contrary, I should cut a more ridiculous figure by refusing him satisfaction. It remains to be seen whether he'll seek it according to the correct code."

"That he won't; at least, I don't think he will. From the way that lot have got their heads together, it looks as if they meant mischief, *now*. They may have been watching their opportunity—to get us two alone. What a pity we didn't see them before our friends went off! They're good fellows, those Yankee officers, and would have stood by us."

"No doubt they would. But it's too late now. They're beyond hailing distance, and we must take care of ourselves. Get your dirk ready, Will, and have your hand close to the butt of that shooting-iron, you took from Mr De Lara."

"I have it that way. Never fear. Wouldn't it be a good joke if I have to give the fellow a pill out of his own pistol?"

"No joking matter to us, if they're meditating an attack. Though we disarmed him in the morning, he'll be freshly provided, and with weapons in plenty. I'll warrant each of the four has a battery concealed under his cloak. They appear as if concocting some scheme—which we'll soon know all about—likely before leaving the house. Certainly, they're up to something."

"Four hundred and ninety dollars, gentlemen!"

The financial statement is made by the office clerk presenting the bill.

"There!" cries Crozier, flinging down a five hundred dollar bill. "Let that settle it. You can keep the change for yourself."

"Thank ye," dryly responds the Californian dispenser of drinks, taking the ten dollar tip with less show of gratitude than a London waiter would give for a fourpenny piece—little as that may be.

Turning to take departure, the young officers again look across the saloon, to learn how the hostile party has disposed itself. To their surprise, the gamblers are gone; having disappeared while the account was being paid.

"I don't like the look of it," says Crozier, in a whisper. "Less now than ever. No doubt we'll find them outside. Well; we can't stay here all night. If they attack us, we must do our best. Take a firm grip of your pistol, with your finger close to the trigger; and if any of them shows sign of shooting, see that you fire first. Follow me; and keep close!"

On the instant of delivering these injunctions, he starts towards the door, Cadwallader following as directed.

Both step out, and for a short while stand gazing interrogatively around them. People they see in numbers, some lounging by the hotel porch, others passing along the street. But none in cloaks or *serapes*. The gamblers must have gone clear away.

"After all, we may have been wronging them," remarks Urozier, as in his nature, giving way to a generous impulse. "I can hardly think that a fellow who's shown such courage would play the assassin. Maybe they were but putting their heads together about challenging us? If that's it, we may expect to hear from them in the morning. It looks all right. Anyhow, we can't stay dallying here. If we're not aboard by eight bells, old Bracebridge 'll masthead us. Let's heave along, my hearty!"

So saying, he leads off, Cadwallader close on his quarter—both a little unsteady in their steps, partly from being loaded with the spoils of "El Dorado," and partly from the effects of the *Parker House* wines, and punches *à la Romaine*.

Chapter Thirty Three
Harry Blew Homeless

While the exciting scene described as taking place in the saloon "El Dorado" was at its height, Harry Blew went past the door. Could the sailor have seen through walls, he would have entered the Hell. The sight of His former officers would have attracted him inside; there to remain, for more reasons than one.

Of one he had already thought. Conjecturing that the young gentleman might be going on a bit of spree, and knowing the dangers of such in San Francisco, it had occurred to him to accompany, or keep close after them — in order that he might be at hand, should they come into collision with any of the roughs and rowdies thick upon the street. Unfortunately, this idea, like that of asking them for a cash loan, had come too late; and they were out of sight ere he could take any steps towards its execution. A glance into the gambling-saloon would have brought both opportunities back again; and, instead of continuing to wander hungry through the streets, he would have had a splendid supper, and after it a bed, either in some respectable hostelry, or his old bunk aboard the *Crusader*.

It was not to be. While passing the "El Dorado," he could know nothing of the friends that were so near; and thus unconscious, he leaves the glittering saloon behind, and a half-score others lighted with like brilliancy.

For a while longer he saunters slowly about, in the hope of yet encountering the officers. Several times he sees men in uniform, and makes after them, only to find they are not English.

At length giving it up, he quickens his pace, and strikes for the office of Silvestre, which he knows to be in the street fronting the water.

As San Francisco is not like an old seaport, where house-room is cheap and abundant, but every foot of roof-shelter utilised by day as by night, there is a chance the office may still be open. In all probability, the shipping-agent sleeps by the side of his ledger; or, if not, likely enough one of his clerks. In which case he, Harry Blew, may be allowed to lie along the floor, or get a shake-down in some adjoining shed. He would be but too glad to stretch himself on an old sack, a naked bench, or, for that matter, sit upright in a chair. For he is now fairly fagged out perambulating the unpaved streets of that inhospitable town.

Tacking from corner to corner, now and then hitching up his trousers, to give freer play to his feet, he at length comes out upon the street which fronts upon the bay. In his week's cruising about the town he has acquired some knowledge of its topography, and knows well enough where he is; but not the office of the shipping-agent. It, therefore, takes him a considerable time to find it. Along the water's edge the houses are irregularly placed, and numbered with like irregularity. Besides, there is scarce any light; the night has become dark, with a sky densely clouded, and the street-lamps burning whale-oil are dim, and at long distances apart. It is with difficulty he can make out the figures upon the doors. However, he is at length successful, and deciphers on one the number he is in search of—as also the name "Silvestre," painted on a piece of tin attached to to the side-post, A survey of the house—indeed, a single glance at it—convinces him he has come thither to no purpose. It is a small wooden structure, not much bigger than a sentry-box, evidently only an office, with no capability of conversion to a bed-chamber. Still it has room enough to admit of a man's lying at full length along its floor; and, as already said, he would be glad of so disposing himself for the night. There may be some one inside, though the one window—in size corresponding to the shanty itself—looks black and forbidding.

With no very sanguine hope, he lays hold of the door-handle, and gives it a twist. Locked, as he might have expected!

The test not satisfying him, he knocks. At first timidly; then a little bolder and louder; finally, giving a good round rap with his knuckles—hard as horn. At the same time he hails sailor-fashion:

"Ahoy, there; be there any one within?"

This in English; but, remembering that the ship-agent is a Spaniard, he follows his first hail with another in the Spanish tongue, adding the usual formulary:

"*Abre la puerta!*"

Neither to question, nor demand is there any response. Only the echo of his own voice reverberated along the line of houses, and dying away in the distance, as it mingles with the sough of the sea.

No use speaking, or knocking again. Undoubtedly, Silvestre's office is closed for the night; and his clerks, if there be any, have their sleeping-quarters elsewhere.

Forced to this conclusion, though sadly dissatisfied with it, the ex-man-o'-war's man turns away from the door, and once more goes cruising along the streets. But now, having no definite point to steer for, he makes short tacks and turns, like a ship sailing under an unfavourable wind—or as one disregarding the guidance of the compass, without steersman at the wheel.

After beating about for nearly another hour, he discovers himself contiguous to the water's edge. His instincts have conducted him thither—as the seal, after a short inland excursion, finds its way back to the beach. Ah! if he could only swim like a seal!

This thought occurs to him as he stands looking over the sea in the direction of the *Crusader*. Were it possible to reach the frigate, all his troubles would soon be forgotten in the cheerful companionship of his old chums of the forepeak.

It can't be. The man-of-war is anchored more than two miles off. Strong swimmer though he knows himself, it is too far. Besides, a fog has suddenly sprung up, overspreading the bay, so that the frigate is hidden from his sight. Even ships lying close in shore can be but faintly discerned through its film, and only the larger spars; the smaller ones, with the rigging-ropes, looking like the threads of a spider's web.

Downhearted, almost despairing, Harry Blew halts upon the beach. What is he to do? Lie down on the sand, and there go to sleep? There are times when on the shores of San Francisco Bay this would not be much of a hardship. But now, it is the season of winter, when the Pacific current, coming from latitudes farther north, rolls in through the Golden Gate, bringing with it fogs that spread themselves over the great estuary inside. Although not frosty, these are cold enough to be uncomfortable, and the haze now is accompanied by a chill drizzling rain.

Standing under it, Harry Blew feels he is fast getting wet. If he do not obtain shelter, he will soon be soaked to the skin.

Looking inquiringly around, his eye rests upon a boat, which lies bottom upward on the beach, appearing through the thick rain like the carapace of a gigantic turtle. It is an old ship's launch that has bilged, and either been abandoned as useless, or upturned to receive repairs. No matter what its history, it offers the hospitality so scurvily refused him at the "Sailor's Home." If it cannot give him supper, or bed, it will be some protection against the rain that has now commenced coming down in big clouting drops.

This deciding him, he creeps under the capsized launch, and lays himself at full length along the shingle.

Chapter Thirty Four
In Dangerous Proximity

The spot upon which the ex-man-o'-war's man has stretched himself is soft as a feather-bed. Still he does not fall asleep. The rain, filtering through the sand, soon finds its way under the boat; and, saturating his couch, makes it uncomfortable. This, with the cold night-air, keeps him awake.

He lies listening to the sough of the sea, and the big drops pattering upon the planks above.

Not long before other sounds salute his ear, distinguishable as human voices—men engaged in conversation.

As he continues to listen, the voices grow louder, those who converse evidently drawing nearer.

In a few seconds they are by the boat's side, where they come to a stand. But though they have paused in their steps, they continue to talk in excited, earnest tones. And so loud, that he can hear every word they say; though the speakers are invisible to him. The capsized boat is not so flush with the sand as to prevent him from seeing the lower part of their legs, from the knees downward. Of these there are four pairs, two of them in trousers of the ordinary kind; the other two in *calzoneras* of velveteen, bordered at the bottoms with black stamped leather. But, that all four men are Californians, or Spaniards, he can tell by the language in which they are conversing—Spanish. A lucky chance that he understands something of this—if not for himself, for the friends who are dear to him.

The first intelligible speech that reaches his ear is an interrogatory:

"You're sure, Calderon, they'll come this way?"

"Quite sure, De Lara. When I stood by them at the hotel-bar, I heard the younger of the two tell one of the American officers that their boat was to meet them at the wooden *muello*—the new pier, as you know. To reach that they must pass by here; there's no other way. And it can't be long before they make appearance. They were leaving the hotel at the time we did, and where else should they go?"

"Not knowing,"—this from the voice of a third individual. "They may stay to take another *copita*, or half-a-dozen. These Inglese can drink like fish, and don't seem to feel it."

"The more they drink the better for us," remarks a fourth. "Our work will be the easier."

"It may not be so easy, Don Manuel," puts in De Lara. "Young as they are, they're very devils both. Besides, they're well armed, and will battle like grizzly bears. I tell you, *camarados*, we'll have work to do before we get back our money."

"But do you intend killing them, De Lara?" asks he who has been called Calderon.

"Of course. We must, for our own sakes. 'Twould be madness not, even if we could get the money without it. The older, Crozier, is enormously rich, I've heard; could afford to buy up all the law there is in San Francisco. If we let them escape, he'd have the police after us like hounds upon a trail. Even if they shouldn't recognise us now, they'd be sure to suspect who it was, and make the place too hot to hold us. *Caspita!* It's not a question of choice, but a thing of necessity. *We must kill them!*"

Harry Blew hears the cold-blooded determination, comprehending it in all its terrible significance. It tells him the young officers are still in the town, and that these four men are about to waylay, rob, and murder them. What they mean by "getting back their money" is the only thing he does not comprehend. It is made clear as the conversation continues:

"I'm sure there's nothing unfair in taking back our own. I, Frank Lara, say so. It was they who brought about the breaking of our bank, which was done in a mean, dastardly way. The Englishman had the luck, and all the others of his kind went with him. But for that we could have held out. It's no use our whining about it. We've lost, and must make good our losses best way we can. We can't, and be safe ourselves, if we let these *gringos* go."

"*Chingara!* we'll stop their breath, and let there be no more words about it."

The merciless verdict is in the voice of Don Manuel.

"You're all agreed, then?" asks De Lara.

"*Si, si, si!*" is the simultaneous answer of assent, Calderon alone seeming to give it with reluctance; though he hesitates from timidity, not mercy.

Harry Blew now knows all. The officers have been gaming, have won money, and the four fellows who talk so coolly of killing them are the chief gambler and his confederates.

What is he to do? How can he save the doomed men. Both are armed; Crozier has his sword, Cadwallader his dirk. Besides, the midshipman has a pistol, as he saw while they were talking to him at the Sailor's Home. But then they are to be taken unawares—shot, or struck down, in the dark, without a chance of seeing the hand that strikes them! Even if warned and ready, it would be two against four. And he is himself altogether unarmed; for his jack-knife is gone—hypothecated to pay for his last jorum of grog! And the young officers have been drinking freely, as he gathers from what the ruffians say. They may be inebriated, or enough so to put them off their guard. Who would be expecting assassination? Who ever is, save a Mexican himself? Altogether unlikely that they should be thinking of such a thing. On the contrary, disregarding danger, they will come carelessly on, to fall like ripe corn before the sickle of the reaper.

The thought of such a fate for his friends fills the sailor with keenest apprehension; and again he asks himself how it is to be averted.

The four conspirators are not more than as many feet from the boat. By stretching out his hands he could grip them by the ankles, without altering his recumbent attitude one inch. And by doing this, he might give the guilty plotters such a scare as would cause them to retreat, and so baffle their design.

The thought comes before his mind, but is instantly abandoned. The fellows are not of the stuff to be frightened at shadows. By their talk, at least two are desperadoes, and to make known his presence would be only to add another victim to those already doomed to death.

But what is he to do? For the third time he asks himself this question, still unable to answer it.

While still painfully cogitating, his brain labouring to grasp some feasible plan of defence against the threatened danger, he is warned of a change. Some words spoken tell of it. It is De Lara who speaks them.

"By the way, *camarados*, we're not in a good position here. They may sight us too soon. To make things sure, we must drop on them before they can draw their weapons. Else some of us may get dropped ourselves."

"Where could we be better? I don't see. The shadow of this old boat favours us."

"Why not crawl under it?" asks Calderon. "There Argus himself couldn't see us."

Harry Blew's heart beats at the double-quick. His time seems come, and he already fancies four pistols to his head, or the same number of poniards pointed at his ribs.

It is a moment of vivid anxiety — a crisis dread, terrible, almost agonising.

Fortunately it is not of long duration, ending almost on the instant. He is relieved at hearing one of them say:

"No; that won't do. We'd have trouble in scrambling out again. While about it they'd see or hear us, and take to their heels. You must remember, it's but a step to where their boat will be waiting them, with some eight or ten of those big British tars in it. If they got there before we overtook them, the tables would be turned on us."

"You're right, Don Manuel," rejoins De Lara; "it won't do to go under the boat, and there's no need for us to stay by it. *Mira!* yonder's a better place — by that wall. In its shadow no one can see us, and the *gringos* must pass within twenty feet of it. It's the very spot for our purpose. Have with me!"

No one objecting, the four separate from the side of the boat and glide silently as spectres across the strip of sandy beach, their forms gradually growing indistinct in the fog, at length altogether disappearing beneath the sombre shadow of the wall.

Chapter Thirty Five
Crusaders, to the Rescue!

"What am I to do!"

It is the ex-man-o'-war's man, still lying under the launch, who thus interrogates himself. He has put the question for the fourth time that night, and now as emphatically as ever, but less despairingly.

True, the conspiring assassins have only stepped aside to a lurking place from which they may more conveniently pounce upon their quarry, and be surer of striking it. But their changed position has left him free to change his; which he at once determines upon doing. Their talk has told him where the man-of-war's boat will be awaiting to take the officers back to their ship. He knows the new wharf referred to, the very stair at which the *Crusaders* have been accustomed to bring to.

It may be the cutter with her full crew of ten—or it may be but the gig. No matter which. There cannot be fewer than two oarsmen, and these will be sufficient. A brace of British tars, with himself to make three, and the officers to tot up five—that will be more than a match for four Spanish Californians. Four times four, thinks Harry Blew, even though the sailors, like himself, be unarmed, or with nothing but their knives and boat-hooks.

He has no fear, if he can but bring it to an encounter of this kind. The question is, can he do so? And first, can he creep out from under the launch, and steal away unobserved?

A glance of scrutiny towards the spot where the assassins have placed themselves in ambuscade, satisfies him that he can. The fog favours him. Through it he cannot see them; and should be himself equally invisible.

Another circumstance will be in his favour: on the soft, sandy beach his footsteps will make but slight noise: not enough to be heard above the hoarse continuous surging of the surf.

All this passes in a moment, and he has made up his mind to start; but hesitates from a new apprehension. Will he be in time? The stair at which the boat should lie is not over a quarter of a mile off, and will take but a few minutes to reach it. Even if he succeed in eluding the vigilance of the ambushed villains, will it be possible for him to get to the pier, communicate with the boat's crew, and bring them back, before the officers reach the place of ambush?

To all this the answer is doubtful, and the doubt appals him. In his absence, the young gentlemen may arrive at the fatal spot. He may return to find their bodies lying lifeless along the sand, their pockets rifled, their murderers gone!

The thought holds him irresolute, doubting what course to take. Should he remain till they are heard approaching, then rush out, give them such warning as he may, throw himself by their side, and do his best to defend them? Unarmed, this would not be much. Against pistols and poniards he would scarce count as a combatant. It might but end in all three being slaughtered together! But there is also the danger of his being discovered in his attempt to slip away from his place of concealment. He may be followed, and overtaken; though he has little fear of this. Pursued he may be, but not overtaken. Despite his sea-legs, he knows himself a swift runner. Were he assured of a fair start, he can hold his distance against anything Spanish or Californian. In five minutes he might reach the pier—in five more be back. If he find the *Crusaders* there, a word will warn them. In all it would take about ten minutes. But, meanwhile, Crozier and Cadwallader may get upon the ground, and one minute—half a minute—after all would be over.

A terrible struggle agitates the breast of the man-o'-war's man; in his thoughts is conflict agonising. On either side are *pros* and *cons*, requiring calm deliberation; and there is no time to deliberate. He must act.

But one more second spends he in consideration. He has confidence in the young officers. Both are brave as lions, and if attacked, will make a tough fight of it. Crozier has also caution, on which dependence may be placed; and at such a time of night he will not be going unguardedly. The strife, though unequal, might last long enough for him, Harry Blew, to bring the *Crusaders*—at least near enough to cry out—and cheer their officers with the hope of help at hand.

All this flits through Harry Blew's brain in a tenth part of the time it takes to tell it. And having resolved how to act, he hastens to carry out his resolution—to proceed in quest of the boat's crew.

Sprawling like a lizard from beneath the launch, he glides off silently along the strand. At first, with slow, cautious steps, and crouchingly, but soon erect, in a rapid run, as if for the saving of his life; for it is to save the lives of others, almost dear as his own.

The five minutes are not up, when his footsteps patter along the planking of the hollow wooden wharf; and in ten seconds after, he stands at the head of the sea-stairway, looking down.

Below is a boat with men in it—half-a-score of them—seated on the thwarts, some lolling over against the gunwales asleep. At a glance he can tell them to be *Crusaders*.

His hail startles them into activity; one and all recognising the voice of their old shipmate.

"Quick!" he cries; "quick, mates! This way, and along with me! Don't stay to ask questions. Enough for you to know that the lives of your officers are in danger."

It proves enough. The tars don't wait for a word more; but spring from their recumbent attitude, and out of the boat.

Rushing up the pier steps, they cluster around their comrade. They have not needed instructions to arm themselves. Harry's speech, with its tone, told of some shore hostility, and they have instinctively made ready to meet it; each laying hold of the weapon nearest to his hand; some a knife, some an oar, others a boat-hook.

"Heave with me, lads!" cries Harry; and they "heave"—at his heels—rushing after, as if to extinguish a fire in the forecastle.

Soon they are coursing along the strand, towards the upturned boat, silently, and without asking explanation. If they did, they could not get it; for their leader is panting, breathless, almost unable to utter a word. But five issue from his throat, jerked out disjointedly, and in hoarse utterance. They are:

"Crozier—Cadwallader—waylaid—robbers—murderers!"

Enough to spur the *Crusaders* to their best speed, if *not* already at it. But they are; every man of them straining his strength to the utmost.

As they rush on, cleaving the thick fog, Harry at their head listens intently. As yet he can distinguish no sound to alarm him; only the monotonous swashing of the sea, and the murmur of distant voices in the streets of the town. But no cries—no shouts, nor shots; nothing to tell of deadly strife.

"Thank the Lord!" says the brave sailor, half speaking to himself; "we'll be in time to save them."

The words have scarce passed from his lips, when he comes in sight of the capsized launch; and almost simultaneously sees two figures upon the beach beyond. They are of human shape, but through the fog looking grand as giants.

He is not beguiled by the deception; he knows it to be the two officers, their forms magnified by the mist. No others are likely to be coming that way; for he can see they are approaching; and, as can be told by their careless, swaggering gait, unsuspicious of danger, little dreaming of an ambuscade, that in ten seconds more may deprive them of existence! To him, hurrying to avert this catastrophe, it is a moment of intense apprehension—of dread chilling fear. He sees them almost up to the place where the assassins should spring out upon them. In another instant he may hear the cracking of pistols, and see flashes through the fogs. Expecting it even before he can speak, he nevertheless calls out:

"Avast there, Mr Crozier! We're *Crusaders*. Stop where you are. Another step, and you'll be shot at. There's four men under that wall waiting to murder ye. D'ye know the names, Calderon and Lara? It's them!"

At the first words, the young officers—for it is they—instantly come to a stand. The more promptly from being prepared to expect an attack, but without the warning. Well-timed it is; and they have not stopped a moment too soon.

Simultaneous with the sailor's last word, the sombre space under the wall is lit up by four flashes, followed by the report of as many pistols, while the "tzip-tzip" of bullets, like hornets hurtle pass their ears, leaving no doubt as to who has been fired at.

Fired at, and fortunately missed; for neither feels hurt nor hit!

But the danger is not yet over. Quick following the first comes a second volley, and again with like result. Bad marksmen are they who design doing murder.

It is the last round of shots. In all likelihood, the pistols of the assassins are double-barrelled, and both barrels have been discharged. Before they can reload them, Harry Blew, with his *Crusaders*, has come up, and it is too late for De Lara and his confederates to use the steel.

Crozier and Cadwallader bound forward; and placing themselves at the head of the boat's crew, advance toward the shadowed spot. They go with a rush, resolved on coming to close quarters with their dastardly assailants, and bringing the affair to a speedy termination.

But it is over already, to their surprise, as also chagrin. On reaching the wall, they find nothing there save stones and timber! The dark space for an instant illuminated by the pistol-flashes, has resumed its grim obscurity.

The assassins have got away, escaping the chastisement they would surely have received had they stood their ground.

Some figures are seen in the distance, scuttling along a narrow lane. Cadwallader brings his pistol to bear on them, his finger upon the trigger. But it may not be they; and stayed by the uncertainty, he refrains from firing.

"Let them go!" counsels Crozier. "'Twould be no use looking for them now. Their crime will keep till morning; and since we know their names, it'll be strange if we can't find them; though not so strange if we should fail to get them punished. But that they shall be, if there's a semblance of law to be found in San Francisco. Now, thanks, my brave *Crusaders*! And there's a hundred pound note to be divided among you. Small reward for the saving of two lives, with a large sum of money. Certainly, had you not turned up so opportunely—But, Harry, how come you to be here? Never mind now! Let us get on board! and you, Blew, must go with us. It'll do you no harm to spend one more night on your old ship. There you can tell me all."

Harry joyfully complies with a requisition so much to his mind; and, instead of tossing discontentedly on a couch of wet sand, he that night sleeps soundly in his old bunk in the frigate's forepeak.

Chapter Thirty Six
A Neglected Dwelling

A Country-House some ten miles from San Francisco, in a south-westerly direction. It stands inland about half-way between the Bay and the Pacific shore, among the Coast Range hills.

Though a structure of mud-brick—the sort made by the Israelites in Egypt—and with no pretension to architectural style, it is, in Californian parlance, a *hacienda*. For it is the headquarters of a grazing estate; but not one of the first-class, either in stock or appointments. In these respects, it was once better off than now; since now it is less than second, showing signs of decay everywhere, but nowhere so much as in the dwelling itself, and the enclosures around. Its walls are weather-washed, here and there cracked and crumbling; the doors have had no paint for years, and opening or shutting, creak upon hinges thickly-coated with rust. Its *corrals* contain no cattle, nor are any to be seen upon the pastures outside. In short, the estate shows as if it had an absentee owner, or none at all.

And the house might appear uninhabited, but for some *peons* seen sauntering listlessly around, and a barefoot damsel or two, standing dishevelled by its door, or in the kitchen kneeling over the *metate*, and squeezing out maize-dough for the eternal *tortillas*.

However, despite its neglected appearance, the *hacienda* has an owner; and with all their indolence, the lounging *leperoa* outside, and slatternly wenches within, have a master. He is not often at home, but when he is they address him as "Don Faustino." Servants rarely add the surname.

Only at rare intervals do his domestics see him. He spends nearly all his time elsewhere—most of it in Yerba Buena, now named San Francisco. And of late more than ever has he absented himself from his ancestral halls; for the *hacienda* is the house in which he was born; it, with the surrounding pasture-land, left him by his father, some time deceased.

Since coming into possession, he has neglected his patrimony; indeed, spent the greater portion of it on cards, and evil courses of other kinds; for the *dueno* of the ill-conditioned dwelling is Faustino Calderon.

As already hinted, his estate is heavily mortgaged, the house almost a ruin. In his absence, it looks even more like one; for then his domestics, having nothing to do, are scarce ever seen outside, to give the place an appearance of life. Fond of cards as their master, they may at most times be observed, squatted upon the pavement of the inner court, playing *monté* on a spread blanket, with copper *clacos* staked upon the game.

When the *dueno* is at home, things are a little different; for, Don Faustino, with all his dissipation, is anything but an indulgent master. Then his *muchuchos* have to move about, and wait upon him with assiduity. If they don't, they will hear *carajos* from his lips, and receive cuts from his riding-whip.

It is the morning after that night when the "El Dorado" *monté* bank suspended play and pay; the time, six o'clock a.m. Notwithstanding the early hour, the domestics are stirring about the place, as if they had something to do, and were doing it. To one acquainted with their usual habits, the brisk movement will be interpreted as a sure sign that their master is at home.

And he is; though he has been there but a very short while—only a few minutes. Absent for more than a week, he has this morning made his appearance just as the day was breaking. Not alone; but in the company of a gentleman, whom all the servants know to be his intimate friend and associate—Don Francisco de Lara.

The two have come riding up to the house in haste, dropped the bridles on the necks of their horses, and, without saying a word, left these to the care of a couple of grooms, rudely roused from their slumber.

The house-servants, lazily drawing the huge door of the *saguan*, see that the *dueno* is in ill-humour, which stirs them into activity; and in haste, they prepare the repast called for—*desayuno*.

Having entered and taken seats, Don Faustino and his guest await the serving of the meal.

For some time in silence, each with an elbow rested on the table, a hand supporting his head, the fingers buried in his hair.

The silence is at length broken; the host, as it should be, speaking first.

"What had we best do, De Lara? I don't think 'twill be safe staying here. After what's happened, they're sure to come after us."

"That's probable enough. *Caspita*! I'm puzzled to make out how that fellow who called out our names could have known we were there. '*Crusaders*' he said they were; which means they were sailors belonging to the English warship. Of course the boat's crew that was waiting. But what brought them up; and how came they to arrive there and then, just in the nick of time to spoil our plans? That's a mystery to me."

"To me, too."

"There were no sailors hanging about the hotel that I saw; nor did we encounter any as we went through the streets. Besides, if we had, they couldn't have passed us, and then come on from the opposite side, without our seeing them—dark as it was. 'Tis enough to make me believe in second-sight."

"That appears the only way to explain it."

"Yes; but it won't, and don't. I've been thinking of another explanation, more conformable to the laws of nature."

"What?"

"That there's been somebody under that old boat. We stood talking there like four fools, calling out one another's names. Now, suppose one of those sailors was waiting by the boat as we came along, and seeing us, crept under it? He could have heard everything we said; and slipping off, after we went to the wall, might have brought up the rest of the accursed crew. The thing seems odd; at the same time it's possible enough, and probable too."

"It is; and now you speak of it. I remember something. While we were under the wall, I fancied I saw a man crouching along the water's edge, as if going away from the boat."

"You did?"

"I'm almost certain I did. At the time, I thought nothing of it, as we were watching for the other two; and I had no suspicion of any one else being about. Now, I believe there was one."

"And now, I believe so too. *Carramba*! that accounts for everything. I see it all. That's how the sailor got our names, and knew all about our design—that to do—*murder*! You needn't start at the word, nor turn pale. But you may at the prospect before us. *Carrai*! we're in danger, Calderon;— no mistake about it. Why the devil didn't you tell me of it—at the time you saw that man?"

"Because, as I've said, I had no thought it could be any one connected with them."

"Well, your thoughtlessness has got us into a fix indeed—the worst I've ever been in, and I can remember a few. No use to think about duelling now, whoever might be challenger. Instead of seconds, they'd meet us with a posse of sheriff's officers. Likely enough they'll be setting them after us before this. Although I feel sure our bullets didn't hit either, it'll be just as bad. The attempt will tell against us all the same. Therefore, it won't do to stay here. So direct your servants not to unsaddle. We'll need to be off, soon as we've swallowed a cup of chocolate."

A call from Don Faustino brings one of his domestics to the door; then a word or two sends him off with the order for keeping the horses in hand.

"*Chingara!*" fiercely exclaims De Lara, striking the table with his shut fist, "everything has gone against us."

"Everything, indeed. Our money lost, our love made light of, our revenge baffled—"

"No, not the last! Have no fear, Faustino. That's still to come."

"How?"

"How I you ask, do you?"

"I do. I can't see what way we can get it now. You know the English officers will be gone in a day or two. Their ship is to sail soon. Last night there was talk in the town that she might leave at any moment—to-morrow, or it may be this very day."

"Let her go, and them with her. The sooner the better for us. That won't hinder me from the revenge I intend taking. On the contrary, 'twill help me. Ha! I shall strike this Crozier in his tenderest part! and you can do the same for Señor Cadwallader."

"In what way?"

"Faustino Calderon, I won't call you a fool, notwithstanding your behaviour last night. But you ask some very silly questions, and that's one of them. Supposing these *gringos* gone from here, does it follow they'll take everything along with them? Can you think of nothing they must needs leave behind?"

"Their hearts. Is that what you mean?"

"No, it isn't."

"What then?"

"Their sweethearts, stupid! And that brings me to what I intend telling you—leastwise to the first chapter of it."

"Which is!"

"That somebody else is going away, too."

"Who?"

"Don Gregorio Montijo!"

"Don Gregorio Montijo?"

"Don Gregorio, daughter and grand-daughter."

"You astonish me! But are they leaving California for good?"

"Leaving it for good."

"That is strange intelligence, startling! Though I can understand the reason; that's well known."

"Oh, yes; the Don's disgusted with things as they now go here; and I suppose the señoritas are also. No wonder. Since these ragged and red-shirted gentry have taken possession of the place, it's not very agreeable for ladies to show themselves about; nor very safe, I should say. Good reason for Don Gregorio selling out, and betaking himself to quieter quarters."

"He has sold out, has he?"

"He has."

"You're sure of it?"

"Quite sure. Rafael Rocas has told me all about it. And for an enormous sum of money. How much do you suppose?"

"Perhaps 100,000 dollars. His property ought to be worth that."

"Whether it ought to be, or is, it has realised three times the amount."

"*Carramba*! Has Rocas said so?"

"He has."

"Has he told you who the generous purchaser is?"

"Some speculating Yankees, who fancy they see far into the future, and think Don Gregorio's pasture-land a good investment. There's a partnership of purchasers, I believe, and they've paid the money down, in cash."

"Already! What kind of cash?"

"The best kind—doubloons and dollars. Not all in coin. Some of it in the currency of California—gold-dust and nuggets."

"That's quite as good. *Santissima*! a splendid fortune. All for a piece of pasture-land, that twelve months ago wasn't worth a tenth part the amount! What a pity my own acres are already hypothecated! I might have been a millionaire."

"No! your land lies too far-off. These Yankees have bought Don Gregorio's land for 'town-lots,' as they call them. In due time, no doubt, they'll cover them with their psalm-singing churches and schoolhouses—though the first building put up should be a prison."

Both laugh together at this modest *jeu d'esprit*; their mirth having a double significance. For neither need be over-satisfied with the sight of a prison.

"By the Virgin!" exclaims Calderon, continuing the conversation; "Don Gregorio has done well, and he may be wise in quitting California. But what the devil are we to do about the girls? Of course, as you say, they're going to!"

"And so it may be. But not before another event takes place—one that may embarrass, and delay, if it do not altogether prevent their departure."

"*Amigo*; you talk enigmatically. Will you oblige me by speaking plainer?"

"I will; but not till we've had our chocolate, and after it a *copita* of Catalan. I need a little alcohol to get my brain in working order; for there's work for it to do. Enough now to tell you I've had a revelation. A good angel—or it may be a bad one—has visited me, and given it. A vision which shows me at the same time riches and revenge—pointing the straight way to both."

"Has the vision shown that I'm to be a sharer in these fine things?"

"It has; and you shall be. But only in proportion as you may prove yourself worthy."

"*Por Dios*! I'll do my best. I have the will, if you'll only instruct me in the way."

"I'll do that. But I warn you, 'twill need more than will—strength, secrecy, courage, determination."

"*Desayuno, señores!*"

This from one of the domestics announcing the chocolate served.

Chapter Thirty Seven
Mysterious Communications

A few moments suffice the ruined gamblers for their slight matutinal repast. After which, a decanter of Catalonian brandy and glasses are placed upon the table, with a bundle of Manilla cheroots, size number one.

While the glasses are being filled, and the cigars lighted, there is silence. Then Calderon calls upon his guest to impart the particulars of that visionary revelation, which promises to give them, at the same time, riches and revenge.

Taking a sip of the potent spirit, and a puff or two at his cigar, De Lara responds to the call. But first leaning across the table, and looking his confederate straight in the face, he asks, in an odd fashion—

"Are you a bankrupt, Faustino Calderon?"

"Of course I am. Why do you put the question?"

"Because I want to be sure, before making known to you the scheme I've hinted at. As I've told you, I'm after no child's play. I ask again, *are* you a bankrupt?"

"And I answer you I *am*. But what has that to do with it?"

"A good deal. Never mind. You *are* one? You assure me of it?"

"I do. I'm as poor as yourself, if not poorer, after last night's losses. I'd embarked all my money in the Monté concern."

"But you have something besides money? This house and your lands?"

"Mortgaged—months ago—up to the eyes, the ears, crown of the head. That's where the cash came from to set up the bank that's broke—breaking me along with it."

"And you've nothing left? No chance for starting it again?"

"Not a *claco*. Here I am apparently in my own house, with servants, such as they are, around me. It's all in appearance. In reality, I'm not the owner. I once was, as my father before me; but can't claim to be any longer.

Even while we're sitting here, drinking this Catalan, the mortgagee—that old usurer Martinez—may step in and turn—kick us both out."

"I'd like him to try. He'd catch a Tartar, if he attempted to kick me out—he or anybody else just now, in my present humour. There's far more reason for us to fear being pulled out by policemen, which makes it risky to stay talking. So let's to the point at once—back to where we left off. On your oath, Faustino Calderon, you're no longer a man of means?"

"On my oath, Francisco de Lara, I haven't an *onza* left—no, not a *peso*."

"Enough. Now that I know your financial status, we will understand one another; and without further circumlocution I shall make you a sharer of the bright thought that's flashed across my brain."

"Let me hear what it is. I'm all impatience."

"Not so fast, Faustino. As I've already twice told you, it's no child's play; but a business that requires skill and courage. Above all, fidelity among those who may engage in it—for more than two are needed. It will want at least four good and true men. I know three of them; about the fourth I'm not so certain."

"Who are the three?"

"Francisco de Lara, Manuel Diaz, and Raphael Rocas."

"And the fourth, of whom you are dubious?"

"Faustino Calderon."

"Why do you doubt me, De Lara?"

"Don't call it doubting. I only say I'm not certain about you."

"But for what reason?"

"Because you may be squeamish, or get scared. Not that there's much real danger. There mayn't be any, if the thing's cleverly managed. But there must be no bungling; and, above all, no backing out—nothing like treason."

"Can't you trust me so far as to give a hint of your scheme? As to my being squeamish, I think, De Lara, you do me injustice to suppose such a thing. The experience of the last twenty-four hours has made a serious change in my way of viewing matters of morality. A man who has lost his all, and suddenly sees himself a beggar, isn't disposed to be sensitive. Come, *camarado!* tell me, and try me."

"I intend doing both, but not just yet. It's an affair that calls for certain formalities, among them some *swearing*. Those who embark in it must be bound by a solemn oath; and when we all get together, that shall be done. Time enough then for you to know what I'm aiming at. Now, I only say, that if the scheme succeed, two things are sure, and both concern yourself, Faustino Calderon."

"What are they? You can trust me with that much, I suppose?"

"Certainly I can, and shall. The first is, that you'll be a richer man than you've ever been in your life, or at least since I've had the honour of your acquaintance. The second, that Don Gregorio Montijo will not leave California—that is, not quite so soon, nor altogether in the way he was wishing. You may have plenty of time yet, with opportunities, to press your suit with the fair Iñez."

"*Carramba*! Secure me that, and I swear—"

"You needn't set about swearing yet. You can do that when the occasion calls for it; and, I promise, you shall have the opportunity soon. Till then I'll take your word. With one in love, as you believe yourself, that should be binding as any oath; especially when it promises such a rich reward."

"You're sure about Diaz and Rocas?"

"Quite so. With them there won't be need for any prolonged conference. When a man sees the chance of getting sixty thousand dollars in a lump lot, he's pretty certain to act promptly, and without being particular as to what that action is."

"Sixty thousand dollars! That's to be the share of each?"

"That, and more, maybe."

"It makes one crazy—even to think of such a sum!"

"Don't go crazed till you've got it; then you may."

"If I do, it won't be with grief."

"It shouldn't; since it will give you a fresh lease of sweet life; and renew your hopes of having the wife you want. But come; we must get away if we wish to avoid being taken away—though, I fancy, there's nothing to apprehend for some hours yet. The *gringos* have gone on board their ship, and are not likely to come on shore again before breakfast. What with their last night's revelry, it'll take them some time to clear the cobwebs out of their eyes after waking up. Besides, if they should make it a law matter, there'll be all the business of looking up warrants, and the like. They do such things rather slowly in San Francisco. Then there's the ten miles out here; even if they strike our trail straight. No; we needn't be in a hurry so far as that goes. But the other's a thing that won't keep, and must be set about at once. Fortunately, the road that takes us to a place of concealment, is the same we have to travel upon business; and that is to the rancho of Rocas. There I've appointed to meet Diaz, who'd have come with us here, but that he preferred staying all night in the town. But he'll be here betimes, and we can all remain with old Rafael till this ugly wind blows past; which it will in a week, or soon as the English ship sails off. If not, we must keep out of sight a little longer, or leave San Francisco for good."

"I hope we'll not be forced to that. I shouldn't at all like to leave it."

"Like it or not, you may have no choice. And what does it signify where a man lives, so long as he's got sixty thousand dollars to live on?"

"True; that ought to make any place pleasant."

"Well; I tell you you'll have it—maybe more. But not if we stand palavering here. *Nos vamos!*"

A call from Calderon summoned a servant, who is directed to have the horses brought to the door.

These soon appear, under the guidance of two ragged grooms; who, delivering them, see their masters mount and ride off they know not whither; nor care they so long as they are themselves left to idleness, with a plentiful supply of black beans, jerked-meat, and *monté*.

Soon the two horsemen disappear behind a ridge of hills; and the hypothecated house resumes its wonted look of desolation.

Chapter Thirty Eight
A Conversation with Quadrumana

Notwithstanding his comfortable quarters in the frigate's forecastle, Harry Blew is up by early daybreak, and off from the ship before six bells have sounded.

Ere retiring to rest, he had communicated to his patron, Crozier, a full account of his zigzag wanderings through the streets of San Francisco, and how he came to bring the cutter's crew to the rescue.

As neither of the young officers is on the early morning watch, but both still abed, he does not wait their rising. For, knowing that the adage, "First come, first served," is often true, he is anxious as soon as possible to present himself at the office of the agent Silvestre, and from him get directions for going on board the Chilian ship. He is alive to the hint given him by Crozier, that there may be a chance of his being made a mate.

As yet he does not even know the name of the vessel, but that he will learn at the office, as also where she is tying.

His request to the lieutenant on duty for a boat to set him ashore, is at once and willingly granted. No officer on that frigate would refuse Harry Blew; and the dingy is placed at his service.

In this he is conveyed to the wooden pier, whose planking he treads with heavier step, but lighter heart, than when, on the night before, he ran along it in quest of *Crusaders*. With weightier purse too, as he carries a hundred pound Bank of England note in the pocket of his pea-jacket—a parting gift from the generous Crozier—besides a number of gold pieces received from Cadwallader, as the young Welshman's share of gratitude for the service done them.

Thus amply provided, he might proceed at once to the "Sailor's Home," and bring away his embargoed property.

He does not; thinking it better first to see about the berth on the Chilian ship; and therefore he steers direct for the agent's office.

Though it is still early, by good luck, Don Tomas chances to be already at his desk; to whom Harry hands the card given him by Crozier, at the same time declaring the purpose for which he has presented himself.

In return, he receives from Silvestre instructions to report himself on board the Chilian ship, *El Condor*; Don Tomas furnishing him with a note of introduction to her captain, and pointing out the vessel—which is visible from the door, and at no great distance off.

"Captain Lantanas is coming ashore," adds the agent; "I expect him in the course of an hour. By waiting here, you can see him, and it will save you boat-hire."

But Harry Blew will not wait. He remembers the old saying about procrastination, and is determined there shall be no mishap through negligence on his part, or niggardliness about a bit of a boat-fare. He has made up his mind to be the *Condor's* first mate—if he can.

Nor is it altogether ambition that prompts him to seek the office so earnestly. A nobler sentiment inspires him—the knowledge that, in this capacity, he may be of more service, and better capable of affording protection, to the fair creatures whom Crozier has committed to his charge.

The watermen of San Francisco do not ply their oars gratuitously. Even the shabbiest of shore-boats, hired for the shortest time, exacts a stiffish fare. It will cost Harry Blew a couple of dollars to be set aboard the *Condor*, though she is lying scarce three cables' length from the shore!

What cares he for that? It is nothing now.

Hailing the nearest skiff with a waterman in it, he points to the Chilian ship, saying:

"Heave along, lad; an' put me aboard o' yonder craft—that one as shows the three-colour bit o' bunting wi' a single star in the blue. The sooner ye do your job, the better ye'll get paid for it."

A contract on such conditions is usually entered into with alacrity, and with celerity carried out. The boatman beaches his tiny craft, takes in his fare, and in less than ten minutes' time Harry Blew swarms up the man-ropes of the Chilian ship, strides over the rail, and drops down upon her deck.

He looks around, but sees no one—at least nothing in the shape of a sailor. Only an old negro, with skin black as a boot, and crow-footed all over the face, standing beside two singular creatures nearly as human-like as himself, but covered with fox-coloured hair!

The ex-man-o'-war's man is for a time in doubt as to which of the three he should address himself. In point of intelligence there seems not much to choose. However, he with the black skin cuts short his hesitation by stepping forward, and saying:

"Well, mass'r sailor-man, wha' you come for? S'pose you want see de cappen? I'se only de cook."

"Oh, you're only the cook, are you? Well, old caboose; you've made a correct guess about my bizness. It's the capten I do want to see."

"All right. He down in de cabin. You wait hya. I fotch 'im up less'n no time!"

The old darkey shuffling aft, disappears down the companion-way, leaving Harry with the two monstrous-looking creatures, whom he has now made out to be orang-outangs.

"Well, mates!" says the sailor, addressing them in a jocular way, "what be your opeenyun o' things in general? D'ye think the wind's goin' to stay sou'-westerly, or shift roun' to the nor'-eastart?"

"Cro—cro—croak!"

"Oh, hang it, no. I ain't o' the croakin' sort. Ha'n't ye got nothin' more sensible than that to say to me!"

"Kurra—kra—kra. Cro—cro—croak!"

"No; I won't do anythink o' the kind; leastways, unless there turns out to be short commons 'board this eer craft. Then I'll croak, an' no mistake. But I say, old boys, how 'bout the grog? Reg'lar allowance, I hope—three tots a day?"

"Na—na—na—na—na—boof! Ta—ta—ta—fuff!"

"No! only two, ye say! Ah! that won't do for me. For ye see, shipmates—I s'pose I shall be callin' ye so—'board the old *Crusader*, I've been 'customed to have my rum reg'lar, three times the day; an' if it ain't same on the *Condor*, in the which I'm 'bout to ship, then, shiver my spars! if I don't raise sich a rumpus as—"

"Kurra—kurra—cro—cro—croak! Na—na—na—boof—ta—ta—pf—pf—piff!"

The sailor's voice is drowned by the gibbering of the orangs, his gesture of mock-menace, with the semi-serious look that accompanied it, having part frightened, part infuriated them.

The fracas continues, until the darkey returns on deck followed by the skipper; when the cook takes charge of the *quadrumana*, drawing them off to his caboose.

Captain Lantanas, addressing himself to the sailor, asks: "*Un marinero?*" (A seaman.)

"*Si, capitan.*" (Yes, captain.)

"*Que negocio tienes V. commigo?*" (What is your business with me?)

"Well, capten," responds Harry Blew, speaking the language of the Chilian, in a tolerably intelligent *patois*, "I've come to offer my sarvices to you. I've brought this bit o' paper from Master Silvestre; it'll explain things better'n I can."

The captain takes the note handed to him, and breaks open the envelope. A smile irradiates his sallow face as he makes himself acquainted with its contents.

"At last a sailor!" he mutters to himself; for Harry is the only one who has yet offered. "And a good one too," thinks Captain Lantanas, bending his eyes on the ex-man-o'-war's man, and scanning him from head to foot.

But, besides personal inspection, he has other assurance of the good qualities of the man before him; at a late hour on the night before he held a communication with Don Gregorio, who has recommended him. The haciendado had reported what Crozier said, that Harry Blew was an able seaman, thoroughly trustworthy, and competent to take charge of a ship, either as first or second officer.

With Crozier's endorsement thus vicariously conveyed, the ex-man-o'-war's man has no need to say a word for himself. Nor does Captain Lantanas call for it. He only puts some professional questions, less inquisitorially than as a matter of form.

"The Señor Silvestre advises me that you wish to serve in my ship. Can you take a lunar?"

"Well, capten; I hev squinted through a quadrant afores now, an' can take a sight; tho' I arn't much up to loonars. But if there's a good chronometer aboard, I won't let a ship run very far out of her reck'nin'."

"You can keep a log-book, I suppose?"

"I dare say I can. I've larned to write, so 'st might be read; though my fist ain't much to be bragged about."

"That will do," rejoins the skipper, contentedly. "Now, Señor Enrique—I see that's your name—answer me in all candour. Do you think you are capable of acting as *piloto?*"

"By that you mean mate, I take it?"

"Yes; it is *piloto* in Spanish."

"Well, capten; 'tain't for me to talk big o' myself. But I've been over thirty year 'board a British man-o'-war—more'n one o' 'em—an' if I wan't able to go mate in a merchanter, I ought to be condemned to be cook's scullion for the rest o' my days. If your honour thinks me worthy o' bein' made first officer o' the *Condor*, I'll answer for it she won't stray far out o' her course while my watch be on."

"*Bueno*! Señor Enrique—B—blee. What is it?" asks the Chilian, re-opening the note, and vainly endeavouring to pronounce the Saxon surname.

"Blew—Harry Blew."

"Ah, Bloo—*azul, esta*?"

"No, capten. Not that sort o' blue. In Spanish, my name has a different significance. It means, as we say o' a gale after it's blowed past—it 'blew.' When it's been a big un, we say it 'blew great guns.' Now ye understan'?"

"Yes; perfectly. Well, Señor Bloo, to come to an understanding about the other matter. I'm willing to take you as my first officer, if you don't object to the wages I intend offering you—fifty dollars a month, and everything found."

"I'm agreeable to the tarms."

"*Basta*! When will it be convenient for you to enter in your duties?"

"For that matter, this minute. I only need to go ashore to get my kit. When that's stowed, I'll be ready to tackle on to work."

"*Muy bien*! señor; you can take my boat for it. And if you see any sailors who want to join, I authorise you to engage them at double the usual wages. I wish to get away as soon as a crew can be shipped. But when you come back we'll talk more about it. Call at Señor Silvestre's office, and tell him he needn't look for me till a later hour. Say I've some business that detains me aboard. *Hasta Luego*!"

Thus courteously concluding, the Chilian skipper returns to his cabin, leaving the newly appointed *piloto* free to look after his own affairs.

Chapter Thirty Nine
The "Blue-Peter"

The ex-man-o'-war's man, now first officer of a merchant-vessel, and provided with a boat of his own, orders off the skiff he has kept in waiting, after tossing into it two dollars—the demanded fare. Then slipping down into the *Condor's* gig, sculls himself ashore.

Leaving his boat at the pier, he first goes to the office of the ship-agent, and delivers the message entrusted to him.

After that, contracting with a truckman, he proceeds to the "Sailor's Home," releases his *impedimenta*, and starts back to embark them in his boat. But not before giving the bar-keeper, as also the Boniface, of that establishment, a bit of his mind.

Spreading before their eyes the crisp hundred pound note, which as yet he has not needed to break, he says tauntingly:

"Take a squint at that, ye land-lubbers! There's British money for ye. An' tho' it be but a bit o' paper it's worth more than your gold-dross, dollar for dollar. How'd ye like to lay your ugly claws on't! Ah! you're a pair of the most dastardly shore-sharks I've met in all my cruzins; but ye'll never have Harry Blew in your grups again."

Saying this, he thrusts the bank-note back into his pocket; then paying them a last reverence with mock-politeness, and giving a twitch of his trousers, he starts after the truckman, already *en route* with his kit.

In accordance with the wishes of Captain Lantanas, he stays a little longer in the town, trying to pick up sailors. There are plenty of these sauntering along the streets and lounging at the doors of drinking-saloons.

But even double wages will not tempt them to abandon their free-and-easy life; and the *Condor's* first officer is forced to the conclusion, that he must return to the ship *solus*.

Assisted by the truckman, he gets his traps into the gig; and is about to step in himself, when his eye chances to turn upon the *Crusader*. There he sees something to surprise him—the *Blue-Peter*. The frigate has out signals for sailing! and he wonders at this; for there was no word of it when he was aboard. He knew, as all the others, that she was to sail soon—it might be in a day or two. But not as the signal indicates,—almost immediately!

While conjecturing what may be the cause of such hasty departure, he sees something that partly explains it. Three or four cables' length from the frigate is another ship, over whose taffrail floats the flag of England. At a glance, the ex-man-o'-war's man can tell her to be a corvette; at the same time recalling what, the night before, he has heard upon the frigate: that the coming of the corvette would be the signal for the *Crusader's* sailing.

While his heart warms to the flag thus doubly displayed in the harbour of San Francisco, it is a little saddened to see the other signal—the "Blue-Peter;" since it tells him he may not have an opportunity to take a more formal leave of his friends of the frigate, which he designed doing. He longs to make known to Mr Crozier and the midshipman the result of his application to the captain of the Chilian ship, and receive the congratulations of the young officers on his success; but now it may be impossible to communicate with them, by the *Crusader* so soon leaving port.

He has half a mind to put off for the frigate in the *Condor's* gig, into which he has got. But Captain Lantanas might, meanwhile, be wanting both him and the boat.

All at once, in the midst of his dilemma, he sees that which promises to help him out of it,—a small boat putting off from the frigate's sides, and heading right for the pier.

As it draws nearer, he can tell it to be the dingy.

There are three men in it—two rowers and a steersman.

As it approaches the pier-head, Harry recognises the one in the stern-sheets, whose bright ruddy face is turned towards him.

"Thank the Lord for such good luck!" he mutters. "It's Mr Cadwallader!"

By this the dingy has drawn near enough for the midshipman to see and identify him; which he does, exclaiming in joyful surprise:

"By Jove! it's Blew himself! Hallo there, Harry! You're just the man I'm coming ashore to see. Hold, starboard oar! Port oar, a stroke or two! Way enough!"

In a few seconds, the dingy is bow on to the gig; when Harry, seizing hold of it, brings the two boats side by side, and steadies them.

"Glad to see ye again, Master Willie. I'd just sighted the frigate's signal for sailin', an' despaired o' havin' the chance to say a last word to yourself, or Mr Crozier."

"Well, old boy; it's about that I've come ashore. Jump out; and walk with me a bit along the wharf."

The sailor drops his oar, and springs out upon the pier, the young officer preceding him.

When sufficiently distant from the boats to be beyond earshot of the oarsmen, Cadwallader resumes speech:

"Harry; here's a letter from Mr Crozier. He wants you to deliver it at the address you'll find written upon it. To save you the necessity of inquiring, I can point out the place it's to go to. Look along shore. You see a house— yonder on the top of the hill?"

"Sartinly, I see it, Master Willie; and know who lives theer. Two o' the sweetest creeturs in all Californey. I s'pose the letter be for one o' them?"

"No, it isn't, you dog; for neither of them. Read the superscription. You see it's addressed to a gentleman?"

"Oh! it's for the guv'nor hisself," rejoins Harry, taking the letter, and running his eye over the direction—Don Gregorio Montijo. "All right, sir. I'll put it in the old gentleman's flippers safe an' sure. Do you want me to go with it now, sir?"

"Well, as soon as you conveniently can; though there's no need for helter-skelter haste, since there wouldn't be time for an answer, anyhow. In twenty minutes we'll weigh anchor, and be off. I've hurried ashore to see you, hoping to find you at the ship-agent's office. How fortunate my stumbling on you here! For now I can better tell you what's wanted. In that letter, there's something that concerns Mr Crozier and myself—matters of importance to us both. When you've given it to Don Gregorio, he'll no doubt ask you some questions about what happened last night. Tell him all you know; except that you needn't say anything of Mr Crozier and myself having taken a little too much champagne—which we did. You understand, old boy?"

"Perfectly, Master Will."

"Good. Now Harry; I haven't another moment to stay. See! The ship's beginning to spread canvas! If I don't get back directly, I may be left here in California, never to rise above the rank of reefer. Oh! by the way, you'll be pleased to know that your friend Mr Crozier is now a lieutenant. His commission arrived by the corvette that came in last night. He told me to tell you, and I'd nearly forgotten it."

"I'm glad to hear it," rejoins the sailor, raising the hat from his head, and giving a subdued cheer; "right gled; an', maybe, he'll be the same, hearin' Harry Blew's been also promoted. I'm now first mate o' the Chili ship, Master Willie."

"Hurrah! I congratulate you on your good luck. I'm delighted to know that, and so will he be. We may hope some day to see you a full-fledged skipper, commanding your own craft. Now, you dear old salt, don't forget to look well after the girls. Again, good-bye, and God bless you!"

A squeeze of hands, with lingers entwined, tight as a reef-knot—then relaxed with reluctance—after which they separate. The mid, jumping into the dingy, is rowed back towards the *Crusader*; while Harry re-hires the truckman; but now only to stay by, and take care of his boat, till he can return to it, after executing the errand entrusted to him. Snug as his new berth promises to be, he would rather lose it than fail to deliver that letter.

And in ten minutes after, he has passed through the suburbs of the town, and is hastening along the shore-road, towards the house of Don Gregorio Montijo.

Chapter Forty
Dreading a "Desafio"

Once more upon the *azotea* stand Carmen Montijo and Iñez Alvarez. It is the morning of the day succeeding that made sacred by their betrothal. Their eyes are upon the huge warship, that holds the men who holds their hearts, with promise of their hands—in short, every hope of their life's happiness.

They could be happy now, but for an apprehension which oppresses them—causing them keen anxiety. Yesterday, with its scenes of pleasureable excitement, had also its incidents of the opposite kind; the remembrance of which too vividly remains, and is not to be got rid of. The encounter between the gamblers and their lovers cannot end with that episode, to which they were themselves witness. Something more will surely come from it.

And what will this something be? What should it? What could it, but a *desafio*—a duel?

However brave on yester-morn the two señoritas were, or pretended to be, however regardless of consequences, it is different to-day. The circumstances have changed. Then, their sweethearts were only suitors. Now, they are affianced, still standing in the relationship of lovers, but with ties more firmly, if not more tenderly, united. For are they not now their own.

Of the two girls, Iñez is less anxious than the aunt, having less cause to be. With the observant intelligence of woman, she has long since seen that Calderon is a coward, and for this reason has but little belief he will fight. With instinct equally keen, Carmen knows De Lara well. After his terrible humiliation, he is not the man to shrink away out of sight. Blackleg though he be, he possesses courage—perhaps the only quality he has deserving of admiration. Once, she herself admired the quality, if not the man! That remembrance itself makes her fear what may come.

She talks in serious tone, discussing with her niece the probabilities of what may arise. The delirious joy of yester-eve—of that hour when she sat in her saddle, looking over the ocean, and listening to the sweet words of love—is to-day succeeded by depression, almost despondency.

While conversing, she has her eyes upon the bay, watching the boats that, at intervals, are rowed off from the warship, fearing to recognise in one the form of him so dear. Fearing it; for they know that her lover is not likely to be ashore again, and his coming now could only be on that errand she, herself, so much dreads—the duel. Duty should retain him on his, the young officer's, ship, but honour may require him once more to visit the shore—perhaps never to leave it alive!

Thus gloomily reflects Carmen, imparting her fears to the less frightened Iñez; though she too is not without apprehension. If they but understood the "Code of Signals," all this misery would be spared them. Since from the frigate's main-royal masthead floats a blue flag, with a white square in its centre, which is a portent she will soon spread her sails, and glide off out of sight—carrying their *amantes* beyond all danger of duels, or shore-scrapes of any kind.

They observe the "Blue-Peter," but without knowing aught of its significance. They do not even try to interpret, or think of it; their thoughts, as their eyes, concentrated upon the boats that pass between ship and shore.

One at length specially arrests their attention, and keeps it for some time fixed. A small craft that, leaving the ship, is steered direct for the town. It passes near enough for them to see there are three men in it; two of them rowing, the other in the stern—this last in the uniform of an officer.

Love's glance is keen, and, aided by an opera-glass, it enables Iñez Alvarez to identify the officer in the stern-sheets as Don Gulielmo. The other two—the oarsmen—are only sailors in blue serge shirts, with wide collars, falling far back.

For what the young officer is being rowed ashore, the ladies cannot guess. If for fighting, they know that another, and older, officer, would be with him. Where is Don Eduardo?

While still conjecturing, the boat glides on towards the town, and is lost to their view behind some sand-hills inshore.

Their glance going back to the ship, they perceive a change in her aspect. Her tall tapering masts, with their network of stays and shrouds, are half-hidden behind broad sheets of canvas. The frigate is unfurling sail! They are surprised at this, not expecting it so soon. With the help of their glasses, they observe other movements going on aboard the war-vessel: signal-flags running up and down their haulyards, while boats are being hoisted to the davits.

While still watching these manoeuvres, the little craft which carries the midshipman again appears, shooting out from behind the sand-hills, and rowed rapidly back to the ship, the young officer still in it.

On reaching the great leviathan, for a short time it shows like a tiny spot along her water-line; but, soon after, it too is lifted aloft, and over the bulwark rail.

Ignorant as the young ladies may be of nautical matters, they can have no doubt as to what all this manoeuvring means. The ship is about to sail!

As this is an event which interests all the family, Don Gregorio, summoned to the house-top, soon stands beside them.

"She's going off, sure enough," he says, after sighting through one of the glasses. "It's rather strange—so abruptly!" he adds. "Our young friends said nothing about it last night."

"I think they could not have known of it themselves," says Carmen.

"I'm sure they couldn't," adds Iñez.

"What makes you sure, *niña*?" asked Don Gregorio.

"Well—because,"—stammers out the Andalusian, a flush starting into her cheeks—"because they'd have told us. They said they didn't expect to sail for a day or two, anyhow."

"Just so; but you see they're setting sail now—evidently intending to take departure. However, I fancy I can explain it. You remember they spoke of another warship they expected to arrive. Yonder it is! It came into port last night, and, in all likelihood, has brought orders for the *Crusader* to sail at once. I only wish it was the *Condor*! I sha'n't sleep soundly till we're safe away from—"

"See!" interrupts Carmen; "is not that a sailor coming this way?"

She points to a man, moving along the shore-road in the direction of the house.

"I think so," responds Don Gregorio, after a glance through the glass. "He appears to be in seaman's dress."

"Would he be coming here?" inquires Carmen, naïvely.

"I shouldn't be surprised; probably with a message from our young friends. It may be the man they recommended to me."

"That's why somebody went ashore in the little boat," whispers Iñez to her aunt. "He's bringing us *billetitas*. I was sure they wouldn't go away without leaving a last little word."

Iñez's speech imparts no information: for Carmen has been surmising in the same strain.

She replies by one of those proverbs, in which the Spanish tongue is so rich:

"*Silencio! hay Moros en la costa*," — (Silence! there are Moors on the coast).

While this bit of by-play is being carried on, the sailor ascends the hill, and is seen entering at the road-gate. There can now be no uncertainty as to his calling. The blue jacket, broad shirt-collar, round-ribboned hat, and bell-bottomed trousers, are all the unmistakable toggery of a tar.

Advancing up the avenue in a rolling gait, with an occasional tack from side to side—that almost fetches him up among the manzanitas—he at length reaches the front of the house. There stopping, and looking up to the roof, he salutes those upon it by removing his hat giving a back-scrape with his foot, and a pluck at one of his brow-locks.

"*Que guieres V., señor?*"—(What is your business, sir?), asks the haciendado, speaking down to him.

Harry Blew—for it is he—replies by holding out a letter, at the same time saying:

"Your honour; I've brought this for the master o' the house."

"I am he. Go in through that door you see below. I'll come down to you."

Don Gregorio descends the *escalera*, and meeting the messenger in the inner court, receives the letter addressed to him.

Breaking it open, he reads:

"Estimable Sir,—Circumstances have arisen that take us away from San Francisco sooner than we expected. The corvette that came into port last night brought orders for the *Crusader* to sail at once; though our destination is the same as already known to you—the Sandwich Islands. As the ship is about to weigh anchor, I have barely time to write a word for myself, and Mr Cadwallader. We think it proper to make known some circumstances which will, no doubt, cause you surprise, as they did ourselves. Yesterday morning we met at your house two gentlemen—as courtesy would then have required me to call them—by name Francisco de Lara and Faustino Calderon. We encountered them at a later hour of the day; when an occurrence took place, which absolved us from either thinking of them as gentlemen, or treating them as such. And still later, after leaving your hospitable roof, we, for the third time, came across the same two individuals, under circumstances showing them to be *professional gamblers!* In fact, we found them to be the proprietors of a monté bank in the notorious 'El Dorado;' one of them actually engaged in dealing the cards! A spirit of fun, with perhaps a spice of mischief, led me into the play, and betting largely, I succeeded in breaking their bank. After that, for a short while we lost sight of them. But as we were making our way to the pier, where our boat was to meet us, we had a fourth interview with these 'gentlemen;' who on this occasion appeared with two others in the character of *robbers* and *assassins!* That they did not succeed in either robbing or murdering us, is due to the brave fellow who will bear this letter to you—the sailor of whom I spoke. He can give you all the particulars of the last, and latest, encounter with the versatile individuals, who claim acquaintance with you. You may rely on his truthfulness. I have no time to say more.

"Hoping to see you in Cadiz, please convey parting compliments to the señoritas—from the Señor Cadwallader and yours faithfully, Edward Crozier."

The letter makes a painful impression on the mind of Don Gregorio. Not that he is much surprised at the information regarding De Lara and Calderon. He has heard sinister reports concerning them; of late so loudly spoken, that he had determined on forbidding them further intercourse with his family. That very day he has been displeased on learning of their ill-timed visit. And now he feels chagrin at something like a reproach conveyed by that expression in Crozier's letter, "The versatile individuals who claim your acquaintance." It hurts his hidalgo pride.

Thrusting the epistle into his pocket, he questions its bearer; taking him into his private room, as also into his confidence.

The sailor gives him a detailed account of the attempt at murder, so accidentally frustrated; afterwards making known other matters relating to himself, and how he has taken service on the Chilian ship—Don Gregorio inquiring particularly about this.

Meanwhile, the young ladies have descended from the azotea, and the ex-man-o'-war's man makes their acquaintance.

They assist in showing him hospitality, loading him with pretty presents, and knick-knacks to be carried on board the *Condor*, to which they know he now belongs.

As he is about to depart, they flutter around him, speaking pleasant words, as if they expected to get something in return—those *billetitas*. For all, he takes departure, without leaving them a scrap!

A pang of disappointment—almost chagrin—shoots through the soul of Carmen, as she sees him passing out of sight. And similarly afflicted is Iñez; both reflecting alike.

Still they have hope; there may be something enclosed for them in that letter they saw him holding up. It seemed large enough to contain two separate notes. And if not these, there should at least be a postscript with special reference to themselves.

Daughters of Eve, they are not long before approaching the subject, and drawing Don Gregorio.

Yes; there is something said about them in the letter. He communicates it:

"Parting compliments to the señoritas!"

Chapter Forty One
The Last Look

"Up anchor!"

The order rings along the deck of the *Crusader*, and the men of the watch stand by the windlass to execute it.

That same morning, Crozier and Cadwallader, turning out of their cots, heard with surprise the order for sending up the "Blue-Peter," as also that the ship was to weigh anchor by twelve o'clock noon. Of course, they were expecting it, but not so soon. However, the arrival of the corvette explains all; an officer from the latter vessel having already come on board the *Crusader* with despatches from the flag-ship of the Pacific Squadron.

These contain orders for the frigate to set sail for the Sandwich Islands without delay; the corvette to replace her on the San Francisco station.

The despatch-bearer has also brought a mail; and the *Crusader's* people get letters—home-news, welcome to those who have been long away from their native land; for she has been three years cruising in the South Sea.

Something more than mere news several of her officers receive. In large envelopes, addressed to them, and bearing the British Admiralty seal, are documents of peculiar interest—commissions giving them promotion.

Among the rest, one reaches Edward Crozier, advancing him a step in rank. His ability as an officer has been reported at headquarters; as also his gallant conduct in having saved a sailor's life—rescued him from drowning—that sailor Harry Blew. In all probability this has obtained him his promotion; but whatever the cause, he will leave San Francisco a *lieutenant*.

There are few officers, naval or military, who would not feel favoured and joyous at such an event in their lives. And so might Edward Crozier at any other time. But it has not this effect now. On the contrary, as the white canvas is being spread above his head, there is a black shadow upon his brow, while that of Cadwallader is alike clouded.

It is not from any regret either feels at leaving California; but leaving it under circumstances that painfully impress them. The occurrences of the day before, but more those of the night, have revealed a state of things that suggest unpleasant reflections, especially to the new-made lieutenant. He cannot cast out of his mind the sinister impression made upon it by the discovery that Don Francisco De Lara—his rival for the hand of Carmen Montijo—is no other than the notorious "Frank Lara," the keeper of a monté table in the saloon "El Dorado!" Now that he knows it, the knowledge afflicts him, to the laceration of his heart. No wonder at the formality of that letter which he addressed to Don Gregorio, or the insinuation conveyed by it. Nor strange the cold compliments with which it was concluded; far stranger had they been warm.

Among other unpleasant thoughts which the young officers have, on being so soon summoned away, is that of leaving matters unsettled with Messrs De Lara and Calderon. Not that they have any longer either design or desire to stand before such cut-throats in a duel, nor any shame in shunning it. Their last encounter with the scoundrels would absolve them from all stigma or reproach for refusing to fight them—even were there time and opportunity. So, they need have no fear that their honour will suffer, or that any one will apply to them the opprobrious epithet—*lâche*. Indeed, they have not, and their only regret is at not being able to spend another hour in San Francisco in order that they might look up the foiled assassins, and give them into the custody of the police. But then that would lead to a difficulty which had better be avoided—the necessity of leaving their ship, and staying to prosecute an action in courts where the guilty criminal is quite as likely to be favoured as the innocent prosecutor. It is not to be thought of, and long before the frigate's anchor is lifted, they cease thinking of it.

Crozier's last act before leaving port is to write the letter to Don Gregorio; Cadwallader's to carry it ashore, and deliver it to Harry Blew. Then, in less than twenty minutes after the returned midshipman sets foot on the frigate's deck, the order is issued for her sails to be sheeted home, the canvas hanging crumpled from her yards is drawn taut, the anchor hauled apeak, and the huge leviathan, obedient to her helm held in strong hands, is brought round, with head towards the Golden Gate.

The wind catches her spread sails, bellies them out, and in five minutes more, with the British flag floating proudly over her taffrail, she passes out of the harbour; leaving many a vessel behind, whose captains, for want of crews, bewail their inability to follow her.

But there are eyes following her, from farther off—beautiful eyes, that express sadness of a different kind, and from a different cause. Carmen Montijo and Iñez Alvarez stand upon the house-top, glasses in hand. Instead, there should have been kerchiefs—white kerchiefs—waving adieu. And there would have been, but for those chilling words: *"Parting compliments to the señoritas."* Strange last words for lovers! *Santissima*! what can it mean?

So reflect they to whom they were sent, as they stand in attentive attitude, watching the warship, and straining their eyes upon her, till rounding Telegraph Hill she disappears from their sight.

A sad cruel shock both have received—a blow almost breaking their hearts.

Equally unhappy are two young officers on the departing ship. They too stand with glasses in hand levelled upon the house of Don Gregorio Montijo. They can see, as once before, two heads over the parapet, and, as before, recognise them; but not as before, or with the same feelings, do they regard them. All is changed now, everything doubtful and indefinite, where it might be supposed everything had been satisfactorily arranged. But it has not—especially in the thoughts of Crozier; whose dissatisfaction is shown in a soliloquy to which he gives utterance, as Telegraph Hill, interfering with his field of view, causes him to take the telescope from his eye.

"Carmen Montijo!" he exclaims, crushing it to its shortest, and returning the instrument to its case. "To think of a 'sport'—a common gambler—even having acquaintance with her—far less presuming to make love to her!"

"More than gamblers—both of them," adds Cadwallader by his side. "Robbers—murderers—anything if they had but the chance."

"Ay, true, Will; everything vile and vulgar. Don't it make you mad to think of it?"

"No, not mad. That isn't the feeling I have; rather fear."

"Fear! Of what!"

"That the scoundrels may do some harm to our dear girls. As we know now, they're up to anything. Since they don't stick at assassination, they won't at abduction. I hope your letter to Don Gregorio may open his eyes about them, and put him on his guard. My Iñez! who's to protect her? I'd give all I have in the world to be sure of her getting safely embarked in that Chilian ship. Once there, dear old Harry Blew will take care of her—of them both."

Cadwallader's words seem strangely to affect his companion, changing the expression upon his countenance. It is still shadowed, but the cloud is of a different kind. From anger it has altered to anxiety!

"You've struck a chord, Will, that, while not soothing the old pain, gives me a new one. I wasn't thinking of that; my thoughts were all occupied with the other trouble—you understand?"

"I do. At the same, I think you make too much of the other trouble, as you call it. I confess it troubles me too a little; though, perhaps, not as it does you. And luckily less, the more I reflect on it. After all, there don't seem so much to be bothered about. As you know, Ned, it's a common thing among Spanish-Americans, whose customs are altogether unlike our own—to have gamblers going into their best society. Besides, I can tell you something that may comfort you a little—a bit of information I had from Iñez, as we were *platicando* along the road on our ride. It was natural she should speak about the sky-blue fellow and my sticking his horse in the hip."

"What did she say?" asks Crozier, with newly awakened interest.

"That he was a gentleman by birth; but falling fast, and indeed quite down."

"And De Lara; did she say aught of him?"

"She did; she spoke of him still more disparagingly, though knowing him less. She said he had been introduced to them by the other, and they were accustomed to meet him on occasions. But of late they had learned more of him; and learning this, her aunt—your Carmen—had become very desirous of cutting his acquaintance, as indeed all of them. And that they intended doing so—even if they had remained in California. But now—so soon leaving it, they did not like to humiliate De Lara by giving him the *congé* he deserves."

Crozier, with eyes earnestly fixed upon Cadwallader, has listened to the explanation. At its close he cries out, grasping his comrade's hand:

"Will! you've lifted a load from my heart. I now see daylight where all seemed darkness; and beholding yonder hill feel the truth of Campbell's splendid lines:—

"A kiss can consecrate the ground,
    Where mated hearts are mutual bound;
The spot, where love's first links are wound,
        That ne'er are riven,
    Is hallowed down to Earth's profound,
        And up to Heaven!"

After repeating the passionate words, he stands gazing on a spot so consecrated to him—the summit of the hill—where, just twenty-four hours ago, he spoke love's last appeal to Carmen Montijo. For the *Crusader* has passed out through the Golden Gate, and is now beating down the coast of the Pacific.

Cadwallader's eyes, with equal interest, are turned upon the same spot, and for a time both are silent, absorbed in sweet reflections; recalling all that had occurred in a scene whose slightest incident neither can ever forgot.

Only when the land looms low, and the outlines of the San Bruno Mountains begin to blend with the purpling sky, does a shadow again show itself on the countenances of the young officers. But now it is different, no longer expressing chagrin, nor the rancour of jealousy; but doubt, apprehension, fear, for the loved ones left behind. Still the cloud has a silver lining, and that is—Harry Blew.

Chapter Forty Two
A Solemn Compact

A Cottage of the old Californian kind—in other words, a *rancho*; one of the humblest of these humble dwellings—the homes of the Spanish-American poor. It is a mere hut, thatched with a species of sea-shore grass, the "broombent" seen growing in the sand-dunes near by. For it is by the sea, or within sight of it; inconspicuously placed by reason of rugged rocks, that cluster around, and soar up behind, forming a background in keeping with the rude architectural style of the dwelling. From the land side it is only approachable by devious and difficult paths, known but to a few familiar friends of its owner.

From the shore, equally difficult, for the little cove leading up to it would not have depth sufficient to permit the passage of a boat, but for a tiny stream trickling seaward, which has furrowed out a channel in the sand. That by this boats can enter the cove is evident from one being seen moored near its inner end, in front of, and not far from, the hovel. As it is a craft of the kind generally used by Californian fishermen—more especially those who chase the fur-seal—it may be deduced that the owner of the hut is a seal-hunter.

This is his profession reputedly; though there are some who ascribe to him callings of a different kind; among others, insinuating that he occasionally does business as a *contrabandista*.

Whether true or not, Rafael Rocas—for he is the owner of the hut—is not the man to trouble himself about denying it. He would scarce consider smuggling an aspersion on his character; and indeed, under old Mexican administration, it would have been but slight blame, or shame, to him. And not such a great deal either under the new, at the time of which we write, but perhaps still less. Compared with other crimes then rife in California, contrabandism might almost be reckoned an honest calling.

But Rafael Rocas has a repute for doings of a yet darker kind. With those slightly acquainted with him it is only suspicion; but a few of his more intimate associates can say for certain that he is not disinclined to a stroke of road robbery or a job at housebreaking; so that, if times have changed for the worse, he has not needed any change to keep pace with them.

It is the day on which the British frigate sailed from San Francisco Bay, and he is in his hut; not alone, but in the company of three men, in personal appearance altogether unlike himself. While he wears the common garb of a Californian fisherman—loose pea-coat of coarse canvas, rough water-boots, and seal-skin cap—they are attired in costly stuffs—cloaks of finest broadcloth, *jaquetas* of rich velvet, and *cahoneras*, lashed with gold lace, and gleaming with constellations of buttons.

Notwithstanding their showy magnificence, the seal-hunter, smuggler, or whatever he may be, does not appear to treat his guests with any obsequious deference. On the contrary, he is engaged with them in familiar converse, and by his tone and gestures, showing that he feels himself their equal.

Two of the individuals thus oddly consorting are already well known to the reader—the third but slightly. The former are Francisco de Lara and Faustino Calderon; the latter is Don Manuel Diaz, famed for his fighting cocks. The first two have just entered under Rocas' roof, finding the cockfighter already there, as De Lara predicted.

After welcoming his newly arrived guests in Spanish-American fashion, placing his house at their disposal—*"Mia casa a la disposition de Vms,"*— the seal-hunter has set before them a bottle of his best liquor—this being *aguardiente* of Tequila. They have taken off their outer apparel—cloaks and hats—and are seated around a small deal table, the only one the shanty contains—its furniture being of the scantiest and most primitive kind.

Some conversation of a desultory nature has passed between them; but they have now entered on a subject more interesting and particular, the keynote having been struck by De Lara. He opens by asking a question:

"Caballeros! do you want to be rich?"

All three laugh, while simultaneously answering:

"Carramba! Yes."

Diaz adds:

"I've heard many an idle interrogatory; but never, in all my life, one so superfluous as yours; not even when there's twenty to one offered against a staggering cock."

Rocas inquires:

"What do ye call rich, Don Francisco?"

"Well," responds the Creole, "say sixty thousand dollars. I suppose you'd consider that sufficient to bestow the title?"

"Certainly," rejoins Rocas; "not only the title, but the substantial and real thing. If I'd only the half of it, I'd give up chasing seals."

"And I cock fighting," put in Diaz; "that is, so far as to look to it for a living; though I might still incline to have a main for pastime's sake. With sixty thousand dollars at my back, I'd go for being a grand ganadero, like friend Faustino here, whose horses and horned cattle yield him such a handsome income."

The other three laugh at this, since it is known to all of them that the ganadero has long since got rid both of his horses and horned cattle.

"Well, gentlemen," says De Lara, after this bit of preliminary skirmishing, "I can promise each of you the sum I speak of, if you're willing to go in with me in a little affair I've fixed upon. Are you the men for it?"

"Your second question is more sensible than the first, though equally uncalled for—at least so far as concerns me. I'm the man to go in for anything which promises to make me the owner of sixty thousand dollars."

It is Diaz who thus unconditionally declares himself Calderon endorses it by a declaration of like daring nature. The seal-hunter simply nods assent, but in a knowing manner. For he is already acquainted with De Lara's design; knows all about it; being, in fact, its real originator.

"Now, Don Francisco! let's know what you're driving at?" demands Diaz, adding: "Have you struck a *veta*, or discovered a rich *placer*? If so, we're ready for either rock-mining or pan-washing, so long as the labour's not too hard. Speak out, and tell us what it is. The thought of clutching such a pretty prize makes a man impatient."

"Well, I'll let you into the secret so far—it is a *veta*—a grand gold mine—a very *bonanza*—but one which will need neither rock-crushing nor mud-cradling. The gold has been already gathered; and lies in a certain place, all in a lump; only waiting transport to some other place, which we can select at our leisure."

"Your words sound well," remarks Don Manuel.

"Wonderful well," echoes Rocas, with assumed surprise.

"Are they not too good to be true?" asks Diaz.

"No. They're true as good. Not a bit of exaggeration, I assure you. The gold only wants to be got at, and then taken."

"Ah! there may be difficulty about that?" rejoins the doubting Diaz.

"Do you expect to finger sixty thousand *pesos* without taking the trouble to stretch out your hand?"

"Oh, no. I'm not so unreasonable. For that I'd be willing to stretch out both hands, with a knife in one, and a pistol in the other."

"Well, it's not likely to need either, if skilfully managed. I ask you again, are you the men to go in for it?"

"I'm one," answers Diaz.

"And I another," growls Rocas.

"I'm not going to say nay," assents Calderon, glancing significantly at the questioner.

"Enough!" exclaims De Lara; "so far you all consent to the partnership. But before entering fully into it, it will be necessary to have a more thorough understanding, as also a more formal one. Are you willing to be bound, that there shall be truth between us?"

"We are!" is the simultaneous response of all three.

"And fidelity to the death!"

"To the death."

"*Bueno*! But we must take an oath to that effect. After which, you shall know what it's for. Enough now to say it's a thing that needs swearing upon. If there's to be treason, there shall be perjury also. Are you ready to take the oath?"

They signify assent unanimously.

"To your feet, then!" commands the chief conspirator. "It will be more seemly to take it standing."

All four spring up from their chairs, and stand facing the table.

De Lara draws a dagger and lays it down before him. The others have their stilettos too—a weapon carried by most Spanish Californians.

Each exhibits his own, laying it beside that already on the table.

With the four De Lara forms a cross—Maltese fashion, and then standing erect, Diaz opposite, Rocas and Calderon on either flank—he repeats in firm, solemn voice, the others after him

"In the deed we this day agree to do, acting together and jointly, we swear to be true to each other—to stand by one another, if need be, to the death; to keep what we do a secret from all the world; and if any one betray it, the other three swear to follow him wherever he may flee, seek him wherever he may shelter himself, and take vengeance upon him, by taking his life. If any of us fail in this oath, may we be accursed ever after. Amen!"

Chapter Forty Three
The "Bonanza"

The infamous ceremony duly ratified, a drink of the fiery spirit of the *mescal* plant—a fit finale—is quaffed. Then they take up their stilettos, replace them in their sheaths, and again sitting down, listen to De Lara, to learn from him the nature of that deed, for doing which they have so solemnly compacted.

In a short time he makes it known, the disclosure calling for but a few words. It is after all but a common affair, though one that needs skill and courage. Simply a "bit of burglary," but a big thing of its kind. He tells them of three hundred thousand dollars' worth of gold-dust lying in a lone country-house, with no other protection than that of its owner, with some half-dozen Indian domestics.

There are but two of them to whom this is news—Diaz and Calderon. Rocas smiles while the revelation is being made; for he has been the original discoverer of the so-called "bonanza." It was that he communicated to De Lara, when, on the day before, he stopped him and Calderon at the *tinacal* of Dolores.

It is not the first time for the seal-hunter to do business of a similar kind in conjunction with the gambler; who, like himself, has been accustomed to vary his professional pursuits. But, as now, he has always acted under De Lara—whose clear, cool head and daring hand assure him leadership in any scheme requiring superior courage, with intelligence for its execution.

"How soon?" asks Diaz, after all has been declared. "I should say the sooner the better."

"You're right about that, Don Manuel," rejoins Rocas.

"True," assents De Lara. "At the same time caution must not be lost sight of. There's two of you aware of what danger we'd be in, if just now we went near the town, or anywhere outside this snug little asylum of Señor Rocas—whose hospitality we may have to trench upon for some time. I don't know, Don Rafael, whether friend Diaz has told you of what happened last night?"

"He's given me a hint of it," replies the smuggler.

"Oh, yes," puts in Diaz; "I thought he might as well know."

"Of course," agrees De Lara. "In that case, then, I've only to add, that there will be no safety for us in San Francisco, so long as the English man-o'-war stays in port. He who broke our bank is rich enough to buy law, and can set its hounds after us by night, or by day. Until he and his ship are gone—"

"The ship *is* gone," says Rocas, interrupting.

"Ha! What makes you say that?"

"Because I know it."

"How?"

"Simply by having seen her. Nothing like the eyes to give one assurance about anything—with a bit of glass to assist them. Through that thing up there,"—he points to an old telescope resting on hooks against the wall—"I saw the English frigate beating out by the Farrallones, when I was up on the cliff about an hour ago. I knew her from having seen her lying in the bay. She's gone to sea for sure."

At this the others looked surprised as well as pleased; more especially Calderon. He need no longer fear encountering the much-dreaded midshipman either in a duel or with his dirk.

"It's very strange," says De Lara. "I'd heard she was to sail soon, but not till another ship came to relieve her."

"That ship has come," returns Rocas—"a corvette. I saw her working up the coast last evening just before sunset. She was making for the Gate, and must be inside now."

"If all this be true," says the chief conspirator, "we need lose no more time, but put on our masks and bring the affair off at once. It's too late for doing anything to-night; but there's no reason why we shouldn't act to-morrow night, if it prove a dark one. We four of us will be strength enough for such a trifling affair. I thought of bringing Juan Lopez, our croupier; but I saw he wouldn't be needed. Besides, from the way he's been behaving lately I've lost confidence in him. Another reason for leaving him out will be understood by all of you. In a matter of this kind it *isn't* the more the merrier, though it *is* the fewer the better cheer. The yellow dust will go farther among four than five."

"It will," exclaims the cockfighter with emphasis, showing his satisfaction at what De Lara has done. He adds: "To-morrow night, then, we are to act?"

"Yes, if it be a dark one. If not, 'twill be wiser to let things lie over for the next. A day can't make much difference; while the colour of the night may. A moonlit sky, or a clear starry one, might get us all where we'd see stars without any being visible—through a noose round our neck?"

"There'll be no moon to-morrow night," puts in the smuggler, who, in this branch of his varied vocations, has been accustomed to take account of such things. "At least," he adds, "none that will do us any harm. The fog's sure to be on before midnight; at this time of year, it always is. To-morrow night will be like the last—black as a pot of pitch."

"True," says De Lara, as a man with some experience of the sea, also having meteorological knowledge. "No doubt, 'twill be as you say, Rocas. In that case we'll have nothing to fear. We can get the job done, and be back here before morning. Ah, then seated round the table, we'll not be like we are now—poor as rats; but every one with his pile before him—sixty thousand *pesos*."

"*Carramba!*" exclaims Diaz, in a mocking tone, "while saying vespers to-night, let's put in a special prayer for to-morrow night to be what Rocas says it will—black as a pot of pitch."

The profane suggestion is hailed with a burst of ribald laughter; after which they set about preparing the *mascaras*, and other disguises, to be used in their nefarious enterprise.

Chapter Forty Four
"Ambre La Puerta!"

Another sun has shone upon San Francisco Bay, and again gone down in red gleam over the far-spreading Pacific, leaving the sky of a leaden colour, moonless and starless.

As the hour of midnight approaches it assumes the hue predicted by Rocas, and desired by Diaz. For the ocean fog has again rolled shoreward across the peninsula, and shrouds San Francisco as with a pall. The adjacent country is covered with its funereal curtain, embracing within its folds the house of Don Gregorio Montijo.

The inmates seem all asleep, as at this hour they should. No light is seen through the windows, nor any sound heard within the walls. Not even the baying of a watch-dog, the bellow of a stalled ox, or the stamping of a horse in the stables. Inside, as without, all is silence.

The profound silence seems strange, though favourable, to four men not far from the place, and gradually, but with slow steps, drawing nearer to it. For they are approaching by stealth, as can be told by their attitudes and gestures. They advance crouchingly, now and then stopping to take a survey of the *terrain* in front, as they do so exchanging whispered words with one another.

Through the hazy atmosphere their figures show weird-like—all the more from their grotesque gesticulations. Even if scrutinised closely, and in clearest light, they would present this appearance; for although in human shape, and wearing the garb of men, their faces more resemble those of demons. They are human countenances, nevertheless, but *en-mascaradas*.

Nothing more is needed to tell who, and what they are, with their purpose in thus approaching Don Gregorio's house. They are burglars, designing to break into it.

It needs not the removal of their masks to identify them as the four conspirators left plotting in the rancho of Rafael Rocas.

They are now *en route* for putting their scheme into execution.

It would look as if Don Gregorio were never to get his gold to Panama—much less have it transported to Spain.

And his daughter! What of her, with Francisco de Lara drawing nigh as one of the nocturnal ravagers? His grand-daughter, too, Faustino Calderon being another?

One cognisant of the existing relations, and spectator of what is passing now—seeing the craped robbers as they steal on towards the house—would suppose it in danger of being doubly despoiled, and that its owner is to suffer desolation, not only in fortune, but in that far dearer to him—his family.

The burglars are approaching from the front, up the avenue, though not on it. They keep along its edge among the manzanita bushes. These, with the fog, afford sufficient screen to prevent their being observed from the house—even though sentinels were set upon its azotea. But there appears to be none; no eye to see, no voice to give warning, not even the bark of a watch, dog to wake those unconsciously slumbering within.

As already said, there is something strange in this. On a large grazing estate it is rare for the Molossian to be silent. More usually his sonorous voice is heard throughout the night, or at brief intervals.

Though anything but desirous to hear the barking of dogs, the burglars are themselves puzzled at the universal silence, so long continued. For before entering the enclosure they have been lying concealed in a thicket outside, their horses tied to trees, where they have now left them, and during all the time not a sound had reached their ears; no voice either of man or animal! They are now within sight of the house, its massive front looming large and dark through the mist—still no stir outside, and within the stillness of death itself!

Along with astonishment, a sense of awe is felt by one of the four criminals—Calderon, who has still some lingering reluctance as to the deed about to be done—or it may be but fear. The other three are too strong in courage, and too hardened in crime, for scruples of any kind.

Arriving at the end of the avenue, and within a short distance of the dwelling, they stop for a final consultation, still under cover of the manzanitas.

All silent as ever; no one stirring; no light from any window; the shutters closed behind the *rejas*—the great *puerta* as well!

"Now, about getting inside," says De Lara; "what will be our best way?"

"In my opinion," answers Diaz, "we'll do best by climbing up to the *azotea*, and over it into the *patio*."

"Where's your ladder?" asks Rocas, in his gruff, blunt way.

"We must find one, or something that'll serve instead. There should be loose timber lying about the *corrals*—enough to provide us with a climbing-pole."

"And while searching for it, wake up some of the *vaqueros*. That won't do."

"Then what do you propose, Rafael?" interrogates the chief conspirator.

The seal-hunter, from a presumed acquaintance with housebreaking, is listened to with attention.

"Walk straight up to the door," he answers; "knock, and ask to be admitted."

"Ay; and have a blunderbuss fired at us, with a shower of bullets big as billiard balls. *Carrai!*"

It is Calderon who speaks thus apprehensively.

"Not the least danger of that," rejoins Rocas. "Take my word, we'll be let in."

"Why do you think so?"

"Why? Because we have a claim on the hospitality of the house."

"I don't understand you, Rocas," says De Lara.

"Haven't we a good story to tell—simple, and to the purpose?"

"Still I don't understand. Explain yourself, Rafael."

"Don't we come as messengers from the man-o'-war—from those officers you've been telling me about?"

"Ah! now I perceive your drift."

"One can so announce himself, while the others keep out of sight. He can say he's been sent by the young gentlemen on an errand to Don Gregorio, or the señoritas, if you like. Something of importance affecting their departure. True, by this they'll know the ship's weighed anchor. No matter; the story of a message will stand good all the same."

"Rafael Rocas!" exclaims De Lara, "you're a born genius. Instead of being forced to do a little smuggling now and then, you ought to be made *administrator-general of customs*. We shall act as you advise. No doubt the door will be opened. When it is, one can take charge of the janitor. He's a sexagenarian, and won't be hard to hold. If he struggle, let him be silenced. The rest of us can go ransacking. You, Calderon, are acquainted with the interior, and, as you say, know the room where Don Gregorio is most likely to keep his chest. You must lead us straight for that."

"But, Francisco," whispers Calderon in the ear of his confederate, after drawing him a little apart from the other two; "about the *niñas*? You don't intend anything with them?"

"Certainly not—not to-night; nor in this fashion. I hope being able to approach *them* in gentler guise, and more becoming time. When they're without a *peso* in the world, they'll be less proud; and may be contented to stay a little longer in California. To-night we've enough on our hands without thinking of women. One thing at a time—their money first— themselves afterwards."

"But suppose they should recognise us?"

"They can't. Disguised as we are, I defy a man's mother to know him. If they did, then—"

"Then what?"

"No use reflecting what. Don't be so scared, man! If I'd anticipated any chance of its coming to extremes of the kind you're pondering upon, I wouldn't be here prepared for only half measures. Perhaps we sha'n't even wake the ladies up; and if we do, there's not the slightest danger of our being known. So make your mind easy, and let's get through with it. See! Diaz and Rocas are getting impatient! We must rejoin them, and proceed to business at once."

The four housebreakers again set their heads together; and after a few whispered words, to settle all particulars about their plan of proceeding, advance towards the door.

Once up to it, they stand close in, concealed by its o'ershadowing arch.

With the butt of his pistol, De Lara knocks.

Diaz, unknown to the family, and therefore without fear of his voice being recognised, is to do the talking.

No one answers the knock; and it is repeated. Louder, and still louder.

The sexagenarian janitor sleeps soundly to-night, thinks De Lara, deeming it strange.

Another "rat-at-tat" with the pistol-butt, followed by the usual formulary:

"*Ambre la puerta!*"

At length comes a response from within; but not the customary "*Quen es?*" nor anything in Spanish. On the contrary, the speech which salutes the ears of those seeking admission is in a different tongue, and tone altogether unlike that of a native Californian.

"Who the old scratch are ye?" asks a voice from inside, while a heavy footstep is heard coming along the *saguan*. Before the startled burglars can shape a reply, the voice continues:

"Damn ye! What d'ye want anyhow—wakin' a fellur out o' his sleep at this time o' the night? 'Twould sarve ye right if I sent a bullet through the door at ye. Take care what you're about. I've got my shootin'-iron handy; a Colt's revolver—biggest size at thet."

"*Por Dios!* what does this mean?" mutters De Lara.

"Tell him, Diaz," he adds, in *sotto-voce* to the cockfighter—"tell him we're from the British man-o'-war with—*Carrai!* I forgot, you don't speak English. I must do it myself. *He* won't know who it is." Then raising his voice: "We want to see Don Gregorio Montijo. We bring a message from the British man-o'-war—from the two officers."

"Consarn the British man-o'-war!" interrupts the surly speaker inside; "an' yur message, an' yur two officers, I know nothin' 'bout them. As for Don Gregorio, if ye want to get sight on him, ye're a preeshus way wide o' the mark. He ain't here any more. He's gin up the house, an' tuk everything o' hisn out o't this mornin'. I'm only hyar in charge o' the place. Guess you'll find both the Don an' his darters at the *Parker*—the most likeliest place to tree thet lot."

Don Gregorio gone!—his gold—his girls! Only an empty house, in charge of a caretaker, who carries a Colt's repeating pistol, biggest size, and would use it on the smallest provocation!

No good their going inside now, but a deal of danger. Anything but pleasant medicine would be a pill from that six-shooter.

"*Carramba! Caraio! Chingara! Maldita!*"

Such are the wild exclamations that issue from the lips of the disappointed housebreakers, as they turn away from the dismantled dwelling, and hasten to regain their horses.

Chapter Forty Five
A Scratch Crew

It was a fortunate inspiration that led the ex-haciendado to have his gold secretly carried on board the Chilian ship; another, that influenced him to transfer his family, and household gods, to an hotel in the town.

It was all done in a day—that same day. Every hour, after the sailing of the *Crusader*, had he become more anxious; for every hour brought intelligence of some new act of outlawry in the neighbourhood, impressing him with the insecurity, not only of his Penates, but the lives of himself and his ladies. So long as the British ship lay in port, it seemed a protection to him; and although this may have been but fancy, it served somewhat to tranquillise his fears. Soon as she was gone, he gave way to them, summoned Silvestre, with a numerous retinue of *cargadores*, and swept the house clean of everything he intended taking—the furniture alone being left, as part of the purchased effects.

He has indeed reason to congratulate himself on his rapid removal, as he finds on the following day, when visiting his old home for some trifling purpose, and there hearing what had happened during the night.

The man in charge—a stalwart American, armed to the teeth—gives him a full account of the nocturnal visitors. There were four, he says—having counted them through the keyhole—inquiring for him, Don Gregorio. They appeared greatly disappointed at not getting an interview with him; and went off uttering adjurations in Spanish, though having held their parley in English.

A message from the British man-of-war! And brought by men who swore in Spanish! Strange all that, thinks Don Gregorio, knowing the *Crusader* should then be at least a hundred leagues off at sea.

Besides, the messengers have not presented themselves at the *Parker House*, to which the caretaker had directed them.

"What can it mean?" asks the ex-haciendado of himself.

Perhaps the sailor who is now first officer of the Chilian ship may know something of it; and he will question him next time he goes aboard.

He has, however, little hope of being enlightened in that quarter; his suspicions turning elsewhere. He cannot help connecting Messrs De Lara and Calderon with the occurrence. Crozier's letter, coupled with the further information received from the bearer of it, has thrown such a light on the character of these two *enhalleros*, he can believe them capable of anything. After their attempt to rob the young officers, and murder them as well, they would not hesitate to serve others the same; and the demand for admission to his house may have been made by these very men, with a couple of confederates—their design to plunder it, if not do something worse.

Thus reflecting, he is thankful for having so unconsciously foiled them—indeed, deeming it a Providence.

Still is he all the more solicitous to leave a land beset with such dangers. Even in the town he does not feel safe. Robbers and murderers walk boldly abroad through the streets; not alone, but in the company of judges who have tried without condemning them; while lesser criminals stand by drinking-bars, hobnobbing with the constables who either hold them in charge, or have just released them, after a mock-hearing before some magistrate, with eyes blind as those of Justice herself—blinded by the gold-dust of California!

Notwithstanding all this, Don Gregorio need have no fear for his ladies. Their sojourn at the hotel may be somewhat irksome, and uncongenial; still they are safe. Rough-looking and boisterous as are some of their fellow-guests, they are yet in no way rude. The most refined or sensitive lady need not fear moving in their midst. A word or gesture of insult to her would call forth instant chastisement.

It is not on their account he continues anxious, but because of his unprotected treasure. Though secreted aboard the *Condor*, it is still unsafe. Should its whereabouts get whispered abroad, there are robbers bold enough, not only to take it from the Chilian skipper, but set fire to his ship, himself in her, and cover their crime by burning everything up.

Aware of all this, the ex-haciendado, with the help of friendly Silvestre, has half-a-dozen trusty men placed aboard of her—there to stay till a crew can be engaged. It is a costly matter, but money may save money, and now is not the time to cavil at expenses.

As yet, not a sailor has presented himself. None seem caring to ship "for Valparaiso and intermediate ports," even at the double wages offered in the *Diario*. The *Condor's* forecastle remains untenanted, except by the six longshore men, who temporarily occupy it, without exactly knowing why they are there; but contented to make no inquiry, so long as they are receiving their ten dollars a day. Of crew, there is only the captain himself, his first officer, and the cook. The orangs do not count.

Day by day, Don Gregorio grows more impatient, and is in constant communication with Silvestre.

"Offer higher wages," he says. "Engage sailors at any price."

The shipping-agent yields assent; inserts a second *aviso* in the Spanish paper, addressed to *marineros* of all nations. Triple wages to those who will take service on a well-appointed ship. In addition, all the usual allowances, the best of grub and grog. Surely this should get the *Condor* a crew.

And at length it does. Within twenty-four hours after the advertisement has appeared, sailors begin to show on her decks. They come singly, or in twos and threes; and keep coming till as many as half-a-score have presented themselves. They belong to different nationalities, speaking several tongues—among them English, French, and Danish. But the majority appear to be Spaniards, or Spanish-Americans—as might have been expected from the *Condor* being a Chilian ship.

Among them is the usual variety of facial expression; though, in one respect, a wonderful uniformity. Scarce a man of them whose countenance is not in some way unprepossessing—either naturally of sinister cast, or brought to it by a career of sinful dissipation. Several of them show signs of having been recently drinking—with eyes bleary and bloodshot. Of strife, too, its souvenirs visible in other eyes that are blackened, and scars upon cheeks not yet cicatrised. Some are still in a state of inebriety, and stagger as they stray about the decks.

Under any other circumstances, such sailors would stand no chance of getting shipped. As it is, they are accepted—not one refused. Captain Lantanas has no choice, and knows it. Without them he is helpless, and it would be hopeless for him to think of putting to sea. If he do not take them, the *Candour* may swing idly at her anchor for weeks, it might be months.

Quick as they came aboard, he enters their names on the ship's books, while Harry Blew assigns them their separate bunks in the forepeak. One, a Spaniard, by name Padilla, shows credentials from some former ship, which procure him the berth of *piloto-segundo* (second mate).

After the ten had been taken, no more present themselves. Even the big bounty offered does not tempt another tar from the saloons of San Francisco. In any other seaport, it would empty every sailors' boarding-house, to its last lodger.

And ten hands are not enough to work the good ship *Condor*.

Her captain knows it, and waits another day, hoping he may get a few more to complete her complement; but hopes in vain, the supply seems exhausted.

Becoming convinced of this, he determines to set sail with such crew as he has secured. But little more remains to be done; some stores to be shipped, provisions for the voyage, the best and freshest San Francisco can afford. For he who authorises their inlay cares not for the cost—only that things may be made comfortable. Don Gregorio gives *carte-blanche* for providing the vessel; and it is done according to his directions.

At length everything is ready, and the *Condor* only awaits her passengers. Her cabin has been handsomely furnished; its best state-room decorated to receive two ladies, fair as ever set foot on board ship.

Chapter Forty Six
"Adios California!"

A bright sun rises over San Francisco, in all likelihood the last Don Gregorio Montijo will ever witness in California. For just as the orb of day shows its disc above the dome-shaped *silhouette* of Monte Diablo, flinging its golden shimmer across the bay, a boat leaves the town-pier, bearing him and his towards the Chilian vessel, whose signals for sailing are out.

Others are in the boat; a large party of ladies and gentlemen, who accompany them to do a last handshaking on board. For, in quitting California, the ex-haciendado leaves many friends behind; among them, some who will pass sleepless hours thinking of Carmen Montijo; and others whose hearts will be sore as their thoughts turn to Iñez Alvarez.

It may be that none of those are present now; and better for them if not; since the most painful of all partings is that where the lover sees his sweetheart sail away, with the knowledge she cares neither to stay, nor come back.

The young ladies going off show but little sign of regret at leaving. They are hindered by remembrance of the last words spoken at another parting, now painfully recalled: "*Hasta Cadiz!*" The thought of that takes the sting out of this.

The boat reaches the ship, and swinging around, lies alongside.

Captain Lantanas stands by the gangway to receive his passengers, with their friends; while his first officer helps them up the man-ropes.

Among the ladies, Harry Blew distinguishes the two he is to have charge of, and with them is specially careful. As their soft-gloved fingers rest in his rough horny hand, he mentally registers a vow that it shall never fail them in the hour of need—if such there ever be.

On the cabin-table is spread a refection of the best; and around it the leave-takers assemble, the Chilian skipper doing the honours of his ship. And gracefully, for he is a gentleman.

Half-an-hour of merry-making, light chatter, enlivened by the popping of corks, and clinking of glasses; then ten minutes of converse more serious;

after which hurried graspings of the hand and a general scattering towards the shore-boat, which soon after moves off amid exclamations of "*Adios!*" and "*Bueno viage!*" accompanied by the waving of hands, and white slender fingers saluting with tremulous motion—like the quiver of a kestrel's wing—the fashion of the Spanish-american fair.

While the boat is being rowed back to the shore, the *Condor* puts out her canvas, and stands away towards the Golden Gate.

She is soon out of sight of the port; having entered the strait which gives access to the great land-locked estuary. But a wind blowing in from the west hinders her; and she is all the day tacking through the eight miles of narrow water which connects San Francisco Bay with the Pacific.

The sun is nigh set as she passes the old Spanish fort and opens view of the outside ocean. But the heavenly orb that rose over Mont Diablo like a globe of gold goes down beyond 'Los Farrallones' more resembling a ball of fire about to be quenched hissing in the sea.

It is still only half-immersed behind the blue expanse, when, gliding out from the portals of the Golden Gate, the *Condor* rounds Seal Rock, and stands on her course West-South-West.

The wind shifts, the evening breeze begins to blow steadily from the land. This is favourable; and after tacks have been set, and sails sheeted home, there is but little work to be done.

It is the hour of the second dog-watch, and the sailors are all on deck, grouped about the fore hatch, and gleefully conversing. Here and there an odd individual stands by the side, with eyes turned shoreward, taking a last look at the land. Not as if he regretted leaving it, but is rather glad to get away. More than one of that crew have reason to feel thankful that the Chilian craft is carrying them from a country, where, had they stayed much longer, it would have been to find lodgment in a jail. Out at sea, their faces seem no better favoured than when they first stepped aboard. Scarce recovered from their shore carousing, they show swollen cheeks, and eyes inflamed with alcohol; countenances from which the breeze of the Pacific, however pure, cannot remove that sinister cast.

At sight of them, and the two fair creatures sailing in the same ship, a thought about the incongruity—as also the insecurity of such companionship—cannot help coming uppermost. It is like two beautiful birds of Paradise shut up in the same cage with wolves, tigers, and hyenas.

But the birds of Paradise are not troubling themselves about this, or anything else in the ship. Lingering abaft the binnacle, with their hands resting on the taffrail, they look back at the land, their eyes fixed upon the summit of a hill, ere long to become lost to their view by the setting of the sun. They have been standing so for some time in silence, when Iñez says:

"I can tell what you're thinking of, *tia*."

"Indeed, can you? Well, let me hear it."

"You're saying to yourself: 'What a beautiful hill that is yonder; and how I should like to be once more upon its top—not alone, but with somebody beside me.' Now, tell the truth, isn't that it?"

"Those are your own thoughts, *sobrina*."

"I admit it, and also that they are pleasant. So are yours; are they not?"

"Only in part. I have others, which I suppose you can share with me."

"What others?"

"Reflections not at all agreeable, but quite the contrary."

"Again distressing yourself about that! It don't give me the slightest concern; and didn't from the first."

"No?"

"No!"

"Well; I must say you take things easily—which I don't. A lover—engaged, too—to go away in that *sans façon* way! Not so much as a note, nor even a verbal message. *Santissima*! it was something more than rude—it was cruel; and I can't help thinking so."

"But there was a message in the letter to grandpapa, for both of us. What more would you wish?"

"Pff! who cares for parting compliments? A *lepero* would send better to his sweetheart in sleeveless *camisa*. That's not the message for me."

"How can you tell there wasn't some other which has miscarried? I'm almost sure there has been; else why should somebody have knocked at the door an' said so. The Americano left in charge of the house has told grandpa something about four men having come there the night after we left it. One may have been this messenger we've missed—the others going with him for company. And through his neglect we've not got letters intended for us. Or, if they haven't written, it's because they were pressed for time. However, we shall know when we meet them at Cadiz."

"Ah! when we meet them there, I'll demand an explanation from Eduardo. That shall I, and get it—or know the reason why."

"He will have a good one, I warrant. There's been a miscarriage, somehow. For hasn't there been mystery all round? Luckily, no fighting, as we feared, and have reason to rejoice. Neither anything seen or heard of your California!! chivalry! That's the strangest thing of all."

"It is indeed strange," rejoins Carmen, showing emotion; "I wonder what became of them. Nobody that we know has met either after that day; nor yet heard word of them."

"Carmen, I believe one *has* heard of them."

"Who?"

"Your father."

"What makes you think so, Iñez!"

"Some words I overheard, while he was conversing with the English sailor who's now in the ship with us. I'm almost certain there was something in Mr Crozier's letter relating to De Lara and Calderon. What it was, grandpa seems desirous of keeping to himself; else he would have told us. We must endeavour to find it out from the sailor."

"You're a cunning schemer, *sobrina*. I should never have thought of that. We shall try. Now I remember, Eduardo once saved this man's life. Wasn't it a noble, daring deed? For all, I'm very angry with him, leaving me as he has done; and sha'n't be pacified until I see him on his knees, and he apologise for it. That he shall do at Cadiz!"

"To confess the truth, *tia*, I was a little spited myself at first. On reflection, I feel sure there's been some mischance, and we've been wronging them both. I sha'n't blame my darling till I see him again. Then if he can't clear himself, oh, won't I!"

"You forgive too easily. I can't."

"Yes, you can. Look at yonder hill. Recall the pleasant hour passed upon it, and you will be lenient, as I am."

Carmen obeys, and again turns her glance toward the spot consecrated by sweetest remembrances.

As she continues to gaze at it, the cloud lifts from her brow, replaced by a smile, and promises easy pardon to him who has offended her.

In silence the two stand, straining their eyes upon the far summit, till shore and sea become one—both blending into the purple of twilight.

"*Adios, California!*"

Land no longer in sight. The ship is *au large* on the ocean.

Chapter Forty Seven
A Tattoo that needs Retouching

The great Pacific current in many respects resembles the Gulf Stream of the Atlantic. Passing eastward under the Aleutian Archipelago, it impinges upon the American continent by Vancouver's Island; thence setting southward, along the Californian coast, curves round horseshoe shape, and sets back for the central part of the South Sea, sweeping on past the Sandwich Isles.

By this disposition, a ship bound from San Francisco for Honolulu has the flow in her favour; and if the wind be also favourable, she will make fast way.

As chance has it, both are propitious to the *Crusader*, and the warship standing for the Sandwich Islands will likely reach them after an incredibly short voyage.

There are two individuals on board of her who wish it to be so; counting every day, almost every hour, of her course. Not that they have any desire to visit the dominions of King Kamehameha, or expect pleasure there. On the contrary, if left to themselves, the frigate's stay in the harbour of Honolulu would not last longer than necessary to procure a boat-load of bananas, and replenish her hen-coops with fat Kanaka fowls.

It is scarce necessary to say that they, who are thus indifferent to the delights of Owyhee, are the late-made lieutenant, Crozier, and the midshipman, Cadwallader. For them the brown-skinned Hawaian beauties will have little attraction. Not the slightest danger of either yielding to the blandishments so lavishly bestowed upon sailors by these seductive damsels of the Southern Sea. For the hearts of both are yet thrilling with the remembrance of smiles vouchsafed them by other daughters of the sunny south, of a far different race—thrilling, too, with the anticipation of again basking in their smiles under the sky of Andalusia.

It needs hope—all they can command—to cheer them. Not because the time is great, and the place distant. Sailors are accustomed to long separation from those they love, and, therefore, habituated to patience. It is no particular uneasiness of this kind which shadows their brows, and makes every mile of the voyage seem a league.

Nor are their spirits clouded by any reflections on that, which so chafed them just before leaving San Francisco. If they have any feelings about it, they are rather those of repentance for suspicions, which both believe to have been unfounded, as unworthy.

What troubles them now—for they are troubled—has nought to do with that. Nor is it any doubt as to the loyalty of their *fiancée*; but fear for their safety. It is not well-defined; but like some dream which haunts them—at times so slight as to cause little concern, at others, filling them with keen anxiety.

But in whatever degree felt, it always assumes the same shape—two figures conspicuous in it, besides those of their betrothed sweethearts—two faces of evil omen, one that of Calderon, the other De Lara's.

What the young officers saw of these men, and what more they learnt of them before leaving San Francisco, makes natural their misgivings, and justifies their fears. Something seems to whisper them, that there is danger to be dreaded from the gamblers—desperadoes as they have shown themselves—that through them some eventuality may arise, affecting the future of Carmen Montijo and Iñez Alvarez—even to prevent their escaping from California.

Escape! Yes; that is the word which Crozier and Cadwallader make use of in their conversation on the subject—the form in which their fear presents itself.

Before reaching the Sandwich Islands, they receive a scrap of intelligence, which in some respect cheers them. It has become known to the *Crusader's* crew that the frigate is to make but short stay there—will not even enter the harbour of Honolulu. The commission entrusted to her captain is of no very important nature. He is simply to leave an official despatch, with some commands for the British consul: after which head round again, and straight for Panama.

"Good news; isn't it, Ned?" says Cadwallader to his senior, as the two on watch together stand conversing. "With the quick time we've made from 'Frisco, as the Yankees call it, and no delay to speak of in the Sandwiches, we ought to get to the Isthmus nearly as soon as the Chilian ship."

"True; but it will a good deal depend on the time the Chilian ship leaves San Francisco. No doubt she'd have great difficulty in getting a sufficient number of hands. Blew told you there was but the captain and himself!"

"Only they; and the cook, an old darkey—a runaway slave, he said. Besides a brace of great red baboons—orangs. That was the whole of her crew, by last report! Well; in one way we ought to be glad she's so short," continues the midshipman. "It may give us the chance of reaching Panama soon as she, if not before her; and, as the frigate's destined to put into that port, we may meet the dear girls again, sooner than we expected."

"I hope and trust we shall. I'd give a thousand pounds to be sure of it. It would lift a load off my mind—the heaviest I've ever had on it."

"Off mine, too. But even if we don't reach Panama soon as the Chilian craft, we'll hear whether she's passed through there. If she have, that'll set things right enough. We'll then know they're safe, and will be so—'Hasta Cadiz'."

"It seems a good omen," says Crozier, reflectingly, "that we are not to be delayed at the Islands."

"It does," rejoins Cadwallader; "though, but for the other thing, I'd like it better if we had to stay there—only for a day or two."

"For what reason?"

"There!" says the midshipman, pulling up his shirtsleeve, and laying bare his arm to the elbow. "Look at that, lieutenant!"

The lieutenant looks, and sees upon the skin, white as alabaster, a bit of tattooing. It is the figure of a young girl, somewhat scantily robed, with long streaming tresses: hair, contour, countenance, everything done in the deepest indigo.

"Some old sweetheart?" suggests Crozier.

"It is."

"But *she* can't be a Sandwich Island belle. You've never been there?"

"No, she isn't. She's a little Chileña, whose acquaintance I made last spring, while we lay at Valparaiso. Grummet, the cutter's coxswain, did the tattoo for me, as we came up the Pacific. He hadn't quite time to finish it as you see. There was to be a picture of the Chilian flag over her head, and underneath the girl's name, or initials. I'm now glad they didn't go in."

"But what the deuce has all this to do with the Sandwich Islands?"

"Only, that, there, I intended to have the thing taken out again. Grummet tells me he can't do it, but that the Kanakas can. He says they've got some trick for extracting the stain, without scarring the skin, or only very slightly."

"But why should you care about removing it? I acknowledge tattooing is not nice, on the epidermis of a gentleman; and I've met scores, like yourself, sorry for having submitted to it. After all, what does it signify? Nobody need ever see it, unless you wish them to."

"There's where you mistake. Somebody *might* see it, without my wishing—sure to see it, if ever I get—"

"What?"

"Spliced."

"Ah! Iñez?"

"Yes; Iñez. Now you understand why I'd like to spend a day or two among the South Sea Islanders. If I can't get the thing rubbed out, I'll be in a pretty mess about it. I know Iñez would be indulgent in a good many ways; but when she sees that blue image on my arm, she'll look black enough. And what am I to say to her? I told her, she was the first sweetheart I ever had; as you know, Ned, a little bit of a fib. Only a white one; for the Chilena was but a mere fancy, gone out of my mind long ago; as, no doubt, I am out of hers. The question is, how's her picture to be got out of my skin? I'd give something to know."

"If that's all your trouble, you needn't be at any expense—except what you may tip old Grummet. You say he has not completed the portrait of your Chilena. That's plain enough, looking at the shortness of her skirts. Now let him go on, and lengthen them a little. Then finish by putting a Spanish flag over her head, instead of the Chilian, as you intended, and underneath the initials 'I.A.' With that on your arm, you may safely show it to Iñez."

"A splendid idea! The very thing! The only difficulty is, that this picture of the Chilian girl isn't anything like as good-looking as Iñez. Besides, it would never pass for her portrait."

"Let me see. I'm not so sure about that. I think, with a few more touches, it will stand well enough for your Andalusian. Grummet's given her all the wealth of hair you're so constantly bragging about. The only poverty's in that petticoat. But if you get the skirt stretched a bit, that will remedy it. You want sleeves, too, to make her a lady. Then set a tall tortoise-shell comb upon her crown, with a spread of lace over it, hanging down below the shoulders—the mantilla—and you'll make almost as good an Andalusian of her as is Iñez herself."

"By Jove! you're right; it can be done. The bit added to the skirt will look like a flounced border; the Spanish ladies have such on their dresses. I've seen them. And a fan—they have that too. She must have one."

"By all means, give her a fan. And as you're doubtful about the likeness, let it be done so as to cover her face—at least the lower half of it; that will be just as they carry it. You can hide that nose, which is a trifle too snub for your *fiancée*. The eyes appear good enough."

"The Chileña had splendid eyes!"

"Of course, or she wouldn't have her portrait on your arm. But how did the artist know that? Has he ever seen the original?"

"No; I described her to him; and he's well acquainted with the costume the Chilian girls wear. He's seen plenty of such. I told him to make the face a nice oval, with a small mouth, and pretty pouting lips; then to give her great big eyes. You see he's done all that."

"He has, certainly."

"About the feet? They'll do, won't they? They're small enough, I should say."

"Quite small enough; and those ankles are perfection. They ought to satisfy your Andalusian—almost flatter her."

"Flatter her! I should think not. They might your Biscayan, with her big feet; but not Iñez; who's got the tiniest little understandings I ever saw under the skirt of a petticoat—tall as she is."

"Stuff!" scornfully retorts Crozier; "that's a grand mistake people make about small feet. It's not the size, but the shape, that's to be admired. They should be in proportion to the rest of the body; otherwise they're a monstrosity—as among the Chinese, for instance. And as for small feet in men, about which the French pride, and pinch themselves, why every tailor's got that."

"Ha, ha ha!" laughs the young Welshman. "A treatise on Orthopoedia, or whatever it's called. Well, I shall let the Chilena's feet stand, with the ankles too, and get Grummet to add on the toggery."

"What if your *Chileña* should chance to set eyes on the improved portrait? Remember we're to call at Valparaiso!"

"By Jove! I never thought of that."

"If you should meet her, you'll do well to keep your shirt-sleeves down, or you may get the picture scratched—your cheeks along with it."

"Bah! there's no danger of that. I don't expect ever to see that girl again—don't intend to. It wouldn't be fair, after giving that engagement ring to Iñez. If we do put into Valparaiso, I'll stay aboard all the time the frigate's in port. That will insure against any—"

"*Land ho!*"

Their dialogue is interrupted. The lookout on the masthead has sighted Mauna-Loa.

Chapter Forty Eight
A Crew that means Mutiny

A Ship sailing down the Pacific, on the line of longitude 125 degrees West. Technically speaking, not a *ship*, but a *barque*, as may be told by her mizzen-sails, set fore and aft.

Of all craft encountered on the ocean, there is none so symmetrically beautiful as the *barque*. Just as the name looks well on the page of poetry and romance, so is the reality itself on the surface of the sea. The sight is simply perfection.

And about the vessel in question another graceful peculiarity is observable: her masts are of the special kind called *polacca*—in one piece from step to truck.

Such vessels are *common enough* in the Mediterranean, and not rare in Spanish-American ports. They may be seen at Monte Video, Buenos Ayres, and Valparaiso—to which last this barque belongs. For she is Chilian built; her tall tapering masts made of trees from the ancient forests of Araucania. Painted upon the stern is the name *El Condor*; and she is the craft commanded by Captain Antonio Lantanas.

This may seem strange. In the harbour of San Francisco the *Condor* was a ship. How can she now be a barque?

The answer is easy, as has been the transformation; and a word will explain it. For the working of her sails, a barque requires fewer hands than a ship. Finding himself with a short crew, Captain Lantanas has resorted to a stratagem, common in such cases, and converted his vessel accordingly. The conversion was effected on the day before leaving San Francisco; so that the *Condor*, entering the Golden Gate a ship, stood out of it a barque. As such she is now on the ocean, sailing southward along the line of longitude 125 degrees West. In the usual track taken by sailing-vessels between Upper California and the Isthmus, she has westered, to get well clear of the coast, and catch the regular winds, that, centuries ago, wafted the spice-laden Spanish galleons from the Philippines to Acapulco. A steamer would hug the shore, keeping the brown barren mountains of Lower California in view.

Instead, the *Condor* has sheered wide from the land; and, in all probability, will not again sight it till she's bearing up to Panama Bay.

It is the middle watch of the night—the first after leaving San Francisco. Eight bells have sounded, and the chief mate is in charge, the second having turned in, along with the division of crew allotted to him. The sea is tranquil, the breeze light, blowing from the desired quarter, so that there is nothing to call for any unusual vigilance.

True, the night is dark, but without portent of storm. It is, as Harry Blew knows, only a thick rain-cloud, such as often shadows this part of the Pacific.

But the darkness need not be dreaded. They are in too low a latitude to encounter icebergs; and upon the wide waters of the South Sea there is not much danger of collision with ships.

Notwithstanding these reasons for feeling secure, the chief officer of the *Condor* paces her decks with a brow clouded, as the heavens over his head; while the glance of his eye betrays anxiety of no ordinary kind. It cannot be from any apprehension about the weather. He does not regard the sky, nor the sea, nor the sails. On the contrary, he moves about, not with bold, manlike step, as one having command of a vessel, but stealthily, now and then stopping and standing in crouched attitude, within the deeper shadow thrown upon the decks by masts, bulwarks, and boats. He seems less to occupy himself about the ropes, spars, and sails, than the behaviour of those who work them. Not while they are working them either, but more when they are straying idly along the gangways, or clustered in some corner, and conversing. In short, he appears to be playing spy on them.

For this he has his reasons. And for all good ones. Before leaving port he had discovered the incapacity of the crew, so hastily scraped together. A bad lot, he could see at first sight—rough, ribald, and drunken. In all there are eleven of them, the second mate included; the last, as already stated, a Spaniard, by name Padilla. There are three others of the same race—Spaniards, or Spanish-Americans—Gil Gomez, José Hernandez, and Jacinto Velarde; two Englishmen, Jack Striker and Bill Davis; a Frenchman, by name La Crosse; a Dutchman, and a Dane; the remaining two being men whose nationality is difficult to determine, and scarce known to themselves—such as may be met on almost every ship that sails the sea.

The chief officer of the *Condor*, accustomed to a man-o'-war, with its rigid discipline, is already disgusted with what is going on aboard the merchantman. He was so before leaving San Francisco, having also some anxiety about the navigation of the vessel. With a crew so incapable, he anticipated difficulty, if not danger. But now that he is out upon the open ocean, he is sure of the first, and keenly apprehensive of the last. For, in less than a single day's sailing, he has discovered that the sailors, besides counting short, are otherwise untrustworthy. Several of them are not sailors at all, but "longshore" men; one or two mere "land-lubbers," who never laid hand upon a ship's rope before clutching those of the *Condor*. With such, what chance will there be for working the ship in a storm? But there is a danger he dreads far more than the mismanagement of ropes and sails—insubordination. Even thus early, it has shown itself among the men, and may at any moment break out into open mutiny. All the more likely from the character of Captain Lantanas, with which he has become well acquainted.

The Chilian skipper is an easy-going man, given to reading books of natural history, and collecting curiosities—as evinced by his brace of Bornean apes, and other specimens picked up during his trading trip to the Indian Archipelago. A man in every way amiable, but just on this account the most unfitted to control a crew, such as that he has shipped for the voyage to Valparaiso.

Absorbed in his studies, he takes little notice of them, leaving them in the hands, and to the control, of his *piloto*, Harry Blew.

But the ex-man-o'-war's man, though a typical British sailor, is not one of the happy-go-lucky kind. He has been entrusted with something more than the navigation of the Chilian ship—with the charge of two fair ladies in her cabin; and although these have not shown themselves on deck, he knows they are safe, and well waited on by the black cook; who is also steward, and who, under his rough sable skin, has a kindly, gentle heart.

It is when thinking of his cabin passengers, that the *Condor's* first officer feels apprehensive, and then not from the incapacity of her sailors, but their bold, indeed almost insolent, behaviour. Their having shown something of this at first might have been excusable, or at all events, capable of explanation. They had not yet sobered down. Fresh from the streets of San Francisco, so lawless and licentious, it could not be expected. But most of them have been now some days aboard—no drink allowed them save the regular ration, with plenty of everything else. Kind treatment from captain and mate, and still they appear scowling and discontented, as if the slightest slur—an angry word, even a look—would make mutiny among them.

What can it mean? What do the men want?

A score of times has Harry Blew thus interrogated himself, without receiving satisfactory answer. It is to obtain this, he is now gliding silently about the decks, and here and there concealing himself in shadow, with the hope of overhearing some speech that will give him explanation of the conspiracy—if conspiracy it be.

And in this hope he is not deceived or disappointed, but successful beyond his most sanguine expectations. For he at length obtains a clue, not *only* to the insubordination of the sailors, but all else that has been puzzling him.

And a strange problem it is, its solution appalling.

He gets the latter while standing under a piece of sailcloth, spread from the rail to the top of the round-house—rigged up by the carpenter as a sun screen, while doing some work during the heat of the day, and so left. The sky being now starless and pitch-black, with this additional obstruction to light, Harry Blew stands in obscurity impenetrable to the eye. A man passing, so close as almost to touch, could not possibly see him.

Nor is he seen by two men, who, like himself, sauntering about, have come to a stop under the spread canvas. Unlike him, however, they are not silent, but engaged in conversation, in a low tone, still loud enough for him to hear every word said. And to every one he listens with interest so engrossing, that his breath is well nigh suspended.

He understands what is said; all the easier from their talk being carried on in English—his own tongue. For they who converse are Jack Striker and Bill Davis.

And long before their dialogue comes to a close, he has not only obtained intelligence of what has hitherto perplexed him, but gets a glimpse of something beyond—that which sets his hair on end, almost causing the blood to curdle in his veins.

Chapter Forty Nine Two
"Sydney Ducks"

Jack Striker and Bill Davis are "Sydney Ducks," who have seen service in the chain-gangs of Australia. They have also served as sailors, this being their original calling. But since a certain voyage to the Swan River settlement—in which they were but passengers, sent out at the expense of Her Britannic Majesty's Government—they have had aversion to the sea, and only take to it intermittently—when under the necessity of working passage from port to port for other purposes. Escaping from a colonisation forced upon them, and quite uncongenial, they had thus made their way into California; and, after a run up the Sacramento, and a spell at gold-seeking, with but indifferent success, had returned to San Francisco; in the Queen City of the Pacific—finding ways of life they liked better than the hard labour of pick, pan, and cradle. Loitering among its low sailor-haunts, they encountered a pleasant surprise, by meeting a man who offered them five thousand dollars each to ship in a merchant-vessel, for the "short trip" to Panama! A wage so disproportioned to the service asked for, of course called for explanation; which the princely contractor gave, after having secured their confidence. It proved satisfactory to the Sydney Ducks, who, without further questioning, entered into the contract. The result was their getting conducted aboard the *Condor*—she being the vessel bound for the port of Panama.

He who had given them this handsome engagement was not the owner of the ship; no more was he her captain or supercargo; but a gentleman representing himself authorised to accept their services, for a somewhat different purpose than the mere working of her sails; and who promised to pay them in a peculiar manner—under certain contingencies, even more than the sum stipulated, notwithstanding its magnificence.

The conditions were partially made known to them before setting foot on the ship; and though an honest sailor would scornfully have rejected them—even in the face of such tempting reward—Jack Striker and Bill Davis have accepted them without scruple or cavil. For they are not honest sailors; but ex-convicts, criminals still unreformed, and capable of any misdeed— piracy, or murder—if only money can be made thereby.

Since coming aboard the *Condor*, and mixing with her crew, they have had additional insight into the character of their contract, and the services required of them. They find that several other men have been engaged in a somewhat similar way; and at a like bounteous wage—for a while wondering at it—till after a mutual comparison of notes, and putting together their respective scraps of intelligence, with surmises added, they have arrived at a pretty accurate understanding of how the land lies, and why their *entrepreneur*—who is no other than the second mate, Padilla—has been so liberal.

Striker, who has seen more of the world, and is the elder of the two "ducks," has been the first to obtain this added information; and it is for the purpose of communicating it to his old chum of the chain-gang, he has asked the latter to step aside with him. For chancing to be cast together in the middle watch, an opportunity offers, which the older convict has all that day been looking out for.

Davis, of more talkative habit, is the first to break silence; which he does on the instant of their ducking under the sailcloth.

"Well, old pal! what d'ye think of our present employ? Better than breakin' stone for them Swan River roads, with twenty pound of iron chain clinkin' at a fellow's ankles. An't it?"

"Better'n that, yes; but not's good as it might be."

"Tut, man, you're always grumblin'. Five thousand dollars for a trip that isn't like to run up to a month—not more than a fortnight or three weeks, I should say! If that don't content you, I'd like to know what would."

"Well, mate; I'll tell'ee what wud. *Thirty* thousand for the trip. An' Jack Striker an't like to be satisfied wi' anythin' much short o' that sum."

"You're joking, Jack?"

"No, I an't, Bill. As you knows, I'm not o' the jokin' sort; an' now mean what I say, sartin as I ever meant anythin' in my life. Both me an' you oughter get thirty thousand apiece o' this yellow stuff—that at the werry least."

"Why, there wouldn't be enough to go round the lot that's in."

"Yes, thar wud, an' will. Old as I am, I hain't yit quite lost hearin'. My yeers are as sharp as they iver wor, an' jist as reliable. Larst night I heerd a whisper pass atween Padilla an' another o' them Spanish chaps, that's put me up to somethink."

"What did you hear?"

"That the swag'll tot up to the total o' three hundred thousand dollars."

"The deuce it will! Why, they said it wasn't half that much. Padilla himself told me so."

"No matter what he's told you. I tell ye now, it's all o' the six figures I've sayed. In coorse, it's their interest to make it out small as they possibly can; seein' as our share's to be a percentage. I know better now; an' knowin' it, an't agoin' to stan' none o' theer nonsense. Neyther shud you, Bill. We both o' us are 'bout to risk the same as any o' the t'others."

"That's true enough."

"In coorse it is. An' bein' so, we oughter share same as them; can, an' will, if we stick well thegither. It's jest as eezy one way as t'other."

"There's something in what you say, mate."

"Theer's every thin' in it, an' nothin' more than our rights. As I've sayed, we all risk the same, an' that's gettin' our necks streetched. For if we make a mucker o' the job, it'll be a hangin' matter sure. An' I dar say theer's got to be blood spilt afore it's finished."

"What would you advise our doing? You know, Jack, I'll stand by you, whatever you go in for."

"Well; I want it to be a fair divide, all round; detarmined it shell be. Why shud the four Spanish fellas get a dollar more'n us others? As I've observed, two of them, Gomez an' Hernandez, have set theer eyes on the weemen folks. It's eezy to see that's part o' theer game. Beside, I heerd them talkin' o't. Gomez be arter the light girl, an' Hernandez the dark un. 'Bout that, they may do as they like for ought's I care. But it's all the more reezun why they oughtent be so greedy 'bout the shinin' stuff. As for Mister Gomez, it's plain he's the head man o' the lot; an' the second mate, who engaged us, is only same's the others, an' 'pears to be controlled by him. 'Twar 'tween them two I overheerd the confab; Gomez sayin' to Padilla that the dust lyin' snug in the cabin-lockers was full valley for three hundred thousan'. An' as theer's eleven o' us to share, that 'ud be nigh on thirty thousan' apiece, if my 'rithmetic an't out o' recknin'. Bill Davis; I say, we oughter stan' up for our rights."

"Certainly we should. But there'll be difficulty in getting them, I fear."

"Not a bit—not a morsel, if we stick out for 'em. The four Spanyards means to go snacks 'mong themselves. But theer be seven o' us outsiders; an' when I tell the others what I've tolt you, they'll be all on our side—if they an't the foolishest o' fools."

"They won't be that, I take it. A difference of twenty thousand dollars or so in their favour, will make them sensible enough. But what's to be the upshot, or, as they call it in the theatre play-bills, what's the programme!"

"Well, mate, so far as I've been put up to it, we're to run on till we get to the coast, somewheer near the Issmus o' Panyma. Theer we'll sight land, and soon's we do, the ship's to be scuttled—we first securin' the swag,' an' takin' it ashore in one o' the boats. We're to land on some part o' the coast that's known to Gomez, he says. Then we're to make for some town, when we've got things straight for puttin' in appearance in a explainable way. Otherways, we might get pulled up, an' all our trouble 'ud be for nowt. Worse, every man-Jack on us 'ud have a good chance to swing for it."

"And the young ladies?"

"They're to go along wi' Gomez an' Hernandez. How they mean to manage it, I can't tell ye. They'll be a trouble, no doubt, as allers is wi' weemen, an' it be a pity we're hampered wi' 'em; mor'n that, it's reg'lar dangersome. They may get the hul kit o' us into a scrape. Howsever, we'll hev to take our chances, since theer's no help for it. The two chaps 'pear to be reg'lar struck with 'em. Well, let 'em carry off the gurls an' welcome. But, as I've sayed, thet oughter make 'em less objectin' to a fair divide o' the dust."

"What's to be done with the others—the old Spaniard and skipper, with the black cook and first mate?"

"They're to go down wi' the ship. The intenshun is, to knock all o' 'em on the head, soon's we come in sight o' land."

"Well, Jack, for the first three I don't care a brass farthing. They're foreigners and blacks; therefore, nothing to us. But, as Blew chances to be a countryman of ours, I'd rather it didn't go so hard with him."

"Balderdash, Bill Davis! What have you or me to do wi' feelins o' that sort? Countryman, indeed! A fine country, as starves ten millions o' the like o' us two; an' if we try to take what by nateral right's our own, sends us out o' it wi' handcuffs round our wrists, an' iron jewellery on our ankles! All stuff an' psalm-singin' that 'bout one's own country, an' fella-countryman. If we let him off, we might meet him somewhere, when we an't a-wantin' to. He'll have to be sarved same as the t'other three. There be no help for't, if we don't want to have hemp roun' our thrapples."

"I suppose you're right, Striker; though it does seem a pity too. But what reason have the Spaniards for keepin' the thing back? Why should they wait till we get down by Panama? As the yellow stuff's lyin' ready, sure it might be grabbed at once, an' then we'd have more time to talk of how it's to be divided? What's the difficulty about our taking it now?"

"'Tant the takin' o' it. That'll be eezy work; an' when the time comes, we'll have it all our own way. We could toss the four overboard in the skippin' o' a flea. But then, how's the ship to be navvygated without the skipper an' first mate?"

"Surely we can do without them?"

"That's jest what we can't. O' all our crew, theer's only them two as hev the knowledge o' charts an' chronometers, an' the like; for him as is actin' second confesses he don't know nothin' 'bout sich. Tharfor, though we're in a good sound craft, without the skipper, or Blew, we'd be most as good as helpless. We're now on the biggest o' all oceans, an' if we stood on the wrong tack, we might niver set eyes on land—or only to be cast away on some dangersome shore. Or, what 'ud be bad as eyther, get overhauled by some man-o'-war, an' not able to gie account o' ourselves. Theer's the diffyculty, don't 'ee see, Bill? For thet reezun the Spanyards have agreed to let things alone till we've ran down nigh Panyma. Theer Gomez says he knows o' a long streetch o' uninhabited coast, where we'll be safe goin' ashore."

"Well, I suppose that'll be the best way, after all. If a man has the money, it don't make much difference where he sets foot on shore; an' no doubt we'll find sport down at Panyma, good as anywheres else."

"Theer ye be right, Bill. When a cove's flush there's pleasurin' iverywhere. Goold's the only thing as gives it."

"With the prospect of such big plunder, we can afford to be patient," says Davis resignedly.

"I an't agoin' to be patient for the paltry five thousand they promised. No, Bill; neyther must you. We've equal rights wi' the rest, an' we must stan' out for 'em."

"Soon as you say the word, Jack, I'm at your back. So'll all the others, who're in the same boat with ourselves."

"They oughter, an' belike will; tho' theer's a weak-witted fool or two as may take talkin' into it. I means to go at 'em the night, soon's I've finished my trick at the wheel, the which 'll soon be on. Ay! theer's the bells now! I must aft. When I come off, Bill, you be up by the night-heads, an' have that Dutch chap as is in our watch 'long wi' ye; an' also the Dane. They're the likeliest to go in wi' us at oncet, an' we'll first broach it to them."

"All right, old pal; I'll be there."

The two plotters step out from under the awning; Striker turning aft to take his "trick" at the wheel, the other sauntering off in the direction of the forecastle.

Chapter Fifty
An Appalling Prospect

Harry Blew stands aghast—his hair on end, the blood coursing chill through his veins.

No wonder, after listening to such revelations! A plot diabolical—a scheme of atrocity unparalleled—comprising three horrible crimes: robbery, the abduction of women, and the murder of men; and among the last, himself.

Now knows he the cause of the crew's insubordination; too clearly comprehends it. Three hundred thousand dollars of gold-dust stowed in the cabin-lockers!

News to him; for Captain Lantanas had not made him acquainted with the fact—the treasure having been shipped before his coming aboard. Indeed, on that same night when he went after Silvestre; for at the very time he was knocking at the ship-agent's office-door, Don Tomas, with a trusty waterman, was engaged in putting it aboard the Chilian ship.

An unfortunate arrangement, after all. And now too certain of ending disastrously, not only for Don Gregorio, but those dear to him, with others less interested, yet linked to his fate.

Though the ex-man-o'-war's man is neither doubtful nor incredulous of what he has just heard, it is some time before his mind can grasp all the details. So filled is he with astonishment, it is natural his thoughts should be confused, and himself excited.

But soon he reflects calmly; and revolving everything over, perceives clearly enough what are the crimes to be committed, with the motives for committing them. There can be no ambiguity about the nature of the nefarious conspiracy. It has all been hatched, and pre-arranged, on shore; and the scoundrels have come aboard specially for its execution. The four Spaniards—or Californians, as he believes them to be—must have had knowledge of the treasure being shipped, and, in their plan to appropriate it, have engaged the others to assist them. Striker's talk has told this; while revealing also the still more fiendish designs of abduction and murder.

The prospect is appalling; and as he reflects upon it, Harry Blew feels his heart sink within him—strong though that heart be. For a dread fate is impending over himself, as well as those he has promised to protect.

How it is to be averted! How he is to save Carmen Montijo and Iñez Alvarez! How save himself?

These questions come crowding together, and repeat themselves over and over; but without suggesting answer. He cannot think of one that is satisfactory; he sees no chance of escape. The crew are all in the plot—every man of them—either as principals, or engaged assistants. The conversation of the two convicts has told this. The second mate same as the rest; which to him, Harry Blew, causes no surprise. He had already made up his mind about Padilla; observing his sympathy with those who were showing insubordination. He had also noticed that whatever was up among them, Gil Gomez was the directing spirit; dominating Padilla, notwithstanding the latter's claim to superior authority as one of the ship's officers; while Velarde and Hernandez seemed also to be controlled by him. The last, Harry Blew has discovered to be a landsman, with no sea-experience whatever; when found out, excusing himself on the plea that he wished to work his passage to Panama. The position of the other seven is understood by what Striker said. All are equal in the scheme of pillage and murder—though not to have equal reward.

Bringing them one after another before his mind; recalling his experience of them—which, though short, has given him some knowledge of their character—the *Condor's* first officer cannot think of one likely to take sides with him. They are all men of iniquity; and in defending the innocent he will have to stand alone. For it will amount to almost that, with no other help than Captain Lantanas, Don Gregorio, and the cook; the first, a slight slender man, with just strength enough to handle a telescope; the second, aged, and something of an invalid; the third, for fighting purposes, scarce worth thinking of. His fidelity might be depended upon; but he is also an oldish man, and would count for little in a conflict, with such desperadoes as those who design making themselves masters of the ship.

All these points present themselves to the mind of the first mate clearly, impressively.

A thought of telling Captain Lantanas what he has discovered, and which at first naturally occurred to him, he no longer entertains. The trusting Chilian skipper would scarce give credit to such an atrocious scheme. And if he did, in all likelihood it would result in his taking some rash step, which would but quicken their action, and bring sooner on the fatal catastrophe.

No; 'twill never do to make him acquainted with the danger, great as it is.

Nor yet should Don Gregorio know of it. The terrible secret must be kept from both, and carefully. Either of them aware of it, and in an hour after, all might be over—the tragedy enacted, and its victims consigned to the sea—himself, Harry Blew, being one of them!

Still crouching under the sail, he trembles, as in fancy he conjures up a fearful scene; vividly, as though the reality were before his eyes. In the midst of the open ocean, or close to land, the tragedy to be enacted will be all the same. The girls seized; the captain, Don Gregorio, the cook, and himself, shot down, or poniarded; after that, the gold dragged out of the lockers; the vessel scuttled, and sunk; a boat alone left to carry the pirates ashore, with their spoils and captives!

Contemplating such a scene—even though only in imagination—it is not strange that the *Condor's* first officer feels a shivering throughout his frame. He feels it in every fibre. And reflection fails to give relief; since it suggests to him no plan for saving himself. On the contrary, the more he dwells on it, the more is he sensible of the danger—sees it in all its stark-naked reality. Against such odds a conflict would be hopeless. It could only end in death to all who have been singled out, himself perhaps the first.

For a time he stands in silent cogitation, with despair almost paralysing his heart. He is unable to think steadily, or clearly. Doubtful, unfeasible schemes shape themselves in his mind; idle thoughts flit across his brain; all the while wild tumultuous emotions coursing through his soul.

At length, and after prolonged reflection, he seems to have made a resolve. As his countenance is in shadow, its expression cannot be seen; but, judging by the words that are muttered by his lips, it is one which should be unworthy of a British sailor—in short, that of a *traitor*.

For his soliloquy seems to show that he has yielded to craven fear— intends surrendering up the sacred trust reposed in him, and along with it his honour!

The words are:

"I must cast my lot in along wi' them. It's the only chance; an' for the savin' o' my own life! *I'll do that Lord help me, I'll do it!*"

Chapter Fifty One
Plot upon Plot

The *Condor* is sailing barge, with a light breeze several points abaft the beam.

Jack Striker is at the wheel; and as the sea is smooth he finds it easy steering, having little to do but keep the barque steady by taking an occasional squint at the compass-card.

The moon—which has just risen—shining in his face, shows it to be that of a man over fifty, with the felon in its every line and lineament. It is beardless, pock-pitted, with thick shapeless lips, broad hanging jowls, nostrils agape, and nose flattened like the snout of a bull-dog. Eyes gosling-green, both bleary, one of them bloodshot. For all, eyes that, by his own boast, "can see into a millstone as far as the man who picks it."

He has not been many minutes at his post when he sees some one approaching from the waist of the ship; a man, whom he makes out to be the first mate.

"Comin' to con me," growls the ex-convict. "Don't want any o' his connin', not I. Jack Striker can keep a ship on her course well's him, or any other board o' this craft."

He is on the starboard side of the wheel, while the mate is approaching along the port gangway. The latter, after springing up to the poop-deck, stops opposite the steersman, as he does so, saying:

"Well, Striker, old chap! not much trouble with her to-night. She's going free too, with the wind in the right quarter. We ought to be making good nine knots?"

"All o' that, I daresay, sir," rejoins Striker, mollified by the affable manner in which the first officer has addressed him. "The barque ain't a bad 'un to go, though she be a queery-rigged craft's ever I war aboard on."

"You've set foot on a goodish many, I should say, judgin' from the way ye handle a helm. I see you understan' steerin' a ship."

"I oughter, master," answers the helmsman, further flattered by the compliment to his professional skill. "Jack Striker's had a fair show o' schoolin' to that bizness."

"Been a man-o'-war's man, hain't you?"

"Ay, all o' that. Any as doubts it can see the warrant on my back, an' welcome to do so. Plenty o' the cat's claws there, an' I don't care a brass fardin' who knows it."

"Neyther need ye. Many a good sailor can show the same. For myself, I hain't had the cat, but I've seed a man-o'-war sarvice, an' some roughish treatment too. An' I've seed sarvice on ships man-o'-war's men have chased—likin' that sort a little better; I did."

"Indeed!" exclaims the ex-convict, turning his eyes with increased interest on the man thus frankly confessing himself. "Smuggler? Or maybe slaver?"

"Little bit o' both. An' as you say 'bout the cat, I don't care a brass fardin' who knows o' it. It's been a hardish world wi' me; plenty o' ups an' downs; the downs oftener than the ups, Just now things are lookin' sort o' uppish. I've got my berth here 'count o' the scarcity o' hands in San Francisco, an' the luck o' knowin' how to take sights an' keep a log. Still the pay an't much considerin' the chances left behind. I daresay I'd 'a done a deal better by stayin' in Californey, an' goin' on to them gold-diggin's up in the Sacramenta mountains."

"You han't been theer, han't ye?"

"No. Never went a cable's length ayont the town o' Francisco."

"Maybe, jest as well ye didn't, Master Blew. Me an' Bill Davis tried that dodge; we went all the way to the washin's on Feather River; but foun' no gold, only plenty o' hard work, wi' precious little to eat, an' less in the way o' drink. Neyther o' us likin' the life, we put back for the port."

For all his frankness in confessing to the cat-o'-nine tails on board a warship, Striker says nothing about a rope of a different kind he and his chum Davis were very near getting around their necks on the banks of that same Feather River, and from which they escaped by a timely retreat upon "'Frisco."

"Well," rejoins Blew, in a tone of resignation; "as you say, maybe I've did the wisest thing after all, in not goin' that way. I might 'a come back empty-handed, same as yerself an' Davis. Ye say liquor war scarce up there. That 'ud never 'a done for me. I must have my reg'lar allowance, or—. Well, no use sayin' what. As an old man-o'-war's man you can can understan' me, Striker. An' as the same, I suppose you won't object to a tot now?"

"Two, for that matter," promptly responds Striker, like all his sort—drouthy.

"Well; here's a drop o' rum—the best Santa Cruz. Help yourself!"

Blew presents a black-jack bottle to the helmsman, who, detaching one hand from the spokes, takes hold of the bottle. Then, raising it to his lips, and keeping it there for a prolonged spell, returns it to its owner, who, for the sake of sociability, takes a pull himself. All this done, the dialogue is renewed, and progresses in even a more friendly way than before; the Santa Cruz having opened the heart of the Sydney Duck to a degree of familiarity; while, on his side, the mate, throwing aside all reserve, lets himself down to a level with the foremast-man.

It ends in their establishing a confidence, mutual and complete, of that character known as "thickness between thieves."

Blew first strikes the chord that puts their spirits *en rapport*, by saying:

"Ye tell me, Striker, that ye've had hard times an' some severe punishment. So's had Harry Blew. An' ye say ye don't care about that. No more cares he. In that we're both o' us in the same boat. An' now we're in the same ship—you a sailor afore the mast, I first officer—but for all the difference in our rank, we can work thegether. An' there's a way we can both o' us do better. Do you want me to tell it ye?"

"Ay, ay; tell it. Jack Striker's ears are allus open to 'ear 'ow he can better his sittivation in life. I'm a listener."

"All right. I've observed you're a good hand at the helm. Would ye be as good to go in for a job that'll put a pile o' money in your pocket?"

"That depends. Not on what sort o' job; I don't mean that. But what's the figger—the 'mount o' the money—how much?"

"Puttin' it in gold, as much as you can carry; ay, enough to make you stagger under it."

"An' you ask if I'm good for a job like that? Funny question to ask—it are; 'specially puttin' it to ole Jack Striker. He's good for't—wi' the gallows starin' him full in the face. Danged if he an't!"

"Well; I thought you wouldn't be the one to show basket-faced 'bout it. It's a big thing I hev on hand, an' there'll be a fortin' for all who go in for it."

"Show Jack Striker the chance o' goin' in, an' he'll show you a man as knows no backin' out."

"Enough, shipmate. The chance is close to hand; aboard o' this ship. Below, in her cabin-lockers, there's stowed somethin' like half a ton o' glitterin' gold-dust. It belongs to the old Spaniard that's passenger. What's to hinder us to lay hands on it? If we can only get enough o' the crew to say *yes*, there needs be no difficulty. Them as won't 'll have to stan' aside. Though, from what I see o' them, it's like they'll all come in. Divided square round, there'd be atween twenty an' thirty thousand dollars apiece. Do that tempt ye. Striker?"

"Rayther. Wi' thirty thousand dollars I'd ne'er do another stroke o' work."

"You needn't then. You can have all o' that, by joinin' in, an' helpin' me to bring round the rest. Do you know any o' them ye could speak to 'bout the bizness—wi' safety, I mean?"

"I do. Two or three. One sartin'; my ole chum, Bill Davis. He can be trusted wi' a secret o' throat-cuttin', let alone a trifle such as you speak o'. An' now, Master Blew, since you've seen fit to confide in me, I'm goin' to gi'e ye a bit o' my confidince. It's but fair 'tween two men as hev got to understan' one the tother. I may as well tell ye that I know all about the stuff in the cabin-lockers—hev knowed it iver since settin' fut in the *Condor's* forc's'l. Me an' Bill war talkin' o't jist afore I coomed to the wheel. You an't the only one as hez set theer hearts on hevin' it. Them Spanish chaps hez got it all arranged arready—an' had afore they shipped 'board this barque. Thar's the four o' 'em, as I take it, all standin' in equal; while the rest o' the crew war only to get so much o' a fixed sum."

"Striker, ye 'stonish me!"

"Well, I'm only tellin' ye what be true, an' what I knows to be so. I'm gled you're agreeable to go in wi' us; the which 'll save trouble, an' yer own life as well. For I may as well tell ye, Master Blew, that they'd made up thar minds to send ye to the bottom o' the briny, 'long wi' skipper an' the ole Spaniard, wi' the black throwed into the bargain."

"That's a nice bit o' news to hear, by jingo! Well, Jack, I'm thankful to ye for communicatin' it. Lord! it's lucky for me we've this night chanced to get talkin' thegether."

"Thar may be luck in't all roun'. Bill an' me'd made up our minds to stan' out for a equal divide o' the dust—like shares to ivery man. Shud there be any dispute 'bout that bein' fair, wi' you on our side, we'll eezy settle it our way, 'spite o' them Spanyards. If they refuse to agree, an' it coomes to fightin', then Jack Striker's good for any two on 'em."

"An' Harry Blew for any other two. No fear but we can fix that. How many do you think will be with us?"

"Most all, I shud say, 'ceptin' the Spanyards themselves. It consarns the rest same's it do us. At all events, we're bound to ha' the majority."

"When do you propose we should begin broachin' it to them?"

"Straight away, if you say the word. I'll try some o' 'em soon as I've goed off from heer. Thar be several on the watch as 'll be takin' a drop o' grog thegether, 'fore we turns in. No better time nor now."

"True. So set at 'em at once, Striker. But mind ye, mate, be cautious how ye talk to them, an' don't commit ayther of us too far, till you've larnt their temper. I'll meet ye in the first dog-watch the morrow. Then you can tell me how the land's likely to lie."

"All right. I'll see to it in the smooth way. Ye can trust Jack Striker for that."

"Take another suck o' the Santa Cruz. If this trip proves prosp'rous in the way we're plannin' it, neyther you nor me 'll need to go without the best o' good liquor for the rest o' our lives."

Again Striker clutches at the proffered bottle, and holds it to his head — this time till he has drained it dry.

Returned to him empty, Harry Blew tosses it overboard. Then parting from the steersman, he commences moving forward, as with the design to look after other duties.

As he steps out from under the shadow of the spanker, the moon gleaming athwart his face, shows on it an expression which neither pencil nor pen could depict. Difficult indeed to interpret it. The most skilled physiognomist would be puzzled to say, whether it is the reproach of conscious guilt, or innocence driven to desperation.

Chapter Fifty Two
Share and Share Alike

In the *Condor's* forecastle.

It is her third night since leaving San Francisco, and the second watch is on deck; the men on the first having gone down below. That on duty is Padilla's; in it Gomez, Hernandez, Velarde, and the two sailors of nationality unknown.

The off-watch consists of Striker, Davis, the Frenchman, who is called La Crosse, with the Dutchman and Dane.

All these five are in the forepeak, the chief mate, as they suppose, having retired to rest.

They have been below for some time, and it is now near eleven o'clock of the night. All have finished their suppers, and are seated, some on the sides of their bunks, some on sea-chests. A large one of the latter, cleated in the centre of the floor, does service as a table. Upon it is a black bottle containing rum—the sailor's orthodox drink. In his hand, each holds his pannikin, while in every mouth there is a pipe, and the forecastle is full of smoke. A pack of playing-cards lies on the lid of the chest; greasy and begrimed, as if they had seen long service; though not any on this particular night, are in the hands of those sitting around, who show no inclination to touch them. They may have been used by the men of the watch now on deck; this, probably enough, since the cards are Spanish, as told by their picturing.

Those occupying the forecastle now have something on their minds more important than card-playing: a question of money; but not money to be made in that way. What they are thinking about, and talking of, is the gold-dust in the cabin-lockers; not how it is to be got out of them, but how it shall be distributed after it is out.

This is not the first time the subject has been before them. There has been talk of it all that day; though only between them in twos, and informally. Since finding out how things stood, and especially after his confab with the first mate, Striker, as promised, has been sounding his shipmates, one after another. He has communicated his purpose to all, and had their approval of it—the four Spaniards excepted. These he has not yet approached; but this night intends doing so—as the others insist that an immediate understanding be arrived at, and the thing definitely settled.

The five are now waiting till those on the watch, not required for deck-duty, come below. All of them have had intimation they will be wanted in the forecastle; and as the night is fine, with no occasion for changing sails or other occupation, only the helmsman need absent himself from a muster, whose summons to most of the second watch has appeared a little strange.

They obey it, notwithstanding; and after a while the two sailors come down—the nondescripts without name; though one goes by the sobriquet of "Old Tarry," the other having had bestowed upon him the equally distinctive, but less honourable, appellation of "Slush."

Shortly after, the second mate, Padilla, makes his appearance, along with him Velarde; the former a man who has seen some forty winters, rugged in frame, with bronzed complexion, and features forbidding, as any that ever belonged to freebooters; the latter in this respect not so unlike him, only younger, of a more slender frame, and less rude in speech, as in manner.

Soon as setting foot on the forecastle's floor, Padilla, as an officer of the ship, speaking in tone of authority, demands to know why they have been summoned thither.

Striker, putting himself forward as the spokesman of the off-watch, replies:

"Hadn't ye better sit down, master mate? The subjeck we're goin' to discuss may take a start o' time an' it's as cheap sittin' as standin'. Maybe ye won't mind joinin' us in a drink?"

Saying this, the ex-convict clutches at the bottle pours some rum into his pannikin, and offers it to Padilla.

The Spaniard accepting, drinks; and passing the cup to Velarde, sits down.

The latter imitating him as to the drink, takes seat by his side; Old Tarry and Slush having already disposed of themselves.

"Now," pursues the second mate, "let's hear what it's all about."

"Theer be two not yit among us," says Striker. "In coorse, one's at the wheel."

"Yes; Gomez is there," responds Padilla.

"Where be Hernandez?"

"I don't know. Likely, along with him."

"Don't much matter," puts in Davis. "I dar' say we can settle the thing without either. You begin, Jack; tell Mr Padilla, and the rest, what we've been talking about."

"'Twon't take a very long time to tell it," responds Striker. "Theer be no great need for wastin' words. All I've got to say are, that the *swag shud be eekilly divided.*"

Padilla starts, Velarde doing the same.

"What do you mean?" asks the former, putting on an air of innocence.

"I means what I've saved—that the swag shud be eekilly divided."

"And yet I don't understand you."

"Yis, ye do. Come, Master Padilla, 'tain't no use shammin' ignorance—not wi' Jack Striker, at all events. He be too old a bird to get cheated wi' chaff. If ye want to throw dust into my eyes, it must be o' the sort that's stowed aft in the cuddy. Now, d'ye understan' me?" Padilla looks grave, so does Velarde. Old Tarry and Slush show no sign of feeling; both being already prepared for the demand Striker intended to make, and having given their promise to back it.

"Well," says the second mate, "you appear to be talking of some gold-dust. And, I suppose, you know all about it!"

"That we do," responds Striker.

"Well, what then?" asks Padilla.

"Only what I've sayed," rejoins the Sydney Duck. "If you weesh, I can say it over 'gain. That theer yellow stuff shud be measured out to the crew o' this craft share and share alike, even hands all roun' without respectin' o' parsons. An', by God! it shall be so deevided—shall, will, an' must."

"Yes!" endorses Davis, with like emphatic affirmation.

"It shall, and it must!"

"*Pe gar*, most it!" adds the Frenchman; followed in the same strain by Stronden the Dane, and Van Houton the Dutchman, chorused by Old Tarry and Slush.

"It an't no use your stannin' out, masters," continues Striker, addressing himself to the two Spaniards. "Ye see the majority's against ye; an' in all cases o' the kind, wheresomever I've seed 'em, the majority means the right. Besides, in this partickler case we're askin' no moren' what's right—refarrin' to the job afore us. I'm willin' to conceed, that you Spanish chaps hev hed most to do wi' the first plannin' o' the thing; as alser, that ye brought the rest o' us into it. But what signify the bringin' in compared wi' the gettin' out? In sich scrapes, 'taint the beginnin' but the eend as is dangersome. An' we've all got to unnergo that danger; the which I needn't particklarly speak o', as every man o' ye must feel it 'bout the nape o' his neck, seein' the risk he'll hev to run o' gettin' that streetched. It's eequil all roun', and tharfor the reward for runnin' it shed be eequil too. So say Jack Striker."

"So I, and I, and I," echo the others; all save Padilla and Velarde, who remain silent and scowling.

"Yis," continues Striker, "an' theer be one who 'ant present among us, as oughter have his share too. I don't mean either Mr Gomez or Hernandez. Them two shud be contented, seein' as they're more after the weemen than the money, an' nobody as I know o' carin' to cut 'em out there. It's true him I refer to hez come into the thing at the 'leventh hour, as ye may say—after 'twar all planned. But he mote a gied us trouble by stannin' apart. Tharfore, I say, let's take him in on shares wi' the rest."

"Whom are you speaking of?" demands Padilla.

"I needn't tell ye," responds the senior of the Sydney Ducks! "If I an't mistook, that's him a comin' down, an' he can speak for hisself."

At the words, a footstep is heard upon the forecastle stair. A pair of legs is seen descending; after them a body—the body of Harry Blew!

Padilla looks scared; Velarde the same. Both fancy their conspiracy discovered, their scheme blown; and that Striker, with all his talk, has been misleading them. They almost believe they are to be set upon and put in irons; and that for this very purpose the first officer is entering the forecastle.

They are soon undeceived, however, on hearing what he has to say. Striker draws it out, repeating the conversation passed, and the demand he has been making.

Thus Harry Blew gives rejoinder:

"I'm with ye, shipmates, to the end, be that sweet or bitter. Striker talks straight, an' his seems the only fair way of settlin' the question. The majority must decide. There's two not here, an' they've got to be consulted. They're both by the wheel. Tharfore, let's go aft, an' talk the thing there. There's no fear for our bein' interrupted. The skipper's asleep, an' we've got the ship to ourselves."

So saying, he leads up the ladder, the rest rising from their seats, and crowding after.

Once on deck, they cluster around the forehatch, and there stop; the first mate having something to say to them before proceeding farther.

The second does not take part in this conference; but stealing past unseen, glides on towards the after-part of the ship.

Soon the others saunter in the same direction, in twos and threes, straggling along the waist, but again gathering into a group around the capstan. There the moonlight, falling full upon their faces, betrays the expression of men in mutiny; but mutiny unopposed. For on the quarterdeck no one meets them. The traitorous first officer has spoken truly: the captain is asleep; they have the ship to themselves!

Chapter Fifty Three
"Castles in Spain"

Gomez is still at the wheel; his "trick" having commenced at the change of the watches. As known, he is not alone, but with Hernandez beside him.

Both are youngish men, neither above thirty; and both of swarthy complexion, though with beards of different colours; that of Gomez black, the other reddish-brown. Besides having heavy moustaches, their whiskers stand well forward on their jaws, and around their throats; growing so luxuriantly as to conceal the greater portion of their faces; the expression upon which it is difficult to determine. Equally to tell aught of their figures, draped as these are in rough sailor toggery, cut wide and hanging loosely about their bodies. Both, however, appear of about medium height, Gomez a little the taller, and more strongly built. On their heads are the orthodox "sou'-wester" hats; that of Gomez drawn slouching over eyes that almost continually glow with a sullen lurid light, as if he were always either angry or on the point of becoming so. At the same time he habitually keeps his glance averted, as though wishing to conceal either his thoughts or his features; it may be both.

Acting in the capacity of a common sailor, he has nevertheless hitherto appeared to control the second mate, as most others of the crew, and more especially the Spaniards.

This, alleged by Striker, has been observed by Harry Blew himself; so that of the conspirators Gomez is unquestionably chief. Though Padilla engaged the hands, the instructions must have proceeded from him, and all were shipped on conditions similar to those accepted by the Sydney Ducks.

Five thousand dollars, for less than a month's service, would be wages too unprecedentedly large to be offered without creating suspicion of some sinister intent. Nor did he, who offered it, leave this point untouched. While promising such big bounty, he exacted a promise in return: that each recipient of it was to bear a hand in *whatever he might be called on to do.*

The men so indefinitely engaged, and on such latitudinarian terms, were not the ones to stick at trifles; and most of them stepped aboard the Chilian ship prepared to assist in the perpetrating of any known crime in the calendar. Since becoming better acquainted with the particulars of what they have been shipped for, not one of them has shown disposition to back out of it. They are still ready to do the deed; but, as seen, under changed conditions.

Gomez is not yet aware of the strike that has taken place; though during the day he has heard some whisperings, and is half expecting trouble with his confederates. Hernandez also, though it is not of this they are now conversing as they stand together at the wheel.

The theme which engages them is altogether different; beauty, not booty, being the subject of their discourse, which is carried on in a low tone, though loud enough to be heard by anyone standing near.

But they are not afraid. *No* one is within earshot. Their comrades of the watch are away in the forward part of the vessel, while those of the off-watch are below in her forepeak—the skipper asleep in his cabin—the passengers in theirs.

It is about two of these last they are talking; and in terms, that, for common sailors, might seem strange—rough ribald men bandying free speech, and making familiar remarks, about such delicate high-born dames as Carmen Montijo and Iñez Alvarez!

But not strange to one acquainted with Gil Gomez and José Hernandez— and too intelligible if knowing their intention towards these ladies. It may be learnt by listening to their conversation; Hernandez, who has introduced the subject, asking:

"About the *muchachas*? What are we to do with them after getting ashore?"

"Marry them, of course," promptly answers the other. "That's what I mean doing with the beautiful Doña Carmen. Don't you intend the same with Doña Iñez?"

"Of course—if I can."

"Can! There need be no difficulty about it, *camarado*."

"I hope not; though I think there will, and a good deal. There's certain to be some."

"In what way?"

"Suppose they don't give their consent!"

"A fig for their consent! We shall force it! Don't be letting that scare you. Whether they're agreeable or not, we'll have a marriage ceremony, or the form of one—all the same. I can fix that, or I'm much mistaken about the place we're going to, and the sort of men we may expect to meet there. When I last looked on Santiago De Veragua—bidding adieu to a place that was rather pleasant—I left behind a few old familiars, who are not likely to have forgotten me, though long years have rolled by since. Some there, who will still be willing, and ready, to do me a service, I doubt not; especially now I have the means to pay for it, and handsomely. If the Padre Padierna be yet alive, he'll marry me to Carmen Montijo without asking *her* any questions; or, if he did, caring what answers she might give to them. It's now nine years since I saw the worthy Father, and he may have kicked up his heels long ago; though that's not likely. He was a tough old sinner, and knew how to take care of himself. However, it won't matter much. If he's under ground, I've got another string to my bow, in the young *extra*, Gonzaga; who, in my time, had charge of souls in a *parrochia*, nearer the place where I hope we shall be able to make shore. He may by this have risen to be grand church dignitary. Whether or not, I've but little fear of his having forgotten old times, when he and I used to go shares in certain little adventures of the amorous kind. So you perceive, *mio amigo*, we're not drifting towards a desert coast, inhabited only by savages; but one where we'll find all the means and appliances of civilisation—among them a priest, to do the little bit of ecclesiastical service we may stand in need of, and without asking awkward questions, or caring a *claco* for consequences. Neither of the two I've spoken of will trouble their consciences on that score, so long as it's *me*. More especially after I've shown them the colour of the stuff with which our pockets will be so plentifully lined. And if neither of my old acquaintances turn up, there are no end of others, who'll be willing to tie the knot that's to make us happy for life. I tell you, *hombre*, we're steering straight towards an earthly paradise. You'll find Santiago all that."

"I hope it may be, as you say."

"You may rest sure of it. Once in the old Veraguan town, with these women as our wives—and they no longer able to question our calling them so—we can enter society without fear of showing our faces. And with this big *bonanza* at our backs, we may lead a luxurious life there; or go anywhere else it pleases us. As for returning to your dear California, as you call it, you won't care for that when you've become a Benedict."

"You've made up your mind, then, that we marry them?"

"Of course I have, and for certain reasons. Otherwise, I shouldn't so much care, now that they're in our power, and we can dictate terms to them.

You can do as you please respecting marriage, though you have the same reasons as myself, for changing your señorita into a señora."

"What do you allude to?"

"To the fact that both these damsels have large properties in Spain, as a worthy friend in San Francisco made me aware just before leaving. The Doña Carmen will inherit handsomely at her father's death, which is the same as if said and done now. I don't refer to his gold-dust, but a large landed property the old gentleman is soon coming into in Biscay; and which, please God, I shall some day look up and take possession of. While the other has no end of acres in Andalusia, with whole streets of houses in Cadiz. To get all that, these women must be our wives; otherwise, we should have no claim to it, nor yet be able to show our faces in Spain."

"Of course I'm glad to hear about all that," rejoins Hernandez; "but, if you believe me, it's not altogether the money that's been tempting me throughout this whole affair. I'm mad in love with Iñez Alvarez;—so mad, that if she hadn't a *claco* in the world I'm willing to be her husband."

"Say, rather, her master; as I intend to be of Carmen Montijo. Ah! once we get ashore, I'll teach her submission. The haughty dame will learn what it is to be a wife. And if not an obedient one, *por Dios*! she shall have a divorce, that is, after I've squeezed out of her the Biscayan estate. Then she can go free, if it so please her."

On pronouncing this speech, the expression on the speaker's countenance is truly satanic. It seems to foreshadow a sad fate for Carmen Montijo.

For some seconds there is silence between the plotters. Again breaking it, Hernandez says:

"I don't like the idea of our putting the old gentleman to death. Is there no other way we could dispose of him?"

"Pah, *hombre*! You're always harping on the strings of humanity; striking discordant sounds too. There's no other way by which we can be ourselves safe. If we let him live, he'd be sure to turn up somewhere, and tell a tale that would get both our throats grappled by the *garrota*. The women might do the same, if we didn't make wives of them. Once that, and we can make exhibit of our marriage certificates, their words will go for nought. Besides, having full marital powers, we can take precautions against any scandal. Don Gregorio has got to die; the skipper too; and that rough fellow, the first mate—with the old blackamoor *cocinero*."

"*Maldita!* I don't feel up to all that. It will be rank wholesale murder."

"Nothing of the sort—only drowning. And we needn't do that either. They can be tied before we scuttle the ship, and left to go down along with her. By the time she sinks, we'll be a long way off; and you, my sensitive and sentimental friend, neither see nor hear anything to give your tender heart a horror."

"The thought of it's enough."

"But how is it to be helped? If they're allowed to live, we'd never be out of danger. Maybe, you'd like to abandon the business altogether, and resign thought of ever having the pretty Iñez for a wife?"

"There you mistake, *amigo*. Sooner than that, I'll do the killing myself. Ay, kill *her*, rather than she shall get away from me."

"Now you're talking sense. But see! What's up yonder?"

The interrogatory is from seeing a group of men assembled on the fore-deck, alongside the hatch. The sky cloudless, with a full moon overhead, shows it to be composed of nearly, if not all, the *Condor's* crew. The light also displays them in earnest gesticulation, while their voices, borne aft, tell of some subject seriously debated.

What can it be? They of the last dog-watch, long since relieved, should be asleep in their bunks. Why are they now on deck? Their presence there, gives surprise to the two at the wheel.

And while engaged in expressing it, and interrogating one another, they perceive the second mate coming aft—as also, that he makes approach in hurried, yet stealthy manner.

"What is it?" asks Gomez.

"A strike," answers Padilla. "A mutiny among the men we engaged to assist us."

"On what grounds?"

"They've got to know all about the gold-dust—even to the exact quantity there is of it."

"Indeed! And what's their demand?"

"That we shall share it with them. They say they'll have it so."

"The devil they do!"

"The old *ladrone*, Striker, began it. But what will astonish you still more; the first mate knows all our plans, and's agreed to go in along with us.

He's at the head of the mutineers, too, and insists on the same thing. They swear, if we don't divide equally, the strongest will take what they can. I've hastened hither to ask you what we'd best do."

"They're determined, are they?"

"To the death—they all say so."

"In that case," mutters Gomez, after a moment or two spent in reflection, "I suppose we'll have to yield to their demands. I see no help for it. Go straight back, and say something to pacify them. Try to put things off, till we have time to consider. *Maldita*! this is an unexpected difficulty—ugly as sin itself!"

Padilla is about to return to his discontented shipmates on the forward-deck; but is saved the journey, seeing them come aft. Nor do they hesitate to invade the sacred precincts of the quarter; for they have no fear of being forbidden. There they pause for a few seconds, and then continue on.

Soon they mount to the poop-deck, and cluster around the wheel; the whole crew now present—mates as men—all save the captain and cook. And all take part in the colloquy that succeeds, either in speech or by gesture.

The debate is short, and the question in dispute soon decided. Harry Blew and Jack Striker are the chief spokesmen; and both talk determinedly; the others, with interests identical, backing them up by gestures, and exclamations of encouragement.

"Shipmates!" says the first officer, "this thing we're all after should be equally divided between us."

"Must be," adds Striker, with an oath. "Share and share alike. That's the only fair way. An' the only one we'll gie in to."

"Stick to that, Striker!" cries Davis: "we'll stand by ye."

"*Pe gar! certainement*," endorses the Frenchman, "Vat for no? *Sacré bleu*! ve vill. I am for *les droits de matelot—le vrai chose democratique*. Vive le fair play!"

Dane and Dutchman, with Tarry and Slush, speak in the same strain.

The scene is as short, as violent. The Spaniards perceiving themselves in a minority, and a position that threatens unpleasant consequences, soon yield, declaring their consent to an equal distribution of the "dust."

After which, the men belonging to the off-watch retire to the forecastle, and there betake themselves to their bunks; while the others scatter about the decks.

Gil Gomez remains at the wheel, his time not yet being up; Hernandez beside him. For some moments, the two are silent, their brows shadowed with gloom. It is not pleasant to lose fifty thousand dollars apiece; and something like this have they lost within the last ten minutes. Still there is a reflection upon which they can fall back well calculated to soothe them— other bright skies ahead.

Gomez first returning to think of this, says:

"Never mind, *amigo*. There will be money enough to serve our present purposes all the same. And for the future we can both build on a good sure foundation."

"On what?"

"On our 'Castles in Spain!'"

Chapter Fifty Four
Coldly Received

The *mal de mer* is no respecter of persons. Voyagers of every age, and either sex, must pay toll to it; the which it indiscriminately, if not equally, exacts from the strong robust youth, and the frail delicate maiden. Even beauty must submit to this merciless malady; at whose touch red lips turn pale, and rose-tinted cheeks show wan and wasted. Afflicting, on first acquaintance with it, it is always more or less disagreeable, and ever ready at offering its hand to those who go down to the sea in ships—that hand whose very touch is palsy.

The voyage Carmen Montijo and Iñez Alvarez are now making is not their first. Both have been at sea before—in the passage out from Spain. But this does not exempt them from the terrible infliction, and both suffer from it.

Stricken down by it, they are for several days confined to the cabin; most of the time to their state-room; and, as ill-luck would have it, without any one of their own sex to wait upon them—a want due to circumstances partially accidental, but wholly unexpected. The Chilian skipper, not accustomed to have a stewardess on his ship, had never thought of such a thing; his whole attention being taken up in collecting that crew, so difficult to obtain; while their own waiting-maid, who was to have accompanied the young ladies on their voyage, failed them at the eleventh hour; having preferred undertaking a journey of a different kind—not to Spain, but the altar of Hymen. At the last moment of embarkation, she was missing; her Californian *amante* having persuaded her to remain behind.

Withal, the lady voyagers have not been so badly attended. The old negro cook—acting also as steward, comes up to the occasion; for he has a tender heart under his rough sable skin, and waits upon them with delicate assiduity.

And Captain Lantanas is equally assiduous in his attentions, placing most of his time at their disposal, with whatever else he can think of likely to alleviate their suffering.

In due course they recover; Carmen first, from being of more robust habit and stronger constitution. But both are at length able to show themselves out of their state-room, and after a day or two waiting for fine weather, they venture upon deck.

During this sojourn below, they have had no communication with any one, save Don Gregorio—who has been like themselves, invalided—and of course the captain and cook. But not any of the officers, or sailors, of the ship. Indeed, on these they have never set eyes, excepting on that day when they sailed out through the Golden Gate. But, then, their thoughts were otherwise occupied—too much engrossed with certain personages absent, to care for any that were present; least of all the sailors of the ship—these scarce getting a glance from them.

Still there is one they have a strong desire to see, and also speak with. Not a common sailor, but the *piloto*, or first officer, of the vessel—for they are aware the English seaman has been promoted to this responsible post.

During their forced confinement in the state-room, they have often held discourse about him; this connected with a subject that gives them the greatest concern, and no little pain. There is still rankling in their breasts that matter unexplained; no letters left by their lovers at their abrupt departure, save the one for Don Gregorio, with salutation to themselves, so coldly, ceremoniously formal. It is to inquire about that, they are so anxious for an interview with Harry Blew, hoping, almost believing him to have been entrusted with some verbal message he has not yet delivered.

From the terms in which Crozier spoke of him while giving account of how he had saved his life, it is natural to suppose, that between preserved and preserver there should be confidence of a very intimate kind. Therefore Carmen still more than half believes the sailor has a word for herself—kept back for the want of opportunity. She recalls certain things he said jocularly, on the day he brought Crozier's letter to the house, and while she was herself showing him hospitality. These went so far as to show, that the ex-man-o'-war's man was not altogether ignorant of the relations existing between her and his old officer. And now she longs to renew conversation with him, hoping to hear more of those same pleasant words—perhaps get explanation of the others not so pleasant—in the letter. Iñez is affected with a like longing, for she too feels the slight they conveyed—if not so much as her aunt, still enough to wish for their true interpretation.

Both thus basing their hopes on Harry Blew, they have been for some time on the lookout for him, though as yet unsuccessfully. Several times have they ascended to the deck; but without seeing him, or only afar off, and, to all appearance, busily engaged with his duties about the ship.

Of course they do not expect him to come to them; and, with the secret purpose they have conceived, dislike summoning him; while he on his part appears to keep aloof, or, at all events, does not draw near—perhaps not desiring to be deemed intrusive. For, although first officer of the vessel, he is still only a rough sailor, and may think himself ill qualified for the company of ladies.

Whatever the reason, they have been several times above, without finding an opportunity to speak with him; and for this they wait with irksome impatience.

At length, however, it seems to have arrived. They have come out on the quarter, in front of the round-house door, and are seated on chairs which the considerate skipper brought up for them. He is himself by their side, endeavouring to entertain them by pointing out the various objects on his vessel, and explaining their uses.

They give but little heed to the technical dissertations of the well-meaning man, and only a passing glance at the objects indicated. Even the two gigantic apes, that go gambolling about the decks—exhibiting uncouth gestures, and uttering hoarse cries—fail to fix their attention; though Captain Lantanas tells them many curious tales of these creatures—*myas* monkeys, he calls them, which he has brought with him from Borneo. Too simple-minded to observe the inattention of his listeners, he is proceeding still farther to illustrate the habits of the orangs, when his lecture on natural history is interrupted, by the necessity for his taking an observation of the sun. It is a few minutes before mid-day, and he must needs determine his latitude. So making apology to the ladies, he hurries down to the cabin to get his quadrant.

His leaving them is a relief, for they see the first mate moving about, and have hopes of being able to accost, and enter into conversation with him. True, he seems busy as ever; but it is nigh the hour when the men of the forecastle go down to their dinners, and then they may have the opportunity while he is disengaged.

For some time they sit watching, and waiting. He is in the waist with several of the sailors around him, occupied about one of the boats, there slung upon its davits.

While regarding him and his movements, the ladies cannot avoid also observing those of the men, nor help being struck by them. Not so much their movements, as their appearance, and the expression seen on some of their countenances. On no one of them is it pleasant, but on the contrary scowling and savage. Never before have they seen so many faces wearing such disagreeable looks, that is, gathered in one group—and they have passed through the streets of San Francisco, where the worst types may be met. Many of them—indeed nearly all—are not only unprepossessing, but positively forbidding; and the young girls, not desiring to encounter certain glances, sent towards them, with an impudent effrontery, turn their eyes away.

Just then, Harry Blew, separating from the sailors, is seen coming aft. It is in obedience to a message which the black cook has brought up out of the cabin—an order from Captain Lantanas for his first officer to meet him on the quarterdeck, and assist in "taking the sun."

But the captain has not yet come up; and, on reaching the quarter, the ex-man-o'-war's man, for the first time since he shipped on the Chilian craft, finds himself alone in the presence of the ladies.

They salute him with an *empressement*, which, to their surprise, is but coldly returned! Only a slight bow; after which he appears to busy himself with the log-slate lying on the capstan-head.

One closely scrutinising him, however, would see that this is pretence; for his eyes are not on the slate, but furtively turned towards the ship's waist, watching the men, from whom he has just separated, and who seem to have their eyes upon *him*.

The young ladies thus repulsed—and almost rudely, as they take it— make no farther attempt to bring on a conversation; but, forsaking their chairs, hasten down the companion-stairs, and on to their own state-room— there to talk over a disappointment that has given chagrin to both, but which neither can satisfactorily explain.

The more they reflect on the conduct of the English sailor, the stranger it seems to them; and the greater is their vexation. For now they feel almost sure that something must have happened; that same thing—whatever it be—which dictated those cruel parting compliments. They seem doubly so now; for now they have evidence that such must have been the sentiment— almost proof of it in the behaviour of Harry Blew.

They are hurt by it—stung to the quick—and never again during that voyage do they attempt entering into conversation with the first officer of the *Condor*, nor with any one belonging to her—save her kindly captain, and the cook, equally kind to them, though in a different way.

Indeed, they no longer care to go on deck; only on rare occasions showing themselves there, as if they disliked looking upon him who has so rudely reminded them of the treason of their lovers.

Can it be treason? And if so, why? They ask these questions with eyes bent upon their fingers—on rings encircling them—placed there by those they are suspecting of disloyalty! The insignia should be proof of the contrary. But it is not, for love is above all things suspicious—however doting, ever doubting. Even on this evidence of its truth they no longer lean, and scarce console themselves with the hope, which that has hitherto been sustaining them. Now farther off than ever seems the realisation of that sweet expectancy hoped for and held out at last parting, promised in the phrase: "*Hasta Cadiz!*"

Chapter Fifty Five
"Down Helm"

"Land, ho!"

The cry is from a man stationed on the fore-topmast cross-trees of the *Condor*. Since sunrise he has been aloft—on the lookout for land. It is now near noon, and he has sighted it.

Captain Lantanas is not quite certain of what land it is. He knows it is the Veraguan coast, but does not recognise the particular place.

Noon soon after coming on, with an unclouded sky, enables him to catch the sun in its meridian altitude, and so make him sure of a good sight. It gives for latitude 7 degrees 20 minutes North, while his chronometer furnishes him with the longitude 82 degrees 12 minutes West.

As the Chilian is a skilled observer, and has confidence in the observations he has made, the land in sight should be the island of Coiba; or an island that covers it, called Hicaron. Both are off the coast of Veragua, westward from Panama Bay, and about a hundred miles from its mouth; into which the *Condor* is seeking to make entrance.

Having ciphered out his reckoning, the skipper enters it on his log:

"Latitude 7 degrees 20 minutes North, Longitude 82 degrees 12 minutes West *Wind West-South-West. Light breeze.*"

While penning these slight memoranda, little dreams the Chilian skipper how important they may one day become. The night before, while taking an observation of the stars, could he have read them astrologically, he might have discovered many a chance against his ever making another entry in that log-book.

A wind west-sou'-west is favourable for entering the Bay of Panama. A ship steering round Cabo Mala, once she has weathered this much-dreaded headland, will have it on her starboard quarter. But the *Condor*, coming down from north, gets it nearly abeam; and her captain, perceiving he has run a little too much coastwise, cries out to the man at the wheel—

"Hard a-starboard! Put the helm down! Keep well off the land!"

Saying this, he lights a cigarrito; for a minute or two amuses himself with his monkeys, always playful at meeting him; then, ascending to the poop-deck, enters into conversation with company more refined—his lady passengers.

These, with Don Gregorio, have gone up some time before, and stand on the port-side, gazing at the land—of course delightedly: since it is the first they have seen since the setting of that sun, whose last rays gleamed upon the portals of the Golden Gate, through which they had passed out of California.

The voyage has been somewhat wearisome: the *Condor* having encountered several adverse gales—to say nothing of the long period spent in traversing more than three thousand miles of ocean-waste, with only once or twice a white sail seen afar off, to vary its blue monotony.

The sight of *terra firma*, with the thought of soon setting foot on it, makes all joyous; and Captain Lantanas adds to their exhilaration by assuring them, that in less than twenty-four hours he will enter the Bay of Panama, and in twenty-four after, bring his barque alongside the wharf of that ancient port, so often pillaged by the *filibusteros*—better known as buccaneers. It is scarcely a damper when he adds, "Wind and weather permitting;" for the sky is of sapphire hue, and the gentle breeze wafting them smoothly along seems steady, and as if it would continue in the same quarter, which chances to be the right one.

After staying an hour or so on deck, indulging in cheerful converse, and happy anticipations, the tropic sun, grown too sultry for comfort, drives them down to the cabin, for shade and *siesta*—this last, a habit of all Spanish-Americans.

The Chilian skipper is also accustomed to take his afternoon nap; and this day, in particular, there is no need for his remaining longer on deck. He has determined his latitude, cast up his dead-reckoning, and set the *Condor* on her course. Sailing on a sea without icebergs, or other dangerous obstructions, he can go to sleep without anxiety on his mind.

So, leaving his second mate in charge—the first being off-watch—he descends to the cabin, and enters his sleeping-room on the starboard side.

But before lying down, he summons the cook, and gives orders for a dinner—to be dressed in the very best style the ship's stores can furnish; this in celebration of the event of having sighted land.

Then, stretching himself along a sofa, he is soon slumbering; profoundly, as one with nothing on his conscience to keep him awake.

For a time, the barque's decks appear deserted. No one seen, save the helmsman at the wheel, and the second mate standing by his side. The sailors not on duty have betaken themselves to the forecastle, and are lolling in their bunks; while those of the working-watch—with no work to do—have sought shady quarters, to escape from the sun's heat, now excessive.

The breeze has been gradually dying away, and is now so light that the vessel scarce makes steerage way. The only vigorous movements are those made by the Bornean apes. To them the great heat, so far from being disagreeable, is altogether congenial. They chase one another along the decks, accompanying their grotesque romping by cries equally grotesque—a hoarse jabbering, that sounds with weird strangeness throughout the otherwise silent ship. Except this, everything is profoundly still; no surging of waves, no rush of wind through the rigging, no booming of it against the bellied sails; only now and then a flap of one blown back, and aboard. The breeze has fallen to "light;" and the *Condor*, though with all canvas spread, and studding-sails out, is scarce making two knots an hour. This too with the wind well upon her quarter.

Still, there is nothing strange about the barque making so little way. What is strange, is the direction in which the breeze is now striking her. It is upon her starboard quarter, instead of the beam, as it should be; and as Captain Lantanas left it on going below!

Yet, since he went below, the wind has not shifted, not by a single point!

The barque must have changed her course; and indeed, has done this; the man at the wheel having put the helm *up*, instead of *down*, causing her to draw closer to the land, in direct contradiction to the orders of the captain!

Is it ignorance on the steersman's part? No, that cannot be. Gil Gomez has the helm; and being a seaman, should know how to handle it. Besides, Padilla is standing beside him; and the second mate, whatever his moral qualities, knows enough for the "conning" of a ship; and cannot fail to observe that the barque is running too much inshore.

Why the skipper's orders are not being carried out, is because they who now guide the *Condor's* course, do not intend that her keel shall ever cleave the waters of Panama Bay.

Why, this is told by the speech passing between them:

"You know all about the coast in there?" inquires Padilla, pointing to land looming up on the port-side.

"Every inch of it; at least, sufficient to make sure of a place where we can put in. That headland rising on the port-bow is Punta Marietta. We must stand well under, taking care not to round it before evening. If we did, and the breeze blow off-shore, which it surely will, we'd have trouble to make back. With this light wind, we won't make much way before nightfall. When Lantanas and the rest are down at dinner, we can put about, and run along till we sight a likely landing place."

"So far as being looked after by Lantanas," observes the second mate, "we need have no fear. To-day the cabin-dinner is to be a grand spread. I overheard his orders to that effect. He intends making things pleasant for his passengers before parting with them. As a matter of course, he'll stay all evening below—perhaps get fuddled to boot—which may spare us some trouble. It looks like luck, doesn't it?"

"Not much matter about that," rejoins Gomez; "it'll have to end all the same. Only, as you say, his staying below will make things a little easier, and save some unpleasantness in the way of blood-spilling. After dinner, the señoritas are sure to come on deck. They've done so every night, and I hope they won't make this night an exception. If Don Gregorio and the skipper keep downstairs, and—"

The dialogue is interrupted by the striking of bells to summon the relief-watch on duty.

Soon as the change is effected, Harry Blew takes charge, Striker replacing Gomez at the helm.

Just at this instant, the head of Captain Lantanas shows above the coaming of the companion stair.

Gomez seeing him, glides back to the wheel, gives a strong pull at the spokes, Striker assisting him, so as to bring the barque's head up, and the wind upon her beam.

"Good heavens!" exclaims the skipper excitedly, rushing on up the stair, and out. For he sees what not only excites his surprise, but makes him exceedingly angry.

Soon as setting his foot on deck, he steps briskly on to the rail, and looks out over the sea—shoreward, towards land, where no land should be seen!

First he glances ahead, then over the port-side, and again in the direction of the vessel's course. What sees he there to make such an impression upon him? A high promontory stretching out into the ocean, almost butting against the bows of his ship! It is Punta Marietta! He knows the headland, but knows, too, it should not be on the bow had his instructions been attended to.

"*Que cosa!*" he cries in a bewildered way, rubbing his eyes, to make sure they are not deceiving him; then to the helmsman:

"What does this mean, sir? You've been keeping too close inshore—the very contrary to what I commanded! Helm down—hard!"

Striker grumblingly obeys, bringing the barque up close to wind. Then the skipper turning angrily upon him, demands to know why his orders have not been carried out.

The ex-convict excuses himself, saying, that he has just commenced his trick, and knows nothing of what has been done before. He is keeping the vessel too on the same course she was on, when he took her from the last steersman.

"Who was the last?" thunders the irate skipper.

"Gil Gomez," gruffly replies Striker.

"Yes; it was he," says the first mate, who has come aft along with the captain. "The watch was Señor Padilla's, and Gomez has just left the wheel."

"Where is Gomez?" asks the captain, still in a towering passion, unusual for him.

"Gone forward, sir: he's down in the forecastle."

"Call him up! Send him to me at once!"

The first officer hurries away towards the head, and soon returns, Gomez with him.

The latter meets the gaze of Lantanas with a sullen look, which seems to threaten disobedience.

"How is this?" asks the Chilian. "You had the wheel during the last watch. Where have you been running to?"

"In the course you commanded, Captain Lantanas."

"That can't be, sir. If you'd kept her on as I set her, the land couldn't have been there, lying almost across, our cut-water. I understand my chart too well to have made such a mistake."

"I don't know anything about your chart," sulkily rejoins the sailor. "All I know is, that I kept the barque's head as directed. If she hasn't answered to it, that's no fault of mine; and I don't much like being told it is."

The puzzled skipper again rubs his eyes, and takes a fresh look at the coast-line. He is as much mystified as ever. Still the mistake may have been his own; and as the relieved steersman appears confident about it, he dismisses him without further parley, or reprimand.

Seeing that there will be no difficulty in yet clearing the point, his anger cools down, and he is but too glad to withdraw from an angry discussion uncongenial to his nature.

The *Condor* now hauled close to wind, soon regains lost weather-way, sufficient for the doubling of Punta Marietta; and before the bells of the second dog-watch are sounded, she is in a fair way of weathering the cape. The difficulty has been more easily removed by the wind veering suddenly round to the opposite point of the compass. For now near night, the land-breeze has commenced blowing off-shore.

Well acquainted with the coast, and noticing the change, Captain Lantanas believes all danger past; and with the tranquillity of his temper restored, goes back into his cabin, to join his passengers at dinner, just in the act of being served.

Chapter Fifty Six
Panama or Santiago?

It is the hour of setting the first night-watch, and the bells have been struck; not to summon any sailor from the forecastle, but intended only for the cabin and the ears of Captain Lantanas—lest the absence of the usual sound should awaken his suspicion, that all was not going right.

This night neither watch will be below, but all hands on deck, mates as foremast-men; and engaged in something besides the navigation of the vessel—in short, in destroying her! And, soon as the first shades of night descend over her, the crew is seen assembling by the manger-board close to the night-heads—all save the man who has charge of the steering, on this occasion Slush.

The muster by the manger-board is to take measures for carrying out their scheme of piracy and plunder, now on the eve of execution. The general plan is already understood by all; it but remains to settle some final details.

Considering the atrocity of their design, it is painful to see the first mate in their midst. A British sailor—to say nought of an old man-of-war's man—better might have been expected of him. But he *is* there; and not only taking part with them, but apparently acting as their leader.

His speech too clearly proclaims him chief of the conspiring crew. His actions also, as they have ever been, since the day when he signified to Striker his intention to join them. After entering into the conspiracy, he has shown an assiduity to carry it out worthy of a better cause.

His first act was backing up Striker's call for an equal division of the bounty. Holding the position of chief officer, this at once established his influence over the others; since increased by the zeal he has displayed—so that he now holds first place among the pirates, nearly all of them acknowledging, and submitting to, his authority.

If Edward Crozier could but see him now, and hear what he is saying, he would never more have faith in human being. Thinking of Carmen Montijo, the young officer has doubted women; witnessing the behaviour of Henry Blew, he might not only doubt man, but curse him.

Well for the recreant sailor, Crozier is not present in that conclave by the night-heads of the *Condor*. If he were, there would be speedy death to one he could not do otherwise than deem a traitor.

But the young officer is far away—a thousand miles of trackless ocean *now* between *Condor* and *Crusader*—little dreaming of the danger that threatens her to whom he has given heart, and promised hand; while Harry Blew is standing in the midst of ruffians plotting her ruin!

O man! O British sailor! where is your gratitude? What has become of your honour—your oath? The first gone; the second disregarded; the last broken!

Soon as together, the pirates enter upon discussion, the first question before them being about the place where they shall land.

Upon this point there is difference of opinion. Some are for going ashore at once, on a convenient part of the coast in sight; while others counsel running on till they enter Panama Bay.

At the head of those in favour of the latter is the chief mate, who gives his reasons thus:

"By runnin' up into the Bay o' Panyma, we'll get closer to the town; an' it'll be easier to reach it after we've done the business we intend doin', Panyma bein' a seaport, an' plenty o' vessels sailin' from it. After gettin' there we'd be able to go every man his own way. Them as wants can cross over the Isthmus, an' cut off on t'other side. An' Panyma bein' full o' strangers goin' to Californey, an' returnin' from it, we'd be less like to get noticed there. Whiles if we land on the coast here, where thar an't no good-sized town, but only some bits o' fishin' villages, we'd be a marked lot— sartin to run a good chance o' bein' took up, an' put into one o' thar prisons. Just possible too, we might land on some part inhabited by wild Indyins, an' lose not only the shinin' stuff, but our scalps. I've heerd say thar's the worst sort o' savages livin' on the coast 'long here. An' supposin' we meet neither Indyins nor whites, goin' ashore in a wilderness covered wi' woods, we might have trouble in makin' our way out o' them. Them thick forests o' the tropics an't so easy to travel through. I've know'd o' sailors as got cast away, perishin' in 'em afore they could reach any settlement. My advice, tharfore, shipmates, be, for us to take the barque on into the Bay; an' when we've got near enough the port, to make sure o' our bein' able to reach it, then put in for the shore. Panyma Bay's big enough to give us plenty choice o' places for our purpose."

"We've heard you out, Mr Blew," rejoins Gomez, "Now, let me say in answer, you haven't given a single reason for going by Panama Bay, that won't stand good for doing the very opposite. But there's one worth all, you haven't mentioned, and it's against you. While running up into the Bay, we'd be sure to meet other vessels coming out of it—scores of them. And supposing one should be a man-of-war—a British or American cruiser, say—and she takes it into her head to overhaul us; where would we be then?"

"An' if they did," returns Blew, "what need for us to be afeerd? Seein' that the barque's papers are all shipshape, they'd have to leave us as they found us. Let 'em overhaul, an' be blowed!"

"They mightn't leave us as they found us, for all that," argues Gomez. "Just when they took it into their heads to board the barque, might be when we would be slipping out of her. How then? Besides, other ships would have the chance of spying us at that critical moment. As I've said, your other arguments are wrong; I'll answer them in detail. But first, let me tell you all, I've got a pretty accurate knowledge of this coast. I ought to have, considering that I spent several years on and off it in a business which goes by the name of *contraband*. Now, all round the shores of Panama Bay there's just the sort of wild forest-covered country Mr Blew talks about getting strayed in. We might land within twenty miles of that port, and yet not be able to reach it, without great difficulty. Danger, too, from the savages, our first officer seems so much afraid of. Whereas, by putting ashore anywhere along here, we won't be far from the old Nicaraguan road, that runs all through the Isthmus. It will take us to the town of Panama; any that wish to go there. But there's another town as big as it, and better for our purpose; one wherein we'll be less likely to meet the unpleasant experience Mr Blew speaks of. It isn't much of a place for prisons. I'm speaking of Santiago, the capital city of Veragua; which isn't over a good day's journey from the coast. And we can reach it by an easy road. Still that's not the question of greatest importance. What most concerns us is the safety of the place *when we get to it*—and I can answer for Santiago. Unless customs have changed since I used to trifle away some time there—and people too—we'll find some who'll show us hospitality. With the money at our disposal—ay, a tenth part of it—I could buy up the *alcalde* of the town, and every judge in the province."

"That's the sort of town for us—and country too!" exclaim several voices. "Let's steer for Santiago!"

"We'll first have to put about," explains Gomez, "and run along the coast, till we find a proper place for landing."

"Yes," rejoins Harry Blew, speaking satirically, and as if exasperated by the majority going against him. "An' if we put about just now, we'll stand a good chance of goin' slap on them rocks on the port beam. Thar's a line o' breakers all along shore, far's I can see. How's a boat to be got through them? She'd be bilged to a sartinty."

"There are breakers, as you say," admits Gomez; "but their line doesn't run continuous, as it appears to do. I remember several openings where a boat, or ship for that matter, may be safely got through. We must look out for one of them."

"*Vaya, camarados!*" puts in Padilla, with a gesture of impatience. "We're wasting time, which just now is valuable. Let's have the barque about, and stand along the coast, as Gil Gomez proposes. I second his proposal; but, if you like, let it go to a vote."

"No need; we all agree to it."

"Ay; all of us."

"Well, shipmates," says Harry Blew, seeing himself obliged to give way, and conceding the point with apparent reluctance; "if ye're all in favour o' steerin' up coast, I an't goin' to stand out against it. It be the same to me one way or t'other. Only I thought, an' still think, we'd do better by runnin' up toward Panyma."

"No, no; Santiago's the place for us. We've decided to go there."

"Then to Santiago let's go. An' if the barque's to be put about, I tell ye there's no time to be lost. Otherways, we'll go into them whitecaps, sure; the which would send this craft to Davy Jones sooner than we intend. If we're smart about it, I dar say we can manage to scrape clear o' them; the more likely, as the wind's shifted, an' is now off-shore. It'll be a close shave, for all that."

"Plenty of sea-room," says the second mate. "But let's about with her at once!"

"You see to it, Padilla!" directs Gomez, who, from his success in having his plan adopted in opposition to that of the Englishman, feels his influence increased so much, he may now take command.

The second mate starts aft, and going up to the helmsman, whispers a word in his ear.

Instantly the helm is put hard up, and the barque paying off, wears round from east to west-nor'-west. The sailors at the same time brace about her yards, and trim her sails for the changed course; executing the manoeuvre, not, as is usual, with a chorused chant, but silently, as if the ship were a spectre, and her crew but spectral shadows.

Chapter Fifty Seven
A Cheerful Cuddy

The *Condor's* cabin is a snug little saloon, such as are often found on trading-vessels, not necessarily for passengers, but where the skipper has an eye to his own comforts, with tastes that require gratification.

Those of Captain Lantanas are refined, beyond the common run of men who follow his profession—usually rough sea dogs—caring little for aught else save their grub and grog.

That the Chilian skipper is not of this class is proved by the appearance of his "cuddy," which is neatly, if not luxuriously, furnished, and prettily decorated. In addition to the instruments that appertain to his calling— telescope, aneroid barometer, sextant, and compass, all placed conspicuously in racks—there is a bookcase of ornamental wood, filled with well-bound volumes; and several squares of looking-glass inlaid between the doors that lead to the four little staterooms—two on each side. There are two settees, with hair-cloth cushions, and lockers underneath the same, in which Don Gregorio's gold-dust is stowed.

Centrally stands a table, eight by six, mahogany, with massive carved legs, and feet firmly fixed to the floor. It is set lengthwise, fore and aft, a stout hair-cloth chair at top, another at bottom, and one at each side—all, like the table, stanchioned to the timbers of the half-deck.

Above a rack, with its array of decanters and glasses; and in the centre, overhead, a swing-lamp, lacquered brass—so constructed as to throw a brilliant glare on the surface of the table, while giving light more subdued to all other parts of the little cabin.

To-night its rays are reflected with more than ordinary sparkle. For the table beneath is spread with the best plate and glassware Captain Lantanas can set forth. And in the dishes now on it are the most savoury viands the *Condor's* cook can produce. While in bottles and decanters are wines of best *bouquet* and choicest vintage.

Around are seated the four guests; the Captain, as host, at the head; Don Gregorio, his *vis-à-vis*, at the foot; the ladies at opposite sides—right and left.

As the barque is going before a gentle breeze, without the slightest roll, or pitch, there is no need for guards upon the table. It shows only the spread of snow-white damask, the shining silver plate, the steel of Sheffield, the ware of Sèvres or Worcester, with the usual array of cut-glasses and decanters. In the centre an épergne, containing fruits, and some flowers, which, despite exposure to the saline breeze, Captain Lantanas has nursed into blooming. But the fruits seem flowers of themselves, having come from California, famed for the products of Pomona. There are peaches, the native growth of San Franciscan gardens, with plums and nectarines; melons and grapes from Los Angelos, further south; with the oranges, plantains, and pine-apples of San Diego. And, alongside these productions of the tropical and sub-tropical clime, are Newtown pippins, that have been imported into California from the far Eastern States, mellowed by a sea voyage of several thousand miles, around the stormy headland of Cape Horn.

The savoury meats tasted, eaten, and removed, the dessert, with its adjuncts, has been brought upon the table—this including wines of varied sorts. Although not greatly given to drink, the Chilian skipper enjoys his glass; and on this occasion takes half-a-dozen—it may be more. He is desirous of doing honour to his distinguished guests, and making the entertainment a merry one.

And his amiable effort has success.

In addition to having seen much of the world, he is by birth and education a gentleman. Although nothing more than the skipper of a merchant-ship—a South Sea trader at that—as already known, he is not one of the rude swaggering sort; but a gentle, kind-hearted creature, as well, if not better, befitted for the boudoir of a lady, than to stir about among tarred ropes, or face conflicting storm.

So kind and good has he shown himself, that his two fair passengers, in the short companionship of less than a month, have grown to regard him with affection; while Don Gregorio looks upon him in the light of a faithful friend. All three feel sorry they are so soon to part company with him. It is the only regret that casts a shadow over their spirits, as they sit conversing around the table so richly furnished for their gratification.

Eating fragrant fruits, and sipping sweet wines, for the moment they forget all about the hour of parting; the easier, as they listen to the tales which he tells to entertain them. He relates strange adventures he has had, on and around the shores of the great South Sea.

He has had encounters with the fierce Figian; the savage New Caledonian; both addicted to the horrid habit of anthropophagy. He has been a spectator to the voluptuous dances of Samoa, and looked upon the daughters of Otaheite, Owyhee, whose whole life is love.

With stories of the two extremes—symbols of man's supreme happiness, and his most abject misery—grim cannibals and gay odalisques—he amuses his guests, long detaining them at the table.

Enthralled by his narration—naïve, truthful, in correspondence with the character of the man—all three listen attentively. The señoritas are charmed, and, strange to say, more with his accounts of Figi and New Caledonia, than those relating to Otaheite and Hawaii. For to the last-named group of islands have gone Edward Crozier and Willie Cadwallader. There these may meet some of the brown-skinned *bayaderes* Captain Lantanas so enthusiastically describes—meet, dance with, and admire them!

But the jealous fancies thus conjured up are fleeting in the shadows of summer clouds; and, soon passing, give place to pleasanter thoughts. Now that land is near, and a seaport soon to be reached, the young ladies are this night unusually elated; and, listening to the vivid description of South Sea scenes, they reflect less sadly and less bitterly on the supposed slight received at the hands of their lovers.

In return, Don Gregorio imparts to the Chilian skipper some confidences hitherto withheld. He is even so far admitted into the family intimacy as to be told how both the señoritas are soon to become brides. To which is added an invitation, that should he ever carry the *Condor* to Cadiz, he will not only visit them, but make their house his home.

Several hours are passed in this pleasant way; interspersed with song and music—for both Carmen and Iñez can sing well, and accompany their singing with the guitar.

At length the ladies retire to their state-room, not to stay, but to robe themselves, with the design of taking a turn in the open air. The smooth motion of the ship, with the soft moonlight streaming through the cabin windows, tempts them to spend half-an-hour on deck, before going to rest for the night; and on deck go they.

Lantanas and the ex-haciendado remain seated at the table. Warmed by the wine—of which both have partaken pretty freely—the Chilian continues to pour his experiences into the ears of his passenger; while the latter listens with unflagging interest.

Supping choice *canario*, his favourite tipple, the former takes no note of aught passing around, nor thinks of what may be doing on the *Condor's* deck. All through the evening he has either forgotten or neglected the duties appertaining to him as her commanding officer. So much, that he fails to notice a rotatory motion of the cabin, with the table on which the decanters stand; or, if observing, attributes it to the wine having disturbed the equilibrium of his brain.

But the cabin *does* revolve, the table with it, to the extent of a three-quarter circle. Gradually is the movement being made—gently, from the sea being calm—silently—with no voice raised in command—no piping of boatswain's whistle—no song of sailors as they brace round the yards, or board tacks and sheets!—not a sign to tell Captain Lantanas has been set upon a course, astray, and likely to lead to her destruction.

Chapter Fifty Eight
Kill or Drown?

Having set the *Condor's* course, with Slush still in charge at the helm, the second mate returns to the fore-deck, where by the manger-board the others are again in deliberation; Gomez counselling, or rather dictating what they are next to do.

The programme he places before them is in part what has been arranged already—to run along coast till they discover a gap in the line of coral reef; for it is this which causes the breakers. Further, they are told that, when such gap be found, they will lower a boat; and having first scuttled the barque, abandon her; then row themselves ashore.

The night is so far favourable to the execution of the scheme. It is a clear moonlight; and running parallel to the trend of the shore, as they are now doing, they can see the breakers distinctly, their white crests in contrast with the dark *façade* of cliff, which extends continuously along the horizon's edge; here and there rising into hills, one of which looming up on the starboard bow has the dimensions of a mountain.

The barque is now about a league's distance from land; and half-way between are the breakers, their roar sounding ominously through the calm quiet of the night. As they were making but little way—scarce three knots an hour—one proposes that the boat be lowered at once, and such traps as they intend taking put into her. In such a tranquil sea it will tow alongside in safety.

As this will be some trouble taken off their hands in advance, the plan is approved of, and the pinnace being selected, as the most suitable boat for beaching.

Clustering around it, they commence operations. Two leap lightly inside; insert the plug, ship the rudder, secure the oars and boat-hooks, clear the life-lines, and cast off the lanyards of the gripes; the others holding the fall-tackle in hand, to see that they were clear for running. Then taking a proper turn they lower away.

And, soon as the boat's bottom touches water, with the two men in it, the painter, whose loose end has been left aboard, is hauled fast, bringing the boat abeam, where it is made fast under a set of man-ropes, already dropped over the side.

Other movements succeed; the pirates passing to and from the forecastle, carrying canvas bags, and bundles of clothing, with such other of their belongings as they deem necessary for a debarkation like that intended. A barrel of pork, another of biscuit, and a beaker of water are turned out, and handed down into the boat; not forgetting a keg containing rum, and several bottles of wine they have purloined, or rather taken at will, from Captain Lantanas' locker bins.

The miscellaneous supply is not meant for a voyage, only a stock to serve for that night, which they must needs spend upon the beach—as also to provision them for the land journey, to be commenced in the morning.

In silence, but with no great show of caution or stealth, are these movements made. They who make them have but little fear of being detected, some scarce caring if they be. Indeed, there is no one to observe them, save those taking part. For the negro cook, after dressing the dinner, and serving it, has gone out of the galley for good; and, now acting as table waiter, keeps below in the cabin.

Soon everything is stowed in the pinnace, except that which is to form its most precious freight; and again the piratical crew bring their heads together, to deliberate about the final step; the time for taking which is fast drawing nigh.

A thing so serious calls for calm consideration, or, at all events, there must be a thorough understanding among them. For it is the disposal of those they have destined as victims. How this is to be done, nothing definite has yet been said. Even the most hardened among them shrinks from putting it in words. Still it is tacitly understood. The ladies are to be taken along, the others to be dealt with in a different way. But how? that is the question, yet unasked by any, but as well understood by all, as if it had been spoken in loudest voice.

For a time they stand silent, waiting for some one who can command the courage to speak.

And one does this—a ruffian of unmitigated type, whose breast is not stirred by the slightest throb of humanity. It is the second mate, Padilla. Breaking silence, he says:

"Let us cut their throats, and have done with it!"

The horrible proposition, more so from its very laconism, despite the auditory to whom it is addressed, does not find favourable response. Several speak in opposition to it; Harry Blew first and loudest. Though broken his word, and forfeited his faith, the British sailor is not so abandoned as to contemplate murder in such cool, deliberate manner. Some of those around him have no doubt committed it; but he does not feel up to it. Opposing Padilla's counsel, he says:

"What need for our killin' them? For my part, I don't see any."

"And for your part, what would you do?" sneeringly retorts the second mate.

"Give the poor devils a chance for their lives."

"How?" promptly asks Padilla.

"Why; if we set the barque's head out to sea, as the wind's off-shore, she'd soon carry them beyond sight o' land, and we'd niver hear another word o' 'em."

"No, no! that won't do," protest several in the same breath. "They might get picked up, and then we'd be sure of hearing of them—may be something more than words."

"*Carrai!*" exclaims Padilla scornfully; "that *would* be a wise way. Just the one to get our throats in the *garrota*. You forget that Don Gregorio Montijo is a man of the big grandee kind. And should he ever set foot ashore, after what we'd done to him, he'd have influence enough to make most places— ay, the whole of the habitable globe—a trifle too hot for us. There's an old saw, about dead men telling no tales. No doubt most of you have heard it, and some have reason to know it true. Take my advice, *camarados*, and let us act up to it. What's your opinion, Señor Gomez?"

"Since you ask for it," responds Gomez, speaking for the first time on this special matter, "my opinion is, that there's no need for any difference among us. Mr Blew's against the spilling of blood, and so would I, if it could be avoided. But it can't, with safety to ourselves; at least not in the way he has suggested. To act as he advises would be madness on our part—nay more, it might be suicide. Still, there don't seem any necessity for a cold cutting of throats, which has an ugly sound about it. The same with knocking on the head; they're both too brutal. I think I know a way that will save us from resorting to either, and, at the same time, ensure our own safety."

"What way?" demanded several voices. "Tell us!"

"One simple enough; so simple, I wonder you haven't all thought of it, same as myself. Of course, we intend sending this craft to the bottom of the sea. But she's not likely to go down all of a sudden; nor till we're a good way off out of sight. We can leave the gentlemen aboard, and let them slip quietly down along with her!"

"Why, that's just what Blew proposes," say several.

"True," returns Gomez; "but not exactly as I mean it. He'd leave them free to go about the ship—perhaps get out of her before she sinks, on a sofa, or hencoop, or something."

"How would *you* do with them?" asks one, impatiently.

"Tie, before taking leave of them."

"Bah!" exclaims Padilla, a monster to whom spilling blood seems congenial. "What's the use of being at all that bother? It's sure to bring some. The skipper will resist, and so'll the old Don. What then? We'll be compelled to knock them on the head all the same, or toss them overboard. For my part, I don't see the object of making such a worry about it; and still say, let's stop their wind at once!"

"Dash it, man!" cries Striker, hitherto only a listener, but a backer of Harry Blew; "you 'pear to 'a been practisin' a queery plan in jobs o' this sort. Mr Gomez hev got a better way o't, same as I've myself seed in the Australian bush, wheres they an't so bloodthirsty. When they stick up a chap theer, so long's he don't cut up nasty, they settle things by splicin' him to a tree, an' leavin' him to his meditashuns. Why can't we do the same wi' the skipper, an' the Don, an' the darkey—supposin' any o' 'em to show reefractry?"

"That's it!" exclaims Davis, strengthening the proposal thus endorsed by his chum, Striker. "My old pal's got the correct idea of sich things."

"Besides," continues the older of the ex-convicts, "this job seems to me simple enuf. We want the swag, an' some may want the weemen. Well, we can git both 'ithout the needcessity o' doin' murder!"

Striker's remonstrance sounds strange—under the circumstances, serio-comical.

"What might you call murder?" mockingly asks Padilla. "Is there any difference between their getting their breath stopped by drowning, or the cutting of their throats? Not much to them, I take it; and no more to us. If there's a distinction, it's so nice I can't see it. *Carramba!* no!"

"Whether you see it or not," interposes Harry Blew, "there be much; and for myself, as I've said, I object to spillin' blood, where the thing an't absolute needcessary. True, by leavin them aboard an' tied, as Mr Gomez suggests, they'll get drowned, for sartin; but it'll at least keep our hands clear o' blood murder!"

"That's true!" cried several in assent. "Let's take the Australian way of it, and tie them up!"

The assenting voices are nearly unanimous; and the eccentric compromise is carried.

So far everything is fixed, and it but remains to arrange about the action, and apportion to every one his part.

For this very few words suffice, the apportionment being, that the first officer, assisted by Davis, who has some knowledge of ship-carpentry, is to see to the scuttling of the vessel; Gomez and Hernandez to take charge of the girls, and get them into the boat; Slush to look after the steering; Padilla to head the party entrusted with the seizure of the gold; while Striker, assisted by Tarry and the Frenchman, is to secure the unfortunate men by fast binding, or, as he calls it, "sticking them up."

The atrocious plan is complete, in all its revolting details—the hour of execution at hand.

Chapter Fifty Nine
The Tintoreras

With all sail set, the barque glides silently on to her doom.

Gomez now "cons" Slush the steering, he alone having any knowledge of the coast. They are but a half-league from land, shaving close along the outer edge of the breakers. The breeze blowing off-shore makes it easy to keep clear of them.

There is high land on the starboard bow, gradually drawing to the beam. Gomez remembers it; for in the clear moonlight is disclosed the outline of a hill, which, once seen, could not easily be forgotten; a *cerro* with two summits, and a *col* or saddle-like depression between.

Still, though a conspicuous landmark, it does not indicate any anchorage; only that they are entering a great gulf which indents the Veraguan coast.

As the barque glides on, he observes a reach of clear water opening inland; to all appearance a bay, its mouth miles in width.

He would run her into it, but is forbidden by the breakers, whose froth-crested belt extends across the entrance from cape to cape.

Running past, he again closes in upon the land, and soon has the two-headed hill abeam, its singular silhouette conspicuous against the moonlit sky. All the more from the moon being directly beyond it, and low down, showing between the twin summits like a great globe-shaped lamp there suspended.

When nearly opposite, Gomez notes an open space in the line of breakers, easily told by its dark tranquil surface, which contrasts with the white horse-tails lashing up on each side of it.

Soon as sighting it, the improvised pilot leaves the helm, after giving Slush some final instructions about the steering. Then forsaking the poop, he proceeds towards the ship's waist, where he finds all the others ready for action. Striker and La Crosse with pieces of rope for making fast the ill-fated men; Padilla and his party armed with axes and crowbars—the keys with which they intend to open the locker-doors.

Near the mainmast stands the first mate, a lighted lantern in his hand; Davis beside him, with auger, mallet, and chisel. They are by the hatchway, which they have opened, intending descent into the hold. With the lantern concealed under the skirt of his ample dreadnought, Harry Blew stands within the shadow of the mast, as if reflecting on his faithlessness—ashamed to let his face be seen. He even appears reluctant to proceed in the black business, while affecting the opposite.

As the others are now occupied in various ways, with their eyes turned from him, he steps out to the ship's side, and looks over the rail. The moon is now full upon his face, which, under her soft innocent beams, shows an expression difficult as ever to interpret. The most skilled physiognomist could not read it. More than one emotion seem struggling within his breast, mingling together, or succeeding each other, quick as the changing hues of the chameleon. Now, as if cupidity, now remorse, anon the dark shadow of despair!

This last growing darker, he draws nearer to the side, and looks earnestly over, as if about to plunge into the briny deep, and so rid himself of a life, ever after to be a burden!

While standing thus, apparently hesitating as to whether he shall drown himself and have done with it, soft voices fall upon his ear, their tones blending with the breeze, as it sweeps in melancholy cadence through the rigging of the ship. Simultaneously there is a rustling of dresses, and he sees two female forms robed in white, with short cloaks thrown loosely over their shoulders, and kerchiefs covering their heads.

Stepping out on the quarterdeck, they stand for a short while, the moon shining on their faces, both bright and innocent as her beams. Then they stroll aft, little dreaming of the doom that awaits them.

That sight should soften his traitorous heart. Instead, it seems but to steel it the more—as if their presence recalled and quickened within him some vow of revenge. He hesitates no longer; but gliding back to the hatch, climbs over its coaming, and, lantern in hand, drops down into the hold— there to do a deed which neither light of moon nor sun should shine upon.

Though within the tropic zone, and but a few degrees from the equinoctial line, there is chillness in the air of the night, now nearing its mid-hours.

Drawing their cloaks closer around them, the young ladies mount up to the poop-deck, and stand resting their hands on the taffrail.

For a time they are silent; their eyes directed over the stern, watching the foam in the ship's wake, lit up with luminous phosphorescence.

They observe other scintillation besides that caused by the *Condor's* keel. There are broad splatches of it all over the surface of the sea, with here and there elongated *sillons*, seemingly made by some creatures in motion, swimming parallel to the ship's course, and keeping pace with her.

They have not voyaged through thirty degrees of the Pacific Ocean to be now ignorant of what these are. They know them to be sharks, as also that some of larger size and brighter luminosity are the tracks of the *tintorera*—that species so much-dreaded by the pearl-divers of Panama Bay and the Californian Gulf.

This night both *tiburones* and *tintoreras* are more numerous than they have ever observed them—closer also to the vessel's side; for the sharks, observantly have seen a boat lowered down, which gives anticipation of prey within nearer reach of their ravenous jaws.

"*Santissima!*" exclaims Carmen, as one makes a dash at some waif drifting astern. "What a fearful thing it would be to fall overboard there—in the midst of those horrid creatures! One wouldn't have the slightest chance of being saved. Only to think how little space there is between us and certain death! See that monster just below, with its great, glaring eyes! It looks as if it wanted to leap up, and lay hold of us. Ugh! I mustn't keep my eyes on it any longer. It makes me tremble in a strange way. I do believe, if I continued gazing at it, I should grow giddy, and drop into its jaws."

She draws back a pace or two, and for some moments remains silent—pensive. Perhaps she is thinking of a sailor saved from sharks after falling among them, and more still of the man who saved him. Whether or no, she soon again speaks, saying:

"*Sobrina!* are you not glad we're so near the end of our voyage?"

"I'm not sorry, *tia*—I fancy no one ever is. I should be more pleased, however, if it *were* the end of our voyage, which unfortunately it isn't. Before we see Spain, we've another equally as long."

"True—as long in duration, and distance. But otherwise, it may be very different, and I hope more endurable. Across the Atlantic we'll have passage in a big steamship, with a grand dining saloon, and state sleeping-rooms, each in itself as large as the main-cabin of the *Condor*. Besides, we'll have plenty of company—passengers like ourselves. Let us hope they may turn out nice people. If so, our Atlantic voyage will be more enjoyable than this on the Pacific."

"But we've been very comfortable in the *Condor*; and I'm sure Captain Lantanas has done all he could to make things agreeable for us."

"He has indeed, the dear good creature; and I shall ever feel grateful to him. Still you must admit that, however well meant, we've been at times a little bored by his learned dissertations. O Iñez, it's been awfully lonely, and frightfully monotonous—at least, to me."

"Ah! I understand. What you want is a bevy of bachelors as fellow-passengers, young ones at that. Well; I suppose there will be some in the big steamer. Like enough, a half-score of our moustached *militarios*, returning from Cuba and other colonies. Wouldn't that make our Atlantic voyage enjoyable?"

"Not mine—nothing of the sort, as you ought to know. To speak truth, it was neither the loneliness nor monotony of our Pacific voyage that has made it so miserable. Something else."

"I think I can guess the something else."

"If so, you'll be clever. It's more than I can."

"Might it have anything to do with that informal leave-taking? Come, Carmen—you promised me you'd think no more about it till we see them in Cadiz, and have it all cleared up."

"You're wrong again, Iñez. It is not anything of that."

"What then? It can't be the *mare amiento*? Of it I might complain. I'm even suffering from it now—although the water is so smooth. But you! why, you stand the sea as well as one of those rough sailors themselves! You're just the woman to be a naval officer's wife; and when your *novio* gets command of a ship, I suppose you'll be for circumnavigating the world with him."

"You're merry, *mora*."

"Well, who wouldn't be, with the prospect of soon setting foot on land. For my part, I detest the sea; and when I marry my little *guardia-marina*, I'll make him forsake it, and take to some pleasanter profession. And if he prefer doing nothing, by good luck the rent of my lands will keep us both comfortably, with something to spare for a town house in Cadiz. But say, Carmen! What's troubling you? Surely you must know?"

"Surely I don't, Iñez."

"That's strange—a mystery. Might it be regret at leaving behind your *preux chevaliers* of California—that grand, gallant De Lara, whom, at our last interview, we saw sprawling in the road dust? You ought to feel relieved at getting rid of him, as I of my importunate suitor, the Señor Calderon. By the way, I wonder whatever became of them! Only to think of their never coming near us to say good-bye! And that nothing was seen or heard of them afterwards! Something must have happened. What could it have been! I've tried to think, but without succeeding."

"So I the same. It is indeed very strange; though I fancy father heard something about them, which he does not wish to make known to us. You remember what happened after we'd left the house—those men coming to it in the night. Father has an idea they intended taking his gold, believing it still there. What's more, I think he half suspects that of the four men—for there appears to have been four of them—two were no other than our old suitors, Francisco de Lara and Faustino Calderon."

She had almost said *sweethearts*, but the word has a suggestion of pain.

"*Maria de Merced!*" exclaims Iñez. "It's frightful to think of such a thing. We ought to be thankful to that good saint for saving us from such villains, and glad to get away from a country where their like are allowed to live."

"*Sobrina*, you've touched the point. The very thought that's been distressing me is the remembrance of those men. Even since leaving San Francisco, as before we left, I've had a strange heaviness on my heart—a sort of boding fear—that we haven't yet seen the last of them. It haunts me like a spectre. I can't tell why, unless it be from what I know of De Lara. He's not the man to submit to that ignominious defeat of which we were witnesses. Be assured he will seek to avenge it. We expected a duel, and feared it. Likely there would have been one, but for the sailing of the English ship. Still that won't hinder such a desperate man as De Lara from going after Edward, and trying to kill him any way he can. I have a fear he'll follow him—is after him now."

"What if he be? Your *fiancé* can take care of himself. And so can mine, if Calderon should get into his silly head to go after *him*. Let them go, so long as they don't come after us; which they're not likely—all the way to Spain."

"I'm not so sure of that. Such as they may make their way anywhere. Professional gamblers—as we know them to be—travel to all parts of the world. All cities give them the same opportunity to pursue their calling—why not Cadiz? But, Iñez, there's something I haven't told you, thinking you might make mock of it. I've had a fright more than once—several times, since we came aboard."

"A fright! what sort of a fright?"

"If you promise not to laugh at me, I'll tell you."

"I promise. I won't."

"'Twould be no laughing matter were it true. But, of course, it could only be fancy."

"Fancy about what? Go on, *tia*: I'm all impatience."

"About the sailors on board. All have bad faces; some of them seem very *demonios*. But there's one has particularly impressed me. Would you believe it, Iñez, he has eyes exactly like De Lara's! His features too resemble those of Don Francisco; only that the sailor has a beard and whiskers, while he had none. Of course the resemblance can be but accidental. Still, it caused me a start, when I first observed it, and has several times since. Never more than this very morning, when I was up here, and saw that man. He was at the wheel, all by himself, steering. Several times, on turning suddenly round, I caught him looking straight at me, staring in the most insolent manner. I had half a mind to complain to Captain Lantanas; but reflecting that we were so near the end of our voyage—"

She is not permitted to say more. For at the moment, a man appearing on the poop-deck, as if he had risen out of it, stands before her—the sailor who resembles De Lara!

Making a low bow, he says:

"Not *near* the end of your voyage, *señorita*; but *at* it," adding with an ironical smile: "Now, ladies! you're going ashore. The boat is down; and, combining business with pleasure, it's my duty to hand you into it."

While he is speaking, another of the sailors approaches Iñez; Hernandez, who offers his services in a similar style and strain.

For a moment, the girls are speechless, through sheer stark astonishment. Horror succeeds, as the truth flashes upon them. And then, instead of coherent speech, they make answer by a simultaneous shriek; at the same time making an attempt to retreat towards the cabin-stair.

Not a step is permitted them. They are seized in strong arms; and half-dragged, half-lifted off their feet, hurried away from the taffrail.

Their cries are stifled by huge woollen caps drawn over their heads, and down to their chins, almost choking them. But though no longer seeing, and only indistinctly hearing, they can tell where they are being taken. They feel themselves lifted over the vessel's side, and lowered down man-ropes into a boat; along the bottom of which they are finally laid, and held fast—as if they had fallen into the jaws of those terrible *tintoreras*, they so lately looked at keeping company with the ship!

Chapter Sixty
The Scuttlers

Harry Blew is in the hold, Bill Davis beside him.

They are standing on the bottom-timbers on a spot they have selected for their wicked work, and which they have had some difficulty in finding. They have reached it, by clambering over sandal-wood logs, cases of Manilla cigars, and piles of tortoise-shell. Clearing some of these articles out of the way, they get sight of the vessel's ribs, and at a point they know to be under the water-line. They know also that a hole bored between their feet, though ever so small, will in due time fill the barque's hold with water, and send her to the bottom of the sea.

Davis, auger in hand, stands in readiness to bore the hole; waiting for the first officer to give the word.

But something stays the latter from giving it, as the former from commencing the work.

It is a thought that seems to occur simultaneously to both, bringing their eyes up to one another's faces, in a fiancé mutually interrogative. Blew is the first to put it in speech.

"Dang me, if I like to do it!"

"Ye've spoke my mind exact, Mr Blew!" rejoins Davis. "No more do I."

"'Tan't nothing short of murder," pursues the chief mate. "An' that's just why I an't up to it; the more, as there an't any downright needcessity. As I sayed to them above, I can see no good reason for sinking the ship. She'd sail right out, an' we'd never hear word o' her again. An' if them to be left 'board o' her shud get picked up, what matters that to us? We'll be out o' the way, long afore they could go anywhere to gi'e evidence against us. Neer a fear o' their ever findin' us—neyther you nor me, anyhow. I dare say, Davis, you mean to steer for some port, where we're not likely to meet any more Spaniards. I do, when I've stowed my share o' the plunder."

"Yes; I'm for Australia, soon's I can get there. That's the place for men like me."

"There you'll be safe enough. So I, where I intend goin'. And we'll both feel better, not havin' a ugly thing to reflect back on. Which we would, if we send these three poor creeturs to Davy's locker. Now, I propose to you what you heerd me say to the rest: let's gi'e them a chance for their lives."

"And not do this?"

As he puts the question, Davis points his auger to the bottom of the ship.

"There an't no need—not a morsel o' good can come from sinkin' her. And not a bit harm in lettin' her slip."

"What will the others say?"

"They won't know anything about it—they can't unless we tell 'em. And we won't be the fools to do that. As I argied to them, with the wind off-shore, as 'tis now, she'll scud out o' sight o' land long afore daylight. Bill Davis! whatsomever the others may do, or think they're doin', let's me an' you keep our consciences clear o' this foul deed. Believe me, mate, we'll both feel better for't some day."

"If you think they won't know, I'm agreed."

"How can they? There an't none o' them to see what we do down here. 'Taint likely there's any listener. Gie a knock or two wi' the mallet!"

The ship's carpenter obeying, strikes several blows against an empty water-cask, the noise ascending through the open hatch. He suspends his strokes at hearing exclamations above; then screams in the shrill treble of female voices.

"You see they're not thinking o' us," says the mate. "Them Spaniards are too busy about their own share o' the job. They're gettin' the girls into the boat."

"Yes; that's what they're doing."

"Sweet girls both be. An't they, Davis?"

"Ay, that they are; a pair of reg'lar beauties."

"Look here, shipmate! Since we've settled this other thing, I want to say a word about them too, and I may's well say it now. Gomez and that land-lubber, Hernandez, are layin' claim to them, as if they had a right. Now they haven't, no more than any o' the rest o' us. Some others may have fancies, too. I confess to havin' a weakness for the one wi' the copper-coloured hair, which is she as Gil Gomez wants to 'propriate. I made no objection to his takin' her into the boat. But soon's we get ashore, I intend to stan' out for my rights to that little bit o' property, which are just as good as his. Do you feel like backin' me?"

"Hang me, if I don't! I'm myself a bit sweet upon the dark 'un, and have been, ever since settin' eyes on her. And though I've said nothing, like yourself, I wasn't going to give that point up, before having a talk about it. You say the word—I'll stan' by you. And if it comes to fightin', I'll make short work with that bandy-legged chap Hernandez, the one as wants her. We can count on Jack Striker on our side; and most like the Dane and Dutchman; La Crosse for certain. Frenchy don't cotton to them Spaniards, ever since his quarrel with Padilla. But, as you say, let's go in for the girls, whether or not. You can claim the light-haired. I'm for the dark one, an' damned if I an't ready to fight for her—to the death!"

"As I for the other!" exclaims the ex-man-o'-war, in eager serious earnest.

"But what's to be done after we go ashore?" asks Davis. "That's what's been bothering me. We're about to land in a strange country, but where these Spanish chaps will be at home, speakin' the lingo, an'll so have the advantage of us. There's a difficulty. Can you see a way out of it?"

"Clearly."

"How?"

"Because the girls don't care for eyther o' the two as are layin' claim to them. Contrarywise, they hate 'em both. I've knowd that all along. So, if we get 'em out o' their clutches—at the same time givin' the girls a whisper about protectin' them—they'll go willin'ly 'long wi' us. Afterwards, we can act accordin' to the chances that turn up. Only swear you'll stan' by me, Bill, an' wi' Striker to back us, we'll bring things right."

"I'm bound to stan' by you; so'll Jack, I'm sure. Hark! that's him, now! He's calling to us. By God, I believe they're in the boat!"

"They are! Let's hurry up! Just possible them Spaniards may take it into their heads—. Quick, shipmate! Heave after me!"

With this, Blew holds out the lantern to light them up the hatch, both making as much haste to reach the deck as if their lives depended upon speed.

Chapter Sixty One
The Barque Abandoned

While the scuttlers are shirking their work in the *Condor's* hold, and simultaneous with the abduction on deck, a scene is transpiring in her cabin, which might be likened to a saturnalia of demons.

The skipper and Don Gregorio, sitting over their walnuts and wine, are startled by the sound of footsteps descending the stair. As they are heavy and hurried, bearing no resemblance to the gentle tread of woman—it cannot be the ladies coming down again. Nor yet the negro cook, since his voice is heard above in angry expostulation. Two of the sailors have just seized him in his galley, throttled him back on the bench, and are there lashing him with a piece of log-line.

They at the cabin-table know nothing of this. They hear his shouts, and now also the shrieks of the young girls; but have no time to take any steps, as at that instant the cuddy-door is dashed open, and several men come rushing in; the second mate at their head. Lantanas, sitting with his face to the door, sees them first, Don Gregorio, turning in his seat, the instant after.

Neither thinks of demanding a reason for the rude intrusion. The determined air of the intruders, with the fierce expression on their faces, tells it would be idle.

In a time shorter than it takes to tell it, the two doomed men are made fast to the stanchioned chairs; where they sit bolt upright, firm as bollard heads. But not in silence. Both utter threats, oaths, angry fulminations.

Not for long are they allowed this freedom of speech. One of the sailors, seizing a pair of nutcrackers, thrusts them between the skipper's teeth, gagging him. Another with a corkscrew, does the like for Don Gregorio.

Then the work of pillage proceeds. The locker lids are forced, and the boxes of gold-dust dragged out.

Several goings and comings are required for its transport to the pinnace; but at length it is stowed in the boat, the plunderers taking their seats beside it.

One lingers in the cabin behind the rest; that fiend in human shape who has all along counselled killing the unfortunate men.

Left alone with them, helpless, and at his mercy, he looks as if still determined to do this. It is not from any motive of compassion that he goes from one to the other, and strikes the gags from between their teeth. For at the same time he apostrophises them in horrid mockery:

"*Carramba*! I can't think of leaving two gentlemen seated at such a well-furnished table, and no end of wine, without being able to hob-nob, and drink one another's health!"

Then specially addressing himself to Lantanas, he continues:

"You see, captain, I'm not spiteful; else I shouldn't think of showing you this bit of civility, after the insults you've offered me, since I've been second officer of your ship."

After which, turning angrily upon Don Gregorio, and going close up, he shrieks into his ears:

"Perhaps you don't know me, Montijo? Can your worship recall a circumstance that occurred some six years ago, when you where *alcalde-mayor* of Yerba Buena? You may remember having a poor fellow pilloried, and whipped, for doing a bit of contraband. I was that unfortunate individual. And this is my satisfaction for the indignity you put upon me. Keep your seats, gentlemen! Drink your wine and eat your walnuts. Before you've cleared the table, this fine barque, with your noble selves, will be at the bottom of the sea."

The ruffian concludes with a peal of scornful laughter, continued as he ascends the cabin-stair, after striding out and banging the door behind him!

On deck, he sees himself alone; and hurrying to the ship's waist, scrambles over the side, down into the boat; where he finds everything stowed, the oarsmen seated on the thwarts, their oars in the rowlocks, ready to shove off.

They are not all there yet. Two—the first mate and Davis are still aboard the barque—down in her hold.

There are those who would gladly cast loose, and leave the laggards behind. Indeed, soon as stepping into the boat, Padilla proposes it, the other Spaniards abetting him.

But their traitorous desire is opposed by Striker. However otherwise debased, the ex-convict is true to the men who speak his own tongue.

He protests in strong determined language, and is backed by the Dutchman, Dane, and La Crosse, as also Tarry and Slush.

"Bah!" exclaims Padilla, seeing himself in the minority; "I was only jesting. Of course, I had no intention to abandon them. Ha, ha, ha!" he adds with a forced laugh, "we'd be the blackest of traitors to behave that way."

Striker pays no heed to the hypocritical speech, but calls to his old chum and Harry Blew—alternately pronouncing their names.

He gets response, and soon after sees Davis above, clambering over the rail.

Blew is not far behind, but still does not appear. He is by the foot of the mainmast with a haulyard in his hands as though hoisting something aloft. The moon has become clouded, and it is too dark for any one to see what it is. Besides, there is no one observing him—no one could, the bulwarks being between.

"Hillo, there, Blew!" again hails Striker; "what be a-keepin' ye? Hurry down! These Spanish chaps are threetnin' to go off without ye."

"Hang it!" exclaims the chief mate, now showing the side; "I hope that an't true!"

"Certainly not!" exclaims Padilla; "nothing of the kind. We were only afraid you might delay too long, and be in danger of going down with the vessel."

"Not much fear of that," returns Blew, dropping into the boat, "It'll be some time afore she sinks. Ye fixed the rudder for her to run out, didn't ye?"

"Ay, ay!" responds he who was the last at the wheel.

"All right; shove off, then! That wind'll take the old *Condor* straight seawart; and long afore sunrise she'll be out sight o' land. Give way there—way!"

The oars dip and plash. The boat separates from the side, with prow turned shoreward.

The barque, with her sails still spread, is left to herself, and the breeze, which wafts her gently away towards the wide wilderness of ocean.

Proceeding cautiously, guarding against the rattle of an oar in its rowlock, the pirates run their boat through the breakers, and approach the shore. Right ahead are the two summits, with the moon just going down behind; and between is a cove of horseshoe shape, the cliffs extending around it.

With a few more strokes the boat is brought into it and glides on to its innermost end.

As the keel grates upon the shingly strand, their ears are saluted by a chorus of cries—the alarm signal of seabirds, startled by the intrusion; among them the scream of the harpy eagle, resembling the laugh of a maniac.

These sounds, despite their discordance, are sweet to those now hearing them. They tell of a shore uninhabited—literally, that the "coast is clear"—just as they wish it.

Beaching the boat, they bound on shore, and lift their captives out; then the spoils—one unresisting as the other.

Some go in search of a place where they may pass the night; for it is too late to think of proceeding inland.

Between the strand and the cliff's base, these discover a beach, several feet above sea-level, having an area of over an acre, covered with coarse grass, just the spot for a camping-place.

As the sky has become clouded, and threatens a downpour of rain, they carry thither the boat's sail, intending to rig it up as an awning.

But a discovery is made which spares them the trouble. Along its base the cliff is honeycombed with caves, one of ample dimensions, sufficient to shelter the whole crew. A ship's lamp, which they have brought with them, when lighted throws its glare upon stalactites, that sparkle like the pendants of chandeliers.

Disposing themselves in various attitudes, some reclined on their spread pilot-coats, some seated on stones or canvas bags, they enter upon a debauch with the wines abstracted from the stores of the abandoned barque—drinking, talking, singing, shouting, and swearing, till the cavern rings with their hellish revelry. It is well their captives are not compelled to take part in, or listen to, it. To them has been appropriated one of the smaller grottoes, the boat-sail fixed in front securing them privacy. Harry Blew has done this. In the breast of the British man-o'-war's man there is still a spark of delicacy. Though his gratitude has given way to the greed of gold, he has not yet sunk to the level of that ruffianism around him.

While the carousal is thus carried on within the cave, without, the overcast sky begins to discharge itself. Lightning forks and flashes athwart the firmament; thunder rolls reverberating along the cliffs; a strong wind sweeps them; the rain pouring down in torrents.

It is a tropic storm — short-lived, lasting scarce half-an-hour.

But, while on, it lashes the sea into fury, driving the breakers upon the beach, where the beat has been left loosely moored.

In the reflux of the ebbing tide, this is set afloat and carried away seaward. Driven then upon the coral reef, it bilges, is broken to pieces, when the fragments, as waifs, dance about, and drift far away over the foam-crested billows.

Chapter Sixty Two
Two Tarquins

It is after midnight. A calm has succeeded the storm; and silence reigns around the cove where the pirates have put in. The seabirds have returned to their perches on the cliff, and now sit noiselessly—save an occasional angry scream from the osprey, as a whip-poor-will, or some other plumed plunderer of the night, flits past his place of repose, near enough to wake the tyrant of the sea-shore, and excite his jealous rage.

Other sounds are the dull boom of the outside breakers, and the lighter ripple of the tidal wave washing over a strand rich in shells.

Now and then, a *manatee*, raising its bristled snout above the surf, gives out a low prolonged wail, like the moan of some creature in mortal agony.

But there is no human voice now. The ruffians have ended their carousal. Their profane songs, ribald jests, and drunken cachinations, inharmoniously mingling with the soft monotone of the sea, have ceased to be heard. They lie astretch along the cavern floor, its hollow aisles echoing back their snores and stertorous breathing.

Still they are not all asleep, nor all within the cavern. Two are outside, sauntering along the shadow of the cliff. As the moon has also gone down, it is too dark to distinguish their faces. Still, there is light enough reflected from the luminous surface of the sea to show that neither is in sailor garb, but the habiliments of landsmen—this the national costume of Spanish California. On their heads are *sombreros* of ample brim; wide trousers—*cahoneras*—flap loose around their ankles; while over their shoulders they carry cloaks, which, by the peculiar drape, are recognisable as Mexican *mangas*. In the obscurity the colour of these cannot be determined, though one is scarlet, the other sky-blue.

Apparelled as the two men are now, it would be difficult to identify them as Gil Gomez and José Hernandez. For all it is they.

They are strolling about without fear, or thought of any one observing them. Yet one is; a man, who has come out of the larger cavern just after them, and who follows them along the cliff's base. Not openly or boldly, as designing to join in their deliberation; but crouchingly and by stealth, as if playing spy on them.

He is in sailor togs, wearing a loose dreadnought coat, which he buttons on coming out of the cavern. But before closing it over his breast, the butt of a pistol, and the handle of a knife, could be seen gleaming there, both stuck behind a leathern waist belt.

On first stepping forth, he stands for a time with eyes fixed upon the other two. He can see them but indistinctly, while they cannot see him at all, his figure making no silhouette against the dark disc of the cave's mouth. And afterwards, as he moves along the cliff, keeping close in, its shadow effectually conceals him from their view. But still safer is he from being observed by them, after having ensconced himself in a cleft of rock; which he does while their backs are turned upon him.

In the obscure niche he now occupies no light falls upon his face—not a ray. If there did, it would disclose the countenance of Harry Blew; and as oft before, with an expression upon it not easily understood. But no one sees, much less makes attempt to interpret it.

Meanwhile the two saunterers come to a stop and stand conversing. It is Gomez who is first heard saying:

"I've been thinking, *compañero*, now we've got everything straight so far, that our best plan will be to stay where we are till the other matter's fixed."

"What other are you speaking of?"

"The marrying, of course."

"Oh! that. Well?"

"We can send on for the *padre*, and bring him here; or failing him, the *cura*. To tell truth, I haven't the slightest idea of where we've come ashore. We may be a goodish distance from Santiago; and to go there, embargoed as we are, there's a possibility of our being robbed of our pretty baggage on the route. You understand me?"

"I do!"

"Against risk of that kind, it is necessary we should take precautions. And the first—as also the best I can think of—is to stay here till we're spliced. One of our two Californian friends can act as a messenger. Either, with six words I shall entrust to him, will be certain to bring back an ecclesiastic, having full powers to perform the flea-bite of a ceremony. Then we can march inland without fear—ay, with flying colours; both Benedicts, our blushing brides on our arms, and in Santiago spend a pleasant honeymoon."

"Delightful anticipation!"

"Just so. And for that very reason, we mustn't risk marring it; which we might, by travelling as simple bachelors. So I say, let us get married before going a step farther."

"But the others? Are they to assist at our nuptials?"

"Certainly not."

"In what way can it be avoided?"

"The simplest in the world. It's understood that we divide our plunder the first thing in the morning. When that's done, and each has packed up his share, I intend proposing that we separate—every one to go his own gait."

"Will they agree to that, think you?"

"Of course they will. Why shouldn't they? It's the safest way for all, and they'll see that. Twelve of us trooping together through the country—to say nothing of having the women along—the story we're to tell about shipwreck might get discredited. When that's made clear, to our old shipmates, they'll be considerate for their own safety. Trust me for making it clear. Of course we'll keep our Californian friends to act as groomsmen; so that the only things wanted will be a brace of bridesmaids."

"Ha, ha, ha!" laughs Hernandez.

"And now to see about our brides. We've not yet proposed to them. We went once to do that, and were disappointed. Not much danger of that now."

"For all that, we may count upon a flat refusal."

"Flat or sharp, little care I. And it won't signify, one way or the other. In three days or less I intend calling Carmen Montijo my wife. But come on; I long to lay my hand and heart at her feet."

Saying which Gomez strides on towards the grotto, the other by his side, like two Tarquins about to invade the sleep of virginal innocence.

Chapter Sixty Three
Within the Grotto

Though the grotto is in darkness, its occupants are not asleep. To them repose is impossible; for they are that moment in the midst of anguish, keen as human heart could feel. They have passed through its first throes, and are for the while a little calmer. But it is the tranquillity of deep, deadening grief, almost despair. They mourn him dearest to them as dead.

Nor have they any doubt of it. How could they? While in the boat, they heard their captors speak about the scuttling of the ship, well knowing what they meant. Long since has she gone to the bottom of the sea, with the living left aboard, or perhaps only their lifeless bodies; for they may have been murdered before! No matter now in what way death came to them. Enough of sadness and horror to think it has come—enough for the bereaved ones to know they are bereft.

Nor do they need telling why it has all been done. Though hindered from seeing while in the boat, they have heard. Cupidity the cause; the crime a scheme to plunder the ship. Alas! it has succeeded.

But all is not yet over. Would that it were! There is something still to come; something they fear to reflect upon, or speak of to one another. What is to be their own fate?

Neither can tell, or guess. Their thoughts are too distracted for reasoning. But in the midst of vague visions, one assumes a shape too well-defined. It is the same of which Carmen was speaking when seized.

She again returns to it, saying:

"Iñez, I'm now almost sure we are not in the hands of strangers. From what has happened, and some voices we heard, I fear my suspicions have been too true!"

"Heaven help us, if it be so!"

"Yes; Heaven help us! Even from pirates we might have expected some mercy; but none from them. *Ay de mi*! what will become of us?"

The interrogatory is only answered by a sigh. The spirit of the Andalusian girl, habitually cheerful, is now crushed under a weight of very wretchedness. Soon again they exchange speech, seeking counsel of one another. Is there no hope, no hand to help, no one to whom they may turn in this hour of dread ordeal? No—not one! Even the English sailor, in whom they had trusted, has proved untrue; to all appearance, chief of the conspiring crew! Every human being seems to have abandoned them. Has God?

"Let us pray to Him!" says Carmen.

"Yes," answers Iñez; "He only can help us now."

They kneel side by side on the hard, cold floor of the cave, and send up their voices in earnest prayer. They first entreat the Holy Virgin that the life of him dear to them may yet be spared; then invoke her protection for themselves, against a danger both dread as death itself. They pray in trembling accents, but with a fervour eloquent through fear.

Solemnly pronouncing "Amen!" they make the sign of the cross; in darkness, God alone seeing it.

As their hands drop down from the gesture, and while they are still in a kneeling attitude, a noise outside succeeds their appeal to Heaven, suddenly recalling them to earthly thoughts and fears.

They hear voices of men in conversation; at the same time the sailcloth is pushed aside, and two men press past it into the cave. Soon as entering one says:

"Señoritas! we must ask pardon for making our somewhat untimely call; which present circumstances render imperative. It's to be hoped, however, you won't stand upon such stiff ceremony with us, as when we had the honour of last paying our respects to you."

After this singular peroration, the speaker pauses to see what may be the effect of his words. As this cannot be gathered from any reply—since none is vouchsafed—he continues; "Dona Carmen Montijo, you and I are old acquaintances; though, it may be, you do not remember my voice. With the sound of the sea so long echoing in your ears, that's not strange. Perhaps the sense of sight will prove more effectual in recalling an old friend. Let me give you something to assist it!"

Saying this, he holds out a lantern, hitherto concealed beneath his cloak. As it lights up the grotto, four figures are seen erect; for the girls have sprung to their feel in apprehension of immediate danger. Upon all, the light shines clear; and, fronting her, Carmen Montijo sees—too surely recognising it—the face of Francisco de Lara; while in her *vis-à-vis*, Iñez Alvarez beholds Faustino Calderon!

Yes, before them are their scorned suitors; no longer disguised in sailor garb, but resplendent in their Californian costume—the same worn by them on that day of their degradation, when De Lara rolled in the dust of the Dolores road.

Now that he has them in his power, his triumph is complete; and in strains of exultation he continues:

"So, ladies! you see we've come together again! No doubt you're a little surprised at our presence, but I hope not annoyed."

There is no reply to this taunting speech.

"Well, if you won't answer, I shall take it for granted you *are* annoyed; besides looking a little alarmed too. You've no need to be that."

"No, indeed," endorses Calderon. "We mean you no harm—none whatever."

"On the contrary," goes on De Lara, "only good. We've nothing but favours to offer you."

"Don Francisco de Lara!" exclaims Carmen, at length breaking silence, and speaking in a tone of piteous expostulation; "and you, Don Faustino Calderon, why have you committed this crime? What injury have we ever done you?"

"Come! not so fast, fair Carmen! Crime's a harsh word, and we've not committed any as yet—nothing to speak of."

"No crime! *Santissima*! My father—my poor father!"

"Don't be uneasy about him. He's safe enough."

"Safe! Dead! Drowned! *Dios de mi alma*!"

"No, no. That's all nonsense," protests the fiend, adding falsehood to his sin of deeper dye. "Don Gregorio is not where you say. Instead of being at the sea's bottom, he is sailing upon its surface; and is likely to be, for Heaven knows how long. But let's drop that subject of the past, which seems unpleasant to you, and talk of the present—of ourselves. You ask what injury you've ever done us? Faustino Calderon may answer for himself to the fair Iñez. To you, Doña Carmen, I shall make reply—But we may as well confer privately."

At this he lays hold of her wrist, and leads her aside; Calderon conducting Iñez in the opposite direction.

When the whole length of the cavern is between the two pairs, De Lara resumes speech:

"Yes, Doña Carmen; you *have* done me an injury—a double wrong I may call it."

"How, sir?" she asks, withdrawing her hand from his, with a disdainful gesture. "How?" he retorts. "Why, in making me love you—by leading me to believe my love returned."

"You speak falsely; I never did so."

"You did, Doña Carmen; you did. It is you who speak false, denying it. That is the first wrong I have to reproach you with. The second is in casting me off, as soon as you supposed you'd done with me. Not so, as you see now. We're together again—never more to part till I've had satisfaction for all. I once hinted—I now tell you plainly, you've made a mistake in trifling with Francisco de Lara."

"I never trifled with you, señor. *Dios mio!* What means this? Man—if you be a man—have mercy! Oh! what would you—what would you?"

"Nothing to call for such distracted behaviour on your part. On the contrary, I've brought you here—for I'll not deny that it's I who have done it—to grant you favours, instead of asking them. Ay, or even satisfying resentments. What I intend towards you, I hope you will appreciate. To shorten explanations—for which we've neither opportunity nor time—I want you for my wife—*want you, and will have you.*"

"*Your* wife!"

"Yes; my wife. You needn't look surprised, nor counterfeit feeling it. And equally idle for you to make opposition. I've determined upon it. So, you must many me."

"Marry the murderer of my father! Sooner than do that, you shall also be mine. Wretch! I am in your power. You can kill me now."

"I know all that, without your telling me. But I don't intend killing you. On the contrary, I shall take care to keep you alive, until I've tried what sort of a wife you'll make. Should you prove a good one, and fairly affectionate, we two may lead a happy life together, notwithstanding the little unpleasantness that's been between us. If not, and our wedded bondage prove uncongenial, why, then, I may release you in the way you wish, or any other that seems suitable. After the honeymoon, you shall have your choice. Now Doña Carmen! those are my conditions. I hope you find them fair enough!"

She makes no reply. The proud girl is dumb, partly with indignation, partly from the knowledge that all speech would be idle. But while angry to the utmost, she is also afraid—trembling at the alternative presented—

death or dishonour; the last if she marry the murderer of her father; the first if she refuse him!

The ruffian repeats his proposal, in the same cynical strain, concluding it with a threat.

She is at length stung to reply; which she does in but two words, twice repeated in wild despairing accent. They are:

"Kill me—kill me!"

Almost at the same time, and in similar strain does Iñez answer her cowardly suitor, who in a corner of the grotto has alike brought her to bay.

After the dual response, there is a short interval of silence. Then De Lara, speaking for both, says:

"Señoritas! we shall leave you now; and you can go to sleep without fear of further solicitation. No doubt, after a night's rest, you'll awake to a more sensible view of matters in general, and the case as it stands. Of one thing be assured; that there's no chance of your escaping from your present captivity, unless by consenting to change your names. And if you don't consent, they'll be changed all the same. Yes, Carmen Montijo! before another week passes over your head, you shall be addressed as Doña Carmen de Lara.

"And you, Iñez Alvarez, will be called Doña Iñez Calderon. No need for you to feel dishonoured by a name among the first in California. Noble as your own; ay, or any in old Spain."

"*Hasta mañana, muchacas!*" salutes De Lara, preparing to take leave. "*Pasan Vs buena noche!*"

Calderon repeating the same formulary, the two step towards the entrance, lift up the piece of suspended sailcloth, and pass out into night. They have taken the lantern along with them, again leaving the grotto in darkness.

The girls grope their way, till their arms come in contact. Then, closing in mutual embrace, they sink together upon the cold flinty floor!

Chapter Sixty Four
Oceanwards

Another day dawns over the great South Sea. As the golden orb shows above the crest of the central American Cordillera, its beams scatter wide over the Pacific, as a lamp raised aloft, flashing its light afar. Many degrees of longitude receive instant illumination, at once turning night into day.

An observer looking west over that vast watery expanse would see on its shining surface objects that gladdened not the eyes of Balboa. In his day, only the rude Indian *balsa, or* frail *periagua*, afraid to venture out, stole timidly along the shore; but now huge ships, with broad white sails, and at rare intervals the long black hull of a steamer, thick smoke vomited forth from her funnel, may be descried in a offing that extends to the horizon itself.

But not always may ships be seen upon it; for the commerce of the Pacific is slight compared with that of the Atlantic, and large vessels passing along the coast of Veragua are few and far between.

On this morning, however, one is observed, and but one; she not sailing coastwise, but standing out towards mid-ocean, as though she had just left the land.

As the ascending sun dispels the night darkness around her, she can be descried as a white fleck on the blue water, her spread sails seeming no bigger than the wings of a sea-gull. Still, through a telescope—supposing it in the hands of a seaman—she may be told to be a craft with polacca-masts; moreover, that the sails on her mizzen are not square-set, but fore-and-aft, proclaiming her a barque. For she is one; and could the observer through his glass make out the lettering upon her stern, he would read there her name, *El Condor*.

Were he transported aboard of her, unaware of what has happened, it would surprise him to find her decks deserted; not even a man at the wheel, though she is sailing with full canvas spread, even to studding-sails; no living thing seen anywhere, save two monstrous creatures covered with rust-coloured hair—mocking counterfeits of humanity.

Equally astonished would he be at finding her forecastle abandoned; sailors' chests with the lids thrown open, and togs lying loose around them! Nor would it lessen his astonishment to glance into the galley, and there behold a black man sitting upon its bench, who does not so much as rise to receive him. Nor yet, descending her cabin-stair, to see a table profusely spread, at either end guest, alike uncourteous in keeping their seats, on the laces of both an expression of agonised despair! And all *this* might be seen on board the Chilian barque, on the morning after she was abandoned by her traitorous and piratical crew, A sad night has it been for the three unfortunates left aboard, more especially the two constrained to sit at the cabin-table. Both have bitterest thoughts, enough to fill the cup of their misery to the brim. A night of anguish for the ex-haciendado. Not because of having seen his treasure, the bulk of his fortune, borne off before his eyes; but from the double shriek which, at that same instant, reached him from the deck, announcing the seizure of things more dear. His daughter and grand-daughter were then made captive; and, from their cries suddenly leasing, he dreaded something worse—fearing them stifled by death. Reminded of an event in Yerba Buena, as also recognising the ruffian who taunted him, made it the more probable that such had been their fate. He almost wished it; he would rather that, than a doom too horrible to think of.

The first mate? He must have been killed too; butchered while endeavouring to defend them? The unsuspicious captain could not think of his chief officer having gone against him; and how could Don Gregorio believe the man so recommended turning traitor?

While they were thus charitably judging him, they received a crushing response; hearing his voice among the mutineers—not in expostulation, or opposed, but as if taking part with them! One, Striker, called out his name, to which he answered; and, soon after, other speeches from his lips sounded clear through the cabin windows, open on that mild moonlight night.

Still listening, as they gazed in one another's face with mute astonishment, they heard a dull thud against the ship's side—the stroke of a boat-hook as the pinnace was shoved off—then a rattle, as the oars commence working in the tholes, succeeded by the plash of the oar-blades in the water. After that, the regular "dip-dip," at length dying away, as the boat receded, leaving the abandoned vessel silent as a graveyard in the mid-hour of night.

Seated with face towards the cuddy windows, Don Gregorio could see through them, and as the barque's bow rose on the swell, depressing her stern, he commanded a view of the sea outside.

There, upon its calm clear surface, he made out a dark object moving away. It was a boat filled with forms, the oar-blades rising and tailing in measured stroke, flashing the phosphorescence on both sides. No wonder at his earnest look—his gaze of concentrated anguish! That boat held all that was dear to him—bearing that all away, he knows not whither, to a fate he dare not reflect upon. He could trace the outlines of land beyond, and perceive that the boat was being rowed for it, the barque at the same time sailing seaward, each instant widening the distance between them. But for a long while he could distinguish the black speck with luminous jets on either side, as the oar-blades intermittently rose and fell, till at length, entering within the shadow of the land, he lost sight of it.

"Gone! all gone!" groaned the bereaved father, his beard drooping down to his breast, his countenance showing he has surrendered up his soul to despair! So, too, Lantanas.

Then both ceased struggling and shouting, alike convinced of the idleness of such demonstrations. The chief officer a mutineer, so must all the others; and all had forsaken the ship. No; not all! There is one remains true, and who is still on her—the black cook. They heard his voice, though not with any hope. It came from a distant part of the ship in cries betokening distress. They could expect no help from him. He was either disabled, or, as themselves, fast bound.

Throughout the night they heard it; the intervals between becoming longer, the voice fainter, till he also, yielding to despair, was silent.

As the morning sun shines in through the stern windows, Don Gregorio can see they are out of sight of land. Only sea and sky are visible to him; but neither to Lantanas, whose face is the other way; so fastened he cannot even turn his head.

The barque is scudding before a breeze, which bears her still farther into the great South Sea; on whose broad bosom she might beat for weeks, months—ay, till her timbers rot—without sighting ship, or being herself descried by human eye. Fearful thought—appalling prospect to those constrained to sit at her cabin-table!

With that before their minds, the morning light brings no joy. Instead, it but intensifies their misery. For they are now sure they have no chance of being rescued.

They sit haggard in their chairs—for no sleep has visited the eyes of either—like men who have been all night long engaged in a drunken debauch.

Alas! how different! The glasses of wine before them are no longer touched, nor the fruits tasted. Neither the bouquet of the one, nor the perfume of the other, has any charm for them now. Either is as much beyond their reach, as if a thousand miles off, instead of on a table between them!

Gazing in one another's faces, they at once fancy it a dream. They can scarcely bring themselves to realise such a situation! Who could! The rude intrusion of the ruffian crew—the rough handling they have had—the breaking open of the lockers—and the boxes of gold borne off—all seem but the phantasmagoria of some horrible vision!

Chapter Sixty Five
Partitioning the Spoil

The same sun that shines upon the abandoned barque lights up the men who abandoned her, still on that spot where they came ashore. As the first rays fall over the cliff's crest, they show a cove of semicircular shape, backed by a beetling precipice. A ledge or dyke, sea-washed, and weed-covered, trends across its entrance, with a gate-like opening in the centre, through which, at high tide, the sea sweeps in, though never quite up to the base of the cliff. Between this and the strand lies the elevated platform already spoken of, accessible from above by a sloping ravine, the bed of a stream running only when it rains. As said, it is only an acre or so in extent, and occupying the inner concavity of the semicircle. The beach is not visible from it, this concealed by the dry reef which runs across it as the chord of an arc. Only a small portion of it can be seen through the portal which admits the tidal flow. Beyond, stretches the open sea outside the surf, with the breakers more than a mile off.

Such is the topography of the place where the mutineers have made landing and passed the night. When the day dawns, but little is there seen to betray their presence. Only a man seated upon a stone, nodding as if asleep, at intervals awakening with a start, and grasping at a gun between his legs; soon letting it go, and again giving way to slumber, the effects of that drunken debauch kept up to a late hour. He would be a poor sentinel were there need for vigilance.

Seemingly, there is none. No enemy is near—no human being in sight; the only animate objects some seabirds, that, winging their way along the face of the cliff, salute him with an occasional scream, as if incensed by his presence in a spot they deem sacred to themselves.

The sun fairly up, he rises to his feet, and walks towards the entrance of the larger cavern; then stopping in front of it, cries out:

"Inside there, shipmates! Sun's up—time to be stirring!"

Seeing him in motion, and hearing his hail, the gulls gather, and swoop around his head in continuous screaming. In larger numbers, and with cries more stridulent, as his comrades come forth out of the cave, one after another—yawning, and stretching their arms.

The first, looking seaward, proposes to refresh himself by a plunge in the surf; and for this purpose starts toward the beach. The others, taken with the idea, follow in twos and threes, till in a string all are *en route* for the strand.

To reach this, it is necessary for them to pass through the gap in the transverse ledge; which the tide, now at ebb, enables them to do.

He who leads, having gone through it, on getting a view of the shore outside, suddenly stops; as he does so, sending back a shout. It is a cry of surprise, followed by the startling announcement:

"The boat's gone!"

This should cause them apprehension; and would, if they but knew the consequences. Ignorant of these, they make light of it, one saying:

"Let her go, and be damned! We want no boats now."

"A horse would be more to our purpose," suggests a second; "or, for that matter, a dozen."

"A dozen donkeys would do," adds a third, accompanying his remark with a horse-laugh. "It'll take about that many to pack our possibles."

"What's become of the old pinnace, anyhow?" asks one in sober strain; as, having passed through the rock-portal, they stand scanning the strand. All remember the place where they left the boat; and see it is not there.

"Has any one made away with it?"

The question is asked, and instantly answered, several saying, no. Striker, the man who first missed it, vouchsafes the explanation:

"The return tide's taken it out; an' I dar say, it's broke to bits on them theer breakers."

They now remember it was not properly moored, but left with painter loose; and do not wonder it went adrift. They care little, indeed nothing, and think of it no longer; but, stripping, plunge into the surf.

After bathing to their hearts' content, they return to the cavern, and array themselves in garments befitted to the life they intend leading. Their tarry togs are cast off, to be altogether abandoned; for each has a suit of shore clothes, brought away from the barque.

Every one rigged out in his own peculiar style, and breakfast despatched, they draw together to deliberate on a plan of future action. But first the matter of greatest moment—the partition of the spoils.

It is made in little time, and with no great trouble. The boxes are broken open, and the gold-dust measured out in a pannikin; a like number of measures apportioned to each.

In money value no one can tell the exact amount of his share. Enough satisfaction to know it is nigh as much as he can carry.

After each has appropriated his own, they commence packing up, and preparing for the inland journey. And next arises the question, what way are they to go?

They have already resolved to strike for the city of Santiago; but in what order should they travel? Separate into several parties, or go all together?

The former plan, proposed by Gomez, is supported by Padilla, Hernandez, and Velarde. Gomez gives his reasons. Such a large number of pedestrians along roads where none save horsemen are ever seen, could not fail to excite surprise. It might cause inconvenient questions to be asked them—perhaps lead to their being arrested, and taken before some village *alcalde*. And what story could they tell?

On the other hand, there will be the chance of coming across Indians; and as those on the Veraguan coast are ranked among the "bravos"—having preserved their independence, and along with it their instinctive hostility to the whites—an encounter with them might be even more dangerous than with any *alcalde*. Struggling along in squads of two or three, they would run a risk of getting captured, or killed, or scalped—perhaps all three.

This is the suggestion of Harry Blew, Striker and Davis alone favouring his view. All the others go against it, Gomez ridiculing the idea of danger from red men; at the same time enlarging on that to be apprehended from white ones.

As the majority have more reason to fear civilised man than the so-called savage, it ends in their deciding for separation. They can come together again in Santiago if they choose it; or not, should chance for good or ill so determine. They are all now amply provided for, playing an independent part in the drama of life; and with this pleasant prospect, they may part company without a sigh of regret.

Chapter Sixty Six
A Tender Subject

The pirates having definitively settled the mode of making their inland journey, there is a short interregnum; during which most of those ready for the road stand idling, one or two still occupied in equipping themselves.

La Crosse has been sent up the ravine, to report how things look landward.

The four Spaniards have signified their intention to remain a little longer on the ground; while the three Englishmen have not said when they will leave. These are together conferring in low voice; but with an earnestness in their eyes—especially Blew's—which makes it easy to guess the subject. Only thoughts of woman could kindle these fiery glances.

Soon all appear ready to depart. Still no one stirs from the spot. For there is something yet: still another question to be determined; to most of them a matter of little, though to some of all consequence.

In the latter light, two at least regard it; since with them it has been the source, the primary motive, the real spur to all their iniquitous action. In a word, it is the women.

The captives: how are they to be disposed of?

They are still within the grotto, unseen, as the sailcloth curtains it. Breakfast has been taken to them, which they have scarce touched.

And, now, the time has come for deciding what has to be done with them; no one openly asks, or says word upon the subject; though it is uppermost in the thoughts of all. It is a delicate question, and they are shy of broaching it. For there is a sort of tacit impression there will be difficulty about the appropriation of this portion of the spoils—an electricity in the air, that foretells dispute and danger. All along it had been understood that two men laid claim to them; their claim, whether just or not, hitherto unquestioned, or, at all events, uncontested. These, Gomez and Hernandez. As they had been the original designers of the supposed deed, now done, their confederates, men little given to love-making, had either not thought about the women, or deemed their possession of secondary importance.

But now, at the eleventh hour, it has become known that two others intend asserting a claim to them—one being Blew, the other Davis.

And these two certainly seem so determined, their eyes constantly turning towards the grotto where the girls are, unconscious of the interest they are exciting.

At length the dreaded interrogatory is put—and point blank. For it is Jack Striker who puts it. The "Sydney Duck" is not given to sentiment or circumlocution.

Speaking that all may hear him, he blurts out:

"Well, chums? what are we to do wi' the weemen?"

"Oh! they?" answers Gomez in a drawling tone, and with an affectation of indifference. "*You've* nothing to do with them, and needn't take any trouble. They'll go with us—with Señor Hernandez and myself."

"Will they, indeed?" sharply questions the chief officer.

"Of course," answers Gomez.

"I don't see any of course about it," rejoins Blew. "And more'n that, I tell ye they don't go with ye—leastwise, not so cheap as you think for."

"What do you mean, Mr Blew?" demands the Spaniard, his eyes betraying anger, with some uneasiness.

"No use your losin' temper, Gil Gomez. You ain't goin' to scare me. So you may as well keep cool. By doin' that, and listenin', you'll larn what I mean. The which is, that you and Hernandez have no more right to them creeturs in the cave than any o' the rest of us. Just as the gold, so ought it to be wi' the girls. In coorse, we can't divide them all round; but that's no reason why any two should take 'em, so long's any other two wants 'em as well. Now, *I* wants one o' them."

"And I another!" puts in Davis.

"Yes," continues Blew; "and though I be a bit older than you, Mr Gomez, and not quite so pretentious a gentleman, I can like a pretty wench as well's yerself. I've took a fancy to the one wi' the tortoise-shell hair, an' an't goin' to gi'e her up in the slack way you seem to be wishin'."

"Glad to hear it's the red one, Blew," says Davis. "As I'm for the black one, there'll be no rivalry between us. Her I mean to have—unless some better man hinders me."

"Well," interpolates Striker, "as 'twas me first put the questyun, I 'spose I'll be allowed to gi'e an opeenyun?"

No one saying nay, the ex-convict proceeds:

"As to any one hevin' a speecial claim to them weemen, nobody has, an' nobody shed have. 'Bout that, Blew's right, an' so's Bill. An' since the thing's disputed, it oughter be settled in a fair an' square—"

"You needn't waste your breath," interrupts Gomez, in a tone of determination. "I admit no dispute in the matter. If these gentlemen insist, there's but one way of settling. First, however, I'll say a word to explain. One of these ladies is my sweetheart—was, before I ever saw any of you. Señor Hernandez here can say the same of the other. Nay, I may tell you more; they are pledged to us."

"It's a lie!" cries Blew, confronting the slanderer, and looking him straight in the face. "A lie, Gil Gomez, from the bottom o' your black heart!"

"Enough!" exclaims Gomez, now purple with rage. "No man can give Frank Lara the lie, and live after."

"Frank Lara; or whatever you may call yerself, I'll live long enough to see you under ground—or what's more like, hangin' high above it wi' your throat in a halter. Don't make any mistake about me. I can shoot straight as you."

"Avast theer!" shouts Striker to Gomez, now calling himself De Lara, seeing him about to draw a pistol. "Keep yer hand off that wepun! If theer must be a fight, let it be a fair one. But, before it begin, Jack Striker has a word to say."

While speaking, he has stepped between the two men, staying their encounter.

"Yes; let the fight be a fair one!" demand several voices, as the pirates come clustering around.

"Look here, shipmates!" continues Striker, still standing between the two angry men, and alternately eyeing them. "What's the use o' spillin' blood about it—maybe killin' one the other? All for the sake o' a pair o' petticoats, or a couple o' pairs, as it be. Take my advice, an' settle the thing in a pacifical way. Maybe ye will, after ye've heerd what I intend proposin'; which I daresay 'll be satisfactory to all."

"What is it, Jack?" asks one of the outsiders.

"First, then, I'm goin' to make the observashun, that fightin' an't the way to get them weemen, whoever's fools enough to fight for 'em. Theer's somethin' to be done besides."

"Explain yourself, old Sydney! What's to be done besides?"

"If the gals are goin' to be fought for, they've first got to be *paid* for."

"How that?"

"How? What humbuggin' stuff askin' such a questyin! Han't we all equil shares in 'em? Coorse we hev. Tharfore, them as wants 'em, must pay for 'em. An' they as wants 'em so bad as to do shootin' for 'em, surely won't objek to that. Theer appear to be four candydates in the field, an', kewrous enuf, they're set in pairs, two for each one o' the gals. Now, 'ithout refarin' to any fightin' that's to be done—an', if they're fools enuf to fight, let 'em—I say that eyther who eventyally gets a gal, shed pay a considerashin o' gold-dust all roun' to the rest o' us—at least a pannikin apiece. That's what Jack Striker proposes first."

"It's fair," says Slush.

"Nothing more than our rights," observes Tarry; the Dane and the Dutchman also endorsing the proposal.

"I agree to it," says Harry Blew.

"I also," adds Davis.

De Lara—late Gomez—signifies his assent by a disdainful nod, but without saying a word; Hernandez imitating the action. In fear of losing adherents, neither dares disapprove of it.

"What more have you to say, Jack?" asks Slush, recalling Striker's last words, which seemed to promise something else.

"Not much. Only thet I think it a pity, after our livin' so long in harmony thegither, we can't part same way. Weemen's allers been a bother ever since I've know'd 'em. An', I 'spose, it'll continue so to the eend o' the chapter, an' the eend o' some lives heer. I repeet, thet it be a pity we shed hev to wind up wi' a quarrel wheer blood's bound to be spilt. Now, why, can't it be settled 'ithout thet? I think I know o' a way."

"What way?"

"Leave it to the ladies theirselves. Gi'e them the chance o' who they'd like for theer purtectors; same time lettin' 'em know they've got to choose 'tween one or t'other. Let 'em take theer pick, everybody unnerstanin' afterwards theer's to be no quarrellin', or fightin'. That's our law in the Australyin bush, when we've cases o' the kind; an' every bushranger hez to 'bide by it. Why shedn't it be the same heer?"

"Why shouldn't it?" asks Slush. "It's a good law—just and fair for all."

"I consent to it," says Blew, with apparent reluctance, as if doubtful of the result, yet satisfied to submit to the will of the majority. "I mayn't be neyther so young nor so good-lookin' as Mr Gomez," he adds; "I know I an't eyther. Still I'll take my chance. If she I lay claim to pronounces against me, I promise to stand aside, and say ne'er another word—much less think o' fightin' for her. She can go 'long wi' him, an' my blessin' wi' both."

"Bravo, Blew! You talk like a good 'un. Don't be afraid; we'll stand by you!"

This, from several of the outsiders.

"Comrades!" says Davis, "I place myself in your hands. If my girl's against me, I'm willin' to give her up, same as Blew."

What about the other two? What answer will they make to the proposed peaceful compromise? All eyes are turned on them, awaiting it.

De Lara speaks first, his eyes flashing fire. Hitherto he has been holding his anger in check, but now it breaks out, poured forth like lava from a burning mountain.

"*Carajo!*" he cries. "I've been listening a long time to talk—taking it too coolly. Idle talk, all of it; yours, Mr Striker, especially. What care we about your ways in the Australian bush. They won't hold good here, or with me. My style of settling disputes is this, or this." He touches his pistol-butt, and then the hilt of *macheté*, hanging by his side, adding, "Mr Blew can have his choice."

"All right!" retorts the ex-man-o'-war's man. "I'm good for a bout with eyther, and don't care a toss which. Pistols at six paces, or my cutlass against that straight blade o' yours. Both if you like."

"Both be it. That's best, and will make the end sure. Get ready, and quick. For, sure as I stand here, I intend killing you!"

"Say, you intend tryin'. I'm ready to give you the chance. You can begin, soon's you feel disposed."

"And I'm ready for *you*, sir," says Davis, confronting Hernandez. "Knives, pistols, tomahawks—anything you like."

Hernandez hangs back, as though he would rather decline this combat *à outrance*.

"No, Bill!" interposes Striker; "one fight at a time. When Blew an' Gomez hev got through wi' theirs, then you can gi'e t'other his change—if so be he care to hev it."

"T'other" appears gratified with Striker's speech, disregarding the innuendo. He had no thought it would come to this, and now looks as if he would surrender up his sweetheart without striking a blow. He makes no rejoinder; but shrinks back, cowed-like and craven.

"Yes; one fight at a time!" cry others, endorsing the dictum of Striker.

It is the demand of the majority, and the minority concedes it. All know it is to be a duel to the death. A glance at the antagonists—at their angry eyes and determined attitudes—makes this sure. On that lonely shore one of the two, if not both, will sleep his last sleep!

Chapter Sixty Seven
A Duel Adjourned

The combat, now declared inevitable, its preliminaries are speedily arranged. Under the circumstances, and between such adversaries, the punctilios of ceremony are slight. For theirs is the rough code of honour common to robbers of all countries and climes.

No seconds are chosen, nor spoken of. All on the ground are to act as such; and at once proceed to business.

Some measure off the distance, stepping it between two stones. Others examine the pistols, to see that both are loaded with ball-cartridge, and carefully capped. The fight is to be with Colt's six-shooters, navy size. Each combatant chances to have one of this particular pattern. They are to commence firing at twelve paces, and if that be ineffectual, then close up, as either chooses. If neither fall to the shots, then to finish with the steel.

The captives inside the cave are ignorant of what is going on. Little dream they of the red tragedy soon to be enacted so near, or how much they themselves may be affected by its result. It is indeed to them the chances of a contrasting destiny.

The duellists take stand by the stones, twelve paces apart. Blew having stripped off his pilot-cloth coat, is in his shirt-sleeves. These rolled up to the elbow, expose ranges of tattooing, fouled anchors, stars, crescents, and a woman—a perfect medley of forecastle souvenirs. They show also muscles, lying along his arms like lanyards round a ship's stay. Should the shots fail, those arms promise well for wielding the cutlass; and if his fingers should clutch his antagonist's throat, the struggle will be a short one.

Still, no weak adversary will he meet in Francisco de Lara. He, too, has laid aside his outer garment—thrown off his scarlet cloak, and the heavy hat. He does not need stripping to the shirt-sleeves; his light *jaqueta* of velveteen in no way encumbers him. Fitting like a glove, it displays arms of muscular strength, with a body in symmetrical correspondence.

A duel between two such gladiators might be painful, but for all, a fearfully interesting spectacle. Those about to witness it seem to think so, as they stand silent, with breath bated, and eyes alternately on one and the other.

As it has been arranged that Striker is to give the signal, the ex-convict, standing centrally outside the line of fire, is about to say a word that will set two men, mad as tigers, at one another—each with full resolve to fire, cut down, and kill.

There is a moment of intense stillness, like the lull which precedes a storm. Nothing heard save the tidal wash against the near strand, the boom of the distant breakers, and at intervals the shrill scream of a sea-bird.

The customary "Ready!" is forming on Striker's lips, to be followed by the "Fire!—one—two—three!" But not one of these words—not a syllable—is he permitted to speak. Before he can give utterance to the first, a cry comes down from the cliff, which arrests the attention of all; soon as understood, enchaining it.

It is La Crosse who sends it, shouting in accent of alarm—

"Mon Dieu! we're on an island!"

When the forest is on fire, or the savannah swept by flood, and their wild denizens flee to a spot uninvaded, the timid deer is safe beside the fierce wolf or treacherous cougar. In face of the common danger they will stand trembling together—the beasts of prey for the time gentle as their victims.

So with human kind; a case parallel, and in point, furnished by the crew of the *Condor* with their captives.

The pirates, on hearing the cry of La Crosse, are at first only startled. But soon their surprise becomes apprehension; keen enough to stay the threatening fight, and indefinitely postpone it. For at the words "We're on an island!" they are impressed with an instinctive sense of danger; and all, intending combatants as spectators, rush up the ravine, to the summit of the cliff, where La Crosse is still standing.

Arrived there, and casting their eyes inland, they have evidence of the truth of his statement. A strait, leagues in width, separates them from the mainland. Far too wide to be crossed by the strongest swimmer amongst them—too wide for them to be descried from the opposite side, even through a telescope! And the inland is a mere strip of sea-washed rock, running parallel to the coast, cliff-bound, table-topped, sterile, treeless—and, to all appearance, waterless!

As this last thought comes uppermost—along with the recollection that their boat is gone—what was at first only a flurry of excited apprehension, becomes a fixed fear.

Still further intensified, when after scattering over the islet, and exploring it from end to end, they again come together, and each party delivers its report. No wood save some stunted bushes; no water—stream, pond, or spring; only that of the salt sea rippling around; no sign of animal life, except snakes, scorpions, and lizards, with the birds flying above— screaming as if in triumph at the intruders upon their domain being thus entrapped!

For they are so, and clearly comprehend it. Most of them are men who have professionally followed the sea, and understand what it is to be "castaways." Some have had actual experience of it, and need no reminding of its dangers. To a man, they feel their safety as much compromised, as if the spot of earth under their feet, instead of being but three leagues from land—were three thousand—for that matter in the middle of the Pacific.

What would they not now give to be again on board the barque sent sailing thither to miserably perish? Ah! their cruelty has come back upon them like a curse.

The interrupted duel—what of it? Nothing. It is not likely ever to be fought. Between the *ci-devant* combatants, mad anger and jealous rivalry may still remain. But neither shows it now; both subdued, in contemplation of the common peril.

Blew, to all appearance, is less affected than his antagonist; but all are cowed—awed by a combination of occurrences, that look as though an avenging angel had been sent to punish them.

From that moment Carmen Montijo and Iñez Alvarez will be safe in their midst, as if promenading the streets of Cadiz, or flirting their fans at a *funcion de toros*.

Safe, as far as being molested by the ruffians around them. Yet, alas! exposed to the danger overhanging all—death from starvation.

A fearful fate threatens the late crew of the Chilian barque, in horror equalling that to which those left aboard of her have been consigned. Well may they deem it a retribution—that God's hand is upon them, meting out a punishment apportioned to their crime!

But surely He will not permit the innocent to suffer with the guilty? Let us hope—pray, He will not.

Chapter Sixty Eight
Long-Suffering

"*Virgen Santissima*! Mother of God, have mercy!"

The cry is heard in the cabin of the *Condor*—Don Gregorio Montijo giving utterance to it.

Several days have elapsed since the desertion of her crew, and she is still afloat, drifting in a south-westerly direction, with all sail set, just as when the pirates put away from her.

Why she has not gone to the bottom is known but to two men—they entrusted with the scuttling.

And just as when left, are the three unfortunate beings aboard: the black cook on his galley bench, the captain and his passenger *vis-à-vis* at the cabin-table, bound to and bolt upright in their chairs.

But though the attitudes of all three are unchanged, there is a marked change in their appearance, especially of those in the cabin. For the white man shown the effects of physical suffering sooner than the Ethiopian.

For over five days Don Gregorio and Lantanas have been enduring agony great as ever tortured Tantalus. It has made fearful inroad on their strength—on their frames. Both are reduced almost to skeletons; cheekbones protruding, eyes sunken in their sockets. Were the cords that confine them suddenly taken off, they would sink helpless on the floor!

Not all this time have they been silent. At intervals they had conversed upon their desperate situation. For the first day, with some lingering hope of being released; but afterwards despairingly, as the hours passed and nothing occurred to change it.

Now and then they have heard cries on deck; knowing they are from the cook; whom they now believe to be, as themselves, bound up somewhere in the forward part of the vessel.

At first they made some attempt to communicate with him, by answering them; but found it an idle effort. He may have heard, but could not help them. And now their feeble strength forbids even such exertion of their voices.

Long since have the two men given up all hope of being able to untie the cords keeping them to their chairs. The knots made by the hands of a sailor would defy the efforts of the most skilled *presti-digitateur*.

And at length also have they ceased to converse, or only at periods long apart. Lantanas, after his first throes of fierce rage, has sunk into a sort of stupor, and, with head drooping down to his breast, appears as if life had left him.

Don Gregorio, on the contrary, holds his erect—at least during most part of the day. For before him is something to be seen—the sea through the stern windows, still open.

On this he keeps his eyes bent habitually; though not with much hope of their seeing aught to cheer him. On its blue expanse he beholds but a streak of white, the frothing water in the vessel's wake, now and then a "school" of tumbling porpoises, or the "spout" of a cachalot whale.

Once, however, an object came within his field of vision, which caused him to start, writhe in his ropes, and cry out to the utmost of his strength. For it was a ship in full sail crossing the *Condor's* track, and scarce a cable's length astern!

He heard a hail and called out in response, Lantanas joining him.

And the two kept on shouting for hours after, till their feeble voices failed them; and they again resigned themselves to a despondency, hopeless as ever.

All their shouts have ever brought them were the Bornean apes, that they often hear scampering up and down the cabin-stair, dashing their uncouth bodies against the closed door.

The Chilian has now quite surrendered to despair; while Don Gregorio, who had also lost hope of help from man, still has faith in Heaven. Hence the prayerful appeal; which with unabated fervour he once more sends up:—

"*Virgen Santissima*! Mother of God, have mercy!"

All at once Lantanas, catching the words, and raising his head, cries out:

"Virgin! Hach! There's no virgin!—No mother of God, nor God neither!"

"Captain Lantanas!"

"Don't captain me! I'm not a captain. I'm a poor miserable creature—starving with hunger—dying of thirst. Merciful Virgin, indeed! Where's her mercy? If she has it, let her show. Let her find me food and drink. Cakes and fruit there! Nothing of the sort. Stones, painted stones! And those other things! Bottles they call them—bottles and decanters. All a deception. They're imps—some demigods! See how they dance. Let's join them! Come, old Zanzibar! Bring your fiddle! And my Bornean beauties, come you. We'll have a grand *fandango*. We'll make a dancing room of the *Condor's* deck, and kick up our heels high as the cuddy head. That's the way we'll do it. Ha—ha—ha! Ha—ha—ha!"

"O God!" groans Don Gregorio, "Lantanas has lost his reason!"

Chapter Sixty Nine
Help from Heaven

For long, the Chilian skipper continues to rave, rolling his eyes about, now and then glaring fiercely at Don Gregorio, as though he wished to stretch across the table and tear him. Fortunate he is confined now.

At first the ex-haciendado spoke kindly, endeavouring to soothe him; but seeing it idle, he has ceased; and now makes no further attempt.

To converse with him would be only painful, and indeed the sight is sufficiently so, suggesting to Don Gregorio what may be his own fate. At times he almost fancies himself the same, as sweeps through his soul the thought of his accumulated calamities.

He wishes that death would relieve him, and has prayed for it more than once. He prays for it again, silently, with his eyes resting on the sea. He awaits the final hour, longing for it to come, his features set in calm, Christian resignation.

Suddenly their expression changes, a ray of renewed hope shooting athwart his face. Not a ray, but a beam, which spreads over his whole countenance, while his eyes kindle into cheerfulness, and his lips become parted in a smile!

Is he about to echo the mad laugh of Lantanas?

No! In that look there is no sign of unseated reason.

On the contrary, he gazes with intelligent earnestness, as at something outside demanding investigation.

Soon his lips part farther, not now to smile, but speak words that involuntarily issue from them. Only two little words, but of large import and greatest cheer:

"A sail!"

For such he has espied; a white speck away off on the line that separates the two blues, but distinguishable from waif of floating foam or wing of gull. Beyond doubt, a sail—a ship!

Once more, hope is in his heart, which bounding up, beats audibly within his breast.

Higher and louder, as the white speck shows larger, and assumes shape. For the tall narrow disc, rising tower-like against the sky, can only be the spread canvas of a ship.

And gradually growing taller, he at length sees she is standing towards the barque!

Intently he continues to watch the distant sail! Silently, without saying aught of it to his companion, or in any way communicating with him. It would be of no use; the mind of the Chilian is closed against outward impressions, and now is not the time to attempt opening it.

Hopefully, Don Gregorio continues gazing, but not without anxiety. Once before he has had disappointment from a similar sight. It may be so again.

But, no; that ship was standing across the *Condor's* track, while this is sailing in the same course—sailing after, apparently, with the intention to come up; and though slowly, surely drawing nearer; as he can tell by her canvas increasing in the bulk, growing broader and rising higher upon the horizon.

A long time elapses—nearly half-a-day—during which he has many hopes and fears, alternating as the hours pass.

But the hopes are at length in the ascendant, and all anxiety passes as the pursuing ship shows her dark hull above the water-line, and he can distinguish her separate sails. They are all set. What joy in his heart as his eyes rest on them! They seem the wings of merciful angels, coming to relieve him from his misery!

And the flag floating above—the flag of England! Were it the banner of his own Spain, he could not regard it with greater gladness, or gratitude. For surely he will be saved now?

Alas! while thus congratulating himself, he sees what causes his heart again to go down within him, bringing back keenest apprehensions. The strange vessel is still a far distance off, and the breeze impelling her, light all along, has suddenly died down—not a ripple showing on the sea's surface—while her sails now hang loose and limp. Beyond doubt is she becalmed.

But the *Condor*! Will she, too, cease sailing?

Yes; she must, from the same cause. Already she moves slowly, scarce making way. And now—now she is motionless! He can tell it, by the glass rack and lamps overhead, that hang without the slightest oscillation. Anon, the barque gradually swings round, and he loses sight of the ship. Through the windows he still beholds the sea, calm and blue, but vacant; no outline of hull—no expanded sail—no flouting flag to keep up his heart, which is once more almost despondent.

But only for a short time; again rising as the barque, sheering round, brings once more her stern towards the ship, and he sees the latter, and something besides—a boat!

It is down in the water, and coming on toward the *Condor*, the oar-blades flashing in the sun and flinging spray-drops that seem like silver stars!

The barque swinging round, he has the boat in view but a short while. What matters it now? He is certain of being saved!

And he looks no longer—only listens.

Soon to hear words spoken in a strong manly voice, to him sweeter than music. It is the hail:

"Barque ahoy!"

In feeble accents he makes answer, and continues to call out, till other voices, echoing along the *Condor's* decks, become commingled with his own.

Then there are footsteps on the quarterdeck, soon after heard descending the cabin-stair.

The handle is turned, the door pushed open, and a swish of fresh air sweeps in, men along with it; as they enter, giving utterance to wild exclamations.

Wrenching his neck around, he sees there are two of them, both in the uniform of naval officers, and both known to him!

Their presence causes him strange emotions, and many—too many for his strength so long and sorely tried.

Overpowered by the sight, he becomes unconscious, as though instead of gladdening, it had suddenly deprived him of life!

Chapter Seventy
Conjectures too True

No need to say that the two officers who have entered the *Condor's* cabin are Crozier and Cadwallader. For she is the polacca-barque chased by a frigate, and that frigate the *Crusader*.

The cry simultaneously raised by them is one of strange intonation, telling less of surprise, than conjecture too fatally confirmed.

While in chase of the barque, and her national colours were first made out, they had no thought of connecting her with the vessel which Don Gregorio Montijo had chartered to take him to Panama. True, they had heard that this was a Chilian vessel, and her skipper of that nation. But they had also been told she was a *ship*, not a *barque*. And as among the many craft in San Francisco Bay, neither had noticed her, how would they think of identifying her with the chased polacca.

Gradually, however, as the frigate drew upon her, certain suspicions of a painful nature began to shape themselves in Crozier's mind; still so vague he did not deem it worth while communicating them to Cadwallader. He remembered having seen a *polacca-masted* vessel in the harbour of San Francisco; besides, that she was a *ship*. And so far as his recollection served, she was of the same size as that running before the frigate. Besides, he could distinctly recall the fact of her flying Chilian colours. The peculiar style of her masting had drawn his attention to her.

And while they were still pursuing the barque, and commenting on the coincident statement of the brig and whaler about men having been aboard of her *covered with red hair*, Crozier also recalled a statement strangely significant, which Harry Blew had made to one of the men who had rowed Cadwallader ashore, on the day the *Crusader* sailed. Blew had been aboard the Chilian vessel, and being asked by his old shipmate what sort of crew she had, laughingly replied: "Only a *black* man, and two *red* ones." Pressed for an explanation about the red ones, he said they were a couple of *orang-outangs*.

Putting these odd *data* together, and comparing them, the *Crusader's* third lieutenant began to have an uneasy feeling, as they followed the retreating vessel. That she was a barque, and not a ship, meant nothing. As a seaman, he knew how easy the conversion—how often made.

When at length both vessels lay becalmed, and an order for boarding was given, he had solicited the command—by a private word to the frigate's captain, as had Cadwallader the leave to accompany him; the latter actuated by impulses not very dissimilar.

When both at length climbed the barque's sides, saw the red monkeys on deck, and the black man in the galley, their apprehension became sharpened to the keenest foreboding—far more than a presentiment of misfortune.

Alas! as they entered the *Condor's* cabin, beholding its fulfilment.

The cry that escaped their lips came on the recognition of Don Gregorio Montijo; followed by other exclamations, as they looked at the two unoccupied chairs, a fan upon the one, a scarf over the back of the other. It was then that Crozier rushing upon deck, sent the cutter off for the surgeon, himself instantly returning to the cabin.

Still wilder—almost a wail—is the shout simultaneously raised by the young officers, when, after dashing open the state-room doors, they look in and see all empty!

They turn to those at the table, asking information—entreating it: one answers with a strange Bedlamite laugh; the other not at all. It is Don Gregorio who is silent. They see that his head is hanging over. He appears insensible.

"Great God! is he dead?"

They glide towards him, grasp table-knives, and cut the cords that have been confining him. Senseless, he sinks into their arms.

But he is not dead; only in a faint. Though feebly, his pulse still beats!

With wine they wet his lips—the wine so long standing untasted! They open his mouth, and pour some of it down his throat, then stand over him to await the effect.

Soon his pulse grows stronger, and his eyes sparkle with the light of reviving life.

Laid gently along the sofa, he is at length restored to consciousness; with sufficient strength to answer the questions eagerly put to him. There are two, simultaneously asked, almost echoes of one another.

"Where is Carmen? Where is Iñez?"

"Gone!" he gasps out. "Carried away by the—"

He does not finish the speech. His breath fails him, and he seems relapsing into the syncope from which he has been aroused. Fearing this, they question him no farther, but continue to administer restoratives. They give him more wine, making him also eat of the fruits found upon the table.

They have also set the skipper free; but soon see cause to regret it. He strides to and fro, flings his arms about in frenzied gesture, clutches at decanters, glasses, bottles, and breaks them against one another, or dashes them down upon the floor. He needs restraining, and they do that, by shutting him up in a state-room.

Returning to Don Gregorio, they continue to nurse him; all the while wishing the surgeon to come.

While impatiently waiting they hear a hail from the top of the cabin-stairs. It is their coxswain, who shouts:—

"Below there!"

He is about to announce the cutter's return from the frigate.

Ah no! It is not that; but something different; which instead of gratifying, gives them a fresh spasm of pain. Listening, they hear him say:—

"Come on deck, Mr Crozier! There's a bank o' black fog rollin' up. It's already close on the barque's starboard bow. It look like there's mischief in't; and I believe there be. For God's sake, hurry up, sir!"

Chapter Seventy One
A Struggle with the Storm

The summons of the coxswain is too serious to be disregarded; and soon as hearing it, the two officers hasten upon deck, leaving Don Gregorio reclining along the settee.

Glancing over the barque's starboard bow, they behold a sky black as Erebus. It is a fog-bank, covering several points of the compass. But while they stand regarding it, it lengthens along the horizon, at the same time rising higher against the heavens. They can see that it is approaching, spreading over the ocean like a pall. And, where it shadows the water, white flakes show themselves, which they know to be froth churned up by the sharp stroke of a wind-squall.

They do not stand idly gazing. All three recognise the threatening danger. They only cast a glance towards the frigate, and, perceiving they can hope for no help from her, at once commence taking measures for themselves. "To the sheets!" shouts Crozier. "Let fly all!"

At the command, the midshipman and coxswain bound off to execute it, the lieutenant himself assisting; since there are but the three to do the work. For the negro, released by Grummet, despite half a pint of rum poured down his throat, is scarcely able to keep his feet. No help, therefore, to be had from him, nor any one else.

But the three strong men, with confidence in their strength, and with knowledge to comprehend the approaching peril, take the proper steps to avert it—these being, as Crozier has commanded, to let go everything.

Working as if for life, they cast off sheets and halyards, and let the canvas flap free. No time for clewing up, or making snug: no thought of either. The sails must take their chance, though they get split into shreds, which they are pretty sure to do.

This actually occurs, and soon. Scarce has her canvas been released from its sheets and tacks, when the barque becomes enveloped in a dense cloud, and the wind strikes like a cannon shot against her sails. Luckily, they were loosed in time. If still stiff set, the masts would have gone by the board, or the *Condor* on her beam-ends. And luckily, too, before struck, Grummet had hold of her helm, and, by Crozier's command, brought her before the wind. To attempt "lying to," with her sails in such condition, would be to court destruction. To "scud" is their only chance for safety.

And away go they before the wind, which, first blowing in fitful gusts, soon becomes a steady gale, with now and then a violent burst catching still another sail, and rending it to ribbons.

Soon there is not a sound one, and scarce aught save strips of torn canvas hanging from the yards, or streaming out like the flags on a signal-staff.

Fortunately the barque well obeys her helm, and the young officers contrive to set storm-stay and trysail, thus helping to hold her steady.

During all this time they have not thought of the frigate. Absorbed in the endeavour to save the craft that carries them, they reflect not on what may be their fate should they get separated from their own ship.

At length, this reflection arises in a form to appal them. The frigate is out of sight—has been ever since the commencement of the gale, the fog having drifted between. They do not now know the direction in which she is; nor can they tell whether she has lain-to, or, like themselves, "run." If the latter, there is a hope she will follow the same course; and, the fog lifting, be again sighted.

Alas! it is more likely she will do the former. Full-manned, she will have taken in sail in good time, and made all snug, so as to ride out the storm; and, aware of the danger in which they on the barque will be placed, she will not forsake the spot, but assuredly lie to.

Just as they have arrived at this conclusion, they hear a gun booming above the blast. They know it is from the frigate, firing to let them know her whereabouts. But, although the sound reaches them with sufficient distinctness, they cannot tell the direction. Who could at sea, in a fog?

Listening, they hear it a second time, and soon after a third.

Then again and again; still distinct, but with the same uncertainty as to its direction. For the life of them they cannot determine the point of the compass whence it comes. Even if they knew, it is a question whether they dare set the barque's head towards it, for the storm has increased to a tempest, and it is touch and go for them to keep the Chilian vessel afloat. Out of trim, she is tossed from wave to wave, shipping seas that threaten to engulf her, or wash everybody overboard.

In this struggle—as it were, for life and death—they lose all hope of being able to keep company with the warship—all thought of it. It will be well if they can but save that they are on from going to the bottom of the sea.

Again they hear the firing, several times repeated—that signal that they are unable to answer, or unable to avail themselves of its friendly warning. Situated as they are, it seems sounding a farewell salute—or it may be their death knell.

Fainter and fainter falls the boom upon their ears; duller and duller at each successive detonation, which tells that the distance between them and the frigate, instead of diminishing, increases. However sad and disheartening, they cannot help it. They dare not put the barque about, or in any way alter her course. They must keep scudding on, though they may never see the *Crusader* again.

At length, no longer do they hear the signal-guns. Whether from greater distance, or louder vociferation of the tempest, they can no more be distinguished amidst its voices.

Throughout all the night the barque scuds, storm-buffeted, shipping huge seas, yet casting them off, and still keeping afloat. Notwithstanding her distressed condition, she rides the gale through to its termination.

As the morning sun gleams over the ocean, along with the subsiding wind, the fog also lifts, leaving both sea and sky clear. And still the *Condor* is afloat, rolling from beam to beam; her tall smooth masts as yet in her, her rigging aright, and her bulwarks unbroken. Only the sails have suffered, and they are all gone.

Grummet is at the wheel, guiding her wayward course; while the two officers stand upon her quarterdeck, with eyes bent abroad, scanning the crests of the big billows that go rumbling along.

But there is no *Crusader* in sight—no frigate—no ship of any kind— nothing but the wide, fathomless ocean!

They are alone upon it, hundreds of leagues from land, aboard a craft they may not be able to manage; and all the more difficult with her sails in shreds. But even were these sound, they have not the strength to set them. They are helpless; but little better off than if they were in an open boat!

In very truth, are they in peril!

But they do not dwell upon it now. A thought still more afflicting is before their minds; and, casting another glance over the ocean—unrewarded as ever—they descend into the cabin, to obtain some particulars of that which has saddened, almost maddened them.

Chapter Seventy Two
A Card Recovered

It is the fourth day since the English officers boarded the Chilian barque. They are still on board of her, and she still afloat—the one a sequence of the other; or, she would now be at the bottom of the sea. A tough struggle they have had of it; only the three to manage so large a craft in a tempest which, though short-lived, was fierce as ever swept over the Pacific. And with no aid from any of the other three. Captain Lantanas is still delirious, locked up in his state-room, lest, in his violence, he may do some harm; while Don Gregorio, weak as a child, reclines on the cabin settee, unable to go upon deck. The negro alone, having partially recovered strength, lends some assistance.

The barque's sails still hang tattered from the spars, for they have since encountered other winds, and had neither the time nor strength to clear them. But they have contrived to patch up the foresail, and bend on a new jib from some spare canvas found in the stores. With these she is making way at the rate of some five or six knots to the hour, her head East and by South. It is twelve o'clock mid-day, and Grummet is at the wheel; the officers on the quarter; Crozier, sextant in hand, "shooting the sun." They have long since given up hope of finding the frigate, or being found by her at sea.

Aware of this, they are steering the crippled vessel towards Panama in hope of their coming across her. In any case, that is the port where they will be most likely to get tidings of her.

A prey to saddened thoughts are the two young officers, as they stand on the quarterdeck of the Chilian vessel taking the altitude of the sun, with instruments her own skipper is no longer able to use. Fortunately, these had not been carried off, else there would be but little likelihood of their making Panama.

At best, they will reach it with broken hearts; for they have now heard the whole story in all its dark details, so far as Don Gregorio could give them.

Having already determined their longitude by the barque's chronometer, they have kept it by log-reckoning, and their present observation is but to confirm them in the latitude.

"Starboard your helm!" shouts Crozier to Grummet. "Give her another point to port. Keep her east-by-south. Steady!"

Then turning to Cadwallader, he says:

"If all goes well, we shall make Panama in less than two days. We might do it in one, if we could but set sail enough. Anyhow, I think old Bracebridge will stay for us at least a week. Ah! I wish that were all we had to trouble us. To think they're gone—lost to us—for ever!"

"Don't say that, Ned. There's still a hope we may find them."

"And found, what then! You needn't answer. Will; I don't wish you to speak of it. I daren't trust myself to think of it. Carmen Montijo—my betrothed—captive to a crew of pirate cut-throats—oh!"

Cadwallader is silent. He suffers the same agony thinking of Iñez.

For a time the picture remains before their minds, dark as their gloomiest fancies can make it. Then across it shoot some rays of hope, saddened, but sweet, for they are thoughts of vengeance. Cadwallader first gives expression to it.

"Whatever has happened to the girls, we shall go after them anyhow. And the robbers, we *must* find them."

"Find, and punish them," adds Crozier. "That we surely shall. If it costs all my money, all the days of my life, I'll revenge the wrongs of Carmen Montijo."

"And I those of Iñez Alvarez."

For a while they stand silently brooding upon that which has brought such black shadow over their hearts. Then Cadwallader says:

"The scoundrels must have plotted it all before leaving San Francisco; and shipped aboard the Chilian vessel for the express purpose of getting this gold. That's Don Gregorio's idea of it, borne out by what he heard from that one of them he knew there—Rocas the name, he says."

"It seems probable—indeed certain," rejoins Crozier. "Though it don't much matter how, or when, they planned the damnable deed. Enough that they've done it. But to think of Harry Blew turning traitor, and taking part with them! That is to me the strangest thing of all, frightfully, painfully, strange."

"But do you believe he *has* acted in such a manner?"

"How can one help believing it? What Don Gregorio heard leaves no alternative. He went off in the boat along with the rest; besides saying words which prove he went willingly. Only to think of such black ingratitude! Cadwallader, I'd as soon have thought of suspecting yourself!"

"His conduct, certainly, seems incredible. I believed Blew to be a thoroughly honest fellow. No doubt the gold corrupted him; as it has many a better man. But let's think no more about it; only hope we may some day lay hands on him."

"Ah! if I ever do that. With my arms around him, I once saved his worthless life. Let me but get him in my embrace again, and he'll have a hug that'll squeeze the last breath out of his body!"

"The chance may come yet, and with the whole scoundrelly crew. What brutes they must have been! According to Don Gregorio's account, they were of all nations, and the worst sort of each. The negro says the same. Among them four that spoke Spanish, and appeared to be Spaniards, or Spanish-Americans. Suppose we pay a visit to the forecastle, and see if we can find any record of their names. It might be of use hereafter."

"By all means!" asserts the lieutenant; "let us." They proceed towards the fore-deck in silence, their countenances showing a nervous apprehension. For there is a thought in their hearts, which neither has yet made known to the other—blacker, and more bitter, than even the thought of Harry Blew's treason.

Unspoken, they carry it into the forecastle; but they are not many minutes there, before seeing what brings it out, without either saying a word.

A bunk—the most conspicuous of the two tiers—is explored first. They turn out of it papers of various sorts: some letters, several numbers of an old newspaper, and a pack of Spanish playing-cards—all pictured. But among them is one of a different sort—a white one, with a name printed upon it.

A visiting card—but whose?

As Crozier picks it up, and reads the name, his blood curdles, the hair crisping on his head:

"Mr Edward Crozier; H.B.M. Frigate Crusader."

His own!

He does not need to be told how the card came there. Too well remembers he when, where, and to whom he gave it—to Don Francisco De Lara on the day of their encounter.

Thrusting it into his pocket, he clutches at the letters, and looks at their superscription—"*Don Francisco de Lara!*"

Opening, he rapidly reads them one after another. His hands holding them shake as with a palsy; while in his eyes there is a look of keenest apprehension. For he fears that, subscribed to some, he will find another name—that of Carmen Montijo! If so, farewell to all faith in human kind. Harry Blew's ingratitude has destroyed his belief in man. A letter from the daughter of Don Gregorio Montijo to the gambler Frank Lara, will alike wither his confidence in woman.

With eager eyes, and lips compressed, he continues the perusal of the letters. They are from many correspondents, and relate to various matters, most about money and *monté*, signed "Faustino Calderon."

As the last of them slips through his fingers, he breathes freely, but with a sigh of self-reproach for having doubted the woman who was to have been his wife.

Turning to Cadwallader—as himself aware of all—he says, in solemn emphasis:

"*Now we know!*"

Chapter Seventy Three
The Last Leaf in the Log

No common pirates then, no mere crew of mutinous sailors, have carried off Carmen Montijo and Iñez Alvarez. It has been done by Francisco de Lara and Faustino Calderon, if or although there is no evidence of the latter having been aboard the barque, it is deducible, and not even doubtful. For a scheme such as that, the confederates were not likely to have parted.

The young officers have returned to the quarterdeck, and there stand gazing in one another's faces; on both an expression of anguish, which the new discovery has intensified. It was painful enough to think of their betrothed sweethearts being the sport of rough robbers; but to picture them in the power of De Lara and Calderon—knowing what they do of these men—is agony itself.

"Yes; it's all clear," says Crozier. "No idea of getting gold has brought the thing about. That may have influenced the others who assisted them; but with them the motive was different—I see it now."

"Do you know, Ned, I half suspected it from the first. You remember what I said as we were leaving San Francisco. After what happened between us and the gamblers, I had my fears about our girls being left in the same place with them. Still, who'd have thought of their following them aboard ship? Above all, with Blew there, and after his promise to protect them! You remember him saying, he would lay down his life for theirs?"

"He swore it—to me he swore it. Oh! if ever I set eyes on him again, I'll make him suffer for that broken oath!"

"What do you propose doing, after we reach Panama? If we find the frigate there, we'll be obliged to join her."

"Obliged! there's no obligation to bind a man situated as I—reckless as this misery makes me. Unless Captain Bracebridge consents to assist us in the search, I'll go alone."

"Not alone. There's one will be with you."

"I know it, Will. Of course, I count upon you. What I mean is, if Bracebridge won't help us with the frigate. I'll throw up my commission, charter a vessel myself, engage a crew, and search every inch of the American coast, till I find where they've put in."

"What a pity we can't tell the place! They must have been near land to have taken to an open boat."

"In sight of—close to it, I've been questioning Don Gregorio. He knows that much and but little beside. The poor gentleman is almost as crazed as the skipper. I wonder he's not more. He says they had sighted land that very morning, the first they saw since leaving California. The captain told them they would be in Panama in about two days after. As the boat was being rowed away, Don Gregorio saw a coast-line through the cabin windows, and not far-off. He saw their boat too, and they appeared making straight for it. Of course they—. That's all I can get out of the poor old gentleman, at present."

"The negro? Can he tell no better story?"

"I've questioned him too. He is equally sure of their having been close in. What point, he has no idea, any more than the orangs. However, he states a particular fact, which is more satisfactory. A short while before they seized hold of him, he was looking over the side, and saw a strangely shaped hill—a mountain. He describes it as having two tops. The moon was between them, the reason for his taking notice of it. That double-headed hill may yet stand us in stead."

"How unfortunate the skipper losing his senses! If he'd have kept them, he could have told us where he was at the time the barque was abandoned. It's enough to make one think the very Fates are against us. By the way, we've never thought of looking at the log-book. That ought to throw some light on the locality."

"It ought; and doubtless would, if we only had it. You're mistaken in saying we never thought of it. I have; and been searching for it everywhere. But it's gone; and what's become of it, I know not. They may have thrown it overboard before forsaking the ship—possibly to blot out all traces. Still, it's odd too, De Lara leaving these letters behind!"

"And the barque under all sail."

"Well, I take it, they were hurried, and of course expected she'd soon go to the bottom. Strange she didn't. No doubt she's met only smooth weather till we came aboard her."

"I wonder where her log-book can be?"

"Not more than I. The old darkey says it used to lie on a little shelf at the turning of the cabin-stair. I've looked there, but no log-book. As you say, it's enough to make one believe the Fates were against us. If so, we may never reach Panama, much less live to—"

"See," cries Cadwallader, interrupting the despairing speech. "Those brutes! what's that they're knocking about? By Jove! I believe it's the very thing we're speaking of!"

The brutes are the Myas monkeys, that, away in the ship's waist, are tossing something between them; apparently a large book bound in rough red leather. They have mutilated the binding, and, with teeth and claws, are tearing out the leaves, as they strive to take it from one another.

"It is—it must be the log-book!" cries Crozier, as both rush off to rescue it from the clutch of the orangs.

They succeed; but not without difficulty, and a free handling of handspikes—almost braining the apes before they consent to relinquish it.

It is at length recovered, though in a ruinous condition; fortunately, however, with the written leaves untorn. Upon the last of these is an entry, evidently the latest made:

"Latitude 7 degrees 20 minutes North; Longitude 82 degrees 12 minutes West. Light breeze."

"Good!" exclaims Crozier, rushing back to the quarterdeck, and bending over the chart. "With this, and the double-headed hill, we may get upon the track of the despoilers. Just when we were despairing! Will, old boy; there's something in this. I have a presentiment that things are taking a turn, and the *Fates will yet be or us.*"

"God grant they may!"

"Ah?" sighs Crozier: "if we had but ten men aboard this barque—or even six—I'd never think of going on to Panama, but steer straight for the island of Coiba."

"Why the island of Coiba?" wonderingly asks Cadwallader.

"Because it must have been in sight when this entry was made—either it or Hicaron, which lies on its sou'west side. Look at this chart; there they are!"

The midshipman bends over the map, and scans it.

"You're right, Ned. They must have seen one or other of those islands, when the Chilian skipper made his last observation."

"Just so. And with a light breeze she couldn't have made much way after. Both the cook and Don Gregorio say it was that. Oh! for ten good hands. A thousand pounds apiece for ten stout, trusty fellows! What a pity in that squall the cutter's crew weren't left along with us."

"Never fear, Ned. We'll get them again, or as good. Old Bracebridge won't fail us, I'm sure. He's a dear old soul, and when he hears the tale we've to tell, it'll be all right. If he can't himself come with the frigate, he'll allow us men to man this barque; enough to make short work with her late crew, if we can once stand face to face with them. I only wish we were in Panama."

"I'd rather we were off Coiba; or on shore wherever the ruffians have landed."

"Not as we now are—three against twelve!"

"I don't care for that. I'd give ten thousand pounds to be in their midst— even alone."

"Ned, you'll never be there alone; wherever you go, I go with you. We have a common cause, and shall stand or fall together."

"That we shall. God bless you, Will Cadwallader! I feel you're worthy of the friendship—the trust I've placed in you. And now, let's talk no more about it; but bend on all the sail we can, and get to Panama. After that, we'll steer for the island of Coiba. We're so far fortunate, in having this westerly wind," he continues, in a more cheerful tone. "If it keep in the same quarter, we'll soon come in sight of land. And if this Chilian chart may be depended on, that should be a promontory on the west side of Panama Bay. I hope the chart's a true one; for Punta Malo, an its name imports, isn't a nice place to make mistakes about. By running too close to it with the wind in this quarter—"

"*Steamer to norrard!*" cries a rough voice, interrupting. It is Grummet's.

The young officers, turning with a start, see the same.

Crozier, laying hold of a telescope, raises it to his eye, while he holds it there, saying:

"You're right, cox: it is a steamer. And standing this way! She'll run right across our bows. Up helm, and set the barque's head on for her!"

The coxswain obeys; and with a few turns of the wheel brings the *Condor's* head round, till she is right to meet the steamer. The officers, with the negro assisting, loose tacks and sheets, trimming her sails for the changed course.

Soon the two vessels, going in almost opposite directions, lessen the distance between. And as they mutually make approach, each speculates on the character of the other. They on board the barque have little difficulty in determining that of the steamer. At a glance they see she is not a warship; but a passenger packet. And as there are no others in that part of the Pacific, she can be only one of the "liners" late established between San Francisco and Panama; coming down from the former port, her destination the latter.

Not so easy for those aboard the steamship to make out the manner of the odd-looking craft that has turned up in their track, and is sailing straight towards them. They see a barque, polacca-masted, with some sails set, and others hanging in shreds from her yards.

This of itself would be enough to excite curiosity. But there is something besides; a flag reversed flying at her mainmast-head—the flag of Chili! For the distress signal has not been taken down. And why it was ever run up, or by whom, none of those now in the barque could tell. At present it serves *their* purpose well, for, responding to it, the commander of the steam packet orders her engines to slow, and then cease action; till the huge leviathan, late running at the rate of twelve knots an hour, gradually lessens speed, and at length lies motionless upon the water.

Simultaneously the barque is "hove to," and she lies at less than a cable's length from the steamer.

From the latter the hail is heard first:

"Barque ahoy! What barque is that?"

"The *Condor*—Valparaiso. In distress."

"Send a boat aboard!"

"Not strength to man it."

"Wait, then! We'll board you."

In less than five minutes' time one of the quarter boats of the liner is lowered down, and a crew leaps into it.

Pushing off from her side, it soon touches that of the vessel in distress.

But not for its crew to board her. Crozier has already traced out his course of action. Slipping down into the steamer's boat, he makes request to be rowed to the ship; which is done without questioning. The uniform he wears entitles him to respect.

Stepping aboard the steamship, he sees that she is what he has taken her for: a line-packet from San Francisco, bound for Panama. She is crowded with passengers; at least a thousand seen upon her decks. They are of all qualities and kinds; all colours and nationalities; most of them Californian gold-diggers returning to their homes; some successful and cheerful; others downcast and disappointed.

He is not long in telling his tale; first to the commander of the steamer and his officers; then to the passengers.

For to these last he particularly addresses himself, in an appeal—a call for volunteers—not alone to assist in navigating the barque, but to proceed with him in pursuit of the scoundrels who cast her away.

He makes known his position, with his power to compensate them for the service sought; both endorsed by the commander of the steamship, who by good luck is acquainted with, and can answer for, his credentials.

Nothing of this is needed; nor yet the promise of a money reward. Among these stalwart men are many who are heroes—true Paladins, despite their somewhat threadbare habiliments. And amidst their soiled rags shine pistols and knives, ready to be drawn for the right.

After hearing the young officer's tale, without listening farther, twenty of them spring forward responsive to his call. Not for the reward offered, but in the cause of humanity and right. He would enlist twice or thrice the number, but deeming twenty enough, with these he returns to the *Condor*.

Then the two vessels part company, the steamer continuing on for Panama; while the barque, now better manned, and with more sail set, is steered for the point where the line of Latitude 7 degrees 20 minutes North intersects that of Longitude 82 degrees 12 minutes West.

Chapter Seventy Four
A Lottery of Life and Death

While these scenes are passing upon the ocean, others of equally exciting character occur upon that desert isle, where, by ill-starred chance for themselves, the pirate crew of the *Condor* made landing.

They are still there, all their efforts to get off having proved idle. But how different now from that hour when they brought their boat upon its beach laden with the spoils of the plundered vessel! Changed not only in their feelings but looks—scarce recognisable as the same men. Then in the full plenitude of swaggering strength, mental as bodily, with tongues given to loud talk; now subdued and silent, stalking about like spectres, with weak, tottering steps; some sitting listlessly upon stones, or lying astretch along the earth; not resting, but from sheer inability to stand erect!

Famine has set its seal upon their faces; hunger can be read in their hollow eyes, and pale sunken cheeks; while thirst shows upon their parched and shrivelled lips.

Not strange all this. For nine days they have tasted no food, save shellfish and the rank flesh of sea-fowl—both in scant supply. And no drink, excepting some rain-water caught in the boat-sail during an occasional slight shower.

All the while have they kept watch with an earnestness such as their desperate circumstances evoked. A tarpauling they have rigged up by oar and boat-hook, set upon the more elevated summit of the two—the highest point on the isle—has failed to attract the eye of any one on the mainland; or if seen, the signal has been disregarded; while to seaward, no ship or other vessel has been observed—nought but the blank blue of ocean, recalling their crime—in its calm tranquillity mocking their remorse!

Repentant are they now; and if they could, willingly would they undo their wicked deed—joyfully restore the stolen gold—gladly surrender up their captives—be but too glad to bring back to life those they have deprived of it.

It cannot be. Their victims left aboard the barque must have long ago gone to the bottom of the sea. In its bed they are now sleeping their last sleep, released from all earthly cares; and they who have so ruthlessly consigned them to their eternal rest, now almost envy it.

In their hour of agony, as hunger gnaws at their entrails, and thirst scorches them like a consuming fire, they reck little of life—some even desiring death!

All are humbled now. Even the haughty Gomez no longer affects to be their leader, and the savage Padilla is tamed to silent inaction, if not tenderness. By a sort of tacit consent, Harry Blew has become the controlling spirit—perhaps from having evinced more humanity than the rest. Now that adversity is on them, their better natures are brought out, and the less hardened of them have resumed the gentleness of childhood's days.

The change has been of singular consequence to their captives. These are no longer restrained, but free to go and come as it pleases them. No more need they fear insult or injury; no rudeness is offered them either by speech or gesture. On the contrary they are treated with studied respect, almost with deference. The choicest articles of food—bad at best—are apportioned to them, as also the largest share of the water; fortunately, sufficient of both to keep up their strength. And they in turn have been administering angels—tender nurses to the men who have made all their misery!

Thus have they lived up till the night of the ninth day since their landing on the isle; then a heavy rainfall, filling the concavity of the boat's sail, enables them to replenish the beaker, with other vessels they had brought ashore.

On the morning of the tenth, a striking change takes place in their behaviour. No longer athirst, the kindred appetite becomes keener, imparting a wolf-like expression to their features. There is a ghoulish glance in their eyes, as they regard one another, fearful to contemplate—even to think of. For it is the gaze of cannibalism!

Yes, it has come to this, though no one has yet spoken of it; the thing is only in their thoughts.

But as time passes, it assumes substantial shape, and threatens soon to be the subject not only of speech, but action.

One or two show it more than the rest—Padilla most of all. In his fierce eyes the unnatural craving is clearly recognisable—especially when his glances are given to the fair forms moving in their midst. There can be no mistaking that look of hungry concupiscence—the cold calculating stare of one who would eat human flesh.

It is the mid-hour of the day, and there has been a long interregnum of silence; none having said much on any subject, though there is a tacit intelligence, that the thoughts of all are on the same.

Padilla, deeming the hour has arrived, breaks the ominous silence:

"*Amigos!*" he says—an old appellation, considering the proposal he is about to make—"since there's no food obtainable, it's clear we've got to die of starvation. Though, if we could only hold out a little longer, something might turn up to save us. For myself, I don't yet despair but that some coasting craft may come along; or they may see our signal from the shore. It's only a question of time, and our being able to keep alive. Now, how are we to do that?"

"Ay, how?" asks Velarde, as if secretly prompted to the question.

"Well," answers Padilla, "there's a way, and only one, that I can think of. There's no need for all of us to die—at least, not yet. Some *one* should, so that the others may have a chance of being saved. Are you all agreed to it!"

The interrogatory does not require to be more explicitly put. It is quite comprehensible; and several signify assent, either by a nod, or in muttered exclamations. A few make no sign, one way or the other; being too feeble, and far gone, to care what may become of them.

"How do you propose, Padilla?"

It is again Velarde who questions.

Turning his eyes towards the grotto, in which the two ladies have taken refuge from the hot rays of the sun, the ruffian replies:

"Well, *camarados!* I don't see why men should suffer themselves to be starved to death, while women—"

Harry Blew does not permit him to finish his speech. Catching its significance, he cries:

"Avast there! Not another word o' that. If any o' as has got to be eaten, it must be a *man*. As for the women, they go last—not first. I, for one, will die afore they do; an' so'll somebody else."

Striker and Davis endorse this determination; Hernandez too, feebly; but Gomez in speech almost firm as that of Blew himself. In De Lara's breast there is a sentiment, which revolts at the horrid proposal of his confederate.

It is the first time he and Harry Blew have been in accord; and being so, there is no uncertainty about the result. It is silently understood, and but waits for one to declare it in words; which Striker does, saying:

"Though I hev been a convick, an' don't deny it, I an't a coward, nor no way afeerd to kick up my heels whensoever I see my time's come. If that he's now, an' Jack Striker's got to die, dash it! he's ready. But it must be a fair an' square thing. Theerfor, let it be settled by our castin' lots all round."

"I agree to that," growls Padilla; "if you mean it to include the women as well."

"We don't mean anythin' o' the sort," says Blew, springing to his feet. "Ye unmanly scoundrel!" he continues, approaching Padilla,—"Repeat your dastardly proposal, an' there'll be no need for drawin' lots. In a minnit more, eyther you or me'll make food, for anybody as likes to eat us. Now!"

The Californian, who has still preserved much of his tenacious strength, and all of his ruffian ferocity, nevertheless shrinks and cowers before the stalwart sailor.

"*Carajo!*" he exclaims, doggedly and reluctantly submitting. "Be it as you like. I don't care any more than the rest of you. When it comes to facing Fate, Rafael Rocas isn't the man to show the white-feather. I only proposed what I believed to be fair. In a matter of life and death, I don't see why women are any better than men. But if you all think different, then be it as you say. We can cast lots, leaving them out."

Padilla's submissive speech puts an end to the strange debate. The side-issue is decided against him, and the main question once more comes up.

After a time, it too is determined. Hunger demands a victim. To appease it one must die.

The horrid resolve reached, it remains but to settle the mode of selection. No great difficulty in this, and it is got over by Striker saying:

"Chums! theer's just twelve o' us, the even dozen. Let's take twelve o' them little shells ye see scattered about, an' put 'em into the boat's pannikin. One o' them we can mark. Him as draws out the marked shell, must—I needn't say what."

"Die" would have been the word, as all understand without hearing it spoken.

The plan is acceptable, and accepted. There seems no fairer for obtaining the fiat of Fate on this dread question.

The shells—*unios*—lie thickly strewn over the ground. There are thousands, all of the same shape and size. By the "feel" it would be impossible to tell one from another. Nor yet by their colour, since all are snow-white.

Twelve of them are taken up, and put into the tin pannikin—a quart measure—one being marked with a spot of red—by blood drawn from Striker's own arm, which he has purposely punctured. Soon absorbed by the porous substance of the shell, it cannot be detected by the touch.

The preliminaries completed, all gather around, ready to draw. They but wait for him who is on watch beside the spread tarpauling, and who must take his chances with the rest in this lottery of life and death. It is the Dutchman who is above. They have already hailed, and commanded him to come down, proclaiming their purpose.

But he neither obeys them, nor gives back response. He does not even look in their direction. They can see him by the signal-staff, standing erect, with face turned towards the sea, and one hand over his eyes shading them from the sun. He appears to be regarding some object in the offing.

Presently he lowers the spread palm, and raises a telescope with which he is provided.

They stand watching him, speechless, and with bated breath, their solemn purpose for the time forgotten. In the gleam of that glass they have a fancy there may be life, as there is light.

The silence continues till 'tis seen going down. Then they hear words, which send the blood in quick current through their veins, bringing hope back into their hearts. They are:

"Sail in sight!"

Chapter Seventy Five
By the Signal-Staff

"Sail in sight!"

Three little words, but full of big meaning, of carrying the question of life or death.

To the ears of that starving crew sweet as music, despite the harsh Teutonic pronunciation of him who gave them utterance.

Down drops the pannikin, spilling out the shells; which they have hopes may be no more needed.

At the shout from above, all have faced towards the sea, and stand scanning its surface. But with gaze unrewarded. The white flecks seen afar are only the wings of gulls.

"Where away?" shouts one, interrogating him on the hill.

"Sou'-westart."

South-westward they cannot see. In this direction their view is bounded; a projection of the cliff interposing between them and the outside shore. All who are able start off towards its summit. The stronger ones rush up the gorge as if their lives depended on speed. The weaker go toiling after. One or two, weaker still, stay below to wait the report that will soon reach them.

The first up, on clearing the scarp, have their eyes upon the Dutchman. His behaviour might cause them surprise, if they could not account for it. As said, the beacon is upon the higher of the two peaks, some two hundred yards beyond the clift's brow. He is beside it, and apparently beside himself. Dancing over the ground, he makes grotesque gesticulations, tossing his arms about, and waving his hat overhead—all the while shouting as if to some vessel close at hand—calling in rapid repetition:

"Ship, Ahoy! Ahoy!"

Looking they can see no ship, nor craft of any kind. For a moment they think him mad, and fear, after all, it may be a mistake. Certainly there is no vessel near enough to be hailed.

But sending their eyes farther out, their fear gives place to joy almost delirious. There *is* a sail, and though leagues off, seeming but a speck, their practised eyes tell them she is steering that way—running coastwise. Keeping this course, she must come past the isle—within sight of their signal, so long spread to no purpose.

Without staying to reflect farther, they strain on towards the summit, where the staff is erected.

Harry Blew is the first to reach it; and clutching the telescope, jerks it from the hands of the half-crazed Dutchman. Raising it to his eye, he directs it on the distant sail—there keeping it more than a minute. The others have meanwhile come up, and, clustering around, impatiently question him.

"What is she? How's she standing?"

"A bit o' a barque," responds Blew. "And from what I can make out, close huggin' the shore. I'll be better able to tell when she draws out from that clump of cloud."

Gomez, standing by, appears eager to get hold of the glass; but Blew seems unwilling to give it up. Still holding it at his eye, he says:

"See to that signal, mates! Spread the tarpaulin' to its full streetch. Face it square, so's to *give* 'em every chance of sightin' it."

Striker and Davis spring to the piece of tarred canvas; and grasping it, one at each corner, draw out the creases, and hold as directed.

All the while Blew stands with the telescope levelled, loath to relinquish it. But Gomez, grown importunate, insists on having his turn, and it is at length surrendered to him.

Blew, stepping aside, seems excited with some emotion he would conceal. Strong it must be, judging from its effects on the ex-man-o'-war's man. On his face there is an expression difficult to describe—surprise amounting to amazement—joy subdued by anxiety. Soon, as having given up the glass, he pulls off his dreadnought, then divesting himself of his shirt—a scarlet flannel—he suspends it from the outer end of the cross-piece which supports the tarpauling; as he does so, saying to Striker and Davis:

"That's a signal no ship ought to disregard, and won't if manned by Christian men. *She* won't, if she sees it. You two stay here, and keep the things well spread I'm goin' below to say a word to them poor creeturs in the cave. Stand by the staff, and don't let any o' them haul it down."

"Ay, ay!" answers Striker, without comprehending, and somewhat wondering at Blew's words—under the circumstances strange. "All right, mate. Ye may depend on me an' Bill."

"I know it—I do," rejoins the ex-man-o'-war's man, again slipping the pilot-coat over his shirtless skin.

"Both o' you be true to me, and 'fore long I may be able to show as Harry Blew an't ungrateful."

Saying this, he separates from them, and hurries back down the gorge.

The Sydney Ducks, left standing by the staff, more than ever wonder at what he has said, and interrogate one another as to his meaning.

In the midst of their mutual questioning, they are attracted by a cry strangely intoned. It is from Gomez, who has brought down the telescope, and holds it in hands that shake as with a palsy.

"What is it?" asks Padilla, stepping up to him.

"Take the glass, Rafael Rocas. See for yourself!"

The contrabandista does as directed.

He is silent for some seconds, while getting the telescope on the strange vessel. Soon as he has her within the field of view, he commences making remarks, overheard by Striker and Davis, giving both surprise—though the latter least.

"Barque she is—polacca-masts. *Carramba*! that's queer. About the same bulk, too! If it wasn't that we're sure of the *Condor* being below, I'd swear it was she. Of course, it can be only a coincidence. *Santissima*! a strange one!"

Velarde, in turn, takes the telescope; he, too, after a sight through it, expressing himself in a similar manner.

Hernandez next—for the four Spaniards have all ascended to the hill.

But Striker does not wait to hear what Hernandez may have to say. Dropping the tarpauling, he strides up to him, and, *sans cérémonie*, jerks the instrument out of his fingers. Then bringing it to his eye, sights for himself.

Less than twenty seconds suffice for him to determine the character of the vessel. Within that time, his glance taking in her hull, traversing along the line of her bulwarks, and then ascending to the tops of her tall smooth masts, he recognises all, as things with which he is well acquainted.

He, too, almost lets drop the telescope, as, turning to the others, he says in a scared, but confident voice:

"*By God, its the Condor!*"

Chapter Seventy Six
A Very Nemesis

Striker's announcement, profanely as emphatically made, thrills the hearts of those hearing it with fear. Not fear of the common kind, but a weird undefinable apprehension.

"*Caspitta!*" exclaims Padilla. "The *Condor!* that cannot be. How could it?"

"It's her for all that," returns Striker. "How so, I don't understan' any more than yourselves. But that yonder craft be the Chili barque, or her ghost, I'll take my affydavy on the biggest stack o' Bibles."

His words summon up strange thoughts which take possession of the minds of those listening. For how can it be the *Condor*, scuttled, sent to the bottom of the sea? Impossible!

In their weak state, with nerves unnaturally excited, they almost believe it an illusion—a spectre! One and all are the prey to wild fancies, that strike terror to their guilty souls. Something more than mortal is pursuing—to punish them. Is it the hand of God? For days they have been in dread of God's hand; and now they seem to see it stretched out, and coming towards them! Surely a Fate—an avenging Nemesis!

"It's the barque, beyond doubt!" continues Striker, with the glass again at his eye. "Everythin' the same, 'ceptin' her sails, the which show patched-like. That be nothin'. It's the Chili craft, and no other. Yonner's the ensign wi' the one star trailin' over her taffrail. Her, sure's we stan' heer!"

"*Chingara!*" cries Gomez. "Where are they who took charge of the scuttling? *Did* they do it?"

Remembering the men, all turn round, looking for them. They are not among the group gathered around the staff. Blew has long ago gone down the gorge, and Davis is just disappearing into it.

They shout to him to come back. He hears; but heeds not. Continuing on, he is soon out of sight.

It matters little questioning him, and they give up thought of it. The thing out at sea engrosses all their attention.

Now nearer, the telescope is no longer needed to tell that it is a barque, polacca-masted; in size, shape of hull, sit in the water—everything the same as with the *Condor*. And the bit of bunting, red, white, blue—the Chilian ensign—the flag carried by the barque they abandoned. They remember a blurred point in the central star: 'tis there!

Spectre or not, with all canvas spread, she is standing towards them—straight towards them—coming on at a rate of speed that soon brings her abreast the islet. She has seen their signal—no doubt of that. If there were—it is before long set at rest. For, while they are watching her, she draws opposite the opening in the reef; then lets sheets loose; and, squaring her after-yards, is instantly hove to.

A boat is dropped from the davits; as it strikes the water, men are seen swarming over the side into it. Then the plash of oars, their wet blades glinting in the sun; as the boat is rowed through the reef-passage.

Impelled by strong arms, it soon crosses the stretch of calm water, and shoots up into the cove.

Beaching it, the crew spring out on the pebbly strand—some not waiting till it is drawn up, but dashing breast-deep into the surf. There are nearly twenty, all stalwart fellows, with big beards—some in sailor garb, but most red-shirted, belted, bristling with bowie-knives, and pistols!

Two are different from the rest—in the uniform of naval officers, with caps gold-banded. One of these seems to command, being the first to leap out of the boat; soon as on shore, drawing his sword, and advancing at the head of the others.

All this observed by the four Spaniards, who are still around the signal-staff, like it, standing fixed; though not motionless, for they are shaking with fear. Their apprehensions, hitherto, of the supernatural, are now real. Even Frank Lara, despite his great courage—his only good quality—feels fear now. For in the officer, leading with drawn sword, he recognises the man who made smash of his Monté bank!

For some moments, he stands in silence, with eyes dilated. He has watched the beaching of the boat, and the debarking of her crew, without saying word. But, soon as recognising Crozier, he clutches Calderon by the arm; more vividly than ever now his crime recalled to him, for now its punishment, as that of them all, seems near. There is no chance to escape it. To resist, will only be to hasten their doom—death.

They do not think of resistance, nor yet flight; but remain upon the hilltop, sullen and speechless.

Calderon is the first to break the silence, frantically exclaiming:

"*Santos Dios*! the officers of the English frigate! Mystery of Mysteries! What can it mean?"

"No mystery," rejoins De Lara, addressing himself to the other three; "none whatever. I see it all now, clear as the sun at noonday. Blew has been traitor to us, as I suspected all along. He and Davis have not scuttled the barque, but left her to go drifting about; and the frigate to which these officers belong has come across, picked her up—and lo! they are there!"

"That's it, no doubt," says Velarde, otherwise Don Manuel Diaz. "But those rough fellows along with them don't appear to be men-of-war's men, nor sailors of any kind. More like gold-diggers, I should say; such as crowd the streets of San Francisco. They must have come thence."

"It matters not what they are, or where from. Enough that they're here, and we in their power."

At this Diaz and Padilla, now known as Rafael Rocas, step towards the cliff's edge to have a look below, leaving the other two by the staff.

"What do you suppose they'll do to us?" asks Calderon of De Lara. "Do you think they'll—"

"Shoot, or hang us?" interrupts De Lara; "that's what you'd say. I don't think anything about it. I'm sure of it. One or other they'll do, to a certainty."

"*Santissima*!" piteously exclaims the ex-ganadero. "Is there no chance of escaping?"

"None whatever. No use our trying to get away from them. There's nowhere we could conceal ourselves; not a spot to give us shelter for a single hour. For my part, I don't intend to stir from this spot. I may as well be taken here as anywhere else. *Carramba*, no!" he exclaims, as if something has occurred to make him change his mind. "I shall go below, and meet my death like a man. No; like a tiger. Before dying, *I shall kill*. Are you good to do the same? Are you game for it?"

"I don't comprehend you," answers Calderon. "Kill what, or whom?"

"Whomsoever I can. Two for certain."

"Which two?"

"Edward Crozier and Carmen Montijo. You may do as you please. I've marked out my pair, and mean to have their lives before yielding up my own—hers, if I can't his. She sha'n't live to triumph over me. No; by the Almighty God!"

While speaking, the desperado has taking out his revolver, and holding it at half-cock, spins the cylinder round, to see that all the six chambers are loaded, with the caps on the nipples. Assured of this, he returns it to its holster; and then glances at his *macheté*, hanging on his left hip. All this with a cool carefulness, which shows him determined upon his hellish purpose.

Calderon, trembling at the very thought of it, endeavours to dissuade him; urging that, after all, they may be only made prisoners, and leniently dealt with.

He is cut short by De Lara crying out:

"You may go to prison and rot there, if it so please you. After what's happened, that's not the destiny for me. I prefer death, and vengeance."

"Better life, and vengeance," cries Rocas, coming up, Diaz along with him, both in breathless haste. "Quick, comrades!" he continues; "follow me! I'll find a way to save the first, and maybe get the last, sooner than you expected."

"It's no use, Rafael," argues De Lara, misunderstanding the speech of the seal-hunter. "If we attempt flight, they'll only shoot us down the sooner. Where could we flee too?"

"Come on; I'll show you where. *Carajo*! Don't stand hesitating; every second counts now. If we can but get ther in time—"

"Get where?"

"*Al boté!*"

On hearing the words, De Lara utters an exclamation of joy. They apprise him of a plan which may not only get him out of danger, but give revenge, sweet as ever fell to the lot of mortal man.

He hesitates no longer, but hastens after the seal-hunter; who, with the other two, has already started towards the brow of the cliff.

But not to stay there; for in a few seconds after the four are descending it; not through the gorge by which they came up, but another—also debouching into the bay.

Little dream the English officers, or the brave men who have landed with them, of the peril impending. If the scheme of the seal-hunter succeed, theirs will be a pitiful fate: the tables will be turned upon them!

Chapter Seventy Seven
Almost a Murder

At the cliff's base, the action, simultaneous, is even more exciting.

Having left their boat behind, with a man to take care of it, the rescuers advance towards the inner end of the cove.

At first with caution: till passing the rock-portal, they see the platform and those on it.

Then the young officers rush forward, with no fear of having to fight. Instead of armed enemies to meet them, they behold the dear ones from whom they have been so long apart. Beside them, half-a-dozen figures, more like skeletons than men—with cowed, craven faces, seeming so feeble as to have a difficulty in keeping their feet!

With swords sheathed, and pistols returned to their holsters, the English officers hasten on, the young ladies rushing out to receive them.

Soon they are together, two and two, breasts touching, and arms enfolded in mutual embrace.

For a while no words—the hearts of all too full for speech. Only ejaculations and kisses, with tears, but not of sorrow.

Then succeeds speech, necessarily brief and half-incoherent, Crozier telling Carmen that her father is still alive, and aboard the barque. He lives—he is safe! that is enough.

Then in answer to his questions, a word or two, on her fide. But without waiting to hear all, he turns abruptly upon Harry Blew, who is seen some paces off. Neither by word, nor gesture, has the sailor yet saluted him. He stands passive, a silent spectator; as Crozier supposes, the greatest criminal on earth. In quick retrospect of what has occurred, and what he has heard from Don Gregorio, how could it be otherwise?

But he will not condemn without hearing him, and stepping up to the ex-man-o'-war's man, he demands explanation of his conduct, sternly saying:

"Now, sir, I claim an account from you. Tell your story straight, and don't conceal aught, or prevaricate. If your treason be as black as I believe it, you deserve no mercy from me. And your only chance to obtain it, will be by telling the truth."

While speaking, he has again drawn his sword, and stands confronting the sailor—as if a word were to be the signal for thrusting him through.

Blew is himself armed with both pistol and knife. But, so far from touching either, or making any sign of an intention to defend himself he remains cowed-like, his head drooping down to his breast.

He gives no response. His lips move not; neither his arms nor limbs. Alone, his broad chest heaves and falls, as if stirred by some terrible emotion.

His silence seems a confession of guilt!

Taking, or mistaking, it for this, Crozier cries out:

"Traitor! Confess, before I run this blade through your miserable body!"

The threat elicits an answer.

"You may kill me, if you wish, Master Edward. By rights, my life belongs to ye. But, if you take it, I'll have the satisfaction o' knowin', I've done the best I could to prove my gratefulness for your once savin' it."

Long before he has finished his strange speech, the impending stroke is stayed, and the raised blade dropped point downward. For, on the hand which grasps it, a gentler one is laid, a soft voice saying:—

"Hold, Eduardo! *Dios de mi alma!* What would you do? You know not. This brave man—to him I owe my life—I and Iñez."

"Yes," adds Iñez, advancing, "more than life. 'Tis he who protected us."

Crozier stands trembling, the sword almost shaken from his grasp. And while sheathing it, he is told how near he has been to doing that which would ever after have made him miserable.

He feels like one withheld from murder—almost parricide. For to have killed Harry Blew, would have been like killing his own father.

The exciting episode is almost instantly succeeded by another, even more stirring, and longer sustained. While Carmen is proceeding to explain her interference on behalf of Blew, she is interrupted by cries coming up from the beach. Not meaningless shouts, but words of ominous import.

"Ahoy, there! help! help!"

Coupled with them, Crozier hears his own name, then the "Help, help!" reiterated; recognising the voice of the man left in charge of the boat— Grummet.

Without hesitating an instant, he springs off toward the strand, Cadwallader and the gold-diggers following; two staying to keep guard over those of the robbers who have surrendered.

On clearing the rocky ledge, they see what is causing the coxswain to sing out in such terrified accents. Grummet is in the boat, but upon his feet, with a boat-hook in his hands, which he brandishes in a threatening manner, shouting all the while. Four men are making towards him fast as their legs can carry them. They are coming along the beach from the right side of the cove.

At a glance the English officers recognise two of them—De Lara and Calderon—sooner from their not meeting them there unexpectedly. For aware that they are on the isle, they were about to go in quest of those gentlemen, after settling other affairs.

No need to search for them now. There they are, with their confederates, rushing direct for the boat—already within pistol-shot of it.

Nor can there be any doubt about their intention to seize upon the boat and carry her off!

Chapter Seventy Eight
The Tables nearly Turned

The sight thus unexpectedly brought before the eyes of the rescuers sends a shiver through their hearts, and draws exclamations of alarm from their lips. With quick intuition one and all comprehend the threatened danger. All at that moment remember having left only two or three men on the barque; and, should the pirates succeed in boarding, they may carry her off to sea, leaving themselves on the isle.

The prospect is appalling! But they do not dwell upon it; they have neither time, nor need. It is too clear, like a flash passing before their minds, in all its dread details! Without waiting to exchange word with one another, they rush on to arrest the threatened catastrophe, bounding over the rocks, crashing through shells and pebbles. But they are behind time, and the others will reach the boat before them!

Crozier, perceiving this, shouts to the coxswain—

"Shove off, Grummet! Into deep water with you!"

Grummet, understanding what is meant, brings the boat-hook point downward, and with a desperate effort, pushes the keel clear, sending the boat adrift.

But before he can repeat the push, pistols are fired, and, simultaneous with their reports, he is seen to sink down, and lie doubled over the thwarts.

A yell of vengeance peals from the pursuing party; and, maddened, they rush on. They will be too late! Already the pirates have reached the boat, now undefended; and all four together, swarming over the gunwale, drop down upon the thwarts, each as he does so seizing hold of an oar, and shipping it.

In agony, Crozier cries out—

"O God! are they to get away—these guilty, redhanded wretches?"

It would seem so. They have already dipped their oar-blades into the water, and commenced pulling, while they are beyond pistol-range.

Ha! something stays them! God is not for them. Their arms rise and fall, but the boat moves not! Her keel is on a coral bottom; her bilge caught upon its rough projections. Their own weight pressing down, holds her fast, and their oar-strokes are idly spent!

They had not thought of being thus stayed; though it proves the turning-point of their fate.

No use their leaping out now, to lighten the boat; no time for that, nor any chance to escape. But two alternatives stare them in the face—resistance, which means death; surrender, that seems the same.

De Lara would resist and die; so also Rocas. But the other two are against it, instinctively holding on to whatever hope of life be left them.

The craven Calderon cuts short the uncertainty by rising erect, stretching forth his arms, and crying out in a piteous appeal for mercy.

In an instant after they are surrounded, the boat grasped by the gunwale, and dragged back to the shore. Crozier with difficulty restrains the angry gold-diggers from shooting them down on the thwarts. Well for them the coxswain has not been killed, but only wounded, and in no danger of losing his life. Were it otherwise, theirs would be taken on the spot.

Assured of his safety, his rescuers pull the four wretches out of the boat; then disarming, drag them up to the platform, and bestow them in the larger cave: for a time to be their prison, though not long. For, there is a judge present, accustomed to sit upon short trials, and pass quick sentences, soon succeeded by their execution. He is the celebrated *Justice Lynch*.

Represented by a stalwart digger—all the others acting as Jury—the trial is speedily brought to a termination. For the four of Spanish nationality the verdict is guilty—the sentence, *death*—on the scaffold.

The others, less criminal, are to be carried on to Panama, and there delivered over to the Chilian consul; their crime being mutiny, with robbery, and abandonment of a Chilian vessel.

An exception is made in the case of Striker and Davis. The "Sydney Ducks" receive conditional pardon, on promise of better behaviour throughout all future time. This they obtain by the intercession of Harry Blew, in accordance with the hint he gave them while they were standing together beside the spread tarpauling.

Of the men sentenced to be hanged, one meets his fate in a different manner. The gold-dust has been recovered, packed, and put into the boat.

The señoritas are cloaked, and impatient to be taken back to the barque, yearning to embrace him they have so long believed dead.

The English officers stand beside them; all awaiting the last scene of the tragedy—the execution of the condemned criminals.

The stake has been set for it; this the level plot of ground in front of the cavern's month. A rope hangs down with a running noose at one end; the other, in default of gallow's arm and branch of tree, rigged over the point of a projecting rock.

All this arranged, De Lara is led out first, a digger on each side of him. He is not tied, nor confined in any way. They have no fear of his making his escape.

Nor has he any thoughts of attempting it; though he thinks of something else, as desperate and deadly. He will not die like a scared dog, but as a fierce tiger; to the last thirsting for blood, to the end trying to destroy—to kill! The oath sworn by him above on the cliff, he still is determined on keeping.

As they conduct him out of the cave, his eyes glaring with lurid light, go searching everywhere, till they rest upon a group some twenty paces distant. It is composed of four persons: Crozier and Carmen, Cadwallader and Iñez, standing two and two.

At the last pair De Lara looks not, the first enchaining his attention. Only one short glance he gives them; another to a pistol which hangs holstered on the hip of a gold-digger guarding him.

A spring, and he has possession of it; a bound, and he is off from between the two men, and rushing on towards the group standing apart!

Fortunately for Edward Crozier—for Carmen Montijo as well—there are cries of alarm, shouts of warning, that reach him in time.

He turns on hearing them, sees the approaching danger, and takes measures to avert it. Simple enough these—but the drawing of his revolver, and firing at the man who advances.

Two shots are heard, one on each side, almost simultaneous; but enough apart to decide which of the two who fired must fall.

Crozier's pistol had cracked first; and as the smokes of both swirl up, the gambler is seen astretch upon the sward—the blood spurting from his breast, and spreading over his shirt bosom!

Harry Blew, rushing forward, and bending over him, cries out:

"Dead! Shot through the heart—a brave heart too! What a pity 'twar so black!"

"Come away, *mia querida!*" says Crozier to Carmen. "Your father will be suffering from anxiety about you. You've had enough of the horrible. Let us hope this is the end of it."

Taking his betrothed by the hand, he leads her down to the boat—Cadwallader and Iñez accompanying them.

All seat themselves in the stern-sheets, and wait for the diggers; who soon after appear, conducting their prisoners, the pirate crew of the *Condor*; short four left behind—a banquet for the *caracaras!*

Chapter Seventy Nine
A Sailor's True Yarn

It is the second day after the tragedy upon the isle, and the Chilian barque has sailed away from the Veraguan coast, out of that indentation known upon modern maps as "Montijo Bay."

She has long since rounded Cabo Mala, and is standing in for the port of Panama. With a full crew—most of them old and able seamen—no fear but she will reach it now.

Crozier in command, has restored Harry Blew to his old rank of first officer; which so far from having forfeited, he is now deemed to doubly deserve. But still weak from his long privation, the ex-man-o'-war's man is excused from duty, Cadwallader doing it for him.

Harry is strong enough, however, to tell the young officers what they are all ears to hear—the story of that *Flag of Distress*. Their time hitherto taken up attending upon their *fiancées*, they have deferred calling for the full account, which only the English sailor can give them.

Now having passed Cabo Mala, as if with that promontory of bad repute all evil were left behind, they are in the mood to listen to the narration in all its details; and for this have summoned the chief officer to their side.

"Your honours!" he begins, "it's a twisted-up yarn, from the start to the hour ye hove in sight; an' if ye hadn't showed yerselves just in the nick o' time, an' ta'en the twist out o' it, hard to say how 'twould 'a ended. No doubt, in all o' us dyin' on that desert island, an' layin' our bones there. Thank the Lord, for our delivery—'ithout any disparagement to what's been done by both o' you, young gentlemen. For that He must ha' sent you, an has had a guidin' hand throughout the whole thing, I can't help thinkin', 'specially when I look back on the scores o' chances that seemed goin' against the right, an' still sheered round to it after all."

"True," assents Crozier, honouring the devout faith of the sailor. "You're quite right in ascribing it to Divine interference. Certainly, God's hand seems to have been extended in our favour. But go on!"

"Well, to commence at the beginnin', which is when you left me at San Francisco. As I told Master Willie, that day he comed ashore in the dingy, I war engaged to go chief mate in the Chili barque. She war then a ship; afterward converted as ye see, through our shortness o' hands.

"When I went aboard her, an' for sev'ral days after, I war the only thing in the shape o' sailor she'd got. Then her captain—that poor crazed creetur below—put advertisements in the papers, offering big pay; the which, as I then supposed, brought eleven chaps, callin' themselves sailors, an' shippin' as such. One o' 'em, for want o' a better, war made second mate—his name bein' entered on the books as Padilla. He war the last o' the three swung up, an' if ever man desarved hangin', he did, bein' the cruellest scoundrel o' the lot.

"After we'd waited another day or two, an' no more makin' appearance, the skipper made up his mind to sail. Then the old gentleman, along wi' the two saynoreetas, came aboard; when we cleared an' stood out to sea.

"Afore leavin' port, I had a suspishun about the sort o' crew we'd shipped. But soon's we are fairly afloat, it got to be somethin' worse than suspishun; I war sartin then we'd an ugly lot to deal with. Still, I only believed them to be bad men—an', if that war possible, worse seamen. I expected trouble wi' them in sailin' the vessel; an' a likelihood o' them bein' disobedient. But on the second night after leavin' land, I found out somethin' o' a still darker stripe—that they war neither more nor less than a gang o' piratical conspirators, an' had a plan already laid out. A lucky chance led to me discoverin' their infarnal design. The two we've agreed to let go off—Jack Striker an' Bill Davis—both old birds from the convict gangs o' Australia—war talkin' it over atween themselves, an' I chanced to overhear them. What they sayed made everythin' clear—as it did my hair to stand on eend. Twar a scheme to plunder the ship o' the gold-dust Don Gregorio hed got in her; an' carry off your young ladies. Same time they war to scuttle the vessel, an' sink her; first knockin' the old gentleman on the head, as well as the skipper; whiles your humble sarvint an' the darkey are to be disposed o' same sweet fashion.

"On listenin' to the dyabolikal plot, I war clear dumfoundered, an' for a while didn't know what to do. 'Twar a case o' life an' death to some o' us; an' for the saynoreetas, somethin' worse. At first I thort o' telling Captain Lantanas, an' also Don Gregorio. But then I seed if I shud, that 'twould only make death surer to all as were doomed. I knowed the skipper to be a man o' innocent, unsuspishus nature, an' mightn't gi'e belief to such 'trocious rascality, as bein' a thing possible. More like he'd let out right away, an' bring on the bloody bizness sooner than they intended it. From what Striker

It scarce needs to tell that the bridegrooms are Edward Crozier and Willie Cadwallader—both now lieutenants. Nor need we say who are the brides; since they are to be given away by Don Gregorio Montijo.

As little necessary to speak of the ceremonial splendour of that double wedding—long time the *novedad* of Cadiz.

Enough to say that present at it are all the wealth and fashion of the old Andalusian city, with foreign consuls, and the commanders of warships in the port: conspicuous amongst these, Captain Bracebridge, and the officers of Her Britannic Majesty's frigate *Crusader*.

Also two other men of the sea—of its merchant service; to hear of whose presence there will, no doubt, make the reader happy, as it does both the brides and the bridegrooms to see them. They belong to a ship lying in the harbour, carrying polacca-masts, on her stern lettered "El Condor;" one of the two being her captain, called Lantanas; the other her chief officer, by name Blew.

God has been just and good to the gentle Chilian skipper, having long since lifted from his mind the cloud that temporarily obscured it. He now knows all, and above all, Harry Blew in his true colours; and, though on the *Condor's* deck they are still captain and mate, when below by themselves in her cabin, all distinction of rank disappears, and they are affectionate friends—almost as brothers.

In the prosperous trading-craft *Condor*, re-converted into her original shape of ship—regularly voyaging between Valparaiso and Cadiz, exchanging the gold and silver of Chili for the silks and sweet wines of Spain—but few would recognise a barque once chased over the South Sea, believed to be a spectre; and, it is to be hoped, no one will ever again see her sailing under a *Flag of Distress*.

and Davis said, I made out that it war to be kept back, till we should sight land near Panyma.

"Well; after a big spell o' thinkin', I seed a sort o' way out of it—the only one appearin' possible. 'Twar this: to purtend joinin' in wi' the conspirators, an' put myself at thar head. I'd larnt from the talk o' the two Sydney Ducks there war a split 'mong them, 'bout the dividin' o' the gold-dust. I seed this would gi'e me a chance to slip in along wi' them. So takin' advantage o' it, I broached the bizness to Striker that same night, and got into his confidence, an' theer councils; arterwards obtaining the influence I wanted.

"Mind, gentlemen, it took a smart show o' trickery and maneuvrin'. 'Mong other things, I had to appear cool to the cabin people throughout all the voyage—specially them two sweet creeturs. Many's the time my heart ached thinkin' o' yourself, Mr Crozier, as also Master Willie—an' then o' your sweethearts, an' what might happen, if I should fail in my plan for protectin' 'em. When they wanted to be free and friendly, an' once began talkin' to me, I hed to answer 'em gruff an' growlin', knowin' that eyes war on me all the while, an' ears listenin'. As to tellin' them what was before, or givin' them the slimmest hint o' it, that would 'a spoilt my plans, an' ruined everything. They'd a gone straight to the old gentleman, an' then it would 'a been all up wi' us. 'Twar clear to me they all couldn't be saved, an' that Don Gregorio himself would hev to be sacrificed, as well as the skipper an' cook. I thought that dreadful hard; but thar war no help for't, as I'd have enough on my hands in takin' care o' the women, without thinkin' o' the men. As the Lord has allowed, an' thank Him for it, all ha'e been saved!"

The speaker pauses, in the fervour of his gratitude; which his listeners, respecting, in silence wait for him to continue the narration. He does so:

"At last, on sightin' land, as agreed on, the day had come for the doin' of the dark deed. It war after night when they set about it, myself actin' as a sort o' recognised leader. I'd played my part, so's to get control o' the rest. We first lowered a boat, putting our things into her. Then we separated, some to get out the gold-dust, others to seize the saynoreetas. I let Gomez look after them, for fear of bringing on trouble too soon. Me an' Davis— who chances to be a sort o' Jack carpenter—were to do the scuttlin'; an', for that purpose, went down into the hold. There I proposed to him to give the doomed ones a chance for their lives, by lettin' the barque float a bit longer. Though he be a convict, he warn't nigh so bad as the rest.

"He consented to my proposal, an' we returned on deck 'ithout tapping the barque's bottom-timbers.

"Soon's I had my head over the hatch coamin', I seed them all below in the boat, the girls along wi' them. I didn't know what they'd done to the

Don an' skipper I had my fears about 'em, thinkin' they might ha'e been murdered, as Padilla had proposed. But I darn't go back to the cabin then, lest they might shove off, an' leave us in the lurch: as some war threatenin' to do, more than one wantin' it, I know. If they'd done that—well, it's no use sayin' what might ha' been the upshot. Tharfore, I had to hurry down into the boat. Then, we rowed away; leavin' the barque just as she'd been the whole o' that day.

"As we pulled shoreward, we could see her standing off, all sails set— same as tho' the crew wor abroad o' her workin' 'em."

"But her ensign reversed?" asks Cadwallader. "She was carrying it so, when we came across her. How came that, Harry?"

"Ah! the bit o' buntin' upside-down! I did that myself in the dark; thinkin' it might get them a better chance o' bein' picked up. I'd just time to do it afore droppin' into the boat."

"And you did the very thing!" exclaims Crozier. "I see God's hand in that surely! But for the distress signal, the *Crusader* would have kept on without giving chase; and—. But, proceed! Tell us what happened afterwards."

"Well; we landed in the island, not knowin' it to be a island. An' theer's another o' the chances, showin' we've been took care o' by the little cherub as sits up aloft. If it hed been the mainland—well, I needn't tell ye, things would now be different. After landin', we stayed all night on the shore; the men sleeping in the biggest o' the caves, while the ladies occupied a smaller one. I took care 'bout that separation myself, determined they shouldn't come to no harm.

"That night theer war a thing happened which I dar say they've told you; an' twar from them I afterwards larned that Gomez an' Hernandez war no other than the two chaps you'd trouble wi' at San Francisco. They went into the cave, an' said some insultin' things to the saynoreetas; I warn't 'far off, an' would 'a made short work wi' them, hed it goed farther than talk.

"Well; up at a early hour next mornin', we found the boat had drifted off seaward, an' got bilged on the breakers. But supposin' we shouldn't want her any more, nobody thought anythin' about it. Then comed the dividin' o' the gold-dust, an' after it the great questyun—leastwise, so far as I war consarned—as to who should take away the girls. I'd been waitin' for this, an' for the settlin' o't I war ready to do or die. Gomez an' Hernandez war the two who laid claim to 'em—as I knowed, an' expected they would. Pertendin' a likin' for Miss Carmen myself, an' puttin' Davis up to what I wanted 'bout the tother, we also put in our claim. It ended in Gomez an' me goin' in for a fight; which must 'a tarminated in the death o' one or other o' us. I hed no dread o' dyin'; only from the fear o' its leavin' the saynoreetas unprotected. But thar war no help for't, an' I agreed to the duel, which war to be fought first wi' pistols, an' finished up, if need be, wi' the steel.

"Everythin' settled, we war 'bout settin' to, when one o' the fellows— who'd gone up the cliff to take a look ahead—just then sung out, that we'd landed on a island. Recallin' the lost boat, we knew that meant a dreadful danger. In coorse it stopped the fight, an' we all rushed up to the cliff.

"When we saw how things stood, there war no more talk o' quarrellin'. The piratical scoundrels war scared nigh out o' thar senses; an' would 'a been glad to get back aboard the craft they'd come out o', the which all, 'ceptin' Davis an' myself, supposed to be at the bottom o' the sea.

"After that, 'twar all safe, as far as concarned the saynoreetas. To them as wanted 'em so bad, they war but a second thought, in the face of starvation; which soon tamed the wolves down, an' kep 'em so till the last o' the chapter.

"Now, young gentlemen; ye know how Harry Blew hev behaved, an' can judge for yourselves, whether he's kep the word he gi'ed you 'fore leavin' San Francisco."

"Behaved nobly, grandly!" cries Crozier. "Kept your word like a man: like a true British sailor! Come to my arms—to my heart, Harry! And forgive the suspicions we had, not being able to help them. Here, Will! take him to yours, and show him how grateful we both are, to the man who has done more for us than saving our lives."

"Bless you, Blew! God bless you!" exclaims Cadwallader, promptly responding to the appeal; and holding Harry in a hug that threatens to crush in his ribs.

The affecting scene is followed by an interval of profound silence; broken by the voice of Grummet, who, at the wheel, is steering straight into the port of Panama, now in sight.

"Mr Crozier!" calls out the old coxswain, "do ye see that craft—the one riding at anchor out yonder in the roadstead?"

All three turn their eyes in the direction indicated; soon as they have done so, together exclaiming:

"*The Crusader!*"

The last incident of our tale takes place at Cadiz, in a grand cathedral church; before the altar of which stand two English naval officers, and alongside each a beautiful Spanish damsel, soon to be his wedded wife.